D0065984

BY THOMAS BERGER

Little Big Man
Killing Time
Regiment of Women
Sneaky People

THE REINHART SERIES

Crazy in Berlin
Reinhart in Love
Vital Parts

Sneaky People

a novel by

THOMAS BERGER

SIMON AND SCHUSTER : NEW YORK

Designed by Irving Perkins
Manufactured in the United States of America
By American Book–Stratford Press, Inc.

1   2   3   4   5   6   7   8   9   10

Library of Congress Cataloging in Publication Data

Berger, Thomas, 1924–
    Sneaky people.
    I. Title.
PZ4.B497Sn[PS3552.E719]   813'.5'4   74-22320
ISBN 0-671-21897-2

To Howard Sackler

Sneaky
People

chapter 1

WHEN BUDDY SANDIFER drove onto his used-car lot he saw that both Leo, his full-time salesman, and Jack, a schoolteacher who sold cars only on Saturday, had clients in hand, while several other potential customers were roaming unsupervised, opening driver's-side doors and peering at the prices whitewashed on windshields. Buddy parked the Buick behind the concrete-block structure that housed the office at one end and at the other the garage where Clarence, a colored flunky, washed, polished, and did minor touch-ups of paint.

Wearing a ripped undershirt, old striped-suit trousers, and rubber knee-boots, Clarence now squatted at the entrance to the garage, scouring the yellowed whitewalls on a blue '36 Plymouth convertible. His brown biceps, operated by cords visible in high relief, throbbed and glistened as he worked the Brillo pad, his head angled to bring his good eye into play. At nineteen he had done some semi-pro boxing and been accidentally half blinded by the right cross of a young Irishman who two years later was mentioned once in a city paper as among the lesser contenders for the light-heavyweight title, but, suffering a series of defeats-by-knockout immediately thereafter, vanished.

Clarence did not look up from the dripping tire; but if he had, his manner would have been polite but not subservient. Buddy had acquired his services when Clarence was caught in the act of trying to steal a car from the lot on, as luck would have it, a night when Buddy had remained late in the darkened office, spread-eagling a woman on the desk. Disengaging at the sound of a suspicious noise outside, he put away his dick and seized a pistol and flashlight from the center drawer just under her buttocks, dashed out, and found Clarence with his dark head and huge shoulders under the opened hood of a '31 Reo.

Buddy was quite cool when armed. "Make me an offer," said he, playing the light on the Negro.

Clarence straightened up slowly. He offered Buddy the wire with which he had been trying to jump the ignition. With stolid dignity he said: "It don't work nohow."

For some strange reason Buddy had a soft spot in his heart for inept men; that this one was colored was even more of a recommendation; and when his flashlight beam illuminated the sightless, milky eye, he saw a combination that gratified him in the extreme.

"You unemployed?" Buddy asked.

"Yeah."

"Can you wash a car?"

"Yeah."

"Show up eight o'clock in the morning and you got yourself a job. Twelve dollars a week."

Clarence asked, but with no interest: "You going shoot me?"

"To hell with that," said Buddy, uncocking his gun and taking it away.

That had been three years ago, and they had not had a longer conversation since. Buddy did not even learn of Clarence's career in the ring until his son, immediately intrigued by the Negro's fantastic musculature, found out about it. But Clarence would answer any question put to him, in the most candid and economical style, e.g., "What happened to your eye?" "Irish Mulvaney." There was some theory around the lot, originated by Leo, that Clarence's brain had also been damaged.

Clarence now earned fifteen dollars a week and presumably lived in Darktown, though nobody was sure about that and the local protocol nicely forbade asking any colored person where he resided or whether he was married to the woman with whom he was probably sharing his abode.

Buddy entered the office by the rear door. He removed his blazer, put it on a hanger, and hooked the wire over the topmost projection of the wooden hatrack which was otherwise empty, the salesmen wearing their jackets when working the lot. Leo today was in badly rumpled seersucker, Jack in a neat Palm Beach suit of tan. Buddy kept his hat on as an anti-sneeze measure against the brief but regular intersection, above his swivel chair, of the drafts of two revolving electric fans, one on each of the walls that flanked his desk.

Ordinarily, with customers outside, Buddy would not have lingered within, though to do so, peering through the venetian blind kept three-quarters louvered against the sun on the west-facing windows, was often a good tactic, building up in a certain type of client a false sense that he was capable of making up his own mind, thereby weakening him for the eventual assault. But today, after a lunch that was exceptionally wretched even for his wife's cuisine, Buddy felt himself the victim, and, behind his natty façade of white flannels, baby-blue shirt, striped tie, tan-and-white shoes, and coconut straw hat with polka-dot band, he was falling into one of his moods.

Leo entered the office at this point. He was wire-haired, anxious, hook-nosed, and his last name was Kirsch, and he was thought by some for these reasons to be a Jew; but he claimed to be of straight German descent and called himself a Lutheran though going to church only on the principal holidays.

He went to his own desk, sat down behind it, found a newspaper, and began to read the classified section, to which it was already opened. Buddy's sneeze startled him.

"I didn't spot you," he said. "You're quiet as a mouse. Sounds like you're coming down with something. You look pretty peakèd too." In sympathy he whipped a handkerchief from his pocket and snorted into it. "Get a Benzedrine inhaler," he said as his nose emerged. "It shrinks the sinuses."

Leo always had a ready suggestion. He saw life for other people as a collection of immediate problems for which simple solutions were available.

"What you got?" asked Buddy, meaning the combination of customer and deal, because what Leo was of course doing was killing time until he could return to the lot and tell the client that he had talked the boss into reducing the price another twenty-five dollars. If that did not suffice, he might return again—perhaps, with a difficult nut to crack, three times—until he had at last reached the basic price which Buddy established for each car and below which no profit would remain. It was not necessary to consult Buddy at any time during this sequence, the schedule for which was long-standing.

"The thirty-five V-eight," said Leo. "The one with the skins." The other Ford, same year, same dark blue, still had a little tread on the tires. It was also priced the same as the one for which Leo had a buyer, had better paint, and the safety glass in the windshield had not yellowed as much. But secretly it was a worse automobile: the clutch slipped and the brake linings were a distant memory. Leo's customer had sense.

He characterized him as "a rube, with his ball 'n' chain." Buddy had in fact noticed the middle-aged couple as he drove in: the man wearing a light-gray hat with a narrow black band and a striped shirt buttoned at the collar without a tie; the woman, a hairnet.

After a while, Leo returned to the lot, but he had miscalculated: the hicks were gone. Jack was talking confidentially to a low-browed young man in a sports shirt with the tails hanging out, alongside a '37 Ford phaeton of which the top was badly worn. But for the local sootfall it would have been displayed in good weather with the canvas furled.

Seeing Leo, Jack angled a finger at him and said to the customer: "Mr. Kirsch will bear me out."

Leo began automatically to nod in support of whatever point Jack was making, and to look sober but unworried. He seldom smiled at a customer; unlike Buddy, he did not have the light touch. Jack however wore a bright grin. He was a large man and had certain effeminate ways though married and with three kids.

"I was just telling Mr. Ballbacher the phaeton's an excellent compromise between a convertible and a family car. He's a family man, like me." Jack always got this information in. Cruel friends in his boyhood had called him a sissy, and it happened occasionally that persons on the other end of the phone thought they were talking to his wife, or if at the office to a stenographer. But he was perfectly normal. He was a better-than-fair bowler and could drink as much brew as the next man, though being a schoolteacher he could not afford to be seen doing it in public.

15

"And," said Leo, continuing earnestly to nod, "you won't find a cleaner model than this here."

"Top is shot to hell," said the young man, flattening his nose shrewdly.

"Last you another year," said Leo. "Then you replace it for a few bucks. Why not? Anyway, you won't have it up much in good weather." He patted Ballbacher's shoulder. The young man wore a Hawaiian-figured shirt and let the ends hang out to conceal the beginnings of a beerbelly. He probably worked in the local pencil factory. When he walked around front and knelt and poked judiciously, meaninglessly, at the grille, in which were stuck some dead leaves from bygone autumns, Leo asked Jack: "Where'd my hayseeds go?"

Jack simpered guiltily. Here Leo was helping him, and yet he hadn't noticed Leo's clients. He felt like a twerp. Therefore he lied. "Said they'd be back in an hour."

"They all say that," Leo noted cynically.

Ballbacher prized a chewing-gum wrapper from the grille. "Clark's Teaberry," he said. Next he peered at the hood and felt it. "Lotta road film. How's the paint underneath?"

"Just wait till the nigger gets through with it," said Leo. "We'd be willing to throw in a Simoniz on this one."

Ballbacher was impressed. "Just wax, or cleaner and wax?"

"The works."

Jack looked at the arm of his Palm Beach suit. There was an ugly smudge on it. He had leaned against more than one car, and while Clarence dusted them all every morning, by noon they were covered with soot.

Leo realized he was doing Jack's work, making a sale for which Jack would get the commission. He saw a young girl in halter and baggy shorts enter the lunch counter across the street.

"I'm going to the Greek's," he told Jack. "I didn't get time to eat lunch yet."

Without warning, Ballbacher suddenly announced that he would take the Ford phaeton at the windshield price, $599, and Jack with soft elation led him into the office to do the paperwork.

Buddy's hat was there, but Buddy was not. He had gone through the side door into the garage, in search of Clarence, whom he had decided to consult on the subject of killing his wife, whose name was Naomi. He had thought about this for ever so long, but not with any detail.

People were always slaughtering each other in Darktown. True, all parties to the killing were colored, which made it a different ballgame, but there must be certain general rules. What Buddy was actually thinking was that Clarence, though incompetent himself, might provide him with a murderer: surely he had some shiftless criminal pal or cousin who would cut his own mother's throat for a fee.

Ralph, Buddy's fifteen-year-old son and only child, had offered to help his mother dry the luncheon dishes, but hardly had he picked up the towel when he saw through the kitchen window that Alice Diefenbaker, a pudgy sixteen-year-old who lived next door, had come out and sat down on the top step of the back porch, her kneecaps as high as her plump milk fund, and her two fat hams, divided by the strained crotch of underpants, shamelessly visible. Her eyes were so pale that at this distance they looked like the empty circles of Little Orphan Annie.

"Be right back," Ralph told his mother, whose arms were up to the elbow in dishwater. He walked smartly to the bathroom, where behind the closed door and with closed eyes he masturbated.

Afterwards he felt the usual degradation and washed his hands several times as if they had been covered with tar. When he returned to the kitchen, he looked out again at

Alice Diefenbaker and recognized her as a big fat ugly slob, and wondered at his recent action. He was prepared to deal with the dishes now, but he had apparently been gone longer than he realized, for the plates were dry and stacked on the drainboard, and his mother was gone.

He went down to the basement to get the lawnmower and found his mother there, filling one of the stationary tubs with household laundry.

"Well," said he, swinging the long handle around so that the blades would not engage while the wheels turned. He trundled the mower to the door that led to the outside stairs. "I guess I'll go to work."

"And a good job you'll do too," said his mother. Nobody else's talked quite like that: almost English, sometimes reminding him of Merle Oberon, though there was no physical resemblance. His mother was skinny and usually wore a housedress; she kept her brown hair in a bun. She never gave him any trouble.

He proceeded to cut two yards that afternoon: one belonged to an old lady named Mrs. Heffelfinger who lived alone, and the other to Leo Kirsch, who worked for his father. The latter was about a mile and a half from home and a half mile from the used-car lot. Although the early September day was no scorcher, Ralph was piss-sweaty from all the walking and pushing. Not being crazy to take the longer route home, he decided to go to the lot, where perhaps he could catch a ride with one of the salesmen on a demonstration drive, or maybe wait until his father was finished, talking meanwhile with Clarence and perhaps helping him wash or wax a car.

He had also to collect his fee from Leo, Leo's mother being some kind of invalid who stayed inside with the blinds drawn and you never saw her throughout the entire job.

While rolling the lawnmower along the sidewalks, Ralph suddenly got a hard-on for no reason at all, which was to say, not thinking of girls, and until it went away, which it did after one block of mental discipline, he had to walk in a kind of duck fashion so as to minimize the bulge in his chino pants. The penis was the strangest of all human organs, except perhaps the nose. In a sex book which a friend named Horse Hauser spirited out of his father's sock drawer, the ejaculation was compared to the sneeze as being inevitable of conclusion after it had once got started. In the same book, written by a medical doctor, they found the assertion that in some women the pubic hair had been known to grow to the *knees*, and they imagined it as a fantastic beard, hanging down.

As Ralph reached the other side of the street from the lot and waited for a Mack truck to rumble by, Leo came out of the Greek's, cleaning his teeth with his tongue.

"Hi, Leo," Ralph said.

"Hi, Ralph," said Leo, immediately going into his pants pocket. "I figure you're ready to bite me for four bits. You got the edges nice, right?" He forked over a half dollar so worn you could hardly see the eagle.

Ralph whipped the clippers from his back pocket and snapped them open and shut. "You bet."

Leo had turned and was looking back. Behind them a stringy-haired girl wearing a slack halter had come out of the Greek's. She had a faceful of pimples and wore glasses.

She said: "Hi, Ralph."

"Hi."

"What are you doing, cutting grass?"

"What's it look like?" riposted Ralph, and pushed the mower over the curb into the gutter.

"Friend of yours?" asked Leo, glancing back as they crossed the street together.

"I hope not," said Ralph. "She's some dope from my class."

Leo was seated at the desk of his mind, writing as follows: *Dearest, you don't know who I am, but I know who you are, and I am passionately in love with you, I don't care about your vision problem or your skin condition, my darling, I want you and need you, a thousand kisses, my dearest precious honey— Your Unknown Admirer.*

He would never actually write this letter. If he had so done, Margie would have swooned, thinking it had come from Ralph, on whom she had a crazy crush and went to sleep every night thinking of, with her toes curled.

Several persons were roaming the lot unattended, Jack no doubt being still inside the office with the buyer of the phaeton and Buddy not having appeared. This annoyed Leo, even though it gave him an opportunity to make up for the theoretical commission he had lost, because in so doing he would be disqualifying himself as a victim of injustice. He was also suffering from heartburn acquired at the Greek's, where he had seated himself at the far end of the counter so that, pretending to keep an eye on the lot across the street, he could ogle the girl, who sat on the first stool inside the door ravenously devouring a jelly doughnut. At 2:30 P.M. nobody occupied the intervening seats.

But hardly had Leo's hamburger been slammed down before him by the Greek, who was always surly after the proper lunch hour had passed, than Leo saw with despair that the girl was mashing the last morsel of doughnut between her lips, soon to be followed by the straw issuing from the bottle of Royal Crown Cola, the last inch of fluid from the bottom of which was sucked up with the appropriate and, to Leo, aphrodisiac sound.

He was forced to gobble his hamburger in two bites and without ketchup or even salt. The patty was grease-hot from the griddle, and Leo's eyes exuded water. He drained his glass of milk. To make it worse, the girl then only feinted at departure, rising merely to pick her back teeth with a forefinger, then sitting down again to order another doughnut.

Her first ferocious bite caused red jelly to squirt onto the countertop, the stingy Greek not providing a plate for small orders.

Thus Leo was compelled to leave before she did. He hoped that Ralph did not make an assumption from the reference to the girl, but he was not really worried. Ralph was a dumb kind of kid, no chip off Buddy's block, taking rather after Naomi, whom Leo respected as wife and mother but who was no great shakes in the upstairs department.

Ralph ran the lawnmower around back and leaned the handle against the wall. He saw his father talking to Clarence inside the open garage, and entered.

"Hi, Clarence." He ignored his father. It was locally customary never to greet your parents in public, since you resided with and were completely dependent upon them. The reverse was not true, however, at least not with Buddy, who was given to demonstrations of conspicuous affection and pride—backslapping, hair-rumpling, etc., which he never did at home. ("C'mere, Ralph, and meet Mr. Plage, vice-president of the Building and Loan. Fred, I'm mighty proud of this boy.") For some reason, Ralph rarely encountered his mother when out of the house, though she issued forth from time to time, walking to the grocery each day and sometimes taking the streetcar into the city for department-store sales, though generally returning home having purchased little.

Ralph was astonished now to hear Buddy say harshly, pointing towards the chain-link fence that separated his compound from the vacant lot in back: "Do you mind, Ralph?"

Ralph retired around the corner of the building, not at all hurt but puzzled as to what kind of confidential business his father would have with a colored man. Had Buddy been talking elbow-to-elbow with Leo or Jack, Ralph of course would have hung back for the green light.

Clarence on the other hand had assumed when Buddy

approached him privately that his employer wanted a piece of dark meat, i.e., wanted to use him as pimp, and behind the mask of his broken nose and milky eye he secretly smirked, believing that, in the inevitable white way, Buddy was impotent and sought black therapy. Before the bout in which Mulvaney had knocked out half his vision, Clarence had seen, when they were getting into their jockstraps in the common dressing room, that his own tool was twice the size of the Irishman's, which looked like a little chicken neck. Clarence knew nothing of Buddy's cocksmanship and would not have believed in it whatever the evidence. Both white women Clarence had himself fucked told him that all men of their race were basically queer, and they should know, being whores.

Jack had brought the Ford phaeton around back for Clarence to Simoniz. This was to impress the purchaser. Actually Clarence would not begin to rub the body until the financing was arranged on Monday with a loan company from which Buddy got a kickback for steering the borrower to its door.

Clarence was rubbing the hood with his forefinger to gauge the depth of the road film when Buddy entered the garage. To do a good job with the Simoniz cleaner would take him an entire day. The buyer would probably show up after his shift let out, Monday afternoon, and expect to drive the car away. Either Clarence would not have finished or the automobile would be imperfectly cleaned and shined. Clarence, who had a sense of craft, constantly had to make decisions of this sort; and whatever the conclusion, he would be blamed, and for the same thing: being colored.

"Hey, Clarence," Buddy said, a bit too loudly, and then lowered his voice for the subsequent remarks. He was not as cool about arranging a murder as he would have liked to be. He did not hate Naomi; he simply wanted to be rid of her. He would have preferred to press a button, causing her to disappear instantly.

"Hey, Clarence, what am I paying you?"

Clarence recognized this as rhetorical and did not answer. He had his dead eye on Buddy and the other angled to inspect Buddy's two-toned shoes.

"Fifteen, I think, and I think you'll admit that's fair considering I didn't turn you over to the police that time." Buddy saw what Clarence was looking at. "These shoes set me back twelve dollars. How you like a pair? Sure you would," said Buddy. "Be a big jitterbug." He pressed the end of his nose as if it were a switch. "Tell you what I need. You supply me and you got yourself a pair of these shoes."

When Clarence was not in his rubber boots he wore a pair of shoes that were cut open in places to ease his two corns and one bunion. He had no vanity about footgear. However he always carried a nice clean handkerchief in his back pocket. If he soiled it—which was seldom, because though his nose was broken it did not exude anything like the amount of snot of the typical white person with the inevitable sinus trouble—he luxuriously threw it away and bought another, encased in cellophane, for five cents at any drugstore, often to the visible amazement of the clerk. He now withdrew the latest and snorted dry into it. He knew how to play a nervous man like a fish.

Buddy said: "I see the idea appeals." He would have preferred though that Clarence had finger-covered one nostril at a time while blowing the other onto the floor and then smeared the deposit glistening across the cement with the sole of his boot. He found no utility in Negro niceties. "I'll make this short and sweet, Clarence. I'm looking for some bird with guts, for a little job I got in mind."

Clarence began to suspect his easy assumption had been in error. Although he was disappointed, he was not a foolishly stubborn man. Thus he had promptly accepted the truth that Irish Mulvaney could outslug him. He extended his lower lip in deliberation and shifted his stance.

"Now I won't mix you up with the details, which are kind of complicated. What I want is a guy who wouldn't have to take much of a chance to earn a nice piece of money, a real nice piece in fact." Buddy lowered his head and leaned towards Clarence's chest, looking from the tops of his eyes past Clarence's chin and as it were up into his flattened nostrils, Clarence having instinctively withdrawn his lip at the movement in his direction.

Clarence now spoke for the first time: "Money."

"It makes the world go round," Buddy said, reducing some of the intensity without diluting the earnestness. He straightened up.

"You don't want to say how much," Clarence stated.

"You know the kind of guy I mean." Neither was Buddy's a question.

Clarence scraped his boot. He was now figuring that Buddy wanted to start a fire that would burn up the cars for the insurance. A Jew had done that to his clothes store in Maywood, which was the proper name for the section known to whites as Darktown and to the colored population as the West Side. A number of people had lived in flats overhead as tenants of the Jew, among them a cousin of Clarence's, and the Jew had got them out of there before setting the fire: which was reckless of him, because when the insurance inspectors came around afterwards and asked the people if they had seen anything unusual, Clarence's cousin had said vengefully: "Just that Jew, carrying a can of gas at midnight." The rooms upstairs had been overrun with rats and the corridor toilet was always full of shit owing to a defective flushing mechanism.

At this moment Ralph came around the corner, and Buddy

sent him away. Next, Leo poked his head through the office door, saying accusingly: "There you are." Buddy failed to acknowledge this statement, and Leo retreated.

"The way I'm thinking," Clarence said suddenly, fixing Buddy with his good eye, "is *how much* leads to *who.*"

Buddy did not relish being eye-pinned by the likes of Clarence, whom in other circumstances he would have stared down. Now, though, it served his needs to be subtle. The less Clarence knew, the better. Once he got hold of the thug, he would conspire to keep Clarence in the dark: surely blood, black blood at that, was not thicker than money. In addition, he and the killer would be linked by murder. Thus he didn't want a moron who could not understand the equation.

"Somebody tough," Buddy said. "But somebody smart." He meant colored-tough, because it would not take much courage to kill a woman; and darky-smart, which was to say capable of an animal shrewdness but not clever enough to match wits with the man who paid him.

"I hears the price going up," said Clarence, who regarded himself as neither tough nor smart but rather *sensible.* The cousin who informed on the Jew was smart, and his ass was generally out.

Buddy had not intended to name a figure to Clarence, whose own fee after all was a pair of twelve-dollar shoes, but he now decided that the Negro was too stupid for jealousy.

"I wouldn't mind letting go of a couple hundred for a real good job. One down and the other when it's finished."

Two hundred for the black man who burned the place down, and thousands for Buddy when the insurance was paid off: the usual white deal.

Clarence squinted. "A hundred for tough, and a hundred for smart."

"You could say that." Buddy was toeing the threshold of impatience now: he had no intention of being analyzed by the likes of Clarence, in whose last statement he detected a hint of mockery.

Clarence let him stew for a while, then said: "When?"

"Don't you worry about that. You just bring me the individual, get your shoes, and forget about it. Keep your nose clean, Clarence. You don't need any more trouble."

This was the second reference of Buddy's to the unsuccessful attempt to steal the car three years before, and it caused the ex-boxer to reflect that having something on another man was in itself a form of insurance. His cousin was a fool: he should have told the Jew, not the insurance people, about the midnight can of gas, threatening to tell *them* unless the Jew paid off. Yes, Clarence could see that now; but he was no happier for the realization.

"When?" he repeated. "When should I bring the individual?"

Mockery again, quoting Buddy's very phraseology. However Buddy had let himself in for it by misinterpreting Clarence's first "when," which he had taken to mean *When must the deed be done?*

He tightened his nuts and said: "Soon as possible."

"Tonight?"

He was strengthened by Clarence's eagerness, having something to deny now. It was not the thought of murder that threatened Buddy: it was rather the need to ask another person for anything.

"No," he said with satisfaction, then arbitrarily named a time: "Tomorrow, eleven A.M."

"Sunday?"

Buddy was quickly derisive. "Sorry to interfere with your weekend drunk."

"I generally goes to church," said Clarence.

Buddy assumed this was more sarcasm. He had had

enough. "Eleven it is. And don't get fresh or you're out of a job." He turned briskly and returned to the office, where Jack was sitting at his, Buddy's, desk, doing the paperwork on the sale of the phaeton, with the purchaser, now looking uneasy, on a camp chair next to him. Leo sat behind his own desk, thumbnailing tablets into his mouth from a cylinder of Tums. Seeing Buddy, he pointed through the window with his other hand.

"We're losing business."

"Then get out there." Buddy took his blazer from the hatrack. "I got an appointment. If I don't get back, you lock up."

"What about the receipts?"

Buddy took the night-deposit key from the end of the golden chain that extended into his right pants pocket from a loop of belt. He handed it to Leo, who recoiled slightly.

"What's eating you? You know where the bank is, and the deposit slips are in the bottom desk drawer. You see me do that every night."

Leo swallowed hard to combat his heartburn. Buddy had never done this before in all the years he had worked for him. Leo was frightened by sudden changes of policy in any area: if his stool was discolored, for example, he was shaken to the core unless the doctor had previously warned him that a certain medication would produce that effect.

Buddy forced the key upon him. "You can't stand to be trusted," he said jovially.

Behind him, Jack was giving the young man a purchase agreement for signature, along with a fountain pen which he had just shaken into the wastebasket, speckling the balled paper with blue. He reversed the pen and indicated the signature-place with its butt. "Right there, Mr. Ballbacher."

Ballbacher began to shake his head. He stood up. "See, I

din't—" He made a ghastly grin. "The facts of the case is
. . . I ain't got that kind of money. I bit off more than I
could chew. See—"

Jack was himself grinning in a loathsome way, trying to
restrain his spite.

"I *told* you, Mr. *Ball*bacher, it's only *thirty*-five dollars
down, and you didn't make *any* objection to that, as I remember, now did you?" Jack felt like prying up the little lever on
the pen and squirting ink in his imbecile face.

"See," said Ballbacher, "I'm getting laid off."

Buddy whirled about in one of his dance steps, came
quickly to the young man, and put out his hand.

"I'm Mr. Sandifer," said he. "That's the name you see on
the sign outside, but they call me Buddy. What do they call
you?"

Ballbacher stood passively while Buddy pumped his hand.
"Dutch."

"Say, Dutch, now we know each other, why don't I knock
off another twenty simoleons in the name of friendship?"
Buddy now claimed Ballbacher's entire right forearm, clamp-
ing it at the elbow while continuing to squeeze the hand.

"I'm real sorry, Mr.—"

"Buddy."

"I ain't got the money, and can't get it." Ballbacher shook
his head doggedly. "Eyes bigger than my stomach." He was
trying to break away from Buddy now. "I got a sick wife, and
my kid has a mastoid—"

"Let's have a private conversation," Buddy said, and by
leverage on the forearm propelled Ballbacher out the front
door in almost a run, though the young man was larger than
he and heavily muscled. There was a physical aspect to sales-
manship; some customers were best manipulated by running
away from them. Ballbacher could be bullied; he admitted
guilt by explaining and apologizing.

"Where you work, Dutch?"

"The foundry."

Buddy turned him so that he looked into the sun.

"Dutch, you know what a verbal contract is?" Buddy did not wait for an answer. "That's when you say you're gonna buy something. You don't have to sign anything. You just have to tell a salesman, 'Yeah, I'll take that phaeton.' Yeah, that's how it works, Dutch."

Ballbacher stank of sweat, but Buddy hung on. "It's the law, Dutch, and nothing you or I can do about it."

Ballbacher frowned. "All I said was 'O.K.' "

Buddy chortled gaily. "Same thing, Dutch. That's what the law calls a verbal contract." He pointed across the street. "Like you go in the Greasy Greek's. You don't say, 'I'll give you fifteen cents for a hamburger.' You say, 'Give me a hamburger.' " Buddy let him go suddenly and slapped his shoulder. "You say *give me*, Dutch, but you're liable for the charge."

Buddy walked away, forsaking Ballbacher, isolating him in the sunshine. In the nearest rank of cars a swarthy little man was opening the driver's door of a '31 Chevy sedan. He slammed it shut, opened it, and slammed it again.

"You'll admit that's a solid body," Buddy said. The man grimaced and shrugged. "Preachers take good care of their machines," said Buddy. "Take a look at that upholstery."

He returned to Ballbacher, who had not moved.

"If you think I'd try to bamboozle a family man, you're wrong," Buddy told him. "I'm one myself. Now, you hit a run of bad luck, get laid off for a while, could happen to anybody in these days. But you got Buddy Sandifer on your side. I need your business, Dutch. I can't afford to make enemies. One word from me down at the loan company, and they'll give you time, Dutch, more time: time's money, Dutch. And in time you'll be back on your feet again."

Ballbacher rubbed his chin and stared bovinely at Buddy. The sun did not seem to trouble him.

He said: "You say I got to buy the automobile even when I didn't sign nothing?"

"I don't say that, Dutch. The *law* says so."

Ballbacher nodded, so heavily that his head stayed down as he walked towards the street.

"Just a minute, fella!" cried Buddy, not following. "You come back here."

Ballbacher responded promptly to this order. He turned, came back, and said deliberately: "Shit on you. You're a goddam chiseler."

Before Buddy's rising fists had got beyond his waist, Ballbacher struck him powerfully in the center of the chest, causing him to back-pedal furiously until he went down on the seat of his white flannels. Ballbacher did not linger to enjoy this, but walked steadily off the lot.

Buddy entered the office and, shoving Jack aside, got his .38 Police Special from the desk. Jack's forehead receded at the appearance of the pistol. He had not seen the prelude to the show of weaponry.

But Leo had and, dropping the roll of Tums he had continued to hold as a talisman, leaped to intercede.

"I'll kill that dicklicker," cried Buddy, waving the gun everywhere.

"No Buddy no Buddy no no no," said Leo, making a desperate song of it. He clasped his boss at the waist, going after the pistol with his other set of fingers. They did a nifty foxtrot between the desks.

"I'll spoil his fucking meat," Buddy said.

Jack was shivering in the chair.

"Jack," said Leo urgently. "For Christ sake." But by the time Jack got to them, Buddy had ceased to struggle except in a rhetorical or symbolic style, gesturing with the pistol and howling indiscriminately.

Clarence could hear this back in the garage, where he was prying a tire off a rim, but he was never curious about the emotional displays of persons socially remote from him.

Ralph, sitting alongside his lawnmower in the shade on the far side of the building, where the blacktop gave way to gravel, heard nothing. Unlike his father he was easily distracted by trivial phenomena. He watched a lone starling peck futilely at stones and wondered how birds fucked. He looked into the waste ground beyond the chain-link fence and developed a fantasy in which, prowling thereupon, he discovered a concrete trapdoor flush with the earth and, lifting it by means of a rusty iron ring, exposed a set of descending stairs, at the bottom of which he found an enormous gambling den full of roulette tables, raucous music, and painted trollops, unbeknownst to the upper world.

John Dillinger had busted out of jail using a gun he had modeled in wood and blackened with shoe polish, and not long afterwards one of the villains in *Dick Tracy* carved a pistol from an Idaho potato, darkening it with tincture of iodine, which turned blue when in contact with starch. There was one of those little eight-page dirty books that showed Dick putting the blocks to Tess Trueheart. All the famous characters looked exactly as they did in the respectable funny-papers, except their peckers and snatches were shown starting on the second page.

Ralph had never yet in all his life seen a real pussy with hair on it, and no bare tits all the way to the nipples except in photographs.

He wondered whether he had waited long enough for his father to finish the conversation with Clarence. Ralph had not possessed an accurate sense of the duration of time since suffering a bad sunburn at the age of eleven, in consequence of which he had been delirious for twenty-four hours. He picked up the clippers, which he had taken from his back pocket before sitting down so that he would not be stabbed in the spine, stood up, and heard the gravel fall clattering from his ass.

After brushing away the rest of it, he went in back and saw his father gunning the car around the corner of the building. He ran and called, but when he gained the corner Buddy had already reached the street, turned onto it, and made his getaway burning rubber.

Inside, Jack was holding the gun. After a slow start, it had been he who finally disarmed Buddy.

Leo shook his head. He felt the effects of the incident. To dispel them, he said: "This has been some day."

Jack returned the pistol to the drawer from which Buddy had taken it. A flat pint of whiskey lay within. Jack could have used a drink, but being a schoolteacher would not dare take one except behind the closed door of his home.

"This ought to be locked," he said. "A child might get hold of it. You know what they say: everybody gets shot with an unloaded gun."

Hearing the nonsensical statement, Leo felt better. "But that one's loaded," said he.

"Would he have shot him, you think?"

"I couldn't say," Leo confessed. "I never saw him do anything like that before. But I never saw him take a sucker punch, either." He paused. "The whole thing was dumb. I don't know what's eating Buddy. Notice he didn't work the lot this afternoon. He stands in the garage, chewing the rag with a jigaboo."

"Where'd he go now?" asked Jack.

Leo made a moue of certainty. "To drive it off, that's for sure." But he remembered that Buddy had already been preparing to leave early, before the set-to. Without thinking of the effect it might have on Jack, he said: "To get his ashes hauled."

Jack's sexual imagination was quite domesticated, however; he had never had a woman before the first night of his honeymoon and none but his wife since, though sometimes when they did it he had fantasies involving movie actresses—oddly enough, the nonsensual types like Irene Dunne. He naturally supposed it was Mrs. Sandifer who quenched Buddy's fire, and he showed no astonishment.

Leo was relieved to see his thoughtless remark fall by the wayside. He never trafficked in sex gossip.

Ralph came into the office at that point, saying: "Shit, I wanted a ride home."

"You talk like that," Leo said disapprovingly, "and you won't get one." Ralph was taken aback. Leo went on, scowling: "A friend of yours told me you stank. I said, 'Like shit!'" Then he showed his teeth, poked Ralph in the belly, and roared. Ralph joined in the laughter. Jack did not, being a schoolteacher. But he prissily loosened the knot of his washable tie and opened his collar.

Leo told Ralph: "Listen, you run up all the windows and lock all the cars, and I'll drop you off."

"Is it closing time already?" Ralph grimaced at what he believed another failure of his inner clock.

Though usually the steadiest of men, Leo had been made disorderly by Buddy's unprecedented loss of control—as Clarence, no schemer, had been led by Buddy's threats to an understanding of blackmail.

"That's right," Leo said recklessly. "Your dad's decided to call it a day." He amazed himself as well as Jack, whose eyebrows arched. Jack had earned no commission whatever, this Saturday; yet, infected by Leo's capriciousness, he made no protest. Instead, he opened the drawer, took out the pint of

Seagram's, unscrewed the cap, and boldly poured whiskey down his throat in full view of Ralph.

Leo was hit hard by this seizing of the initiative. He did not himself imbibe.

"Hey, Ralph," he said desperately. "You want a drink?"

Ralph said: "Sure." He always enjoyed Leo's badinage.

But Jack cried: "Leo!" And put the bottle away posthaste, avoiding Ralph's eyes. Better to ride it out than to ask Ralph to say nothing. Jack knew better than to put himself at the mercy of a schoolboy. But he struck back at Leo.

"What about the receipts?"

Leo decided Jack was getting too big for his breeches: he found the question even more insolent than the drinking.

"You just let me worry about that," said he. "You can take off now if you want." In the absence of Buddy, Leo considered himself boss. Jack flipped his hands and went into the little washroom in the far corner; already he had begun to feel the effects of the whiskey. If he went home having earned no money and with alcohol on his breath, his wife would think the worst.

Leo went to the short, squat safe behind Buddy's desk. Its door was never closed, the only valuables, the checks and cash of the day, being kept within in a green metal box, locked by a key of which Buddy and Leo had examples, but not part-time employee Jack. Before leaving the lot each evening, Buddy emptied the box and prepared a deposit slip, then drove to the bank and dumped the tan envelope in the night chute. As Buddy himself had said just before the run-in with Ballbacher, Leo had seen him do this many times.

Yet having now to do it himself made Leo uneasy. He liked money but feared its physical reality. He paid all bills immediately, in cash, going in person to the Light & Power and Bell Telephone offices. His expenditures for living were modest; his invalid mother did not cost him as much as he let people assume, the doctor having long since announced that her ailments were imaginary and prescribed only sugar pills. It would have been much more expensive to keep her in a madhouse; she was harmless enough, all the more so when she believed she was dying and stayed in bed. Leo's earnings averaged out, give or take, at thirty-five per week.

He took the cashbox from the safe and put it on Buddy's desk, saying to Ralph: "Your dad's still working on his first million."

Jack could be heard urinating. Embarrassed by the sound and fearful that the schoolteacher would also fart, as some men did while so engaged, Ralph said: "I'll lock up the cars," and exited.

Leo found a deposit slip and, having opened the cashbox, began to record the amounts of the cashiers' checks therein. This done, he turned to the greenbacks, some crumpled and almost black from use, others so crisp and fresh as to look bogus. His first count came to $387. Incredulous, he recounted and arrived at the even more unlikely sum of $429. He had himself made only one cash sale all day: a '33 Ford station wagon, with sides of rotten wood, for an adjusted price of $85. Buddy, and perhaps Jack as well, must have sold several cars either under his nose or behind his back: remarkable in such a small organization.

He looked for the vouchers which should have been placed in the box along with the money for each sale, but, aside from his own for the $85, found only those for transactions by check.

Jack emerged from the toilet. Leo was about to seek his help on the problem at hand, but noticed that a glimpse of Jack's shirttail was available in the wrong place: namely, his fly.

"Better close the barn door before the horse gets out," he said, pointing.

35

Nodding in despair, the schoolteacher fastened the lower button of his suit jacket, the skirt of which was however too short to conceal the delinquency.

"My shorts and shirttail both are caught in the zipper," said he, rolling his eyes. "Some kettle of fish."

"Get a pliers from Clarence."

"Say, that's an idea," said Jack. "I was going to sneak to the car and drive home." He went into the garage.

Clarence saw him approaching with his fly open, and determined to hit the big fairy with a tire iron if he tried anything funny.

In the office Leo counted the cash a third time: $325. On the deposit slip he listed only the $85 he had himself collected. He put the slip, this money, and the checks into the manila envelope and closed but did not seal the flap. The remainder of the cash, rolled, went into his left pants pocket, where it exerted an interesting pressure against his genitals lodged nearby.

Ralph returned with all the car keys, each with its dirty-white tag listing the model. Leo dropped these into the bottom of an old candy box and put the box in Buddy's wastebasket, covering it with the discarded paper.

"How come not the safe?" asked Ralph.

"They could blow it open. But nobody'd ever look here."

Leo poked his head into the garage and saw Jack working with the pliers at his crotch. He waved the envelope. "Lock up, willya? I'm going to the bank."

Jack distractedly agreed to that. He had his own key; he was often first to arrive on Saturday morning, eager to make the most of his day. Clarence was rolling a wire wheel, which bore a soft tire, towards the air hose out back. Nobody had told him they were closing.

"Hey, Champ," Leo shouted. "You're through for the day." Clarence let the wheel fall crashing where he was and went to wash up at the hose with Lava Soap. He had never been invited to use the office lavatory; he had in fact never been inside the office.

"No dice," said Leo when he came out the front door onto the lot and saw Ralph bringing the lawnmower around the side of the building.

"It'll go in the trunk, Leo," said Ralph.

"The handle won't, and that's illegal unless you tie on a red rag and I ain't got one." He pointed to his faded blue four-door '34 Plymouth. "Get in and leave the mower here. I'm telling you, Ralph."

The luxurious thought of stealing the money was infecting Leo with rudeness. Of course it was all playacting, his plan being to retain the cash only until he could account for it properly. Yet here he was, climbing behind the wheel, about to leave the lot for the weekend with a pocketful of filthy lucre for which he had made three sums, each inconsistent with the others, and he had not even queried Jack as to the missing vouchers, nor had he looked in the sales ledger in which all transactions were entered by Buddy, the first record he should have consulted for enlightenment when the cash-box proved cryptic.

Without a clue to this, Ralph wondered why his friend Leo was acting so pricky all of a sudden.

chapter 2

LAVERNE'S TOP-FLOOR FLAT, in the rear of the two-story building, was reached by an outside staircase. In his current state, Buddy did not trouble to take the giant step that would evade the fourth tread, which shrieked at the imposition of weight. Ordinarily he liked to arrive silent as a burglar and apprehend Laverne in the act of bleaching her hair with cotton balls dipped in a saucer of peroxide or washing her step-ins. Buddy delighted in the particulars of illicit domesticity, whereas in his proper home the sight of a basinful of Naomi's slimy wet hose was greatly offensive to him.

Now however he had other needs. Gasping from the immediate climb, his skin prickly-heated from the several rushes and recessions of blood as anger alternated with shame—he had been tricked into an ineffective defense of his honor, humiliated before his employees, and not by Ballbacher, that shitheel, but by himself; made *disorderly*—aching, panting, and with a smudge on the seat of his white flannels, not covered by the tail of his blazer, he opened Laverne's never-latched screendoor and entered her living room.

The shades were drawn against the heat even on this not hot day, and it was warmer inside than out. The room as usual had an odor that reminded him of firecracker punk, though actually it came from the incense she often burned in the belly of a little brass Buddha on the whatnot shelf alongside the hand-colored portrait photo of herself taken at the time of her confirmation: the expression slightly petulant owing to the onset of her first period, for which her mother had not prepared her; staring into the camera, her pants full of blood. Fastidious Buddy disliked such reminiscences.

"Izzat you, stinkpot?"

Buddy was in no mood to give the traditional Bronx cheer in reply. He silently went through three feet of hallway, entered the bedroom, and was struck over the head with a stuffed animal.

Laverne was plastered against the wall just inside the door, smirking, blouseless, her white-brassiered boobies looking even more tremendous than usual. Buddy retrieved the pink ᵃlephant from the floor. For an instant he considered hurling it back at her, having at the moment no stomach for accepting even a tender attack without retaliation, but as always the presence of Laverne's aggressive flesh worked its marvelous magic.

While she stripped, he fitted the animal between the cheeks of his ass, threading its trunk between his legs to emerge in front, where he swung it in clockwise revolutions. For her part she extended and waggled her tongue, then said, in an artificially rough contralto: "I can take all you got and then some." Causing him to drop the limp synthetic member and expose the real one, stiffened by her boast. She seized it and led him around the room as if he were a little red wagon.

In no time at all Buddy's chagrin had decamped. . . .

After knocking one off in the summertime, Buddy liked to stay in bed awhile, lying in his sweat, though in winter he immediately jumped up and dressed so as not to risk a chill. With two long blood-red talons, Laverne peeled the fishskin from his member and took it away.

The toilet exploded in a flush, and she returned, purple-tipped bazooms wobbling. She sat down on the edge of the bed, reached under the pink-shaded lamp, claimed the pasteboard box of Sheffields, then slid the little drawer out and plucked up one of the cigarettes. She had a lighter that was shaped like an automatic pistol: you pulled the trigger and a flame sprang up through a tiny trapdoor on top of the barrel about halfway along.

Having fired up her cigarette, Laverne said: "Did you tell her?"

Buddy spotted a piece of flaking paint on the ceiling almost directly overhead. If the roof leaked the plaster would eventually fall; that could be lethal to an occupant of the bed.

"Ralph was there."

"Today was the day you were going to tell her."

"Ralph sat there, eating like a horse. I don't know where he puts it." Buddy patted his plumpish midsection and in so doing encountered a large fluff of lint in his navel though he had showered that morning. "He stays skinny as a rail."

Laverne nodded and spewed smoke from lips from which she had wiped the smudged color while in the bathroom disposing of the fishskin.

"You're going to do it, though, right, Buddy? You're gonna find the occasion. You promised."

"You got my word on it."

"I don't know, Bud," said Laverne. "You been saying that since the Year One. What would you do if I cut off the nookie supply?"

She made this threat periodically. As usual, Buddy dismissed it with levity.

"I'd just have to whip my willie by hand," said he. He raised himself on the near elbow and, pivoting, swung his legs to the floor on the far side of the bed.

With his back to her, he said soberly: "Look, baby—"

"You're not gonna do it, are you, Buddy? You're not ever going to do it."

"I been working on it. You don't know how hard—"

"And you can't do it."

"No, no," said Buddy. "You ain't got it straight. You don't know what I mean, kid." He adjusted his tool, which was still shrinking inside the foreskin. "I been thinking for a long time. Some things are hard to put into words."

Suddenly he twisted around. "Where would she go if I dumped her?"

Laverne continued to stare at him. He put a hand on her shoulder cap. "I'm working on an idea." Laverne of course knew nothing of his plan to have Naomi killed. It was not the sort of thing you could reveal even to its beneficiary. "You know I love you, baby. But I wanna do right by all concerned: that's the kind of monkey I am. Besides, I don't have any grounds on her, so she'd have to be the one who files against me, and how would that look for the business if it gets messy? And I don't relish the thought of bringing you into it, getting you smeared with filth."

Buddy got up and walked off the woolly bedside rug. He stole a look to see how Laverne was taking this and saw that the cigarette had fallen from the slot of the undersized ashtray and was burning the surface of the night table. He went to put it out and saw several other scars on the varnish. The pink satin shade on the lamp had separated here and there from the top ring of wire. He tried the switch.

"Hey, the bulb is out."

41

"I don't go in the grocery store any more, Buddy. They give me funny looks."

To forestall the expansion of this statement, he said quickly: "Oh screw them, Laverne. You should care about some little pissants in dirty aprons. Besides, I told you to order by phone."

"Yeah, great, so that delivery boy wants more than a nickel, I can tell you."

Buddy turned from the table and peered down at the dark roots in her scalp. "What's that supposed to mean?"

"He hangs around," cried Laverne. "He thinks I'm a fast one, Buddy."

"That little punk!" Buddy thrust his lightly haired chest out beyond his belly. "I'll hand him his head." He punched a fist into a palm. "I'll sour his milk."

"He wouldn't do it if you was here."

"What's he do?"

"It's the way he looks. He don't have respect."

Buddy walked to the foot of the bed and put a hand on either upright of the bedstead and leaned in.

"Look," he said. "This thing is driving me wild too. All I want is a life with you. Is that too much to ask? We got a right to happiness!" He took a deep breath and felt the area of soreness where Ballacher had struck him.

"The way you talked back then, it was so simple."

"It wasn't that long ago."

"Well," said Laverne, "it was March and here we are at the beginning of September."

"I thought at first we'd just have a few laughs, and then this thing hit me like a ton of bricks. I can name the exact minute—"

"When the band played 'Always' at the Palm Terrace," said Laverne. " 'That refers to us, baby,' you said. 'Not for just an hour, not for just a day, not for just a year, but always.' I want a whole life with you, sweetheart, all of you, all the time."

Buddy also recalled that shortly thereafter he felt an alien hand on his shoulder, opened his eyes, and saw, partly through Laverne's hair, the figure of the bouncer, who said: "House rule. No intimacies on the dance floor." And those pricks collected a dollar cover charge per person.

"I wasn't talking through my hat then," he said, "and I have not changed since."

Leo was going to take Ralph home before driving to the bank, though the latter was much nearer the lot than the Sandifer house, but at the crucial turn he suddenly altered his plan, wheeled to the right, and went along Philathea Street in a southerly direction.

"I got to drop this off," said he, taking his hand from the black gearshift knob and tapping the fat brown envelope on the seat between them. "It's full of mazuma, and I don't want to get stuck up."

"Did anybody ever knock over this bank? Baby Face Nelson or Homer Van Meter or one of those guys?"

"You'd of heard about it if they did," said Leo, sucking his teeth.

"Anybody ever pick the lock of the night deposit?"

"Wouldn't do them any good. You can't reach down to the basement."

"What about a long wire?" Ralph asked. "With a hook on the end of it."

Leo found himself enjoying this juvenile conversation. It postponed the moment at which he must decide what to do about the money in his pocket.

"There's a swinging shelf or door inside, at the top of the chute, sort of," he said. "It swings down but not the other way, so if you was pulling something up it would close and you would run up against it, more or less." He punched Ralph's bony knee. "You got to think up a better way to make your bundle."

"Yeah, cutting grass," said Ralph, and made a face. He thought with annoyance of the lawnmower still down at the lot.

Leo pulled in to the curb, scraping the sidewalls of the tires with a horrible sound. "Here," he said, taking the key ring from the pocket of his seersucker jacket. "You make the deposit." His voice assumed a nasty edge. "You're the son and heir. It'll all be yours someday anyhow."

That is, if Buddy didn't blow it all on his chippies. Leo was intoxicating himself with resentment, as a faint-hearted man gulps alcohol in preparation for an approach on a woman guarded by taboo: race, loyalty, or law. The moment lay at hand. He could still add the diverted cash to the contents of the envelope, correct the slip, punctiliously initialing the changes, seal the flap, and present the package to Ralph for deposit. But to do so, he must once again count the stack of money which in each of the three previous tallies had emerged with a different total from the last.

As it happened, Ralph took the decision from him, seizing key and envelope, and in a trice the boy had crossed the sidewalk to the bronze trapdoor and only his fumbling at the lock gave Leo time to shout from the window.

"Seal that envelope! The flap is open."

The stickum tasted slightly of menthol. Ralph pressed the envelope against the smooth yellow brick of the bank's wall and fingered the flap down. He unlocked the entrance to the chute and dropped the envelope within, not seeing the hinged barrier of which Leo spoke. Depositing money in this fashion was like dropping crap into a toilet: down the sewer, never to be seen again in its current form. "Did you ever realize,"

Horse Hauser once asked, "how much dissolved shit is in the oceans of the world?"

Leo said nothing en route to Ralph's house, though his lips moved from time to time as if he were sucking on a Sen-Sen. One long black hair grew from his right ear. A lot of adult guys let things like that go: nose-shrubbery, hickeys, etc. As yet Ralph had good skin, but he was eternally vigilant for pimples. Several kids in his class were acned like the surface of the moon, and many had blossoms on their cheeks. Candy was said to bring these out on girls; on boys, jacking off. Ralph always inspected his face carefully after yanking his crank.

At the conclusion of the sloppy U-turn that brought the car before the Sandifer house, this time about a yard from the curb—for an auto salesman, he was a lousy driver—Leo finally spoke.

"How's your mom these days?"

"Swell," said Ralph.

"I ain't seen her in a coon's age."

"Well, she's always there." Ralph opened the door and stepped over the running board, to which he had some ritualistic aversion, onto the paved square that interrupted the continuous strip of grass.

Leo was about to move off when Ralph turned and came back. He stuck his head through the window. "I forgot to say thanks for the lift."

"I thought I had a flat or something," said Leo. "Don't mention it, sport." He liked nice manners in a boy.

With the money in his pocket, Leo postponed going home. He wandered around town in his car. After the second tour of the business district, he went across the railroad tracks and then followed the creek for a mile, passing the dairy, the ice plant, and a siding full of boxcars. Through the open door of one of the last he saw two hoboes. He exchanged bleak stares

45

with them. The life of the road held no allure for Leo: coffee in a can, going to the toilet in a field, getting rousted by the railroad cops, would outweigh the romantic rewards if any.

Though in the earlier Depression years many ruined millionaires, unemployed executives, and forgotten war heroes were alleged to have become bindlestiffs, the tramps you saw locally had low foreheads and if refused a doorstep meal could turn surly unless you had or pretended to have superior force. Leo did not own an animal, yet he had posted on his gate a sign reading: BEWARE OF DOG. Kids pulled it down the next Halloween, having it in for him because he would not contribute to the trash drive by which they hoped to raise money for softball sweaters.

Leo held on to his old newspapers, iron objects, and tinfoil (he had accumulated a sphere the size of an orange) to sell himself to the Hunky junkman who came around twice a month with a horse and wagon, crying some gibberish. If Leo saw a pop bottle in gutter or empty lot he would add it to the collection of such vessels he kept in a milk crate in the trunk of his car, redeeming them for two cents each when his supply exceeded one dozen.

He was that sort of guy. On the other hand, he bought good food, always specifying ground beef and not hamburger (which could contain anything from pig's guts to human fingers lost to the chopping machine). And he enjoyed the extravagance of paying Ralph Sandifer fifty cents to cut his lawn every Saturday, so that his own Sundays were free for slow and repeated perusals of the rotogravure section of the newspaper, which often printed pictures of young girls at swimming pools throughout the metropolitan area ("The bevy of local cuties above, l. to r.: Suejane Criswell, Ellen Reingold, Dorjean Wattle"). Sitting on the cistern cover in the shade of a half-dead elm, the smell of mown grass around him, Leo would peer at Dorjean's little pointy breasts and write one of his imaginary letters: *Dear Miss Wattle, I couldn't help but being passionately attracted to you on the basis of your recent photo as published in The Graphic* . . . This would be more stilted, less inordinate than the note to the girl, Ralph's acquaintance, he had followed into the Greek's, because he had seen Dorjean only in the paper.

But here he was, this careful man, driving about with several hundred dollars which as yet could not be termed stolen but in no event could be called his property.

chapter 3

LAVERNE WAS PREPARING one of Buddy's favorite suppers: fried pork chops, fried potatoes, fried apples. Standing at the stove, she wore his favorite costume: a short frilly pink apron over black-lace step-ins and brassiere, long-gartered silk stockings, and platform shoes.

Buddy relished the sight of her from behind in this garb. Sometimes he would steal up and pinch her bottom. Otherwise he sat at the kitchen table, fully dressed in his street clothes, including necktie but not blazer. He had even brushed his teeth with the Squibb toothbrush he maintained in a celluloid case in the medicine chest.

Laverne was a robust woman, only two inches shorter than his own five-nine, and weighing a good 130: a big blonde, a real armful. She lifted the edge of the pan top with which she had covered the skillet so as not to be spattered with sizzling fat and peered underneath. She squealed and dropped it instantly: a flying grease drop had escaped and smitten her wrist.

"Dagnab it!" Even when hurt she would not curse: Buddy liked that trait.

Concerned, he half rose. "Want the Unguentine?"

She wiped her arm with a quilted potholder and raised it to her squinting eyes. Laverne was farsighted but refused to consider glasses. Because of her attire the windowshade was lowered, and the light was far from good.

"Naw, it's nothing."

"Next time," said Buddy, "hold the lid like a shield; you know, like King Arthur."

"That's what *she* does, right?"

"Come on, honeypot, don't be a dope. I figured that out sitting here right now. I figure out a lot of things from time to time. I ought to get a patent on them."

"Oh, yeah?" Using his suggested trick, Laverne determined that the chops were done on one side and levered them over with a spatula. "Like what?" This was no wiseguy, doubting question: she was always interested in hearing his ideas.

"Well, the other day when you had your period, remember, you said how it embarrassed you to go inna drugstore and buy Kotexes if a man waits on you."

"Worse if it's some smarty-pants kid," she said. She seemed to be developing an obsession about teen-aged boys. Buddy thought privately that if it were Ralph, the lad would be more ashamed than she, but he agreed diplomatically.

"Sure, sure. I used to feel like that if I had to buy cundrums from a woman."

"You have to call 'em that, Buddy?"

"Sweetie, I told you that's not a dirty word. It's the right name. It doesn't come from 'cunt.' "

"You don't see it on the package, do you? Why can't you say 'prophylactics,' huh?"

Buddy sighed. "O.K. What I'm getting at is, you know Ralph, he sends away for a lot of free catalogues and samples.

49

Last year the kid bought a dollar's worth of penny postcards and sent all hundred out . . ."

Laverne frowned and turned away. She had nothing against Ralph, whom she had never seen, except that he was part of Buddy's other life—and that Buddy had only an hour ago used him as an excuse for not telling Naomi he wanted a divorce. Buddy was insensitive to this, though he never mentioned Naomi to her if he could help it.

"And you know I get my fishskins by mail, in plain wrapper —could be a box of cigars. They sell everything that way nowadays. Convenience. In your own home, see?"

Laverne had the potatoes all sliced and ready, and the apples as well. She salted the former and dusted the latter with sugar and a sprinkling of cinnamon, the aroma of which reached Buddy and implemented the sense of well-being that had already been created in him by the lovemaking, the shower, Laverne's costume, and the bouquet of pork chops frying in bacon grease. Ballbacher and, for that matter, even Naomi were distant unpleasantnesses.

"Now, here's my idea: how about Kotexes by mail order? The feature is, a woman's period comes up every month on schedule. You could have a standing order. Every thirty days, see, a box of Kotex is automatically mailed to the woman, like a magazine subscription. Plain wrapper, comes right to the house. No embarrassment of drugstores. Also, it would probably be cheaper because of the guaranteed order, like a magazine costs less by mail than on a newsstand."

"Yeah, I subscribe to *Silver Screen* for that very reason," said Laverne, who read more about movie luminaries than she saw pictures. One of her ambitions was to visit Hollywood and take the bus tour of the stars' homes, as had been done by a female acquaintance who won the trip in a marathon dance contest some years earlier. More than once Laverne had mentioned to Buddy that California would be a nifty place for a honeymoon.

"See," said Buddy, "that's the kind of idea I ought to get a patent on. Kotex-of-the-Month Club."

"That's a swell idea, Bud." In taking the pork chops from the skillet she dropped one, and it skidded across the linoleum almost to Buddy's shoes. "Oops," said she, "wrong number." She retrieved it and went to the sink, where she rinsed it under the hot-water faucet. "I'll take this one," she said.

"Don't be dumb," said Buddy.

"No, the juice is all washed off." She was a wonderful girl, always concerned for his welfare. Buddy went over and put his hands under her apron.

When Leo got home his mother said: "You missed it, Leo." She lay on the davenport under an afghan. From the corner the parrot screeched.

Leo said: "I'll bet." He went to the parrot's cage. The bird turned its scruffy green head upside down and uttered a piercing whistle. Leo had owned him for almost twenty years. God knew how old it was. Some said they lived to eighty or more. Leo had been willed it by an old lady to whom he had delivered newspapers as a lad.

The parrot greeted him with its own name: "Hi, Boy."

"Hi, Boy," Leo answered, and then clucked with his tongue.

Boy brought his head to its normal position and laughed cacophonously. This was an affectionate utterance: Boy was fond of Leo. Boy and Leo's mother ignored each other. Boy detested all strangers, but had seen few if any in years.

"You missed my hemorrhage," explained Leo's mother.

51

"Blood gushed from my nose and throat. I left a trail throughout the house."

Leo did not trouble to seek the evidence. In earlier years he would have said he saw no blood, and his mother would have answered that she had cleaned it up, and he would have said the carpet was not damp, and she would have answered that it had dried quickly on such a warm day, and he would have said that it wasn't especially warm today, and she would have responded with a smug smile.

You couldn't get an argument out of his mother, who had the peculiarity of talking to herself when addressing him, though she never did it when alone, as he had frequently observed from places of hiding.

"Bum!" Boy cried fondly, behind his back.

With the money in his pocket and the heartburn in his midsection, Leo had little interest in food. Without hope he said: "I guess if you're so sick you won't want much of a supper. I was thinking I'd open a can of tomato soup—"

"And then?" asked his mother, her eyes full of gluttonous glee. She had never needed glasses and did not have a single filling. At fifty-eight she looked as if she had been a beauty at twenty; yet old photos did not support this assumption, showing her as rather plain.

"Uh-huh," Leo said stoically, "you want me to heat the pot roast and make mashed potatoes and peas 'n' carrots?" His mother was nodding vigorously. "Feed a hemorrhage, starve a fever," said he. "Well, let me go and get washed first."

He went through the beaded curtain into the hallway and began deliberately to climb the stairs.

"Leo," called his mother. "What's dessert?"

He supported himself on the banister and pondered. 'There's some devil's-food left and then I could open a can of apricots."

In his room Leo took off the seersucker jacket, examined the collar, saw quite a ring of oily dirt, and hung the garment on the closet doorknob so he would remember to deal with it on the morrow. Looking down at his pants, he saw a conspicuous bulge so near his crotch that a neutral observer might have taken it for an erection: the wad of money. He withdrew it and placed it on the dresser between a cigar box that contained collar studs, a penknife, and other items owned by his late father and a faded photograph of the man in the uniform of the Spanish-American War, in which his father had claimed to serve as one of Teddy Roosevelt's Rough Riders; but once when he had one too many he confessed he had actually been some kind of rear-area supply clerk.

From time to time it had occurred to Leo that his father might have jumped, and not fallen, off the roof, where he had ostensibly gone to search for a persistent leak. This was an absurd thought, given his father's happy-go-lucky temperament: the man was grinning in this very picture. Though if you looked very long at a frozen, photographic smile it turned into a grimace of hatred.

Leo removed his pants and put them on a hanger. He stood now in his sagging BVD's and dark-green white-clocked lisle socks, navy-blue garters, and light-tan oxfords. Leo was mildly bowlegged—not enough to illustrate his father's old joke: "If he stood next to a sawbuck he'd spell OX"—but otherwise he had a decent build of the sinewy type. He took good care of himself generally, drinking a pint of milk every day and always starting out with a hearty breakfast of the country-fresh eggs that were delivered once a week by a farmer. The greasy hamburger had been an aberrant snack.

He thought of counting the money again, but he was under an even worse pressure here than at the office, his mother expecting her supper momentarily so that she could be finished by the time her radio programs came on. A sense of responsibility was Leo's principal trait of character.

After he washed the dishes he would take his Saturday night bath, go to bed, and sleep soundly unless awakened by the sound of his mother's vomiting in the bathroom. She did this, whether really or in simulation, several nights a week, continuing to retch until she had routed him from bed.

However, Leo was not basically a bitter man. He found his mother no more alien than any other full-grown woman.

Ralph could not have cut the back yard anyway: it was full of wet wash on ropes stretched between iron standards and supported here and there with splintery wooden clothes props. No one but his mother would have done the wash on Saturday; she was unrepresentative in that as well as other areas, and also inconsistent: by accident she might even occasionally do the laundry on Monday.

He found her in the kitchen, opening a can of salmon.

"You know I said at lunch I would cut our grass?"

Naomi dumped the solid pink cylinder into a bowl and began to mash it. "And you can't because of the wash."

"That would sure be a good excuse, but the truth is I left the lawnmower down at the lot. I just wanted you to know why I didn't keep my word."

"Ralph, do you think that sometimes you are too honest?" She turned the bowl over and violently shook its contents onto a plateful of lettuce.

"Maybe," he said soberly. "But the truth is the truth."

"Oh, I don't know," said his mother. "Maybe it is all made up." She carried the plate to the table. Supper was that and soda crackers, followed by a chocolate cupcake moist with sweat from the cellophane.

After eating, Ralph walked a few blocks to Horse Hauser's, went to the back steps, and called: "Hey, Hauser!" This was the protocol. Not until you had completed high school did you mount the stairs and knock or ring; not unless you got a formal invitation to a party did you ever use the front.

It took two or three of such cries before Hauser appeared behind the screendoor, wiping his mouth on his hand and that on his ass. He said: "Hi, Fartface."

"You coming out?"

"When I finish my pie."

Ralph sat on the steps and waited. After about fifteen minutes Hauser emerged, letting the screendoor slam behind him with a loud report. He was about the same height as Ralph but considerably heavier, and most of the difference was in muscle. Ralph did not like to engage in warm-weather sports with Horse, owing to his own comparative frailness, which Hauser lost no opportunity to mention when they had their shirts off.

By way of greeting Horse gave him a painful punch in the upper arm. Ralph winced, and Hauser said jovially: "What a fruit!"

Before they had taken two strides, Hauser's father, an enormous bald man wearing an undershirt, loomed in the doorway and shouted: "You slam that screendoor once more, you little pup, and I'll put my shoe up your asshole."

Hauser slunk cravenly around the corner, but once in the side yard he showed Ralph he was giving his old man the Finger.

They walked down to the business district. Ralph took care when they passed certain yards because of Hauser's tendency to maneuver him to the inside and push him into a hedge. Hauser was childishly treacherous, but Ralph had always been attracted by his ebullience.

When they passed the city hall with its side door marked

POLICE, Hauser said: "Why is a police station like a men's room?" Ralph didn't know. "That's where the dicks hang out." Ralph did not respond as soon as Hauser wished and got an elbow in the ribs for his delay. "You don't get it."

"Sure I do," said Ralph, looking down the street because he thought he spotted the lush figure, surmounted by the dish-water-blond head, of Imogene Clevenger, a subject of his fantasies though in real-life encounters she never seemed to see him. To gain prestige with Hauser he said: "Boy, would I like to put it to that."

Horse however stared at a passing car that was jammed full of colored people. Soberly he asked: "Listen, Sandifer, do you think you could jazz a coon girl?"

"What a question."

"I'm asking you, no shit. You know Corky Barker? He went down to see his relatives in the South this summer. He says white guys fuck nigger girls all the time down there."

"Did *he?*"

"Naw, he was scared. He said he thought it would be weird, but I know he was scared."

"I guess it would be weird," Ralph admitted.

"That's because you're a fruit." Hauser guffawed and punched Ralph right on the bruise he had given him earlier.

"Knock it off for Christ's sake," said Ralph, rubbing his arm. In response Hauser gave him still another blow. "You son of a bitch," said Ralph, squaring off, "I'm telling you."

"Hoho," said Hauser, hands on his hips, "you're going to apologize. You're not man enough to call me that."

Hauser was the far better boxer, but Ralph could out-wrestle him. Once Ralph had got him on the ground and, scissoring his legs around the neck, applied pressure until Hauser turned maroon.

"All right," said Ralph. "I'm sorry I said S.O.B., but if you punch me one more time we're going to tangle."

Hauser accepted both apology and warning, nodding his thick burr head, and shook hands.

"Fair deal."

An illustration of why Ralph and Horse, who had little in common except an interest in sex, stayed friends: every now and then they made these gentlemen's agreements, and Hauser was good as his word once he gave it. It occurred to Ralph that Hauser deliberately provoked him so that they could make a pact. Hauser loved rituals, as opposed to Ralph, who observed them really because he thought he should. The other thing to be said for Hauser was that he was only superficially tough. One time when they had had a real fight, a year or so before, and Hauser cut Ralph's lip with a blow to the mouth, it was Horse burst into tears and ran away. Neither ever referred to this incident.

At length they reached Elmira's, the local hangout. From outside it looked as if all the booths were filled with people eating potato chips and drinking Cokes, a combination that cost a dime. Ralph had made a dollar fifty that day, counting his allowance, but being rather a skinflint, had put a dollar forty into a little bank that was constructed in the form of a book, its leatherette cover inscribed, "*The Secret of Wealth,* by I. M. Rich." A burglar presumably would not discern it among orthodox volumes.

Hauser on the other hand was a glutton and a spendthrift.

"Come on," he said when Ralph showed signs of wanting to linger on the sidewalk. "I'm hungry."

"You just ate."

"Not much. My old man upsets my stomach." Ralph had eaten with the Hausers. It was true that Horse's father upbraided him incessantly, but without apparent effect: he devoured enormous quantities of food and had the table manners of a hog.

"I want to stay out here and see what quiff is on the street."

57

"It's all inside," said Hauser. But Ralph was uneasy to be very near girls in a social interior; outdoors you could trail them at a distance and make derisive remarks to your male companions. Horse went into Elmira's, however, and Ralph couldn't very well follow girls by himself, which would be weird and perhaps interpreted as the act of a sex maniac, so he followed his friend.

Hauser threw insulting greetings at various persons as they moved along the aisle: "Pigface, Filthy Fred, Hick," etc., and got as good as he gave: "Pimp, Jerk, Crud." Ralph did not engage in this corny crap.

The very last booth on the right was empty. Hauser having stopped to chaff some acquaintances, Ralph took the lead; but before he could choose the back bench, from which you could watch new arrivals, Horse pushed roughly past him and claimed it.

"Goddam," said Ralph, "you got the manners of an ape."

Hauser good-naturedly made a monkey face and pretended to scratch fleas. Then he banged on the table with the ketchup bottle. "Service!" The Heinz label caught his eye. "Warnie Warren went to Pittsburgh this summer. They let you go through the Heinz factory and give you free pickle samples and also a pin shaped like a pickle. You can go through the Hershey factory, too, in Hershey, Pennsylvania, and they give you free chocolate. You could probably travel all over the U.S.A. and get enough free samples to live on. Like them little loaves of Wonder Bread they gave away in that booth at the fair."

Elmira herself, a tall and buxom middle-aged woman who either dyed her hair red or wore a wig—there was an argument about this—came to take their orders. She nodded grimly at the ketchup bottle and said: "You break that and you bought it."

Hauser put the bottle down and fished a dollar bill from his pants pocket. Narrowing his eyes and speaking in what he thought was an imitation of George Raft, he said: "Baby, there's a lot more where this came from. I could buy and sell this joint."

Elmira neatly plucked the bill from his fingers. She said: "I'll settle for you paying your tab."

Horse howled. "Me?"

"Yes, you, hotshot. You owe me something from last week, remember?"

"You're some Jew," Hauser said. "If you was a man your name would be Izzy."

Elmira snorted. She never smiled but was a good-hearted soul who put a lot of kids on the cuff, and also was a soft touch for people collecting for various projects and causes: glee club, Community Chest, sandlot ball teams, etc. It was said her husband had been sent to the pen for bootlegging during Prohibition. Perhaps because of this Elmira was herself a teetotaler, and if she caught a kid with a pint of wine she banned him from her place for life.

"Hi, Ralph," she said, dismissing Hauser with her nose.

"Hi, Elmira."

"Say," she said, "I was thinking of getting a little machine for myself. I was thinking of coming around and seeing your dad."

"He'd certainly be glad to see you," Ralph said. "I know that."

"What I was thinking, it's the end of summer now and the prices will probably go down."

Ralph nodded judiciously. "They might, at that."

"You tell him I'm in the market for a good buy, a little coupe maybe. I ain't driven in years though. Years back, the late mister had a little flivver. I could drive that real good, but they've changed since, I hear. You used to shift gears with your feet in those days."

59

"Old Doc Klingman," Horse said, "still drives a Model T."

"I wouldn't call that old sawbones if I was dying from hydrophobia," said Elmira. She took their orders: a bowl of chips and a Coke for Ralph, and for Hauser a chocolate malted and a banana split.

"You're gonna get a potgut one of these days," said Ralph when Elmira had gone. Horse's father had a big beerbelly.

"Naw," said Hauser. "Everything I eat turns to shit." He took something from his pocket. "Hey, look." He showed Ralph a little tin of Between the Acts miniature cigars.

"If you light up in here Elmira will throw you out," Ralph said.

Hauser opened the box and, shielding it from the aisle with one hand, displayed the contents: a coiled rubber.

"New or used?"

"Brand-new Sheik," said Hauser, closing the tin and putting it away. "Stole it from my father's chiffonier. He keeps 'em under his socks. He's got a fuck-book there, too: *Maggie 'n' Jiggs.*"

Ralph spoke disparagingly. "He'll kill you." But the sight of the rubber inflamed him all the same, as did ladies' underwear when seen on a clothesline, unless it belonged to close female relatives.

"Naw," said Hauser. "He don't count 'em."

Ralph sneered and went into his tough idiom: "You ain't got no use for it, except to put it on when you beat your meat."

Hauser looked dramatically smug, turning his mouth down and raising his eyebrows. "The hell you say."

Ralph got a lump in his throat. He cleared it. "What's that supposed to mean?"

"That's for me to know and you to find out."

"Screw you, Hauser."

Their orders came and Hauser plunged into his, alternately slurping malted through the straws and shoveling into his mouth heaps of banana, three flavors of ice cream, chopped nuts, maraschino cherry, whipped cream, and butterscotch sauce.

Munching his spartan potato chips, Ralph grimaced and said: "Jesus, you make me sick."

"Make you sicker if you saw the nookie I'm smelling," said Horse, his mouth full of multicolored glop.

Ralph refused to be lured into the trap, knowing Hauser had far less patience than he with a story.

He turned and looked at a portion of the room he could see without cracking his neck. Sure enough, across and one booth behind that which was lateral with his own, there sat Imogene Clevenger, facing the door, so that he saw the back of her blond bob, a round of cheek, a tip of nose, and, through the inverted V made by her trunk and the arm elbowed on the tabletop, a swell of sweatered breast. She was with another girl—as always with the good-lookers, a beast who had pimples and wore glasses.

This latter person reacted immediately to Ralph's stare, which had passed over and rejected her with the speed of light. She smiled and waved. It was that Margie he had run into in the afternoon with Leo, across from the lot. Ralph feebly returned the wave and turned back.

Hauser said: "Boy, you know the dogs."

"Should I be nasty?" Ralph hated being back on the defensive.

Hauser wiped his mouth on the back of his hand, though a container of napkins was right there. He had already finished the entire order. "Like I always say," said he, "with the ugly ones you put an American flag over their head and fuck for Old Glory."

"She ain't got much of a body either."

Suddenly Hauser pulled several paper napkins all at once from the chromium holder and scrubbed his sticky hands. "Hey, Sandifer," he said in a low, confidential voice, "you want to hear about this whore I found or not?"

Ralph's stomach joined his testicles.

Horse leaned into the table. "Swear you won't spread it around?"

"Not me."

"Only you and me in on it, O.K.?"

"Scout's honor."

"You know that grocery I deliver for? I never told you this before, on account of I knew you would say I was full of shit—"

Ralph groaned in relief. He had actually thought Hauser *had* found a whore and would expect him to do something about it. "You mean that big blonde you claim gives you the eye?"

Hauser leaned back and pursed his lips. "Oh, I did tell you?"

"Only about a hundred times."

Hauser's wide face came across the table again. "Well, how about this then: I saw her pussy today."

The anxiety rushed back. Ralph let some Coke exhaust its effervescence on his palate.

"She showed it to you?"

"Let's put it this way: she sure knew I was looking at it. She had this kimono on, and it was open, and she was sitting on the couch, and you could see right up between her legs, and there was her big hairy twat."

Ralph sneered again. "That was accidental, for God's sake."

"So why didn't she close up when I was looking, I ask you?" Hauser answered himself: "She's a whore, that's why. Who else is dressed like that, at home in the middle of the day? She don't go out to work and she ain't married."

"How do you know?"

"I never see no husband around there."

"Well," said Ralph, "her husband would be out to work when you delivered, wouldn't he? Whereas if she was a whore, there'd *be* guys around." Ralph figured this out for himself. He had never seen a "whore" in his life.

"The guys come at night, you asshole," said Hauser.

"How'd you know? You ain't seen 'em."

"I don't have to. That's just the way whores work."

"The voice of experience," Ralph said scornfully.

"Lester told me," said Hauser. Lester was his older brother, a sailor who occasionally came home on leave.

"Lester's a big whoremaster?"

"Not him," said Horse. "He don't have to pay for it. Girls put out for him left and right. He says it's a pretty poor man who has to buy his poongtang. Old Lester sees a girl he likes and goes right up to her and says let's fuck."

Ralph shook his head. "He must get slugged a lot."

Hauser howled. "You'd be surprised at all the ass he gets."

You could never tell with Horse what was a joke or just a lie. Ralph couldn't imagine a decent girl even going on a date with Lester Hauser, who had big ears and an undershot jaw and old acne craters on his cheeks. He was bowlegged in his uniform and his sailor hat was always soiled around the bottom with sweat, dirt, and hair oil.

Hauser reached into his pocket and came out with a handful of dollar bills. "Lookie here," he said, "and I got a few more where they came from."

"What'd you do?" asked Ralph. "Rob a bank?"

Hauser leered. "I got my sources. How much are you carrying?"

"A dime."

"The stingiest man in town," said Hauser, rolling his eyes. He counted the four bills in his hand. "All right, I'll loan you two bucks."

"For what? All I got is a Coke and chips."

Hauser leaned over and whispered: "For the whore, stupid."

Ralph's head-skin tightened from nape to eyebrows, but his face remained bland.

"That's what they get: two bucks," said Hauser. "Everybody knows that."

"I got to get home," said Ralph. He put his dime on the table and drank the remaining swallow of his Coke.

"You were all ready to walk around town for a couple hours, following girls. You're yellow, Sandifer. That's what ails you."

"I don't feel too good. I think I got a touch of sunstroke cutting grass today."

"You got a yellow streak a mile wide running down your back."

Ralph said levelly: "You wanna come outside and repeat that?"

"I'll holler it from the housetops. You're just going to pull your pud all your life. Look, I'm offering you the money." He thrust two bills across the table.

Ralph realized that Hauser was not challenging him in a personal way. He pulled in his jaw and became realistic. "You mean, go over there now? You don't really know she's a whore. Second, it's against the law. Third, what about getting a disease?"

Hauser replied: "She's one all right!" He pushed out of the booth, saying: "If you're a man, you'll follow me."

Ralph felt as though he might hemorrhage through ears, nose, and mouth if he were forced to make an irrevocable decision. He was a deliberative sort. For something like this he had to study days, weeks, years; until he was about twenty would be more like it.

Passing Imogene Clevenger's oblivious back, he thought: If you had ever looked at me, I wouldn't be in this hideous situation. He ignored Margie's obsequious smile and did not reply to her "Bye, Ralph. Don't do anything I wouldn't do."

Hauser was waiting inexorably on the sidewalk.

Ralph said: "For Christ's sake, it's still light."

"Damn right it is. So we go down to the drugstore and get us some port wine, have a few drinks till it gets dark, see?"

This was getting crazier and crazier. "Are you nuts, Hauser? Doc won't sell us any wine at our age."

Horse was somber. Then he brightened. "I got it. I'll tell him it's for my old man."

"You'd need a note for that," said Ralph. "Like for cigarettes."

"We'll forge one. Go inside and get a piece of paper and a pencil from Elmira."

"You go."

Horse squinted for a moment and then decided not to make a point of it. "Naw. She'll know something's fishy. How about going to your house and you steal some of your father's booze? He won't miss it."

"My dad doesn't keep any around. I don't think he drinks."

"At my house, the liquor's kept in the kitchen and my old man sits in there guzzling it all night."

"Let's forget this whole thing until some other night when the time is ripe," said Ralph.

"No," Hauser said emphatically. "A quitter never wins and a winner never quits. I'll figure out something, goddammit. It's got to be tonight."

He got the bright idea to hang around in front of the drug-

65

store in hopes some older guy they knew would come along and they could persuade him to make the purchase for them. But after waiting about five minutes without success, Horse got restless and began to goose Ralph and to hoot stupidly. When he started this, Ralph walked away and looked in the window of the hardware store. A Colt Woodsman .22 pistol was displayed there on a card showing pictures of a crow, a woodchuck, a squirrel, and a rabbit, a bull's-eye target super-imposed on each.

After a bit Hauser stopped shouting and, joining Ralph at the show window, turned serious. "Boy, point that at a coon and he'd go white."

"You know Clarence, that colored guy who works for my dad?" asked Ralph. "He's got biceps the size of sugar melons."

Hauser rolled his short sleeve to the shoulder and made a muscle. "Let's see yours," he said.

Ralph ignored the invitation. "He used to be a terrific boxer till he lost an eye. You should see him with his shirt off. His stomach muscles look like a lot of little squares, kind of a checkerboard. I never saw a build like that on anybody."

Horse was jealous. "Yaa," he sneered. "Boogies are all yellow." He looked lovingly at the distended biceps alongside his ear and made it jump.

"What about Joe Louis?"

"Who'd he ever beat? Primo Carnera, that stupid Dago. And Maxie Baer's a Jewboy. Somebody white would kill him, like Jack Dempsey or Gene Tunney." Hauser lowered his arm and said: "Sandifer, you're just a nigger lover." He stared over Ralph's shoulder. "Hey, here comes my brother."

Ralph turned. Sure enough, there was Lester Hauser in his sailor suit, coming along the sidewalk, white bellbottoms flapping at the end of his bowlegs.

66

"Hi, Lester," said Horse.

"Hi, kid," Lester replied in his superior manner. He ignored Ralph as always.

"Would you do me a big favor, Lester?"

Lester stared down at Horse. His sailor hat was on the back of his head, allowing a bunch of greasy curls to protrude in front.

"I ain't got no extra moolah, Horace, if that's what you got in mind."

Horse produced a quarter. "Would you go in Doc's and get me a pint of wine?"

Lester frowned. "Can you handle that, buster? 'Cause if you can't and the old man takes a ball bat to you, I ain't gonna be no part of it."

"Sure. I know what I'm doing."

"If you got another one of them quarters, I'll get a pint for myself."

"Sure, Lester," Horse said. "That's swell." He gave the coins to his brother.

"Was that port or sherry?" Lester asked.

"Port."

Lester swaggered into the drugstore.

Hauser said: "The old man used to kick the shit out of Lester until he went in the Navy. He's scared of him now. Lester's as rough as a cob: he'd kick him in the nuts."

Before long Lester emerged with two flat pints in separate paper bags.

He gave one to Horse. "Just keep out of my part of the park," he said. "Over back of the war monument, you know? That bunch of bushes? Soon's it's dark I'm going to take that Imogene Clevenger over there, get her loaded, and screw her little ass off."

"I'll be damned," Horse said admiringly.

67

"I done it more than once," said Lester, and he walked up the street towards Elmira's.

"Gimme some of that booze," Ralph cried madly, snatching the paper bag from Hauser's hand. "Then let's go find that fucking whore."

chapter 4

HORSE SHOWED THE EFFECTS of the wine before Ralph did, though Ralph was scarcely a veteran of the bottle. They had gone down to the railroad station for their drinking. The station was closed at this hour, but trains would whistle through from time to time throughout the evening. The boys found a place of concealment beneath a baggage truck, sat on the cold concrete of the platform, and passed the pint back and forth, Ralph wiping its mouth at every one of his own turns. He also worried about getting piles, sitting there on the cement, which was supposed to happen according to folk wisdom. He felt injured and reckless, yet was prudent even in his distress.

Hauser on the other hand began to speak in a slurred voice after his second drink.

"How old's your brother?" asked Ralph.

"Twenty," said Hauser. "He had the clap last year. Old Lester drinks whiskey like it was Coke. He's done just about everything. When he was in high school, him and some other

69

guys smoked weed in the toilet, and he got expelled. Once a bunch of nigger kids come in Elmira's and Lester jumped up and says, 'I think you got the wrong place,' and they backed down and left nice as pie."

Ralph was getting sick of Lester. "Oh yeah?"

"Yeah," said Horse, "they would have stunk up the place."

Ralph had but lately noticed that he himself stank under the arms when he sweated. He sniffed at Hauser. "You could use some Mum yourself."

Hauser laughed, took another swig, and said: " 'Hi, girls,' said the blind man as he passed the fish store."

In this fashion they passed the time till twilight. At one point an express train hurtled through with a whistle and a blur of windows, too fast to wave at anybody on board, and Hauser began to sing the well-known parody to the tune of "Humoresque."

"Please refrain from flushing toilets while the train is in the station . . ."

The bottle was half empty now, but Ralph still did not have a sense of drunkenness, though it seemed to take longer than usual to move the feet at the end of his outstretched legs. The high emotion he had felt earlier had also receded.

"How do you feel?" he asked Horse.

Hauser's eyes were hooded in the fading light. He licked his lips ever so slowly and said: "Goddam," He crawled out from under the baggage wagon on all fours and took forever to get upright. At last he stood, swaying. "We better get going. That's a mile or so of a walk."

It took Ralph even longer to emerge. He shook his head.

"You're drunk," said Hauser, but Ralph denied it and demonstrated by treading along the very edge of the platform, above the rails. About a hundred yards from the station, a half-witted kid had two years before fastened a spike to the track with electrician's tape. Coming through at sixty, the Flyer's locomotive and three cars were derailed, with several killed and many injured. It made a big splash in the city papers.

"Is Wilmer Wilson still in the asylum?" Ralph asked.

Horse said: "I sure hope so. They should of put him away when he used to shit his pants in school. That whole family is crazy. You know his sister Clara? They caught her screwing herself with a Nehi bottle."

"A lot of nuts live in this town," said Ralph. They had come to the end of the platform, from which it was a three-foot drop to the ground. "You know Leo Kirsch, who works for my dad? His mother's a loony."

"Warren Small's brother," Horse said. "He's thirty years old, with the mind of a little kid. They got to feed him by hand." He leaped off the platform and fell sprawling on the gravel.

They began to walk through a quiet neighborhood where people sat on swings or gliders in the shadows of front porches. As they approached the iron bridge over the creek, streetlights came on behind and ahead of them, and they went into the darkness under a large elm and hit the bottle again. When Ralph got his turn, there was only about an inch of wine left. He carried it until they reached the bridge.

"Christ," said Horse, "don't that water stink!"

Ralph drained the bottle into his throat and threw it off the bridge. The expected splash was a breaking noise instead. Apparently it hit a rock.

A heavy, angry question issued from beneath the bridge: "Who done that?"

Hauser answered in a false, hoarse voice: "Who wants to know?"

"By God, I'll come up there and you'll be sorry to find out."

"Kiss my royal red American ass, you shitheel," Hauser

71

cried, and he and Ralph ran across the bridge and continued for three blocks.

When they finally stopped, panting, Ralph said: "Who do you think that was?"

"Could of been a Hunky who went under there to take a dump, or a tramp." Hauser peered up the street. "Hey, we're right around the corner from the store."

"Already?" Ralph's sense of elapsed time had been deranged by the wine. He had expected a longer journey. Still, he did not return to the dread of yore. Nor for that matter had he been frightened by the voice from beneath the bridge; he would have held his ground had Hauser not fled.

Hauser said: "I could use a beer." He hunched his thick shoulders and lowered his head as a car turned the corner and approached them. "Act normal." Although he wasn't doing so. In fact, he went into a funny, mincing walk.

Ralph, in the assurance of alcohol, stared boldly at the automobile as it passed them.

"Wasn't that the police cruiser?" asked Hauser.

"No," said Ralph. "Certainly not."

"Is it stopping?" As Ralph, to satisfy him, turned and looked, Hauser whispered desperately: "Don't let them see you looking!"

"What's wrong with you?"

Hauser left the sidewalk to put his head against a curbside tree. "I did a dumb thing," he said, his voice breaking. "I took—" He began to sob. "Oh, dear God . . ." He wept into his crossed arms.

Ralph was losing his patience at this horseplay. "Come on, Hauser, for Christ sake. I'm leaving."

Horse wiped his face on his two short sleeves. "All that money I got—I took it from the cash register. The drawer was open, and Bigelow was down cellar and the butcher was in the icebox. I didn't even think about it. I saw my chance and grabbed a handful, and then some woman come in and I couldn't put it back, and then Bigelow come up from the cellar with a case of pop and then it was closing time and he gave me my pay—" He broke down again.

Ralph breathed deeply four or five times. "Uh-huh," he said. He patted Hauser's beefy shoulder. "I'm thinking. . . . I'm thinking."

"I'm sick," said Hauser and bent over to vomit in the gutter.

Ralph was indeed searching his mind as the retching went on. The alcohol had honed his faculties as well as making him immune to panic.

"You haven't spent any of it yet," he said. "Or anyway, not much. There was the dollar at Elmira's and the fifty cents for the port wine. I guess you had that much from your pay?"

He waited while Horse wiped his mouth on a wrist, and the wrist on his behind as usual. Hauser then made an affirmative mumble, but returned to his misery.

"I must have been nuts. How could I—" He rubbed his head with his clean hand. Suddenly he took refuge in anger. "That lousy bastard Bigelow, leaving the register open. He did it to trap me, is what he did. I see it all now. You know I don't get no discounts? I got to pay full price for Pepsis and Nabisco wafers and stuff? I want to make a sandwich or eat a pickle, I got to pay? He hates my guts, that prick."

"We've got to stick to your problem," said Ralph. "At this moment you're a crook, Horse. Your pockets are full of money you stole."

Hauser burst into tears again.

"But," Ralph continued, "there's a perfect answer, so you can stop bawling right now." Hauser persisted, however, and Ralph spoke sharply. "Get hold of yourself, man!"

All at once Horse straightened up like a soldier. "I guess I'll have to take my medicine," said he, blubbering only a little.

73

"I'll tell you what we're going to do," said Ralph. "We're going to the store. We're going to pick the lock or break a window, and we're going to put the money back."

It took Hauser a while to understand that this suggestion was sober and not a cruel mockery of him in his vulnerability.

Ralph also explained: "See, not in the register, which he probably empties at night like most businessmen. We put the dough someplace where it could have fallen by accident—under the counter, you know, or in the potato bin."

"What would money be doing in a potato bin?"

"Then you name a place," Ralph said sharply. "The fact is, you took it."

"You'll never let me live that down!" Horse cried. "But if you think you can blackmail me, Sandifer, forget it." With his face still glistening from the tears—and Ralph also could see, by the nearest streetlamp, that Hauser's nose exuded snot—he had turned truculent.

"Christ, use your handkerchief," said Ralph, walking away.

At length the chastened Horse caught up, saying when they gained the corner, "This way." They turned left and soon reached the grocery, which occupied the ground floor of a two-story frame building; upstairs the windows were lighted.

"Who lives up there?" asked Ralph.

Hauser whispered: "Bigelow."

"C'mon." Ralph continued to walk along the pavement. "We can't afford to be seen loitering in the vicinity." Hauser plodded heavily at his elbow. "Did you ever pick a lock?"

"No."

"Neither did I. I guess that's out." He was also out of plans. With the owner living upstairs they could hardly break a window. The truth was, it was hopeless. But it was also truly none of his affair. Ralph himself had never swiped a penny from anyone. He was so scrupulous in regard to other people's money that if the paper boy or milkman came to collect and his mother called to him from the basement: "Get it from my purse," he would not delve within that intimate container but rather took it down to her. This though he was aware that a lot of people believed that swiping money from close relatives was not a crime.

He had been ignoring his own drunken condition since this matter had come up, but he was about to take advantage of it now and throw Hauser to the dogs. But Horse suddenly linked arms with him and said: "You won't desert me, will you, Ralphie?" The wheedling note was unprecedented in their long relationship. "You'll keep thinking, won't you? You got to save me."

There was something structurally wrong with this appeal— Hauser with his superior size, age, and initiative having always been the leader—but also something enormously gratifying.

Ralph, who hated to be touched, got out of his grasp, and brutally, shoving the beefy Hauser away. But at the same time he said: "You can count on me." The project really had a perfect morality about it: the restoration of stolen funds by thievish methods; better than the Robin Hood sort of thing, which he had always recognized as, underneath all the charitable motives, still robbery.

They had reached the end of the block, where the lamp was out. Hauser had become a quiet, stolid presence in the dark. Like an obedient hound he followed Ralph across the street, and they started down the opposite sidewalk, going back in the direction of the grocery.

When the moment approached for Buddy's leave-taking, Laverne as usual had turned sullen and fled into the bathroom to wash her undies. Formerly he would hang about and cajole her, but he had given up this practice after it had consistently resulted only in tearful demonstrations. Also he admired her for hating goodbyes, tending himself to oversentimentality on such occasions, swan songs, debilitating regrets. She had trained him to square his shoulders and march crisply out the door.

He did not sneak down the steps, but neither did he turn on the outside light at the top landing. The windows of the first-floor flat were to the rear of the diagonal staircase; he was farther from them at each phase of the descent. It was his practice coolly to ignore the fat couple on the ground floor if they were sitting on their porch. He worked on the principle that an obvious slyness called attention to itself. As a used-car merchant he enjoyed a great latitude in his social connections. He might be demonstrating, delivering, or collecting an automobile, wherever or with whomever he was seen.

Beyond this, boldness created its own immunity. In the early days of their association, it had happened more than once that while downtown in the city with Laverne he had recognized local persons, but always from the side or back, and a magical force restrained them from turning towards him. For some time now, the rewards of the domestic experience had kept the lovers at home. So much the worse for any observers who might be counting his visits.

Most people were too yellow to go beyond clandestine gossip and, say, write Naomi a poison-pen letter; and if they did and she read and understood it, he was still her meal ticket, and she was not noted for her pride. Anyway, he planned to have her killed soon. But then would not his association with Laverne, which it stood to reason had been noticed by someone, be incriminating? Not if he had an iron-clad alibi. He was indifferent to suspicions that could not be legally implemented. In the time to come a strained reputation might even bring him more business: he knew that much about the human race. A divorce would hurt him worse, being negative. Buddy had thought about this for a long time, but in fits and starts, not continuously. He was impulsive, no plodder.

He found his car around the corner, eased it away from the curb, made one turn, drove a block and made another, heard the crash of breaking glass, and saw two boys running along the sidewalk. When they reached the streetlight he recognized one as Ralph. He had no concern for the other, who anyway broke from the pavement as the car approached and plunged into a darkened side yard.

Buddy swept into the gutter and flung open the door on the passenger's side. Ralph halted as if a net had been thrown over him.

"Hey."

"Yes," Ralph said, without apparent recognition. He came obediently to the car. "You see—oh . . ."

"Surprise," Buddy said. Then, pointing to the seat: "You just get in and keep your trap shut."

Ralph obeyed, and Buddy drove rapidly until they were across the iron bridge. "Now," he said, slowing down, "I want to know why I oughtn't take you to the police station—or maybe the mental asylum."

Ralph was looking into his own lap. "I can't give you any good reason."

"Then I'll tell you why," Buddy said levelly. "Buddy Sandifer's boy up on vandalism charges: that would be swell for business." He whipped his head towards Ralph and then back. "Have you possibly turned into a rotten little punk? Tell me I'm wrong, if you can."

He had stopped the car now. Ralph looked out and saw the railroad station again. It was depressively fascinating to think that in this place, not long ago, though drunk, he had not been in any trouble.

"I certainly wish I could," said he.

77

"You're talking like a bum, Ralph. Who was that other kid?" He revved the engine and then turned off the ignition. Crickets were singing in the weeds below the platform. "I can sit here till the cows come home."

"It's an outlandish story," said Ralph. "I'll admit that. You know what was tied to that brick we threw in the window? Money."

Buddy repeated the word without expression.

"I knew you wouldn't believe it."

"*Money?*"

"Six or seven dollars, I think," said Ralph, "though I never counted it, true. Whatever the original amount was, plus a dollar for the window, which was the basement window. The main window is plate glass, and if you broke it, it would certainly cost more than a dollar, so we—"

"You're talking junk now, Ralph," Buddy said in despair. "Nobody throws money away for a cheap laugh."

"Well, it's the God's honest truth that that brick had money tied to it with a shoelace." In fact the lace was Ralph's own. Consequently he hadn't been able to run well; his gym shoe threatening to fall off, he had surrendered at the appearance of the car. He had rather be caught than lose one Ked. "Actually it won't cost a dollar to replace that small amount of glass, so there's something extra for the inconvenience caused Mr. Bigelow."

Buddy sighed. For once Ralph looked at him, and saw a weird, wolfish grin in the light from the dashboard.

"It wasn't vandalism," Ralph assured him. "You could check that tomorrow. You could go around there and I'll bet he would tell you."

Buddy maintained his queer, sinister expression until Ralph turned away. "I wasn't an angel myself at your age." said he. "I helped myself to something from the collection plate once in Sunday school, and ate ice cream till I got sick. But I never

destroyed property and can't understand anybody who does."
He changed pace with a harsh accusation: "I guess you think
it's exciting to break glass?"

"Not me."

"It's dumb, Ralph, is what it is. What have you accomplished?"

"You're not getting the point. You're not paying attention
to what I said."

As could be expected, neither did his father listen to this.
"Tell you what you're going to do, Ralph. Tomorrow you're
going around to that store and make a clean breast of it to the
owner. You're going to have to take a chance he'll have you
arrested. But I don't think that will happen. I think he will
realize the courage it took on your part and your honest desire
to make good on the damage."

Buddy lifted a hip and fetched the wallet from his back
pocket. "Here." He handed a bill to Ralph. "You give him
that." He started the car, but before pulling away from the
station he said: "I bet he'll end up thinking more of you than
if you hadn't broken the window at all. People are like that."

Ralph closed his eyes in acquiescence, though his father
wasn't looking at him. He opened them as they passed under
a streetlight and saw that the bill was a two-dollar note, the
standard fee for a whore, if you could believe Horse Hauser,
who had quoted his brother Lester, who if you could believe
him, was by now screwing Imogene Clevenger under a bush in
the park.

"So far as I'm concerned, I'll never mention it again," said
Buddy.

When they got home Ralph went to his room, realized he
had been stinking drunk for hours, fell onto the bed, and
went to sleep with his clothes on.

Naomi sat in the living room, reading a book. She was
wearing the same housedress as at lunch and sheenless cotton

stockings, in view from the calf down. Her skirt never climbed very far up when she sat, but her stockings invariably drooped in whatever attitude.

She peeped over the top of the volume at Buddy's entrance. "You must be devastated after a day like this. I trust you had a bite somewhere. If not, there's some salmon left."

"And *how*," said Buddy, sitting down on the couch. He ignored the mention of food. Naturally he abhorred salmon. "I ran across Ralph and gave him a lift."

"Wasn't that lucky," said Naomi, lowering the book to her lap.

"Say," said Buddy, "you see more of him than I do. How's he getting along?"

"Oh, you never need worry about Ralph. He's very self-sufficient."

Buddy grimaced inwardly at her pretentious lingo; what showed was a smile. "You know how it is with a kid that age. He plays his cards close to his chest. The last guy he'll shoot straight with is his old man. I was like that myself. I wonder if he's tried smoking yet. I sneaked a few drags on my pop's pipe once, made me sick as a dog, haven't smoked again till this day. God rest his soul." All of Buddy's immediate family were dead, except a sister who moved to Massachusetts and hadn't been heard from since, nor had she been sought. He was a loner.

He regretted having introduced this subject. Naomi went to the drumtop table and took a cigarette from a brass box, now greened, which had been a wedding gift years before.

Buddy resumed: "If I could find the time I ought to take Ralph fishing or to a ballgame."

Back in her chair, Naomi slowly released the smoke from her first draught. "I wonder."

"Don't he like baseball?"

"If so, it had better be tomorrow. High school begins on

Monday." She returned deliberately to the cigarette, placing it in an ashtray on the little disc-shelf affixed midway down the shaft of the floorlamp.

Buddy repressed most of his annoyance. "It was just an idea. I'd like to do something for him."

Naomi thought about this. Then she said: "Well, no one need be embarrassed by good motives."

When she was dead Buddy intended to put Ralph in a military school.

Oddly enough, though they usually retired at different hours, Buddy and Naomi slept together in a double bed. He even put it to her occasionally. It was not altogether without satisfaction that he ran her skinny body through with his lethal weapon. This however was not one of those nights. He pretended to be asleep when she slopped in, semicircled the bed in her old nightgown, got into the far side, and, tilting the lampshade and leaving it askew, turned out the light.

chapter 5

NEXT MORNING Buddy arrived at the lot fifteen minutes early for his appointment, opened the safe to get the money, and found the cashbox empty.

However, after a moment of panic he remembered his instructions to Leo and realized that the latter had taken all the cash to the night depository, including the sum that had been kept for the hiring of a killer. Buddy had assembled a fund of approximately three hundred and fifty dollars by diverting amounts from the cash payments for car sales. This lode remained always available in the metal box, which lay behind the locked door of the safe at night and on weekends. A burglar might of course blow the safe and be rewarded. But if, after Naomi's death, suspicious investigators checked Buddy's bank accounts they would find no large withdrawals that could not be innocently justified.

Now of course this careful provision had been destroyed, and Buddy could blame nobody but himself. How could he have made such an error? Going back over the events of the day before, he recalled that he had already asked Leo to make the deposit before the sorry incident with Ballbacher. Having arranged the appointment with Clarence, he had been over-eager to join Laverne. It was as if Naomi had already been disposed of. This was his initial mistake. The resulting elation had vanished with the blow of Ballbacher's fist. Buddy's luck, good or bad, was often serial, having a run, in whichever direction, until the god in power was appeased.

His job now was to arrest and reverse the momentum of failure. Above all he must keep his head: no more unwarranted glee, no loss of control when surprised, no surrender to confusion when as now he was discomfited by his own blunder. Calm reasoning revealed that, the bank being closed all weekend, Leo's deposit would not be dealt with until at least 9 A.M. on Monday, at which time Buddy could report there and correct it.

That left the matter of the colored hoodlum whom Clarence was due to bring around momentarily. It had been Buddy's intention, after establishing, as well as you could in an interview, that the man was capable of performing the deed, to pay him something down. Now that the supply of money was not at hand, no such deposit could be issued.

Buddy's sole argument being cash on the barrelhead, he had no idiom in which to negotiate. Until he retrieved his treasure next morning, his proposition must be theoretical. For twenty-four hours there would be extant a colored hoodlum who was privy to his plan and, having taken no money, without personal implication. Were he arrested for another crime during the night, he might seek favor with the authorities by informing them of Buddy's proposal.

In a town this size, a merchant like Buddy knew all members of the modest-sized police force, remembered them at

Xmas, and gave them special consideration on purchases. In return he got no traffic citations for either his personal infractions or those made in the name of his business, for example if a client or salesman had too heavy a foot on a test drive: younger customers often wanted to try the "pickup" of a given car when starting off at a green light.

The cops would not, certainly, be eager to believe the story told by a Negro under arrest, yet all who heard it would remember if Naomi subsequently died of other than natural causes.

Buddy retained his self-possession, but he had not worked out an answer to the problem by the time Clarence arrived at the office. Therefore he was relieved to see that the ex-boxer was alone, even though the lone appearance implied that he still would not have his hired killer.

Clarence wore a black suit so often pressed as to show a glint, a glaring white shirt, and a dull black tie bearing a series of small red figures. Buddy had never seen him dressed in other attire than work clothes. His bearing went with the suit: Buddy saw it as pompous.

In ambivalent reaction he said derisively: "I see you flopped."

Clarence gravely strode behind Leo's desk and, unbuttoning his jacket, sat down.

"That's the ticket," Buddy said. "Make yourself to home. Maybe you'd like a cigar."

"I don't use them," said Clarence, apparently without intentional irony, though his dead eye always provided some, willy-nilly.

"Well now, that's very interesting, *sir*. I figure all big muckety-mucks smoked El Ropos." Buddy exposed his teeth and spoke through them. "What the hell's your idea coming here empty-handed and all dressed up like a Christmas tree? Didn't I warn you about getting fresh?"

Clarence put his big hands onto Leo's desk and shot each white cuff. Then he leaned back deliberately. "I got that man you wanted."

Buddy felt a twinge of fear, and, outraged by it, he reinforced his snarl. "You leave him tied up outside like a dog?"

Clarence frowned. Buddy saw that the sarcasm was too obscure for him. "I told you to bring him here this morning, and I don't see nobody. Now, when I asked you yesterday you could have told me you didn't have nobody, but you had to play the big shot and come here in that suit and sit down like you owned this place and—" Buddy cleared his throat violently.

Clarence chose this moment, during the clamor, to speak.

Buddy shouted: "What, what?"

"You looking at him."

Buddy amazed himself by understanding this statement instantly. Clarence of course was the perfect man for the job, subhuman, moronic, disposable, and otherwise useless. Buddy realized he might have had him in the ulterior mind for some such purpose as long ago as the night on which he had apprehended the one-eyed Negro in the attempt to steal a car.

Yet he was cautious, shouting: "*You?* You couldn't even steal an automobile!"

"Maybe that is so," said Clarence, all at once producing a bold yet also sly smile, which was at odds with his ministerial attire. His teeth were not of the notorious Negro white, but rather yellow in contrast to his dazzling shirt collar. "But I can sure strike a match."

Now Buddy was baffled. "You already drunk at eleven A.M.?"

"Only thing is," Clarence proceeded to say, "if I roast the meat, I want a nice slice."

Buddy made an expression in which the rest of his face

85

converged on his nose. "Well," he said, "if you are talking the English language, I'm a sheep-fucker."

"You want me burn this place down so's you can get the insurance," said Clarence. "I know that soon's you open you mouth."

Buddy imitated a carp with bulging eyes and protruded lips, and then he laughed so hard he felt it in his gut.

Clarence extended the reach of his own grin. "When them gas tanks go you will have something."

Buddy ended his laugh with: "Whooee! Goddam, you are one smart cookie." He frowned suddenly. "But what gets me if you got that much upstairs is why you wash cars for a living instead of being on the brain trust down in Washington, D.C." He poked a finger at the ex-boxer. "You just let me do your thinking for you, Clarence. I don't want you laid up with brain damage."

Buddy rose from the one-buttocked perch on the window-sill, kicked the cramp from his leg, loosened the fabric that clung to his crotch, and plunged both hands into his side pockets.

"I tell you though," said he, "I might buy the idea you're the bozo I been looking for. I might just do that, Clarence." He squinted as if smoke had been blown into his eyes.

"Figured you would."

"Oh you did, did you? Well, you just wipe off that grin now, because you are full of condensed horseshit, see." Buddy punched a finger at him. "You don't know what or why or how, sonny boy."

Clarence leaned back in the chair, his expanding chest putting tension on the buttonholes of his shirt. He had added weight since his ring days, owing to a diet of canned spaghetti, potato salad, baked beans, and the packaged bakery goods he got from the day-old shelves at the A & P. A forty-five-year-old widow who lived down the hall in his rooming house would

86

sometimes invite him in for a warm meal, but she expected the use of his tool in return, feeling for it with her stockinged toe under the card table while he ate; and since losing the sight of one eye, there was nothing in the world he so hated as to be bought by a woman.

Buddy smirked. "It ain't setting fire to nothing either, like Sid Birchbaum."

Clarence pinched his own nose.

"I refer," said Buddy, "to the Yiddish gentleman who got caught over in your neck of the woods."

Clarence seldom heard anyone's name if they were white; he thought of them according to their professions or locations. Among his own kind he usually knew only a one-word designation per person: first, last, or nick-. As to his own name, which was properly Clarence Honeywell, he had fought as Kid Hammond.

Clarence could have called himself anything he wished; he possessed no identifying documents. He had never been arrested, married, licensed to drive, or enrolled with Social Security. Behind the glassine window in his imitation alligator skin wallet the identification card stayed blank.

He understood now that Buddy meant the Jew who had set fire to the store underneath his cousin's room: the very reference Clarence had made to himself the day before. This evidence of his employer's shrewdness caused his confidence to wither somewhat. He respectfully brought his chair back to the upright position and put his hands in his lap.

Buddy changed gears. "Clarence, you got family around here?"

"Not me."

"You don't live with a woman?"

"Not lately."

"No folks at all?"

"Huh-uh." The cousin had expected to get a reward for

fingering the Jew and when rejected went downtown and in another futile exercise of vengeance tried to burglarize the offices of the insurance company, was caught, and sentenced to five to ten in the state prison.

"Ain't you a local boy?"

"Huh-uh." Clarence was local to noplace, having been taken as an infant from rural Mississippi, which he did not remember, to Detroit, from which as an adolescent he had run away. He was much more widely traveled than Buddy, who had never been farther than say 150 miles in any direction from his source.

Needing no more assurance, Buddy moved towards Leo's desk, staying on the side of Clarence's good eye.

"I'm not going to beat around the bush," he said. "I want to get somebody taken care of." He swiveled his head as if to loosen a stiffening neck. This movement reminded the ex-Kid Hammond of someone he had once faced in the ring, a pimple-shouldered wop who did that in the corner while waiting for Hammond to take the count of eight, which meant he was feeling the effects of the Kid's left hand, which had been jabbing his head for two rounds. He never suspected a dumb nigger would be watching for things like that. Hammond got up and when the wop came out gave him another left. The wop came underneath with a right and knocked the Kid down and out.

Buddy put his soft white hands on the desktop and leaned at Clarence. "For keeps," he added. Still seeing no comprehension on the dark face, he said irritably: "Shit, I mean I want someone knocked off."

He pushed himself away and, with his chin down, strolled in a circle. He was wearing a white sports shirt with black windowpane checks and powder-blue slacks without belt loops. The waist could be adjusted by means of little straps and buckles at the sides. These were half hidden by the bulge

88

of flesh created by this stricture. If Buddy had seen himself in a mirror at this point he might have puffed out his shirt around his middle, though that would have destroyed the sleekness with which, in front, it now swooped under the taut waistband.

Before he came all the way around he asked, inspecting the shine on his wingtip oxfords: "Am I getting through to you, Clarence?"

"Uh-huh." This was not true. Clarence was playing for time. Throughout his life he had seen various persons get killed, generally by other individuals to whom they were related by blood, sexual connection, or friendship. But these people were all colored, and he was smart enough to reflect that Buddy would scarcely have a motive to want a Negro done away with, when he would not even sell one a car. That Buddy's business was Jim Crow was all Clarence knew or cared to know. Just as he did not understand Buddy's view of him, he was ignorant of Buddy's reason for maintaining this policy: though one dollar was as green as the next, irrespective of the hand that paid it, there were white customers who might be lost if they saw a colored individual buy a more expensive automobile than *they* could afford, a notorious Negro practice.

If black was therefore out of the question, then Buddy was proposing that Clarence kill a white man. Clarence had once known a girl who claimed to have gone to New York and in the practice of whoring helplessly met a white man who took her out to dinner and to a show on Broadway, an experience so perverse that she returned to the provinces forthwith. "Up there they crazy." Unlike down South, locally you were not required to give way on the sidewalk to white people, but if you were a woman you did not *date* one. If a man, you might even in extreme circumstances, such as private argument or race riot, shed one's blood; but you never killed one with premeditation. It simply was not done, and Clarence had always been a stickler for custom.

Therefore he rose, shook the wrinkles from his jacket, and felt that the knot of his tie was still snug.

"I guess you ain't looking *at* the man you was looking *for*."

Buddy raised his eyes but not his head. Silently he watched Clarence rebutton the jacket.

When this job was completed he said: "Sit down. I want to talk turkey." Clarence remained standing, but Buddy went on anyway. "Now you been working for me for some time, and you know I'm hard but fair. I could of sent you to jail but I give you a job instead, and I believe I am right in saying that every Xmas since, I have raised your wages a dollar though you are doing the same amount of work as when you started, which ain't never been enough to kill you. I have to tell you there are them who don't like people of your race, but I'm not one."

He went back of his own desk, got his chair, and rolled it, not without some difficulty from the balky wheels, to a position in front of Leo's desk, back of which Clarence was now unbuttoning his jacket though still standing.

Within a few seconds Buddy had addressed more language to him than in all their previous association. As it happened, Clarence enjoyed fluent talk; that was why he usually spent most of Sunday in the church, the preacher and some of the elders as well being noted orators.

For his own part, Buddy was in his natural element when it came to selling a reluctant customer a bill of goods.

"You had much experience with women?"

Clarence now took a seat. He wet his lips, felt an earlobe, and clasped his hands before him.

"Some."

Buddy indulged in a bit of levity by way of preface. "Like the fellow says, turn 'em upside down, they're all the same."

Take any white man, you would get a smile at this, but Clarence showed no reaction. Not joking, Buddy said: "They're a pain in the ass sometime, the best of them."

"That's right!" Clarence spoke with great feeling.

Buddy saw he had found a nerve. "Damn right! And when it comes to the worst, you got a living hell."

With even greater vehemence Clarence repeated his assent. He was no stranger to woman trouble.

Buddy lifted his hand like a traffic cop. "I say a man's got a right to respect."

"You tell it." Clarence was now responding as if in church. He was impressed with Buddy's command of this subject.

"If God meant it to be the other way around," said Buddy, "he would of given the man a hole and the lady a club between her legs."

He unintentionally had struck Clarence's funnybone. The ex-boxer chuckled so heartily that his good eye blurred.

Buddy brought down his hand and clapped it with the other. "By God, I hate to see a man take shit from a woman."

Clarence blinked to clear his eye and said seriously: "It don't hurt to take a stick to some."

"Thing to do is not let a woman get her hooks in you to begin with. But that's easier said than done. Maybe you got a business to build up and don't have time to run around chasing pussy. When you're young maybe all you want's a nice home to go to after a hard day, with a hot supper and a pipe to smoke in your slippers."

Clarence looked pensive.

"Say this happened to a young fella," Buddy went on. "You could see how easy he would get the problem we was talking about." Clarence seemed to have fallen into a coma. Buddy waved at him. "See what I'm getting at?"

Clarence's good eye looked from right to left. He lowered his chin onto the knot of his necktie. Buddy wondered why he was trying to justify himself to a colored flunky. "Well, goddammit, yes or no? I don't like to talk to myself."

The ex-boxer brought his chin up and scratched it reflectively. "I don't know if I right," he said at last, "but you trying to deal with—" He started again, speaking very patiently: "When I come in here you was talking about killing, and now you talking about being married?"

"Sure," said Buddy in relief. "You ever been married, Clarence?"

The car washer shook his head.

Buddy nodded. "Uh-huh. Well then, it might be hard for you to appreciate what the setup is like when it goes bad. You work hard to give a woman everything she wants, and what you get back is shit. You got things on your mind, but you can't talk to her about them. She sits there reading a fucking book. She don't fix her hair any more. Hell, she don't even wash it regular, and when she does she don't clean the fucking sink, so it don't drain; it's full of dirty hair and green grease! Makes you want to puke."

Clarence could appreciate that. There was nothing as bad as a filthy woman.

"She'll fry you an egg with the yellow hard all the way through," Buddy went on. "Burn the toast black. She won't shave her legs and lets them get hairy as an ape's. She's got no pride. She'll let her stockings fall down to her ankles. She's got yellow fingers from smoking, and so's her teeth. Lets a bagful of garbage set on the sink till if you lift it the bottom falls out. You give her a shirt she'll scorch it."

For some moments Clarence had been aware that the job for which Buddy was recruiting him was not only the murder of a white, but a white woman. This was too bizarre to provoke him into rising, as he had before, and uttering a refusal. Instead he sat there soberly and tried to understand why Buddy had picked him, though true it had been by default; but Buddy had expected the candidate would be colored. Apparently any Negro would do. Perhaps it was a compliment.

"Well sir," he said finally, "you got a problem all right, but I just wash the cars."

Buddy was silent for a while. Then he said: "Christ, Clarence, you could do it easy as falling off a log." He let several seconds pass again. "How else could you make two hundred bucks all at once?"

Clarence smiled in wonderment. This man was asking him to kill his wife.

"I see," said Buddy, "you're beginning to like the idea. *Two hundred dollars.*"

It was the craziest proposal Clarence had ever received his life long, crazier by far than the one made by a man who came into his dressing room after a bout and represented himself as a promoter with an interest in Clarence's career and took him to his apartment, where he handcuffed himself to a bedstead and offered Clarence ten dollars to whip his big fat white ass with a bundle of twigs tied together.

"It'd be *easy,*" said Buddy. "And you can't get in no trouble, because I let you in myself and then afterwards give you plenty of time to get away before calling the cops."

Clarence kept grinning.

"First thing tomorrow morning," Buddy said, "I'll go to the bank and get you half. You put a hundred in your pocket, and we'll get the details down pat."

What the ex-boxer was thinking now was that if it was so easy to kill his wife, why didn't he do it?

"Way I figure," said Buddy, "we make it look like burglary. You come in the outside cellar door, come up the steps, and you're right across the hall from the bedroom." He closed his eyes in thought. "After you got the main job out of the way, you open dresser drawers and spill stuff on the floor."

The office door opened behind him, and Buddy almost snapped his head off his neck. It was Ralph.

"I didn't know you'd be here. I just dropped by to get the lawnmower I left, and I saw the car. I didn't know you were coming here on Sunday."

"*I thought you promised*," said Buddy in a deliberate fury, "*to keep your nose clean from now on*."

Ralph wrinkled his nose. "Huh?"

"Since when do you open a closed door without knocking?"

Clarence stolidly closed his eyes. He had no stake in this.

"No backtalk, please," said Buddy in a calmer voice. He pointed to the door.

"Can I use the bathroom, please?" Ralph asked, and before Buddy could decide whether this was an elaboration of the insolence he slipped into the little lavatory and locked the door.

Buddy rushed to the plywood panel and pounded upon it. "Come out of that place!" He feared Ralph would settle down for a long crap. He was answered almost immediately by the sound of the flushing mechanism. Ralph came out, buttoning the top of his fly. He was a lightning-swift pisser.

"Sorry," he said to his father. "I didn't know you had to go that bad."

To save face, Buddy went inside and took a leak for himself. He had to wait a longer time than usual for his waterworks to function. He wondered whether he had been jazzing too violently of late: that could happen.

In the office Ralph said hi to Clarence.

Clarence nodded silently, then looked at the desktop, trying to discourage the expected questions about his career in the ring.

"I guess back in the old days you'd be out now doing roadwork," said Ralph. "Even on Sunday." Clarence shrugged. "Then back to the training camp for a big steak and

94

half a dozen eggs. I guess Primo Carnera would eat half a dozen *steaks*. He had a glass jaw though, didn't he? You ever fight him?"

Clarence twitched his chin.

"I guess he was dangerous if he fell on you," said Ralph.

Clarence did not smile at the jest. He was thinking that even when he won the rare purse he could seldom afford steak for supper, let alone breakfast. He wished this kid would go away.

"He was *too* big, wasn't he? I guess the right size is like Louis?"

Clarence avoided bars the nights on which Louis fought; he didn't need that. Not that he meanly wanted to see him defeated by a white man, just because he, Clarence, had been half blinded by one. But neither did he childishly exult in the man's persistent victories as if they reflected glory on him, as did the stupid janitors and shoeshine boys. What Clarence would have liked was that some other colored fighter give Joe a good beating. But when John Henry Lewis fought him, Joe knocked out John Henry in the first minute of the first round.

"I was thinking," said Ralph, "if I got a pair of gloves, maybe you might show me a few pointers if you had the time."

This suggestion depressed Clarence even further. He almost yearned for the return of that evil man from the toilet.

He mumbled, scraping his upper lip with the rake of his lower span of teeth. One wanted him to commit a murder, and the other wanted boxing lessons. Whites ran the world without knowing how to do anything for themselves.

Buddy emerged at that point and asked Ralph: "Why aren't you in Sunday school?"

"It's over."

Buddy nodded. "All right, Ralph. You can run along."

"See you, Clarence," Ralph said and departed.

Buddy peered out the window to see if he was actually leaving. He saw Ralph run the lawnmower out to the sidewalk and then stop and rudely scratch his butt in public. That no one was around at this hour on a Sunday was neither here nor there; the gesture was loutish.

Turning, he said to Clarence: "Let's let the details go until I pick the exact time. You might forget 'em otherwise or get to boozing and shoot your mouth off. I hope you got sense enough afterwards to keep your trap shut. They got an electric chair up at the pen. . . . What I figure is maybe sometime the middle of the week, but I gotta check. Sometimes her sister comes to visit and stays the night."

He seized his chair and ran it back behind his desk. "Tomorrow you get your hundred. Bring some kinda coat and hang it in the corner of the garage. When you go home, feel in the pocket for a envelope."

Clarence rose and buttoned his suit. Services continued all day at the Abyssinian Baptist Church, and he intended to spend the afternoon there.

It occurred to Buddy that there would be no need to give Clarence the second half of the fee. Once he had performed the job, to whom could he complain?

chapter 6

RALPH WAS JUST FINISHING his bread pudding when he heard Horse Hauser calling "Hey, Sandifer" outside the back door.

"May I be excused?" he asked his father.

Buddy grimaced. "Isn't that kid old enough to knock on the door like a decent human being?"

At this point Hauser shouted again, and Ralph said: "I'd better go out there or he'll keep yelling."

"You tell him to knock on the door from now on. I don't want to hear any more hog-calling outside my house."

Naomi smiled at this turn of speech. For Sunday dinner they sat at the round table in the dining room. Concealed by the mashed-potato bowl was a burn hole in the white tablecloth, made by a fallen candle some years before at the last Christmas get-together of the relatives prior to the death of Ralph's remaining grandma, Naomi's mother.

Ralph took his dirty dish and glass to the kitchen and went

out the other exit. Hauser howled once again before he reached the door.

"Who let you out of your cage?" Ralph said, descending the back steps.

Hauser said coldly: "C'mere." He walked over by the garage and turned to confront the attendant Ralph. "Sandifer, if you ratted on me last night, I'll get you for it."

"Me?"

"I'll trim your ass, is what I'll do."

Ralph extended his jaw. "Any time you want to try . . ."

Hauser diminished the depth of his already low forehead. "Frankly," he said with pomposity, "I thought better of you."

"In the first place," said Ralph, "I don't know what you are talking about."

"The cruiser got you."

Ralph struck himself in the brow. "That was my father. A car suddenly pulled up, and it was my old man of all people! He didn't recognize you, and I didn't tell him."

"Sure about that?" Hauser peered at him like a movie detective grilling a suspect.

Ralph had enough of this. "Look, you prick." He poked Hauser's chest with two knuckles. "I got you out of a jam that I had nothing to do with, so don't come around here and give me any shit."

This sent Horse into retreat. He backed up against the side of the garage, saying humbly: "Appreciate it, Sandifer. You're a real good man."

Mollified, Ralph said: "Let's forget it. The money's back and you're clear."

Hauser's mouth sagged. "But I tell you this: I can't ever go back to that job again. I can't show up there tomorrow. I'd give it away for sure. That's the way I am. I can't hide nothing."

Ralph sought to pass this off with a jest. "Bragging or complaining?"

"I'm serious."

Bored, Ralph looked at the tiny tree he had planted near the garage last spring. It had been dead all summer. On the annual Arbor Day every student was given a little sapling to take home and put into the ground. Ralph's never took root though he faithfully carried out the planting instructions on the mimeographed slip included and religiously supplied water. Hauser and most other guys used their baby trees for whip-fights or re-creations of the duels between Errol Flynn and Basil Rathbone, dropping the shredded results in the gutter.

"Well," Ralph said, "let's go down to Elmira's and have a Coke or something." He started to walk away, but Horse did not follow, so he came back. "Look, if you feel that way, why don't you make a clean breast of it to Bigelow? After all, he's got his money."

"I could easier cut my throat. No, I'm finished." He looked accusingly at Ralph. "I don't get no allowance like you, Sandifer. My old man don't give me the sweat off his balls."

"I only get fifty cents, and I work damn hard for that." Nevertheless, Horse made him feel guilty. "If you want to cut grass, you could take over some of my customers to tide you over. Like Leo Kirsch. You can have Leo. Or I got an idea: we could become partners and split all profits. With two of us, we could mow a lawn in half the time. We could take on more customers, and both of us would make at least as much as I do alone. Then when the fall settles in, we'll rake leaves, and shovel snow in the wintertime. Maybe wash windows for spring housecleaning."

Hauser was sneering. "Maybe you like nigger work, but it's not for me."

99

Ralph was miffed. "Well, you wanted my advice."

Hauser made his mouth into an O. "Since when? I came over here to do *you* a favor, Sandifer. There ain't nothing you can do for me."

"Screw you."

"Now you're being childish," said Horse. "What I wanted to tell you was Bigelow will need a new delivery boy, and you can be it if you go over there after school tomorrow."

"You serious? You giving it up?"

"I told you I was. You calling me a liar?"

Ralph looked at his feet. "Nice of you, Hauser."

"It beats cutting grass. I generally raked in three, maybe three and a half a week. He pays two-fifty, and then sometimes you get tips or they let you keep the deposit on the returned bottles. And you get stuff at Christmas, though not always money. Get a rear basket for your bike, along with the front one you already got, so you can take a couple sacks at the same time. It's two hours a day, and four on Saturday afternoon. If you ain't delivering he will want you to carry stock up from the cellar, but I always took it easy on that. Told him I was ruptured."

"I might just go over there," Ralph said. "I was thinking of going out for football, but I'm too light."

"Yeah," said Hauser, who though husky had little interest in sports. "At Christmastime you generally get something from most of them. Maybe a little hard candy at least." He spoke sadly.

"I guess you'll miss it," said Ralph. "Sorry how it worked out."

Hauser suddenly stared at him in defiance. "Don't bleed at the asshole for me. I'll get by all right. I got what it takes."

"Come on," Ralph said expansively. "Let's go down to Elmira's. It's on me."

"Jesus," said Horse. "I never thought I'd see the day when

you'd spring for anything. Bet the moths will fly out when you open your pocketbook."

Ralph was happy to see that Horse had regained his pride in spite of all. He had despised the hysterical figure of the night before.

After a dinner of stewed chicken and noodles, and an apple pie he had timed so it would come fresh and hot to the table, where his mother ate one stout wedge, and then another, with alternate forkings of rat-trap cheese, Leo let the dishes soak in the sink and took his long leisurely postprandial defecation while reading the newspaper supplement called *This Week*. He used the basement facility, which was situated within a compartment of rough boards in the corner near the coal bin. His mother never came down cellar, so he left the door open. When he looked up from the paper he had a view of the furnace and beyond it the standing pool of water that had leaked through the concrete-block walls during the last rainstorm: beneath it was a clogged drain.

He had left the undeposited money on his dressertop all night while he slept more soundly than usual, not for once being awakened by his mother's midnight retching. When he awakened in the morning and dressed, returning the small change and keys to his pants pockets, he saw the bills, which the night's rest had caused to straighten from a wad into a sloppy pile. He felt a certain resentment, as if they had been forced upon him against his will. He took the stack by one end and slapped it irritably upon the dresser, raising some dust. It was housecleaning day.

After he had prepared and delivered to her bed his mother's breakfast of four soft-boiled eggs broken over fragments of toast and crumbled bacon, a mug of hot water and lemon for her bowels, he went into his room, rolled the bills tightly again, and put them into his pocket. They were still there, in the pants that now lay around his ankles as he sat upon the commode.

He did not consciously think of them, yet it was they that distracted him from the articles in *This Week*, of which he had read two as well as a page of jokes with so little attention that he could not have described the subjects thereof or have retold the jokes as it was his practice to do on Mondays to customers at the lot. Leo had to get his material from such sources; he did not have Buddy's talent for original wit.

Finally he gave up, flushed the toilet, went out, and looked at the water on the floor. It had dwindled somewhat in recent days owing to evaporation, leaving a white ring to mark the circumference of the original collection. The wall nearby was stained with damp. He suspected the tree roots again had broken through the drainpipe that ran between the cellar and the sewer under the street, but to have a plumber verify that with his "snake" would cost at least a dollar and a half and to have him grind the pipe free might go as high as five dollars. And the water did no harm where it was.

Leo toiled up the steep steps, which took more effort than usual; the money seemed to weigh him down. He emerged into the kitchen and gazed negligently at the sinkful of soapy water and dishes. Normally he would deal with that before going outside, in good weather, or to his room in bad, and having his session with the young girls in the rotogravure section. Today however, in a renegade mood, he continued past the sink and through the dining room into what his mother called the parlor. As usual she was lying there on the davenport.

"Hi, Boy," said the parrot, then leaped from the perch to the wire wall of the cage, turned itself upside down, and began slowly to descend with fastidious claws. Leo inserted his index finger through the wires, and Boy halted his downward progress to rub the side of his beak against it. But had Leo rubbed Boy, the bird would have nipped him. Boy, a tyrant, had to take the initiative. Leo respected that, however, as a note of pride on the part of a totally dependent creature who furthermore lived in a prison. He could not have tolerated an obsequious pet.

He had not looked directly at his mother, who no doubt would speak soon enough, in complaint or with some importunity. He kept his shoulders stiff as he claimed the rotogravure section and walked from the room. Only when he reached the back door did he relax, yet he could hardly believe he had got away scot-free. Perhaps she had fallen asleep. As he turned the key in the door he kept locked against tramps, he heard the horrible gurgling cough for which she had been noted for years and which the doctors said issued from no organic cause. He plunged onto the back steps to escape its vile sound, walked across the lawn that Ralph had mowed the day before, and sat on the cracked wooden cover of the disused cistern under a large old elm that had been dying for years of the blight but so slowly that half of it was still in leaf—luckily, the half that shaded the cistern.

Leo lived in the old part of town. His next-door neighbor's garage had been converted from a barn. When Leo was a boy his father had kept chickens in a henhouse, now gone, at the bottom of the property, which extended for about a hundred fifty feet, beyond which was empty land full of the goldenrod and ragweed that tormented the asthmatic.

Instead of perusing his favorite section, with its pictures in brown monochrome, Leo let it fall from his slack hand and told himself uncompromisingly that tomorrow morning he must return the money to the cashbox in the safe. If he did this before Buddy reached the lot, the explanation, if required, would be simple. He had deposited precisely the amount for which there were sales records; he had left in the box that for which there were none.

Having made the decision, Leo was almost overwhelmed by a sense of well-being. He rose from his seat as if inflated, bent to retrieve the roto section, sat down again, and leafed through it. No bathing beauties were therein; it was too late in the season. But there was a picture of a thin, lank-haired girl in a tartan skirt and saddle oxfords, holding a sphere about the size of a coconut, with a caption that read: "Thelma Wilhelm, Washburn freshman, shows ten-pound ball of tinfoil she's been collecting since 1936. When it reaches basketball size, says the fifteen-year-old, she'll sell it, giving proceeds to Community Chest."

A pity he had sold his own tinfoil ball to the junkman. He could otherwise have offered it to Thelma to incorporate into hers. Leo adored the earnest good will of young girls.

Dear Miss Wilhelm: Under separate cover please find my contribution to your worthy efforts in behalf of charity. You are a fine, upstanding young person. I trust you do not smoke tho, and you get your cigarette foil from father, uncle, etc., and other adults. A Friend

The thought of Thelma opening the package with a little chirp of pleasure, and cupping his silver ball in her slender white hands on which the nails were all chewed, was very erotic to Leo.

He sat there on the cistern cover, enjoying a nonphysical orgasm that violated no laws, and when he heard a shout from behind, his reaction was guiltless.

He turned and saw Jim Plum, his neighbor, waving at him with a sickle. He waved back with the roto section. On that encouragement, Plum came over. He was a medium-sized man, but lumbered when he walked as if he were much heavier.

"How you doin', fella?" he asked.

"I can't complain," said Leo.

"Smell the skunk last night?"

"Can't say I did."

"Dog must of got after him. Ever had a dog that got sprayed by a skunk?" Plum was a genial man whose questions however had a certain belligerency about them. He toyed with the sickle as if he might give Leo a taste of it unless he got the expected answer.

"No, I never."

"You wash him in tomato juice."

"Is that a fact," said Leo.

"Some people say milk, but they're wrong. No soap will touch it, for sure. I don't know about turps. But tomato juice's the ticket."

"Pretty expensive, I bet," said Leo.

"Depends on the size of your dog. A fox terrier will take a whole number-ten can. Now, you got a collie, you need a lot more."

"I bet," said Leo, shaking his head dolefully.

"But you got to do something," Plum said, rubbing his buttock with the back of the sickle blade. "He'll stink so much you can't bear him around. I never owned a dog myself. You know who told me that? A boogie. They know everything about dogs. You ever know any colored people, Leo?"

"There's one down at the lot."

"I've known quite a few in my time," Plum said, propping one foot in a high-topped shoe onto the cistern cover alongside Leo and leaning over him in amiable menace. "I don't mind saying I learned a lot from 'em. You know, they'll eat carp, when nobody else will touch it. The secret is you pull out the mud vein, then you got something that tastes as good as bluegill or perch. I never eat any kind of fish myself. Life's too short for that."

105

Plum had a way of talking with special enthusiasm of things he did not do.

"What's your favorite food?" he asked. "Steak or roast beef?"

"Roast beef, I guess."

"Then steak, and then?"

Leo said: "Roast pork would have to come in there."

Plum frowned. "Not ham? Covered with pineapple pieces and cloves? Man, that's eating, for my money. Then you got sandwiches from it at night, with lots of mustard. Next morning, a big fat slice with your eggs! The ham what am, like they say."

Leo was getting uneasy with Plum hanging over him. "That what you had for dinner, huh?"

Plum backed away and raised his eyebrows. "The fact is, we had chicken."

"Me too."

"I be damned," said Plum. "That's a coincidence for you. Like old Hoover used to say, a chicken in every pot. I read Roosevelt and Eleanor eat wieners now and again. You can't tell what's in a sausage though; might be a rat fell in the grinder, for God's sake."

Leo wrinkled his nose.

Plum said: "But you don't think of that if you're in a ball-park, and the hotdog guy comes around and you eat one, you want another. He laughed at this folly. "I haven't seen a ballgame in six-seven years though." Still smiling, he said: "How's Sandifer these days?"

Plum did not like Buddy. Though Leo lived next door, Plum had acquired his last car at a lot in neighboring Oldenburg, where he ran a radio-repair shop.

"He's always treated me all right."

"Ever see his latest floozy?"

Leo made a stern mouth. "That's none of my business, the way I see it."

"She lives in the second-floor-back over on Myrtle, just off Chandler. I delivered a set across the street there the other day and saw him come out. Then later I see this blond head at the window."

Leo said in a dampening tone: "We sold her a machine. He was dropping it off."

"He drove away in a car. If he delivered one for her, who drove his over?"

"Jack did and then walked home for lunch. He lives over that way."

Plum said: "That was four o'clock or so."

In the first place Leo was exasperated by having to tell the lie; then to have it questioned was unfair in the extreme.

"Jack *left it there* at lunch. Buddy picked it up later. *I* picked Jack up at his house and took him back to the lot."

Plum was not insensitive. "Don't get me wrong, Leo. I'm not grilling you. It's just with that bird's reputation . . ."

Throughout the years Leo had always got unwanted information about Buddy's love life by such means, and while always publicly denying its authenticity, he invariably accepted it privately as truth. The resulting tension was very unpleasant, and it was never relieved by any personal knowledge: not once had he seen Buddy in a compromising situation.

He rose from the cistern. "You sure couldn't prove it by me."

Plum looked kindly at him. "You know, Leo, you've got a clean mind. You're too decent a human being to maybe know how rotten some people are."

Plum had embarrassed himself by making this statement, he whose usual role was to relate facts with which he had no

107

personal connection to someone for whom they had no use. "I have to take the little lady for a spin," he said abruptly, turned, and lumbered towards home.

Leo was touched by Plum's opinion, but wondered whether the theory held water. He actually knew a great deal of dirt, though he never sought it out nor did he pass it on. For example, he knew what had inspired Plum's bias against Buddy. Dave Hunnicut, who owned the Flying Red Horse station, had told Leo that in 1937 Buddy had put the blocks to Plum's wife. "She's a nympho," said Hunnicut, leaning close and giving Leo the benefit of his halitosis.

Leo rarely saw Grace Plum though she lived next door. She worked in a beauty shop in the city, taking an early streetcar every morning. At Xmas time, according to Plum, she got a lot of nice gifts from her clients, some of whom were well-to-do. Unless it rained, Plum always took her for a ride of a Sunday afternoon. Sometimes they would stop for a game of Tom Thumb golf, then get grilled-bratwurst sandwiches at the cafe nearby and bring them home for supper. That was all Leo knew about the Plums' home life, and it was rather more than he knew about the Sandifers'.

Leo's period of recreation having reached its end, he got up from the cistern and headed inside to vacuum the house from top to bottom. For a few precious hours the roar of the old Hoover would obscure his mother's sounds. At the back steps he lifted the lid of the garbage can and dropped in the rotogravure section, the only part of the paper that he did not preserve for the basement collection which would in time be sold to the junk dealer.

The picture of What's-her-name and her tinfoil ball fell face down upon the broken eggshells and the blackened starfish of a banana skin. Leo was ruthless after he had had his way with a girl.

He crept quietly along the hall to the closet which held the vacuum cleaner, hoping to get it out and running before his presence was detected. Nevertheless the parrot heard him cross a loose floorboard and screeched: "Bum!" He waited for his mother's ax to fall, but apparently she was still dozing on the weight of her enormous dinner, at which she had devoured the entire chicken except the drumstick he had served himself, three helpings of noodles, two of pie. She ate like a laborer, spent most of her day on sofa or bed, and still had the figure of a young girl. Perhaps her nocturnal vomiting provided the answer.

Leo had equipped the vacuum with an extension cord which, added to the long wire that unwrapped from the hooks on the handle, gave him twenty feet to play with, so that he could plug it into a hall socket and enter the living room with the machine already whirring and nod and smile while his mother's mouth worked inaudibly. Before the development of this technique he had been at her mercy; he did not have the stomach to throw the switch once she had begun to talk. Though, in truth, it was all the same to her whether she could be heard or not.

She had been a different woman when his father was alive. His father had been the talker. Funny, Leo had no precise memory of what his father had talked about, but it was always good-natured and often accompanied by a finger in the area of his bellybutton, followed by a little popping vibration of his father's lips. His father would also address him with joke names like "Schnickelfritz" or "Buster Brown," and sometimes from no other motive than high spirits give him a penny for jawbreakers. Leo usually salted these coins away, but he would come around with his tongue stuck in his cheek and say something so his father could suggest: "Better finish the candy before trying to bejabber."

In those days his mother did all the housework. Sometimes she would take a moment in the late afternoon just before supper to pedal a roll through the player piano, though she never sang. She was up in the morning before everybody else, and stayed up at night until all were in bed. She knitted mufflers, crocheted doilies, canned every variety of fruit and vegetable, and baked all the bread and cake they ate. In the spring she cleaned the wallpaper of every room in the house with that pink putty that soon turned black. When repapering was called for, she did that as well, first soaking the old layer with a sponge and then stripping the plaster bare with a triangular scraper. She would set up a pasting rig like a professional, boards across sawhorses, shoot the roll along it, mark, cut, and slap on the flour-and-water mix with the big white-bristled brush; then climb the stepladder and drop the segment along the wall. On the finished job you could not see where the patterns joined unless you went right up to the seams.

In her day she never had the electrically powered instrument now wielded by Leo. His mother did the job with a carpet sweeper, and better than he, as she had been a better cook, a better housekeeper all around; indeed a better person until his father had fallen off the roof, because she had a job commensurate with her talents and interests.

Whereas Leo had felt misplaced all his life. What was he doing selling used cars? He was no extrovert like Buddy, and his interest in money was rather in saving what he had than in making more, the reverse of the salesman's proper mystique.

While vacuuming each Sunday, Leo simultaneously carried out the accumulation of trash from his soul, cleaning it for another week of balanced existence. Why was his sex life confined exclusively to writing imaginary notes to schoolgirls? Why did he have no friends and furthermore feel no need to have any? Why was he without hobbies and avocations? For he was aware, from articles in *This Week* as well as the attitudes of such associates as Jack his co-worker and Plum the neighbor, that the way he lived might seem restricted, even bleak, to others; to some who were not aware that he supported his mother, perhaps even downright odd. But if you had no friends, there were fewer persons to speculate on such matters.

If you had short-lived, fantasy relationships with females, you spent no time or money; and if they were with teen-aged girls, the make-believe was not rich enough to distract you from reality. Leo feared the consequences of even imagining an association with, say, a Grace Plum, in whose large breasts and deep hips one might disappear as if in quicksand. Therefore he sensibly averted his eyes when he saw her come out to sunbathe attired in shorts and halter.

As to hobbies, he had scarcely enough leisure in which to perform his tasks.

This left, to last, what was always the first question of his Sunday stocktaking: his job. True, he was by nature no salesman, but at least since he had worked for Buddy he had been offering for sale a product that customers were in the market for, else they would not have come on the lot. Previously, in the worst years of the Depression, after being laid off as clerk at the coal company, a job he had had since dropping out of school, he was forced to go from door to door with the kind of merchandise nobody sought of their own volition: a one-volume encyclopedia, then a line of shoddy brushes in imitation of Fuller, and finally the real Realsilk hosiery, a product that was decent enough but required calling on housewives with an intimate item when they were home alone. No doubt Buddy would have made a bundle at this, as well as an enormous commission in flesh, but Leo preferred the hostile women who slammed the door in his face to those who did not even open it.

Finally, there was security in working for Buddy. Their personalities were compatible. At the rare moments when

Buddy's control failed, as in the incident with Ballbacher—which was unprecedented in the appearance of the gun—Leo's own gift came into play. Had Ballbacher been his own customer, of course, no trouble would have arisen. One problem Leo could handle beautifully was the last-minute loss of nerve by a certain type of client. When Ballbacher had hesitated, Leo would have taken the initiative in negation, denied him the pen and the purchase agreement, and made a display of compassionate superiority. "Let's look at something else that's not too rich for your blood." This might have led to a lesser sale or none at all, but it might also have stung the man's pride in a subtle way, suggesting that in considering a car he could not afford *he* had been the fraud, and not the salesman.

. . . All this while Leo had been methodically vacuuming the hallway, with its long, dun-colored runner that was worn through to the backing along the center line. Reaching its end, he ran the machine across the bare patch of floor between hall and living room, from which it evoked a thunderous reverberation. Across the faded maroon-and-blue carpet he steered for the area under the parrot's cage, with its week's collection of the sunflower seeds, whole, fragmented, or husks, either dropped by Boy with his insouciant eating habits or flung out deliberately. He seemed to enjoy the machine and always clung to the near bars, head cocked to watch its progress below; though if Leo bumped the standard that supported his abode, Boy would beat his wings and squawk shrilly enough to be heard above the motor.

Boy was supposed to be about the same age as Leo, according to the old lady who had given him the bird when he was fifteen. Despite the parrot's manifest affection for him, Leo sometimes looked at the merciless yellow eye and wondered how they both would fare if Boy were five feet eight and he were a tiny man behind bars.

Without relaxing its attention, without even a tremor of tail, the parrot suddenly ejected a spurt of liquid excrement, which solidified instantly when it hit the newspapers on the cage floor, forming another oyster-colored clump with seeds, chaff, and gravel.

Leo deftly swung the machine around and rumbled across the rug towards the davenport, keeping his eyes down until the first row of orange-and-pink, octagonal segments of afghan intruded into the top of his vision. There was nothing for it now but to look up and see his mother's mouth working.

But a sudden tension of the power cord caused him instead to turn and see he had encircled the vertical standard of the birdcage. Another inch of forward motion would have toppled it over. He had never done this before.

He switched off the motor, creating an awful silence. Boy was back on his swing, green head stolidly pulled down neckless into his sloping shoulders, eyes self-righteously closed.

Leo turned. His mother never noticed his activities unless he made a mistake while performing them. She would not have missed this error, which he was fully prepared to admit had been idiotic.

The afghan had fallen to the floor, and she was all blood from her chin to the waist of the old dressing gown. If her past hemorrhages had been only in fantasy, this one was real, and she was white-faced and dead.

Even in the throes of horror, Leo realized he must clean up here before carrying the Hoover upstairs.

chapter 7

ACCORDING TO an alphabetical scheme, Ralph
and Hauser were assigned to different home rooms in high
school. On the first day, after an assembly attended by the
entire student body, everyone was dismissed until the following morning. The two friends found themselves in the crowd
and started the familiar walk home. The high school adjoined
the grade school to which they had gone for eight years.

As freshmen they were allowed one elective, and Ralph had
chosen Speech. Hauser had predicted he would himself opt
for Manual Training, which had been compulsory in the
seventh and eighth grades, but now he announced that he too
had decided on Speech.

"It's supposed to give you poise," said Ralph. "That comes
in handy in business and I guess in whatever other field you
might go into in later life."

"Listen, Sandifer," said Horse, "until I learn the ropes I
hope you don't try to crack me up when I have to make a
speech." He compressed his lips earnestly. "You know, like

make a monkey face or give me the old—" He thumbed his nose.

Some other kids went by on bikes. One cried: "You eat it, Hauser."

"Christ, why would I do that?" asked Ralph in amazement.

"You want to make an agreement? You won't try to crack me up, and I won't do it to you. O.K.?"

"It's a deal." They shook on it.

"Listen," Ralph said. "I think I'll take you up on that job, if you still mean it. I think I'll go over there about three P.M."

"Sure." Hauser looked morose. But suddenly he brightened. "How about that brick we threw through Bigelow's window! I bet he didn't know whether to shit or go blind when he found that." Without warning he rammed Ralph with his hard hip. Taken by surprise, Ralph fell against a low retaining wall at the edge of someone's property.

"God *damn* you," he cried as he rose. He examined the seat of his trousers. "If you've torn these new pants of mine—"

Across the street on the other sidewalk he saw Darlene and Doreen Montgomery, twins who were in their class, and realized Hauser had knocked him down to show off to them. They made identical grimaces. One shouted: "You think you'd grow up now you're in high school."

Hauser, usually so quick with a rejoinder, turned his head away, smiling foolishly and in silence. He had a crush on the twins.

When they had walked snippishly on, he said in a sickeningly sentimental voice: "Gee, I'm crazy about those cuties. Aren't they just the *cutest* things imaginable?" He seemed to be talking to himself. "They got real good taste in clothes too. Look at them little tams on the backs of their heads."

"You're going crazy, Hauser," Ralph said sourly. "I don't know what you see in those snotty bitches."

"Class," said Horse. "See how clean they keep their saddle oxfords, and their skirts ain't never wrinkled. I bet you they go to Florida again in November like they did last year, and come back with lovely suntans in the winter."

Mrs. Montgomery was a cousin of the Flegenbaums, the brewery family. Before Prohibition they had been bootleggers. Mr. Montgomery, a sallow little man, had been given a managerial job at the beer plant, which made him well-to-do in the local context: he drove a Chrysler, and the twins sported a different outfit every schoolday. However, they were far from being the rich girls portrayed by Katharine Hepburn, with their own tennis courts and a uniformed flunky who served breakfast from silver-covered dishes; and to show you how provincial they were, once when Ralph borrowed an ascot from his father to wear inside his sports-shirt collar to hide the top of a frayed undershirt, the Montgomery twins snickered and asked if he had a throat-cold.

Hauser watched the girls until they turned the corner. They walked briskly, in step, their pleated skirts swinging in unison.

"They slay me, those two," said he.

"Yeah, yeah."

"Sandifer, I want to ask you man to man: do you think I've got a chance?"

"With which one?"

Hauser hung his head. "It's weird. Either one. Both, I guess. The idea of twins is devastating. I can't imagine one without the other. I can't tell one from the other. I'd like to get married to them both."

"Married? What the hell you want to get married for?"

"Why," said Hauser, frowning, "because you fall in love."

Ralph snorted. "You're a fifteen-year-old kid, for Christ sake."

"I guess you're thirty-five."

"When I am," said Ralph, "I won't be married."

"You'll be jacking off in some boardinghouse someplace: that's what you'll be doing."

Ralph had not intended to get into this argument, but he could not endure Hauser in a sentimental phase. "I'll be going out with movie stars!"

They had stopped walking. Hauser seized the crook of his elbow and said: "Tell me this then: suppose you had the chance to get married to Merle Oberon?"

"She's already married. That's no example." He did not know this for a fact about Merle. If he came across an article about her in a newspaper or movie mag he quickly turned the page. He could not bear learning about her personal life. He wanted stars to live only on the silver screen, vanishing into a limbo between pictures. He had heard that his favorite male performer, Errol Flynn, was a big drunk and sex fiend in real life. He hated to hear that kind of information.

"By time you're thirty-five maybe she'll be divorced. You know movie stars."

Ralph said stiffly: "I don't want to talk about it. It's ridiculous."

Hauser jeered. "You're afraid to admit you're madly in love with Merle. I notice you never talk dirty about her, either. That's what I mean, Sandifer. A man just don't go through life fucking whores. He wants to find the girl of his dreams and settle down in a little love nest and have kids."

"A glamorous star like Merle in a little love nest?"

"Go on," said Hauser, throwing up his shoulder caps, "be sarcastic. You don't hurt my feelings none. Someday when you're an old bum, you come around my house where I'm living with Doreen—or Darlene—and we'll give you a hot meal on the back steps."

"O.K.," said Ralph. "Then you come for cocktails in my New York penthouse, and be sure to wear your tuxedo because if you don't the butler won't let you in."

They had reached Horse's home, a two-story structure from which the paint was flaking. The long porch ran downhill at the north end, where a post was disintegrating from rot or termites. A blackened dump-truck sat in the twin mud tracks that constituted the driveway. Hauser's father was a driver for the coal company.

"Oh-oh," said Horse, seeing the truck. "The big prick is home for lunch."

"See you," said Ralph.

"Not if I see you first," Horse cried without turning his head.

Buddy went to the bank as soon as it opened, poked his head into the frosted-glass cubicle of Charlie Furst, the president, and asked for the return of the erroneous night-deposit envelope.

Charlie was dunking a teabag into a china cup. "Sure, Bud," said he. "Mary just went down to bring them up." He hung the tiny tag over the side of the cup. "Say, I'm going to buy a new machine and if Hellman Buick won't give me enough on the trade-in, I might come around and see you."

"You'd do all right over there," said Buddy. "They need your business." Furst had approved a loan for Buddy some years before and ever since had been threatening to ask for the return of what was not that big a favor. He would expect top dollar for his car. Buddy had better friends now at the Building & Loan Society. Still, this was not the time for reluctance; he could save that until Furst showed up at the lot. "But if they don't," he said, "come on over and we'll see what we can do."

"Thirty-seven Buick four-door, clean as a whistle. You know the car. Less than fifty thousand mileage?" He was asking how much it would bring.

Buddy would not accept the question. "We'll be glad to

take a gander if it don't work out with Hellman. But I know him to be fair."

Furst raised his eyebrows. "I thought he was the competition." Hellman had his own used-car lot next to his showroom.

"Charlie," Buddy said sententiously, "I never try to succeed by knocking someone else."

Furst held his cup over the metal wastebasket and plucked out the dripping teabag, which however he did not discard but rather tucked onto the saucer for later use. He was a middle-aged man of no great local popularity, having had to foreclose mortgages on various people during the Depression.

"That's a real manly attitude," said he.

Buddy gave him a one-fingered salute and went to the last teller's window, which was unattended. Through the bars he saw that Mary Wentworth had brought the night deposits up from the basement in a Werk Soap carton, which she was now emptying onto her desk.

He called to her, and she came to the window. Mary was a widow in her late thirties. Her trunk was slender but she had a plump face and a large round behind. Recently she had taken to hennaing her brown hair, no doubt because of the arrival of some gray.

After hearing Buddy's problem in sullen silence, she returned to her desk, found the envelope, and brought it to him. "I never thought *you'd* make a mistake," she said sourly and went back to work.

"Obliged, Mary," said Buddy. It had been Mary he was pronging in the office that night when Clarence tried to steal a car. She had come originally to the lot to sell her late husband's automobile, which she could not drive, and anyway she was in grievous need of money, her uninsured spouse having left her with two children and no profession. Buddy gave her more for the old Hupmobile than he could ever sell

119

it for, and he also made her a gift of his tool for several months until her gratitude became obnoxious. She of course called it love, but Buddy knew it was rather that she had been badly in need of confidence. He had done a lot for her, even put in the good word with Charlie Furst that got her hired at the bank; but since he had turned off the sex, all she had for him was the peevishness of the spurned.

Now you take Laverne: he sensed a potential ferocity in her, which perhaps she herself was not aware of. He believed she might kill him if he ever rejected her. In the throes of her passion he often felt as if she might tear his dick out at the roots. Afterwards he was sometimes strangely disappointed to find it still in place, though having in his late frenzy been obsessed with its imminent disappearance. Buddy had looked all his life, without realizing it, for a woman who overwhelmed, even terrified him when fucking and then climbed out of bed, hunger satiated, to display an equable temperament.

When he reached the lot and parked behind the office he saw Clarence in the garage. He waved the envelope at him, but the one-eyed Negro did not seem to get the significance of the gesture. Around front, Buddy had to unlock the door. Leo was rarely known to be late, but his tardiness now served Buddy's ends.

Buddy opened the envelope and shook its contents out upon his desk. He saw immediately that the murder fund was not included, but took a while to accept that fact, counting and recounting and examining the deposit slip. Then he went to the safe and took out and unlocked the cashbox, though he knew the effort would be fruitless.

But there, secured by a rubber band, were the bills. Buddy thumbed their edges reflectively, but did not count them. Were it not for the rubber band, he might have assumed that somehow he had overlooked the money the day before when he had searched the box. But he understood immediately that, having no matching sales slips for this sum, Leo had brought it back. But when?

Leaving the money where it was, he locked the box and replaced it in the safe. He unlocked the door to the garage and saw Clarence, who was prying at the thread of his rubber boot with a screwdriver.

"Leo been in here?"

"No," said Clarence.

Buddy closed the door and went to look out front. It was rare to see a customer this early on a Monday morning. He and Leo generally used the time to reconsider prices on cars that had been around for a while without attracting much interest. Then after Clarence cleaned the old figures off the windshields, Leo would whitewash the new ones on, making certain flourishes, such as long tails on the digits that permitted and underlining special bargain prices or following them with one or more exclamation marks.

As it happened, the morning proved more profitable than most Mondays before noon. A Methodist minister, who had been given a hundred dollars to purchase a replacement for his '29 Ford, bought a '31 LaSalle that had been on the lot for months, did not try to jew Buddy down, accepted the offer of twenty-five dollars for his old car, and drove off oblivious to the blue smoke pouring from the tailpipe.

Buddy was about to get into the old A-model and drive it back for Clarence's cleanup when he heard footsteps behind him. He turned and saw Ballbacher.

Before he had time to react, the young man spoke: "I want to buy a Ford phaeton if you got one."

He showed no recognition of Buddy whatever. He was some kind of nut.

Buddy stared at him for a moment and then said: "Well, we ain't got one."

Ballbacher's square face was suddenly segmented by a grin. He pulled a handful of greenbacks from his pants pocket. "I got the cash right here."

Buddy looked and saw twenties and tens.

"Whatjuh do, rob a bank?"

"Pinochle."

"Tell you what," said Buddy. "I'll take a look. You just give me a minute."

He returned to the office and opened the lowest drawer in the right-hand pedestal of the desk, intending to put the gun in his pocket, for purposes of protection, not revenge. He believed that in dealing with Ballbacher he was skating on thin ice. He saw him now as a warped individual and not as the straightforward adversary who had dropped him with Saturday's sucker punch.

But the pistol was not in the drawer. Buddy ransacked the rest of the desk and then searched Leo's, because he remembered that he had been disarmed by his salesmen and supposed that Leo, either ignorant of its proper home or with an idea of making it unavailable for sudden passionate uses, had stowed the weapon elsewhere. That would be like Leo, the man of reason. But neither was it in Leo's desk.

Buddy burst into the garage, where Clarence, having poured some sand onto an oil spill, was watching it turn dark before applying his broom. On Monday mornings he always spruced up his shop.

"All right," Buddy said fearlessly, though he knew Clarence was armed, "you just give me that gun."

Clarence took his weight off the broom handle. "I ain't got no gun."

Buddy decided on diplomacy. "Listen, that deal we got, I don't want you to use a gun, see. You got the wrong idea."

The statement caused Clarence to smile enigmatically.

Buddy said: "You just turn it over. It ain't healthy for you."

Clarence sighed, dropped the broom, and raised his arms. He had been frisked many times by the police, who often stopped him capriciously in his neighborhood after dark. These searches, which were never explained, invariably proved futile. The cop's apology generally took the form of slapping Clarence on the rump and saying: "You just keep clean."

Clarence spread his legs to make his crotch accessible, because a professional frisk went that high, though how there'd be room in there for a gun or knife along with your cock was beyond him.

Buddy at first backed away in the idea that the ex-boxer was threatening him with a bear hug, but he now got the idea. "I don't figure you got it on you. You got it hid someplace." He scanned the garage in an abstract fashion. Already he had abandoned his suspicion. Facing Clarence, seeing his dead eye, he could not seriously believe him capable of guile.

The Negro lowered his arms and spoke in a tone so sympathetic that, if he had not been a moron, it might have been taken as irony: Buddy was always alert to that note. "Somebody done stole your gun?"

"Humh," Buddy grunted, disposing of the matter. He started away. "You was going to give me some money," said Clarence.

Buddy stopped and said without turning: "I was gonna stick it in your coat pocket hanging on a nail." He whirled around. "You got to remember details like that."

"I remember," said Clarence, bending to pick up his broom, "but I never saw you do it yet." Erect again, he pointed to a dark garment hanging in the corner above an oil drum full of sand. "That there is the coat, in case you was looking for it."

"I wasn't," Buddy said tartly. "I was looking for my pistol, and a while back I was looking for Leo, and you couldn't do me no good with either." He made a sudden decision. "Listen, I can't give you that money till just before the job."

"Shit then," said Clarence.

Buddy marched up and stuck a finger in his face. "You get your fucking ass out of here." He was fuming. "You ain't got a deal, and you ain't even got a job pushing that broom. I don't take that kind of talk from anybody I pay."

Clarence stood his ground, and when Buddy stopped shouting for a moment, he said earnestly but not obsequiously: "I never said shit on *you*. What I says was shit for me if I don't get no money ahead, for killing ain't like taking a tire off a wheel, specially when it come to killing somebody you ain't got nothing against."

Buddy was arrested by this speech of unprecedented length.

"So," Clarence concluded, "I will sure go away if that's what you want, on account of you is the boss and this here is your property and no mistake." He meant the broom, and handed it at Buddy, who did not take it but stared at him for a while.

Then Buddy made a barking laugh. "Clarence, I never thought you couldn't take a joke." He even clapped the ex-boxer on the shoulder, the first time he had ever touched him. It was like striking stone: he felt only the huge cap, large as a baby's head. "The deal is still on, and you'll get your cash. Jesus, I forgot my customer." He turned and trotted to the office.

Through the window he saw that Ballbacher was still standing obediently where he had been left.

Buddy went outside. "It turns out we got just what you're looking for, my friend. It's your lucky day."

"My lucky day," Ballbacher repeated, but his voice was lugubrious.

"It's over here." Buddy started down the nearest aisle between the cars, but stopped when he heard no following footsteps on the blacktop. Ballbacher was still in place.

"Let's take a look at that phaeton," said Buddy. "It's in the back row."

Ballbacher put his hand to his mouth and pushed the lower lip almost to his nose. He dropped his fingers and looked belligerently at Buddy.

"What am I doing here? My kid needs an operation. My wife'd kill me if I drove up in somepin like that." He now changed his expression, showing Buddy a vulnerable look of dilated eyes. "I been playing pinochle all night and drinking white lightning from a jug." He shrugged and walked staunchly away, no suggestion of alcohol in his stride.

"Come again, sir," said Buddy to the receding back. He felt as if a burden had been lifted from his own.

The pencil factory's noon whistle sounded from across town. Where the hell was Leo? Buddy went inside and picked up the phone.

Leo answered on the first ring.

"Leo," said Buddy, "what in the hell are you doing?"

Leo's voice had a weird energy though what he said was reasonable enough. "I got up real early and took your money to the office. I put the night-deposit key on top the medicine chest in the toilet."

"You did the right thing," Buddy said hastily. He was on the defensive. "I made a couple sales I forgot to write up. I ain't been feeling up to snuff lately. Hey, that crazy sonbitch Ballbacher showed up again this morning and pulled the same stunt again." Buddy laughed hollowly. "I kept my head this time."

Leo said: "I been thinking about it ever since the undertaker came, and I—"

"What undertaker?"

"—finally saw through your trick. I don't know how I was so dumb all along, but when a man is left all alone in the world he sees things he didn't suspect when he had somebody to take care of."

"Huh?"

"Yeah," said Leo.

"Undertaker?"

"All the years I worked for you I never even borrowed a quarter to eat at the Greek's from the petty cash. So somebody put his mitts in the cashbox, and you don't suspect the pansy or the coon, no. You set your trap for Leo."

"Trap?"

"Count those bills, you skunk. You won't find a dollar missing."

"Jesus, Leo," Buddy said. "It's beginning to dawn on me." He spoke intensely through pursed lips. "This is the damnedest thing imaginable. I assure you, one, nobody's got sticky fingers around the lot, so, two, I wasn't ever laying a trap for anybody, most of all you, who are honest as the day is long, which is why you got the only other key to the box, so nobody can get in there but me 'n' you. You handle all Jack's cash, him being part-time, as you are well aware. But . . ."

Buddy cleared his throat and began an effort to turn the tide. "All things being equal like the fellow says, I don't mind telling you you hurt my feelings plenty with your nutty goddam theory, because if a man's close associates don't trust him he travels under a cloud in this world of ours. I always took you for a man of integrity, Leo, and I always thought the feeling was mutual."

Leo was suspiciously silent.

Buddy said: "Leo, are you still there?"

Leo screamed into the phone: "You, of all people, to cast aspersions on my character. You filthy dirty pig with all your whores." He laughed cruelly. "I know about every one: Mary

Wentworth and Plum's wife and that blonde on Myrtle just off Chandler."

Buddy was not inclined to panic under this sort of attack, which after all was flattering.

"Now Leo, this ain't like you," he said quietly. "You've always been a squareshooter."

"And the Dago woman at the Motor Vehicle Bureau, and that redhead who gives manicures in the barbershop of the Stinson Hotel downtown—and I could name a dozen more but I won't. You are steeped in evil."

Buddy said: "I can tell you're worked up in some kinda mood where you won't listen to reason, Leo. The facts of the case is you're acting like a woman driver, wandering all over the road. I don't mind telling you, I wouldn't take this from anybody else of the male race, but for the fact I have known you for years, and this is the first time I can recall you have a wild hair in your ass."

"You make a mockery of womanhood," said Leo, his voice breaking.

Buddy essayed a wisecrack: he was really getting tired of Leo. "Well sir, being a man, how is it any skin off your rump?"

"Your wife is a mother," said Leo. Buddy was startled to receive what sounded like a Bronx cheer, blown directly into the phone. For an instant he believed this whole thing was a hoax, though Leo had always been humorless. But, with Leo going on to make the identifiable gasps of weeping, Buddy realized he had heard not a mock salute but a burst of grief.

Putting this together with the cryptic reference to the undertaker, Buddy said gravely: "Leo, tell me if I'm wrong, but has there been a death in your family? I hope and trust it's not your mom."

Leo screamed: "Don't soil her name on your slimy lips!" And hung up.

As to Leo's knowing about his girls Buddy was unconcerned. He lived comfortably in the truth that a reputation such as his evoked jealousy from men and attracted women. No, what he worried about was his gun. Raving with grief, whatever its cause—he had not answered the question about his mother—Leo might be planning to blow out his brains.

Buddy hastily turned all the locks, got into his car, and accelerated in the direction of Leo's house, without a word to Clarence, who, not permitted to use the office toilet, was urinating into the drain in the center of the garage floor, his broad back discreetly turned to the open entrance.

chapter **8**

BIGELOW THE GROCER was a large, bald man
in an apron that was smudged from toting cartons from the
cellar. He used his big belly a lot, not only as a prop for
burdens but also as a kind of threat to smaller customers. He
pushed it now at Ralph; it was restrained by the edge of the
counter.

"What can I do you for?" He seemed altogether neutral,
neither smiling nor projecting any menace but his abdomen,
which after all was merely dumb flesh. Ralph was anyway
inclined to trust fat people.

Speaking levelly himself, Ralph said: "You know Horace
Hauser who delivers for you, well, he can't come to work any
more. I don't know why, maybe he's sick or something or his
folks won't let him, but he said I could take his place if it was
all right with you. If you don't believe me, you can call him
up." Ralph flushed and rubbed his head. "Well, no, I guess
you can't do that because they haven't got a phone. Anyway,
I'm not lying."

Bigelow stared at him for a time, then lowered the bald head and pushed the meaty face across the counter. "He wasn't worth a good goddam, that little snot. He was always into the loose candy or stinking up the crapper." He threw his fat hand towards an open door at the rear, through which could be seen the beginning of a flight of descending steps, presumably to the basement. Ralph was happy to hear there was a toilet on the premises; they weren't easy to find when you were out.

"I don't mind Number One if nature calls," said Bigelow. "But I say you oughta take your dumps at home except in unusual circumstances." He put on a pious expression. "Like if you was sick."

"I agree with that," said Ralph.

Bigelow turned mocking. "Oh you do, do you? You think all there is to the job is how you act about the toilet?"

"Well, no, I don't—" Ralph was talking to himself, Bigelow having left abruptly, and very swiftly for a man of his bulk, at the tinkle of the bell over the entrance. Before the customer, a middle-aged woman wearing a green hat, had closed the door, he was in position at the top of the counter. As she marched along, he kept parallel stride behind the glass candy case, which was neck-high, his face towards her and beaming in expectancy.

When he reached the clearing where the cash register and scales were mounted, he flushed Ralph from the area with a scowl, and the woman entered the gap, spitefully thumping her purse upon the counter.

"Well, Harry," said she, "here I am again, a glutton for punishment." She opened her handbag and snatched from it a fragment of paper.

"What can I do you for today, Miz Hugel? Got some fresh eggs just in from the farm, still warm from the hens."

"I *bet* they are," said Mrs. Hugel. "And you break 'em in a pan and you'll have fried chicken. Harry, your eggs wasn't even fresh last year when they was first put in cold storage, you old horse thief. The only reason I step in here is I'm too lazy to get to the A and P, so I keep making you rich."

"Show me a fellow at the A and P though who is fresh as me," said Bigelow. "If I thought the wife wouldn't catch me, I'd ask you out." He bunched his lips and simpered at her.

"Why, you old goat!" Mrs. Hugel said, cackled merrily, and with both hands adjusted her hat, which was decorated with artificial cherries. "You'd order one soda and two straws: that'd be your idea of a date, you tinhorn."

Up to this point Ralph had believed she spoke with genuine ill will, and because he recognized her from church, where she sang contralto in the choir, had continued to back away in embarrassment. Now that he understood the joking nature of the exchange, he stepped forward and said: "Hi, Mrs. Hugel." Then, in response to her frown, he added: "Ralph Sandifer."

Her brow cleared. "Oh hi, Ralph. I'm getting blind as a bat these days. My, you're shooting right up there. Say, are you still in the junior choir?"

"No, ma'am, not since my voice changed."

She continued to nod amiably at him. "I figured that. Well, what arc you doing over in this neck of the woods?" She cocked her head at Bigelow and said: "You sure didn't come this far for a bargain."

Bigelow, perhaps jealous at the loss of attention, said quickly: "He's my delivery boy."

"Yes, ma'am," said Ralph.

"Your dad's business going under, so he put you out to work?" asked Mrs. Hugel.

The edge of nastiness probably meant nothing. Ralph was aware that women of her age were often sarcastic for no apparent reason; it seemed to go with their hats and what was called middle-aged spread.

"No, ma'am. I always have some kind of job."

"It's good for a boy to make his own spending money, *I* think," she said, as if in argument. "My Clyde started his paper route when he was twelve. Some said, my, that's child labor, but he never suffered for it and by time he was eighteen he had a hundred and eleven dollars in the bank, and that ain't hay. He learned the value of money, I say."

"He still bookkeeping at the pencil factory?" Ralph asked politely.

"He *certainly* is," said Mrs. Hugel, again with the cryptic defiance, which may have been just a personal quirk of style. She turned to Bigelow and said belligerently: "Gimme a bunch of your bananas and try to include a few that ain't all black."

Bigelow winked at her. "Sure thing, Toots."

"And just keep a civil tongue in your head."

When Mrs. Hugel had left, Bigelow led Ralph to the cellar and directed him to bring certain cartons upstairs. Ralph discreetly looked for and saw the window he had busted Saturday night. It was masked with a piece of cardboard. The broken glass had been taken away.

"Whenever you ain't got no deliveries to go on," said the grocer, "you make yourself useful down here. I don't wanna see you standing around with your finger up your rear end." He leered at Ralph. "You got muscle enough to handle these babies?" He lifted a carton of Carnation Milk and thrust it at Ralph, who taking a deep breath managed to accept it without plunging to his knees, though it was so heavy that he did not dare speak in answer lest his chin collapse.

Bigelow said, chuckling: "You get ruptured, it ain't my responsibility." In a bit of grandstanding he seized two of the cartons for himself and clumped up the stairs. Like so many fat men he was extremely strong, yet Ralph believed that someone as tall and wide, but without the belly, could probably take him.

Had Ralph been alone he might have rested the box against the stair railing about halfway up—he was getting old and out of condition—but knowing that unless he followed hard upon Bigelow's heels the grocer would needle him, he climbed onward, trying the method of breath control advanced in the pamphlet he had bought by mail on *The Secrets of Oriental Self-Defense,* the only useful technique explained therein (unless you were attacked by an adversary armed with a Samurai sword or a sharpened bamboo stave). Before long he sensed that he was turning purple, but two steps from the top he got a psychological boost from noticing that Bigelow's pace had slowed considerably.

Emerging into the store, Bigelow coughed and lowered his burdens, really dropped them, in the middle of the floor. In relief Ralph placed his carton atop the other two. He was adjacent to the meat department. Working with a cleaver at the butcher's block was a much younger man than Bigelow. He had sandy hair and wore a bloodstained apron, also a dirty-white overseas cap.

He gave Ralph a merry grin and said: "Hi, Small Change. Your breath is coming in short pants." He crashed his cleaver into a hunk of meat, and from the latter fell a clean pork chop, suddenly taking form as it were; a neat thing to see.

Ralph immediately took to this friendly, deft fellow. After he caught his breath he said: "I'm working here now after school."

"I got eyes," the butcher said in his jolly-snotty way. "What happened to Horse? He flush himself down the kibo?" He cut two more chops and added them to the first, weighed the trio, tore a length of brown paper from the roll mounted on the counter, wrapped them, and tied the parcel with string from a ball on a spindle, going through this series in what seemed one continuous motion, finally slapping the package down and writing the price upon it with a black crayon.

"Catch," he cried and tossed the parcel at Ralph, who luckily was far enough away to react efficiently before it reached him. "Miz Slingerland, two twenty-eight Randolph. Know the neighborhood?"

"I can find it," said Ralph. "Should I go right now?"

"Well, I think so," the butcher said, winking, "unless you want to go in the icebox and beat your dummy." He was a real joker.

Before Ralph got to the door Bigelow called to him: "Hey, where you headed? C'mere. You always check, see, if there's other stuff to go." He threw some final items in a big bag already quite full and pushed it at Ralph. "Hummel, one ninety-four Constance." He claimed from behind his ear the pencil that he wore there and handed it over. "Write-um down until you got-um memorized. That Hauser used to get-um all messed up." He put out his hand. "And gimme that new pencil back. You get yourself a stub from Red." He pointed to the meat department. Ralph started back the aisle, but Bigelow said: "Not now. When you come back. Get going and step on it. You got a bike I hope."

"Yes, sir."

"Then you oughta be fast. I don't pay you to stop and jaw with nobody or watch them put out a fire. Hauser would go around the corner and stay an hour. He wadn't worth a fart in a windstorm. Keep your nose clean and you'll do awright." Bigelow suddenly and for the first time smiled: he wasn't the world's worst.

"Sure thing."

The grocer returned to his habitual ill humor. "Get going then, for Pete's sake."

When Ralph returned from these deliveries, which owing to his unfamiliarity with the neighborhood took him longer than he had anticipated, Bigelow, waiting on several customers at once, took time to cock an eye at the wall clock and grumble, then pointed to two big sacks and a cardboard carton. These turned out to be loaded to capacity with cans and clinking bottles and displayed crayoned addresses. They were too much for the front basket on Ralph's bike, and he had not yet bought the rear one suggested by Hauser, because he had not known whether he would get the job.

Eventually he balanced the carton across the rim of the basket—it was too large to fit within—and straddling the frame of the bicycle, holding a bag in the crook of each elbow, clutching the handlebars, he walked the vehicle to the first address, passing en route two kids he knew, who derided him.

His satisfaction in having dealt successfully with the problem now went out of memory: he realized he must cut a preposterous figure and could only hope he met no attractive girls before he had got rid of his load. His luck held in that respect, though failing him in another. At the next corner he met that Margie, who came along the intersecting street.

She proceeded to exploit her unusual opportunity. "You just let me," she said triumphantly, and wrested the bag from his left elbow, which was too weary to resist. She hugged it ardently against the flat chest of her mud-brown blouse.

"You're gonna get it if there're eggs in there," Ralph said disagreeably, feeling against his will an enormous easing of the muscles of his free arm. However, he was off center now, and had to correct quickly so as not to favor his right side, on which he held yet another sack. This movement unsettled the so carefully placed carton on the basket: it began to slide leftwards.

"You sap!" he cried at Margie, leaned over the handlebars to arrest the box, and inadvertently turned the front wheel to the wrong side. The heavy carton slid off the tilted basket, past his grasping fingers, and hit the sidewalk with a heart- and bottle-breaking sound. He watched Coke foam on the pavement, and then the slower oleaginous formation of spilled cream. The ketchup bottle was also broken, but its torpid contents did not escape the vessel, remaining an integral mass of red paste and glass.

He assailed the buttinsky. "Goddam, you stupid twerp! Lookit that."

Margie did as ordered, water appearing behind her lenses, which, Ralph also noticed, were dirty.

Her thin lips quivering in shame, she said: "I'll pay the damages." She wept silently but made snuffling noises when the tears reached her nostrils. Actually her nose was well shaped, and its skin was nice too, without blackheads or enlarged pores. The pimples on her cheeks were really the ruins of old ones, pale-violet blemishes. Brushing her hair once in a while would help. It looked clean enough but ratty.

"Here, hold this bike," Ralph ordered, gave her the remaining bag as well, climbed out of the frame, and knelt to see what he could do about the mess. Only the bottles he had seen from above were smashed. Two other Cokes had survived. A can of tomatoes was dented, a loaf of Taystee Bread bent. Cream covered one end of a package of meat.

"Gimme your handkerchief if you've got one."

Behind the bags she said: "I don't." The bike was leaning against her hip and looked unreliable. Ralph rose and took it to a telephone pole; its backstand was broken.

"You can put the sacks down now if you want," said he. Luckily he kept his eye on her. "No, not in that dog dirt!"

She came away from the curb. "I don't mind holding them, really."

He got out his own handkerchief, which had stayed fresh and pressed all day, and cleaned the sheen of cream from the meat parcel. He balled the soiled cloth and returned it to his rear pocket. He put the carton right side up and agitated it so that the contents would settle. Whoever opened those Cokes during the next hour would spatter their ceiling. He carried the box to the bicycle.

Margie tearfully stared between the bags at the sidewalk. "I insist on paying for the damages."

With what? She carried no purse and had no visible pockets in her clothes. However, Ralph did not ask this obvious question. No use making a jerk feel worse; the result would be more jerkiness.

"Tell you what you *could* do," said he. "You could go home and get a broom and dustpan and clean this mess up."

"I don't live near here." In answer to his exasperated groan she said: "I was on my way to the library. I always go this way because I like to walk across the iron bridge and look at the water."

Ralph merely groaned again and proceeded gingerly to place the carton upon the bike basket without dislodging the vehicle from its place of support. Succeeding in the effort, he called for the bags.

"Well, one thing I can do," said Margie. "I can just tote these sacks for you."

Ralph weighed the suggestion. Her company would embarrass him if he encountered acquaintances; but he had been mocked already by those boys for being overburdened as a lone hand. If she carried the bags, he could mount the seat and ride the bike, a situation of some dignity. Walking briskly behind his slow pedaling, she would be identifiable as an assistant and not a girl friend. In an emergency he could even sprint far ahead, leaving her in obscurity.

"All right," he said. Then, as she began with the side of her shoe to scrape the largest fragment of glass towards the gutter: "Don't do that! Cars park there."

137

"Oh, yeah." She peeped worshipfully between the bags. "Gee, you sure have a quick mind, Ralph. I'm scatterbrained I guess."

"So I noticed." He climbed on the bike seat.

Whenever he got too far ahead, which happened occasionally because the bags were heavy for her and she was careful to avoid further spillage, Margie cried out, and he stopped. After the first bag was disposed of, at a house seven blocks from the store, she was able to quicken her pace en route to the second destination, going indeed into an outright trot when Ralph, in mischief, turned on a burst of speed for the final fifty yards—and overshot the address, for harsh braking would have projected the carton to the pavement again.

He waited for her to come up puffing, sweating, her glasses fogged. Suddenly he felt shitty for pulling that stunt. At the first house, after receiving a lecture on balancing the box, she had held the bike while he carried the sack to the back door, waited in vain, and finally left it on the steps.

But now his conscience inspired him to say: "Go ahead, you can take it in."

Her glasses had slipped down on the sweat of her upper nose. She stared over them, panting from the run, sweating copiously on the forehead, and clutching the bag in an attitude of endless apology.

"You mean it, Ralph?" As if he did not, she quickly opened the gate in the picket fence that surrounded this place and, having got inside, closed it firmly, speaking again only after she had got behind the barrier. "Gee, that's nice of you."

Ralph looked away. When he turned back he saw the dope had gone up on the *front* porch, violating the protocol of which everyone was aware, but before he could shout, the door opened and the housewife appeared. Ralph averted his eyes again and kept them so until Margie returned through the gate.

"Can't you do anything right?"

Boldly ignoring the question, she said: "Here, this is yours." She opened her fist, displaying exceptionally delicate slender fingers, though the palm was dirty and the nails chewed. She held a nickel.

Ralph drew back. "No, you keep it."

"No, it's yours!"

"You did the work. It's only right."

"But it's your job," she said with a wail. "And then I broke that junk, so here's a nickel against it. That takes care of the Coke. I still owe for a half pint of cream and a bottle of Heinz's catchup."

Ralph could not help seeing the flaw in this computation. Without her aid he would not have broken the bottles and he would have put the tip in his pocket. Result: five cents ahead rather than still as much as thirty cents in the hole. Also there was a two-cent deposit on the Coke bottle. However, mean logic aside, he thought better of her than he ever had before: she meant well.

He accepted the coin in a judicious manner. "O.K. then. But the accident wasn't all your fault by any means." He coughed and said: "It was nice of you to help." He put one foot on a pedal. "O.K., listen, I'll see you around."

She pointed at the box. "You don't need help with that?"

"Huh-uh."

"See, I don't have anything to do. I was going to the library, but I forgot my card. I could carry in that box for you, and the tip would be all yours." She pushed the glasses up her nose.

"Thanks," said Ralph, "but this is my first day on the job. I've got to make time, and I'm behind schedule right now." She looked so woeful that he tarried another moment. "I got it. Why not go see your pal Imogene Clevenger?" The suggestion also gave him an opportunity to pronounce that name, the magic of which had returned after the progress in which his spiteful feelings of Saturday night had given way by next morning to a conviction that Lester Hauser had surely lied about her.

"She's no pal of mine! The other night she went off with that awful sailor."

Ralph squashed his testicles against the forward projection of the bicycle seat; there was some rotten pleasure in that. He said feebly: "That old guy?"

"He's immoral too. He drinks like a fish." Margie put her grubby hand to her mouth. "I'm sorry, Ralph. I forgot Horace is your best friend."

"Lester is only his brother. You don't have to like brothers of friends." Ralph added pompously, impersonally: "You don't even have to like friends of friends. Frankly, I can't stand your friend Imogene.

"I just hate her," Margie cried enthusiastically. "I don't intend to ever see her again."

"Yeah," he said curtly. "See you." He took off at a speed that threatened to throw the box back over the handlebars.

All the shades in Leo's house were pulled down, but there was no black wreath on the front door. Buddy opened the screen and knocked on the wood. The door had a window of clear glass, but it was hung with inside curtains through which nothing could be seen of the interior. Buddy had his eye there nevertheless, trying to look within, when the curtains parted at the bottom of the pane and Leo's face appeared.

Though below Buddy's level, and given Leo's hysteria on the telephone, it looked normal enough. Buddy flashed his well-known grin. Leo's heavy eyebrows came up though his head stayed low. The curtains closed and the door opened.

Leo wore an ancient spinach-green bathrobe, spotted with food stains. Taking the bit in his teeth, Buddy boldly pushed in without waiting for an invitation. The hallway was dark and had a queer odor.

Buddy began to talk with energy. "Gee, Leo, you give me quite a scare. You were talking so screwball on the phone, I figured you had gone haywire, but here I find you safe and sound, old son, and that sure takes a load off." For effect he rolled his eyes, looking at nothing, and said: "Gee, what a nice place you've got here. I don't believe I been inside in all these years. Well, sir . . ." He reached at Leo as if to touch him but did not, wanting no part of that filthy robe. "So I come over right away, anyhow."

Leo closed the door and stood silently between it and Buddy, with the only available light behind him. Buddy could hardly see his face.

"Tell me I did the right thing," said Buddy. "Have you got trouble?" He was astonished to hear his voice quaver and realized he was frightened. He needed a response; this gloomy dump was getting under his skin.

Leo spoke somberly. "It's early. I'm not dressed yet."

"Oh," said Buddy with no conscious irony, "I thought it was noon, Leo."

"She'll be on view at four."

Whatever that meant. Buddy had momentarily forgotten Leo's grief on the phone, being obsessed with his missing gun.

"Listen, Leo," he began, "I looked all over the office for that—" And then he remembered. "Good gravy, was I right when I asked about your dear mom?"

Leo lowered his head and his shoulders heaved.

"My sincere condolences," said Buddy. "I never had the good fortune to know that fine lady, but I know what she meant to you, Leo. You have to walk the harsh road of life alone now." He clapped his shoulder. "But at least you got a friend in Buddy Sandifer. Anything I can do, you name it."

Leo's head came up. "Excuse me. I ain't being much of a host. I'll give you some coffee."

Anything to get out of that hall. Buddy followed his employee along the passageway to the rear. The farther they went, the feebler the light. But at last Leo opened a door that turned out to be the entrance to the kitchen.

Buddy felt a rush of well-being. "Swell place, Leo, real swell." The room looked spotless; the linoleum had such a high sheen that Buddy walked gingerly. "Shame to track up this fresh polish," said he, keeping his heels in the air. He took a seat at the oilcloth-covered table and observed that even the ketchup bottle there was crustless around the cap though not new.

Leo himself though was a mess in the light: unshaven, uncombed, and with yellow egg on the bosom of the robe.

"Must be hell for you," Buddy said compassionately. "If the insurance don't cover the arrangements, you just say the word and I'll help out."

Though he had been crazy on the phone and abstracted thus far in person, Leo now reassumed the personality he had always displayed at the lot. "That's mighty white of you, Buddy." Yet the contrast between his appearance and his sudden reasonable manner was bizarre.

Buddy watched him go to the stove and get the coffeepot, already filled and presumably warm. However, after Leo had poured him a cup, brought the milk bottle from the Frigidaire, and indicated the sugar bowl, he found the coffee stone-cold.

"Walsh's is making the arrangements, I guess?" Buddy asked, naming the best-known of the local funeral homes. When they bought their new hearse, the Walsh brothers got a better deal from Buddy for the old one than if they had used it as trade-in. Buddy felt a superstitious need to oblige morticians. Then he made a nice profit from the eight college boys who bought it in common and decorated the panels with comic slogans like "Life goes from bed to hearse."

Leo nodded. But then, just as Buddy had thought he was back to normal, he stirred his own cold coffee with a dirty forefinger. He narrowed his reddened eyes. "You take me for a fool, don't you?"

"What the devil," said Buddy.

"Hoho, I got you figured out."

If fool there was, it was Buddy, for coming here. "Let's not start that nutsy stuff again, Leo." He shot his hand into the air. "Reason I came, if you wanna hear it, is my gun is missing from the office. I thought the crazy way you was talking, you might of taken it to do away with yourself."

"Don't worry about that," Leo said, leaning back in his chair and smiling grandly.

Buddy pushed his cup away and rose. "In view of your recent loss, I won't get into a argument with you. But I'll say this, Leo: I wish you'd ask the doc for a bromide or something. You need rest. You had a shock, nothing to be ashamed of—"

Leo took the pistol from a pocket of his bathrobe. Just as Buddy's heart collided with his tonsils, however, Leo reversed the weapon and pushed it butt-first across the tablecloth.

Buddy seized the gun and dropped it into his jacket. He breathed deeply. "Much obliged, Leo. Now, whyn't you try to get some rest before going down the funeral home? Take a shot of Nervine if you got any or at least a couple aspirin."

The man was cracked, but without his gun he was harmless. If Leo stayed in this state after his mother was under ground, Buddy planned to see old Doc Klingman on the matter. Maybe Leo could use a term in Greenlawn, the local nut hatch. When Buddy was twelve he found his own mother had been there for the two months following his birth. Few families went without a relative, if only an in-law's cousin, who was, had been, or would be in Greenlawn; it was no disgrace.

Leo said stolidly: "The Walsh boys are bringing her here. She wanted to be laid out in the living room. I couldn't never count how many times she told me that. She didn't go down the business district in maybe fifteen years, and definitely did not want to break her record when she was dead. Course, they had to take her down there for embalming; no way to get around that."

"Got to honor the wishes of the departed," said Buddy. "There used to be a lot of that when I was a kid: laying-out in the home of the deceased. That thing seemed to go out with the horse. I for one don't know why. It's kinda nice."

"Well, it's homey," said Leo. He looked and sounded normal again, and Buddy would have loved to know why he took the pistol, but did not dare ask and perhaps set him off again.

"Gee," said Buddy. "It's quick, ain't it? I gather she passed away yesterday some time."

Leo brightened. "Walsh's didn't have any other bodies on hand. I guess that was lucky anyway."

Buddy said: "Now, Leo, you get some rest like I said."

"I got to make a lot of coffee and get some cake at the bakery."

"For pity sake, Leo, people don't come to laying-outs for the refreshments. You don't get none if the body is laid out at the funeral home."

"You get coffee," Leo said stubbornly.

"But that's only if you do business with the Walshes, like us. They take you in the office, where they got that electric percolator. But they never have cake."

"But this," Leo said defiantly, "was her *home*."

Buddy opened the kitchen door onto the gloom of the

144

hallway. "I'll send a floral arrangement soon as they can get it here. You stay where you are. I can find my own way out."

Leo looked at him desperately. "Say, Buddy," he said, "I should of asked you before borrowing the gun."

Buddy waved at him, pretending indifference. "I won't mention it again."

"I had to do a job," said Leo, his eyes flickering. "I had this parrot, see, ever since I was a kid. He didn't like women. He hated my mother, but funny, when he saw she died, he started screaming and wouldn't stop unless the cage was covered. And even after the Walshes come and took her away, Boy still screamed if you took the cover off. So that's no life for a bird. So he wouldn't touch his sunflower seeds when I dosed them with rat poison, and I lived with him for years, I couldn't bear to wring his neck or use a butcher knife, so I went over and returned that money and got your gun, and come back, and I took him outside and opened the cage door. He wouldn't come out at first because one time I did that and opened the door and when he was on the grass I sprayed him with the hose and he was mad as hell and yelled, 'Fire!' which I never heard him say before nor since. Generally the only thing he said was 'Hi, Boy' and 'Bum.' So he had his eye on that pistol, which must of looked like a hose to him, and I put it in my pocket till he walked out onto the pile of dried grass Ralph stacks at the end of the yard, which I cover the flowerbeds with in the winter along with the leaves. A grasshopper walks out of it, and Boy sees it, looks down, I get the pistol out and blow his head off."

Leo plunged his own head into his folded arms and moaned in grief.

"You can get mighty attached to a pet," said Buddy.

Leo's tear-stained face came up, howling: "I shouldn't of done it! I could have given him away. I could have given him to Ralph."

145

Buddy regarded this as a close call. He now observed that Leo's real anguish was due to the loss of the parrot and not his mother. They might keep him in Greenlawn forever once they got hold of him.

"You had enough tragedies for one day," he said, conscious of the weight of the gun in his pocket. He put his hand there so it would not swing against the doorjamb as he turned and went along the hall.

He opened the front door on four men who were mounting the porch with a large packing crate. One of the pair at the leading corners was a Walsh.

"Hi, Buddy," said he. "Catch that screendoor, willya?"

"Hi, Roy." Buddy did as requested, stepping aside. Howie Walsh and a colored helper had the back end.

Howie, who was younger than Roy, shook his head at the sight of the entrance. "This baby'll never make that," said he. The Negro seemed to echo these sentiments with a shining grin.

"It's them screendoor hinges," said Roy. "Buddy's got her as far back as she'll go, right?"

"Right," said Buddy.

"Say, Bud, ya mind? Ask Leo for a screwdriver to get them hinges off. I'd ask him, but he's the bereaved."

"I'll go, Roy," said the white helper, a husky, tanned young fellow who worked summers as a lifeguard at the public pool.

"Wait a minute," Buddy said, getting out his combination penknife/nail file. Holding the door with his ass, he found that the screwheads yielded to his file.

They put the box down while he worked. The colored guy began to whistle softly. "Cut that out," Roy ordered.

When Buddy was done he jiggled the screws in his hand and said: "Plain pine box, huh?" He raised his eyebrows at Leo's stinginess.

Roy peered within the doorway to see whether Leo was

146

nearby, then said discreetly, within a cupped hand: "It just goes in the ground; that's the way he figures."

"What's it inside, just wood full of splinters for Jesus' sake?" asked Buddy.

Roy leaned closer to him. "She won't be laid out in it. We're supposed to arrange her on the couch, like she fell asleep."

"With the *Woman's Home Companion* in her hand," Howie said. The Negro joined him in a snicker.

"You ain't serious."

"Well, the magazine is just Howie's joke," said Roy, bending to take his corner. "The rest is correct." He looked up. "Hey, Leo's here, isn't he? I don't want to act on my own responsibility in a matter like this. People get riled up about little details."

They maneuvered the coffin through the door. "*Now* what?" said Howie as they halted in the entrance hall.

Buddy squeezed past them, saying he would get Leo. But when he reached the kitchen his employee had vanished. Where would he go in that filthy bathrobe? Through the window he got an answer: Leo was down at the end of the yard, staring at a flowerbed. It did not seem tasteful to shout, so Buddy left the house and walked to him.

"They're here with the body."

Leo was looking at a mound of fresh earth. "I don't know if I ought to leave him here. Some alley cat might dig him up."

Buddy returned to the house. "He's out there at the grave of his fucking parrot," he told Roy. "This thing has loosened his screws. You better go ahead. I'm gonna call Doc Klingman to give him a sedative."

"I gotta have authorization from somebody for the arrangement of this body," said Roy. "I can't just dump it on the davenport." The Negro chuckled. Dressed in dark clothing, he was hard to discern in the darkened hall now the door was closed.

"He works for you, Buddy," said Howie. "How about it? He don't have any relatives I know of."

Buddy said: "Better find the living room first."

Roy Walsh opened a door on the right, looked in, and said: "This is it."

Buddy entered the room, which was even darker than the hall. Not only were the window shades down; the heavy opaque curtains were closed. The four men plodded in with the coffin. Buddy squinted about in search of light, but found only one lamp, a floor model with a thick shade from which hung a beaded fringe.

"Hell with this," he said, opening the curtains and running the shade up on a window. "We can close them again when you're done, if he wants that."

It was an old room, wallpapered in a brown figure against a tan ground. Buddy hated dreary wallpaper. The sofa was upholstered in green plush. Above it hung two silhouettes on silver paper: George Washington and Abraham Lincoln.

"Wait a minute," said Buddy to the advancing men and removed a magazine holder from the floor just ahead of them. It held several clean copies of *The National Geographic* and a crinkled, damp-stained *Liberty* that looked as if it had been used under a flowerpot: you could see the ring.

"Catch that rocker, too, willya, Bud?" said Howie, who wanted to swing his end around. Buddy scooted it away on its runners.

They lowered the box to the carpet. Realizing the corpse would shortly be revealed, Buddy grew queasy.

Addressing Roy, he said: "You guys know your business. You don't need me. Leo'll be in in a minute." He headed out.

Howie called: "Hey, Buddy." When Buddy turned, the

cover was already off the coffin; must have been on there loose, could have fallen off it if they had tripped. "I think you have to agree we did a nice job," Howie said, smiling smugly down on the deceased.

There was nothing for it but that Buddy come back and admire. He saw a younger face than he had expected, painted in bright rouge and brighter lipstick.

Roy said, standing back, hands on hips: "What do you think?"

"I never knew the lady," said Buddy.

"Is that a fact?"

"Not a gray hair on her head." He could see no great resemblance to Leo. No doubt she had been a good-looker when young, with a nose that was at once delicate yet strong. "Awful lot of make-up."

"Them was the instructions," said Roy, reaching in to take the shoulders of the body.

At this Buddy went away again and stared at the china figures on a whatnot shelf in the corner, not turning back until the four men had lifted the dead woman out and put her on the davenport.

"Now what do you think about this afghan?" Roy asked. "Like this, maybe?" He had spread it over her lower body.

Howie said: "She wouldn't be laying here with her shoes on."

Roy agreed, and Howie took them off and paired them neatly on the floor at the end of the sofa.

The four men stood back and regarded the tableau. The young white helper pointed at a maroon satin cushion, the decorative kind never used practically, which lay flat on a footstool, the golden corner-tassels dangling.

"Pillow'd be nice."

"That's a crackerjack idea," Roy said with verve. He fetched it and put it under her head, which had previously been mounted on the little end-bolster of low elevation, part of the upholstery.,

Buddy couldn't get over the garish make-up job, to complete which Roy now pulled from his pocket a box of Coty powder, removed the puff, and patted the corpse's face with it. Suddenly he handed the box to Howie and put the index finger of his freed hand under his nose to inhibit a sneeze.

"Now," he said, stepping back, "what do you think, Buddy?" As soon as he took his finger away he sneezed anyhow.

"Swell from where I stand, Roy. But maybe Leo—"

"Good enough for me," Roy said. "We got to get back. Two more bodies come in just as we were leaving: old Jack McCord and the little Hunnicut boy who died of infantile paralysis, poor little shaver. It never rains but it pours." He looked at the box. "I'd like to leave this here, but no matter where you stick it, people fall over it. Also it gives what you call a ghoulish impression. Tell Leo we'll be back tomorrow morning."

The four men bent to pick up the coffin.

"See you, Bud," said Howie, going out the door.

"Not soon, I hope," Buddy replied. The colored guy favored him with one last grin over the shoulder.

Alone with her, Buddy looked again at Leo's mother. She must have been real nice-looking as recently as twenty years before, when he had been seventeen. He had started out a year earlier, with a woman of forty-two.

But it was creepy to think of sex in the presence of a corpse, even one painted like a whore. Nor did he have the patience to encounter Leo again.

He went out to his car.

chapter 9

In contrast to Leo's late mother, Laverne wore no make-up whatever, and her hair was up in curlers. She had on an old opaque slip that was more modest than most of her dresses.

"You never come this early," she said sullenly.

"Thanks for the big welcome," said Buddy, who on entering had clasped her from behind, hands on breasts, groin between the bulbs of her bottom, but she had coldly twisted away. He sat at the kitchen table, still brooding over the rebuff.

"I had a bad time this morning," he said.

"Who didn't?"

What could be her beef, with the rent paid and nothing to do but curl her hair? But he did not say this aloud. Instead he gave a simplified version of his annoyances: Leo's mother's death, Leo's crackup.

"If he don't come out of it, I need me a new salesman."

Laverne's curlered head did not turn. Seen from the back,

her slip was sacklike, with no shape at all. Down towards the hem it bore a pointed scorch mark from the tip of an iron. Buddy put more self-pity in his voice. "As if I needed another problem."

This brought her around. "What other problems have you got?"

There was a kind of jealousy in her question. Buddy pulled back his chin. "What's eating you, Laverne?"

"Oh, nothing, nothing at all, Buddy. I really like sitting here day after day, waiting for you to come and get your ashes hauled and then run home."

"Well, do you have to get foul-mouthed about it? We been through that time and time again and I explained it thoroughly. What did I just tell you yesterday?"

"To turn over so you could do it dog-style."

Buddy flushed with repulsion. "For Christ's sake, Laverne, come on up out of the sewer."

She grinned bitterly. "Yesterday was Sunday, and that's all I can recall. Saturday you said you was working on the situation. Yesterday you never referred to it. You never do refer to it unless I ask, in all these months." She pulled a chair from under the table and plumped herself down upon it. "I've been thinking a lot this whole weekend."

"I been doing more than thinking," said Buddy, leaning earnestly across the bare enamel tabletop.

She knitted her penciled eyebrows. "Which means?"

He leaned back, as if in assurance. "You just trust me."

She left her quizzical expression as it was.

"Listen, Laverne, I just been with a dead body. That shakes you up on a Monday before lunch. I mean, in a living room it's real creepy, and then some. In a funeral parlor you are prepared."

"Well, I'm among the living, Buddy, though you may not know it."

He put on a lascivious smile. "Baby, how could I forget?" He put his hand across the table, trying to reach a tit, but she drew back.

"Buddy, I'll be glad to give you the conclusion I arrived at," she said coldly.

"Aw, Laverne." He put his face in his bracketed hands, which deformed it slightly, orientalizing his eyes, and tried a bit of japery: "No tickee, no washee." But she stayed stern, pale-faced, and in curlers. "Where's your funnybone today?" he asked. Then: "You got anything for a sandwich?"

"Sure, Buddy, coming right up!" This was said sardonically. She rose, marched to the refrigerator, opened it, and looked inside. "We have one slice of ham sausage. We have a tomato. We have one egg."

Buddy made a disdainful nose. "No kind of real meat?"

"We didn't know we would be serving lunch today, sir," Laverne said, bending to open the hydrator. "We can make a tomato sandwich with lettuce and mayonnaise."

"That's woman's food," Buddy said. "All right, fry me that egg—unless you was saving it for yourself."

"We thank you very much," said Laverne, "but we aren't eating, ourself, because we just weighed ourself and found we was too fat from sitting home here alone all the time with nothing to do but chew candy."

"All right, all right, I feel the needle. Now just be a good girl and fix that egg."

For the first time ever, she fried it hard all the way through, Naomi-style, and the toast that clutched it was butterless and burned almost black. Buddy's mouth felt as if full of dust.

"You wouldn't have a Coke?"

"No, I wouldn't. The order hasn't come yet." She sat across from him again. Now her expression was blank. This was worse, given her passionate nature, than anger, which in time he could always convert into lust.

"Well, some coffee then, Laverne?" On the sibilant a tiny fragment of desiccated toast flew from his lips. "*Excuse* me," he said loftily, plucking it up.

Like Leo, Laverne had some breakfast coffee still in the pot. Unlike him, she heated it until an unpleasant odor told Buddy it was boiling. Meanwhile she was running water in the sink, as if in impatience to wash the dish on which she had served him the sandwich—which was furthermore a saucer, not a plate. Buddy hated that kind of error, which signified the inattention of the server. Incredulously he watched her compound it: she lifted the saucer, blew the crumbs from it, and put the coffee cup into its well.

Buddy lowered his half-eaten sandwich to the table, pushed his chair back, and stood up. Consulting his watch, he said: "Gee, I forgot nobody's at the lot. I better get back pronto." This was a bluff-calling test. Laverne ordinarily whined if he stayed less than an hour. Nor was there precedent for a visit of whatever length in which he did not plow her within, say, fifteen minutes after arriving.

Now, though, she stood in her old petticoat, holding the marble-enameled coffeepot in one hand and the cup in the other, and said in a tone of eminent reason: "You better do that."

"Yeah, I better," said Buddy and waited for her to surrender. She returned the coffeepot to the stove and put the cup and saucer in the standing water of the sink. She wrung out the string dishcloth and with it swept the crumbs from the tabletop into her free palm. She picked up the garbage from his egg sandwich and went to the trashcan and pedaled its top open.

This was unbearable. "For Christ's sake, Laverne," said Buddy in disbelieving exasperation.

Laverne dropped the rubbish in the can and wiped her

hand with the wet gray rag. After the top came down with a clang, she said: "If you was thinking of pussy for dessert, you can forget it."

Buddy let the screendoor slam and thundered down the outside stairs. It was monstrously unfair that he should have to suffer this treatment only now that he had hired a killer. She had caused no real trouble in all the months he had done nothing. As usual when he was the victim of an injustice Buddy soon felt defenseless, and in this case he couldn't go to Laverne for succor, as he had done when felled by Ballbacher's sucker punch.

As he got into the car he had wild, desperate thoughts of calling Mary Wentworth at the bank, ordering her to meet him after work, perhaps sodomizing her brutally on his desk; or lying in wait at the corner on which Grace Plum deboarded from the bus and getting blown as he drove home. Though ordinarily Buddy deplored deviate acts as ends in themselves, he now needed ardently to defile some female while at the same time not violating his vow never to make love to anyone but Laverne. Even if she now revealed a unique nastiness, he was still so crazy about that woman that he would have gone back upstairs and kissed her ass had he thought she would thereby be mollified.

With his understanding of the female sex, he knew however that such a move would be useless at this time. Women operated on the principle: Sin in haste, repent at leisure. Left to cool her heels, Laverne would develop a usable shame; regret would stimulate her appetite, and his answering magnanimity would ignite her. Two-three days without cock would put her at the limits of her endurance. Indeed, he loved her so much—despite her current mood—that were it not a subtle kindness he could not have submitted her to this cruel denial.

155

Ralph was on one of his earlier deliveries when his father drove out of the neighborhood by another street. And for once their routes did not coincide. Neither his father nor his mother knew he had gone to apply for the job at Bigelow's. He might in fact not tell them for days. For example, they were utterly ignorant that he had tried caddying at the outset of the summer. For no special reason, unless it was an instinctual or hereditary strain of paranoia, of which he was unconscious, Ralph played his cards close to his chest. For their parts, his parents had never been snoops.

The address crayoned on the side of the carton was, cryptically, 23-B Myrtle; no name accompanied it. Ralph found the street, and he found the number but not the supernumerary letter on a big, old, gray, square house with almost no yard: the kind of place that looked as if it would be populated with residents to match. He removed the box, lowered the bike to the grassy strip above the curb, there being no nearby pole or tree, and went around the corner of the building, at which point the concrete path gave way to loose gravel. There he also came upon his "23-B" in unpainted zinc figures affixed to the post of an outside stairway.

With a simultaneous inflation of his chest, he hefted the carton onto his right shoulder and, securing it with one hand and a flattened ear, he ascended to the top landing, where he did not knock but called through the screendoor: "Bigelow's delivery!"

There was no response from within. Given the current angle of the sun, the light of which was detained by the crosshatching of the screen, much of which was clogged with soot, he could see nothing of the interior.

The carton having begun to hurt his ear and shoulder, he lowered it to the boards of the landing. As his head was rising he saw the bottom of the screendoor swing towards him, and he slid the box away from its projected route. Still bent, he saw upon the threshold a pair of those ladies' slippers called "mules," of pink satin with fuzzy pompoms on the toes. The ankles above them were blue-white as skim milk, as were the shins and so on to the beginning of the swell of calf. At this point bare flesh was succeeded by more pink fuzz, now along the hem of what in the Sears, Roebuck catalogue, that classic sourcebook for masturbatory images, was called a negligee. The body of this garment was of a pink satin one shade darker than that of the mules, which were perhaps faded.

Ralph looked only as far as the belt, but he was conscious, through his upper peripheral vision, of two substantial bulges just above and flanking the loose, slippery satin knot.

He lifted the carton in both hands and propped it, Bigelow-style, against his midsection, though skinny as he was he had no shelf there. With an automatic smile he looked then at her face, and saw the sexiest woman he had ever laid eyes on—bright yellow curls and sky-blue eyes fringed with enormous lashes, cheeks of rose and lips of flame.

"Hi," she said. "You're a new one."

Only those remarkable eyes could have kept his own glance from falling to her fantastic breasts, which now his lower peripheral sight told him were unconfined behind the negligee, and he was dying to see whether there were nipple bumps on the sleek satin.

He nodded and mumbled, and adjusted his burden, which caused the remaining bottles to clink, reminding him of the breakage.

"See, I had a little accident—it actually wasn't my fault—" But suddenly, standing there before the muzzles of those breasts, he understood it would be unmanly to blame Margie. Deserve it though she did in one sense, in another her error could be seen as arising from her attraction to him. He might himself, with this fascinating woman, commit some disgrace for the same motive. The world could use more tolerance.

"What really happened was: a couple of things in your order got busted somehow." His eyes disappeared into his forehead. "Let's see now, a Coke and catchup and . . ." He had forgotten the third item.

With her free hand she gestured to him to enter. "You're letting the flies in." She gave him room, but not much, and as he stepped across the threshold, compressing himself so strenuously that had he been carrying a bag and not a box he would have crushed it, his forearm slid along and over not one but both warm, weighty, sleek-surfaced, superficially yielding yet immanently dominant, massive but lyrical extrusions of bosom. He wore a short-sleeved summer shirt.

The accident he had anticipated, and forgiven himself for by exploiting Margie's example, happened at this point: his sneaker was imprisoned briefly at the threshold, perhaps fouled on the rubber stair tread often encountered in such a place, its lip curled to trap and trip the unwary toe. In freeing his foot Ralph projected himself forward with a violence which, after the liberation of the sneaker, was too much for his equilibrium.

So as not to fall, he ran right across the living room, reaching the entrance of the hallway before he gained his balance. He did not however drop the carton.

She was chuckling behind him.

"Sorry," said he, coming back with the blood roaring in his ears. "I better get rid of this before anything else happens."

"Right in here, on the table," said she. Her satin back led him to the kitchen. Owing to the carton, he could not see the swell of her behind. He was conscious for the first time, though it had been everywhere throughout, of her sense-reeling scent: not that of known flowers, but a compound of fragrances from imaginary jungles, gaudy fruits deliquescing into syrup, the mating odors of fur-bearing animals, along with the sophisticated essences poured from cut-glass decanters into crystal balloons and sipped with closed eyes by tuxedo-clad epicures.

Putting down the carton at last, he remembered for no reason at all: "Cream was the other thing broken." Again he blushed, remembering its thick, opaque ooze on the pavement, very like ejaculated semen in the palm of the hand.

"Listen!" he said hastily, rudely, then revised it: "I mean, you don't have to worry, ma'am. I'll make a special trip back to the store and get those items replaced. Five minutes, maybe less."

She crossed her arms beneath her sumptuous breasts and smiled gorgeously, but also kindly. "I'm not worried, for gosh sake. Accidents can happen to anybody."

Ralph just gawked helplessly at her blue eyes. He was smitten by her angelic combination of beauty and generosity.

"A penny for your thoughts," she said at last.

Ralph emerged from his coma. "It's nice of you not to be mad."

She frowned amiably. "When you think how short life is, you concentrate on the real important matters and don't cry over spilled milk."

"Cream," said Ralph, and regretted doing so; she might consider it a correction.

"Oh, sure!" She snapped her wrist at him and giggled marvelously. She bent to look into the box, favoring him with her golden crown. "Hey, here's two Cokes that are still O.K. Why don't you have one?"

Ralph was overcome.

"I'll tell you," she said, "I don't use the stuff myself." She bared her flawless teeth and tapped an incisor with a red fingernail. "I say it's no good for the enamel. It's got caffeine in it, and that's acid you know." Her expression froze for an

159

instant. She slapped herself on the forehead. "So why am I asking you to drink it then, huh? How inconsiderate can you get?"

She was an inch or so taller than he, but in another year they would be about the same size, given his rate of growth, which had so far proved normal.

"Oh, that's all right," said Ralph. "I don't drink much pop anyway. I don't like the fizz."

Even her grimace was enchanting. "Yeah, I know what you mean. Like beer, I never cared for it." She brightened. "But champagne now, that's different."

"I never tasted it."

"Well then, you got something to look forward to." Her smile now was rather shy. "I've just had it on special occasions."

"Like New Year's Eve."

"Right!" she exclaimed, as if it were a remarkable observation. She certainly could enhance a routine give and take. Ralph yearned to have a really brilliant thought that would devastate her.

Straining too hard, he said: "Coca-Cola was invented around the turn of the century by a druggist, as a kind of medicine."

This was a mistake. Saying, "I oughtn't hold you up. You got work to do," she walked rapidly into the living room, her mule-heels clacking, and soon returned, bosoms in motion, with a red handbag already open. She took from within a little red change purse and plucked out a coin.

It was a quarter. "I can't take this," said Ralph. "With what I broke and all."

"You'll have to pay," she said. "I know how bosses are. I spilled some tea once on some gingham in a dry-goods store where I worked as a kid, and I had to pay for it. So"—she pressed the quarter on him—"I'm splitting the cost of the damage with you. I can afford it better than you. So you just take it or I'll get mad, and you don't want to get me mad or I'm a devil."

He simply stood there in wonderment.

She went on: "See, what I could do is say forget all about what was broken, because the Coke and the whipping cream were not for me but for my gentleman friend, and he and I won't be seeing one another any more, and speaking of the catchup, I still got enough in the old bottle—you can always add hot water and get some more out. So you could just go back and not mention it to the boss, and we'd be even-Steven for all I cared.

"But I'm not going to do that. Why? Do you have any idea?" She turned her glorious face at an angle to her swan neck.

Ralph shook his head in adoration. He hoped she would take hours to explain, in that musical voice and exuding that fragrance, eyes sparkling and hair glowing.

"I'll tell you," she said. "You might call me mean, but I think nothing in the world is more important than a sense of responsibility in a man. Like it might not of been your fault for the accident, but delivering those groceries is your *responsibility*, and you want to make it good. So if I was to say forget *all* about it, I would be taking away your chance to be a man who stands for something." She blinked dramatically. "Does that make any sense? I guess it's pretty complicated."

Ralph felt faint. Her intelligence and moral character were comparable to her heavenly beauty.

"Oh, yes," he said. "It makes a whole lot of sense." He nodded so vigorously he felt a catch in his nape.

She extended her hand. "Let's shake on it. Put 'er there, partner."

Her hand was no larger than his, but warmer, softer, and with more strength; his own was happily helpless.

"You going to be regular or is it just for today?" she asked. "Frankly, I never have much cared for that kid Horace. He's an example of what I'm talking about. Now when he breaks something, he never comes clean like you; he tries to sneak it past me."

With a disloyalty that could be called divine—considering the deed he had performed for Hauser on Saturday night—Ralph said: "He's not much of a guy. I got his job."

"Well," said she, "since we'll be seeing each other a lot, my name's Laverne."

"I'm pleased to meet you, Miss Laverne."

"No, that's my *first* name, unless you're talking like a colored person from *Gone with the Wind*. My last name's Lorraine, and my middle is Linda, all L's, but I wish you would call me just Laverne. We're just plain folks here." Her giggle was like the ringing of a silver bell.

"Mine's Ralph."

"Hi, Ralph."

"The whole thing's Ralph V. Sandifer." He shrugged. "The middle's actually Virgil. My dad was stuck with that for a first name, but he doesn't use it, either, except for legal matters." Noticing her queer look, he assumed that he had somehow offended her, given her great moral sensitivity, with this kind-of-apology. "I guess names don't matter really." But hers did, magnificently: Laverne Linda Lorraine was a song in itself.

She walked briskly to the sink and clattered things there. Whatever the reason, she had, he saw definitely, enough of him at the moment.

He said: "I have to get back to work."

She made no response. But as he reached the doorway she asked: "That your dad who's got the car lot?"

He turned and saw her more beautiful than ever. Now, despite her coloring, she looked dark, vulnerable, tragic in fact, with shadowed eyes like Merle Oberon's. Of what exquisite variations she was capable! Laverne Linda Lorraine, I love you with all my being. But what he said was merely: "Yes."

"It's not your uncle or anything like that?"

"No." He fled in a disorder of feeling.

When he got to the curb he discovered his bicycle had been stolen.

Buddy brooded resentfully for the rest of the afternoon, which he spent sitting in the office behind the closed door, ignoring the customers, if such there were, outside. Few cars sold themselves. Only one person breached his privacy. This fellow entered without knocking. He was young, with steel-rimmed glasses and a smirk.

"Hey," he said brashly, "you know that thirty-seven Chevy two-door of yours—they got one in better condition at Loewenfels', down on the Milltown Pike near the infirmary—for fifty dollars less."

"Then you go over and scoop it up, fella."

The young man's smirk grew broader. "Oh, yeah? I figured we could do a little negotiating."

"Take a look at the rubber on that baby."

"The muffler's rusted out, and the paint on the hood is shot: engine heat's faded it."

"I know the car," Buddy said frostily. "You wanna make a quick deal, I'll go down twenty-five."

"I'm going to take another look at Loewenfels'," said the guy. He hesitated at the door, waiting in three-quarter profile, one shoulder high, for another offer, but it being in Buddy's psychological interest, which was predominant at the moment, to deny him, he heard nothing further, and left.

Buddy had the feeling that things were coming to a head. His decision, made as usual on impulse, to let Laverne stew in her own juice for a few days was in retrospect seen as impracticable, like an unenforceable law such as that, still on the books in some states, forbidding unorthodox sex practices even by spouses.

Already he felt a growing pressure in his groin. Unless his testes were regularly evacuated they became the seat of his central nervous system and sent throughout his body venomous communications in the forms of neuralgia, dyspepsia, and a twitching of the inner eyelid, maddening though not visible to others.

In this condition in the old days he would have gone instantly to the nearest woman and relieved himself inside her. He could not be resisted when under the force of this need, though several times it had happened that his partner, met but an hour earlier in one roadhouse and under the assumption she was being taken to another, interpreted as rape his assault on her in the parking lot—but dropped the charges long before his climax, which invariably succeeded two or even three of hers.

Such a measure was unthinkable now. A latecomer to monogamy, like all converts Buddy was a zealot. He could not abstain from Laverne, and he could not do otherwise with any other female.

To boot, in the area of his profession he was as it were emasculated by Leo's defection: strange but true. By cracking up, Leo had stolen his thunder, had become the romantic, the focus of concern and attention. Leo might come out of it once his mother had been buried; but his potentiality for disorderliness under stress would not be forgotten. In a word, Leo, previously the soul of reliability, could never be trusted again.

Buddy seized the phone, called the authoress of all his ills, and listened hatefully to her pretentious announcement.

"Naomi Sandifer speaking. Hello."

"Say, Nay," Buddy said. "Leo Kirsch's mom passed away

yesterday. She's laid out at his house. We better look in there about five-thirty, so hold the supper."

"How dreadful," said Naomi. "I gather it was unexpected."

"Yeah, yeah," Buddy said with an unusual display of open impatience. "You didn't know the lady."

"Still—"

Before she could make some fucking philosophical statement about death, Buddy said: "I got business to do, and I'm all alone here, but I'll get away by five and pick you up."

"I'll be here."

You could count on that. She would throw on a shapeless dress, powder her face sloppily, with a spill on the collar, and be ready. You never had to wait on the bathroom because of her: insufficient compensation for the embarrassment of escorting her into the world, if Leo's living room could be called public.

"Okey-doke," said Buddy and was about to hang up when he was halted by an unpremeditated thought. "Say, is Gladys coming this week?"

Her sister, who lived about ten miles away, was wont to visit Naomi once or twice a month, by bus. If the matter of departure escaped her mind until evening, she often stayed overnight. Despite Buddy's business, her husband, a limp mailman, owned no car, but would take no favors from his brother-in-law. She was two years older than Naomi, freckled and sinewy, athletic in appearance and in action as well, had played volleyball in high school and nowadays bowled on some team of neighborhood women. She had by her own admission never come close to having a child, for reasons undisclosed. She was one of the few females with whom Buddy had had social contact and yet never thought about in positive sexual terms, Gladys being more masculine than her husband, against whom Buddy also had the moral bias of the self-made man when contemplating a Civil Service malingerer.

"There's a coincidence," said Naomi, with her meaningless enthusiasm over a banal event. "She had intended to come today, but won't be able to because of some breakdown, I believe, in the plumbing."

Under stern control, Buddy converted his emotion into exaggerated sympathy. "Gee, that's too bad."

"Oh," said Naomi, who was always vivified by an expression of regret, "it's not a tragedy."

"Huh," said Buddy.

"It's not life-or-death, by any means," Naomi said.

Buddy hung up, went to the safe, then found a blank envelope in his desk and put the money therein. This sequence had been brisk, but he entered the garage in a dreamy fashion. Clarence was not in evidence. Probably he was out on the lot dusting the merchandise. Buddy put the envelope in the inside breast pocket of the old jacket, the lining of which was so frayed that towards the tail it hung in ribbons.

He headed back to the office, now in a saunter. He reassumed his seat behind the desk. Unbeknown to himself, he began to work his face in a manner that looked to his employee Jack, who had heard about Leo's loss at the gas station and come to the lot and opened the office door at this moment, like an epileptic fit. Being a devotee of first-aid tips in newspapers, magazines, and pamphlets given away free at drugstores, Jack knew the danger was that the subject would swallow his own tongue, and he loped towards Buddy, flexing en route the index finger he must thrust down his employer's throat.

Since receiving Ballbacher's sucker punch, Buddy had been instinctively on guard against another unprovoked, maniacal attack. Had Leo chosen to make one when in possession of the gun, he would of course have been helpless. Jack was another matter: a large man, but flabby and sissified; lumbering urgently but slowly, his hand clawed like a girl's, he would go for the eyes.

Buddy grasped a heavy glass paperweight shaped like half an ostrich egg and prepared to let Jack have it with a roundhouse to the temple. His reaction was so quick and Jack's advance so sluggish that there was even time to gloat:

"Come and get it, sucker."

This and the raised paperweight put Jack on ice. He stopped and asked: "Are you O.K.?"

"You better believe it."

Buddy knew instantly that he had mistaken Jack's intentions. He however carried it off deftly. He lowered his hand and dropped the paperweight onto the desktop from a height of three inches. Hard upon the report, he said grinning, as if in farce: "Never know who might jump you these days."

Jack peered anxiously at him. Buddy expatiated: "I oughtn't joke about it though. Leo's mom died yesterday and he has lost his marbles, I hope only temporary. He took my gun without permission and shot his parrot."

"Maybe you should sit down again," Jack said in concern.

Buddy said irritably: "I'm perfectly O.K., like I said. It's Leo. His mother . . ." He went through it again, but this time added: "And he's laid the old lady out on the livingroom sofa, like she drifted off to sleep."

Jack said: "I heard about his loss, poor devil. He'll be all right. Leo's got his two feet on the ground." He proposed their going in together on the flowers.

Buddy looked slightly indignant. "The wife and I already sent ours."

Jack shrugged. "It was only a thought." He had another: "We've—*my* wife and I—have been wanting for some time to ask you and Mrs. Sandifer to come see us. Maybe tonight after we all come back from Leo's you would stop in for coffee."

Buddy looked at his watch. "We're going over there pretty soon now."

"Oh," said Jack. "Well then, maybe another time soon."

"Sure thing," said Buddy.

When Jack left, Buddy went into the garage again. Clarence was polishing a dark-green '38 Packard, the best car currently on the lot. He was buffing the hood with a mitt made of sheepskin and looking at his reflection in green.

"Hi," Buddy said almost shyly. "Did you look in your coat lately?"

Clarence stopped polishing, removed the mitt, went to the corner, took his jacket from above the oil drum, and found the envelope in the pocket. He took out the currency and counted it, provoking anxiety in Buddy.

"It's all there. Come here. I want you to get this straight."

Clarence was in no hurry. Having finished his deliberate count, he replaced the money in the envelope and the envelope in the jacket.

"It's tonight," Buddy said. "I got it all worked out. I want you to listen."

Clarence ambled back. He wore an exceptionally stupid expression, his mouth slack and the lid of his good eye three-quarters shut. He returned the mitt to his right hand and began again to rub the gleaming hood.

"Knock that off," said Buddy. "Listen to this." Clarence kept his sheepskin-covered hand on the hood, but stopped moving it in circles. "You go around the back of the house. There's this outside door to the cellar. I'm gonna unlock it. Soon as you get in, there's the stairs to the upstairs on your left. At the top of them there's a door to the hall. Now, in the hall, first door on your right's the bathroom. A few feet further along, only across on the left side, is the bedroom where she'll be."

He peered into Clarence's wooden face. "I better make a map." He trotted about the garage, looking for a piece of paper, but the place was neat as Leo's kitchen. At last in the oil drum that served as a trash barrel he found a crumpled brown bag. He smoothed it out on the hood of the Packard, produced a pencil, and avoiding the grease spots on the paper, made a sketch of the ground floor of his residence.

"Here you go." Buddy used the pencil as pointer. Clarence moved around to the other side of him so as to employ his good eye. Buddy indicated the murder route with a series of tiny arrows. "This room here is the boy's." He put the pencil point onto the square next to that which symbolized the master bedchamber. "He sleeps like a log."

He realized the Negro smelled of perfume. No, make that sweet soap: Cashmere Bouquet, to be exact. Buddy's nostrils were acute to scents. Laverne bathed with this very brand. Call it perverse, but Buddy was reassured by the identification, though reacting with superficial annoyance. He reared back and asked sharply: "Are you getting all of this?"

Clarence nodded.

Buddy left the map on the car and strutted to the back of the garage and its wall-mounted workbench. He soon found what he was looking for, and touched it with the point of his pencil. "Come here. . . . This here monkey wrench. Take it. Screw the jaws closed. Yeah, that'll do it."

Clarence swung the big Stillson at the end of his arm and looked appraisingly at Buddy.

"One good shot of that . . ." said Buddy. He shut his eyes and shook his head. He was no sadist. It would be over in an instant, she being asleep at the time. Back at the car he seized the map again and waited for Clarence to join him.

"Here, I'll put in the location of the bed." He drew a

rectangle and flanked it with two tiny squares. "Night tables, see. She sleeps on the inside, away from the door, so this table is hers. It'll have a lamp on it and maybe a glass of water and a few hairpins and whatnot. Don't lean on it or something might fall off. Afterwards we'll mess up the whole room."

"We?" Clarence asked.

"Yeah," said Buddy, and then, as if he were explaining it to himself: "It's the only way to be sure. I been over and over it. If I was out, like at a meeting or something, how would I be sure she went to bed same as usual? And there ain't no meetings of anything I belong to tonight, the Kiwanis or Masons or whatnot. If I was out in a bar with somebody, it'd look phony because I never go to bars with guys, and my goose would be cooked if I went with a woman, wouldn't it?"

He looked pleadingly towards Clarence though not at him. "I got to be at the scene, and I certainly don't relish it. I got to be in my pajamas, in that room, in bed or pretending I was in bed and asleep when he comes in and opens the dresser, and she wakes up and screams and he lets her have it with the wrench, and I wake up and struggle with him and get hurt bad enough to make it believable that he could get away."

Clarence asked: "*You* gets hurt?"

Buddy winced. "I ain't looking forward to it, but I think my left hand oughta get broke maybe. I need everything else that would be likely to be busted in a fight in the dark with a killer." He would also mess up his hair and tear his pajamas, but before that he would open the dresser drawers and throw their contents to the floor, having already, when Naomi was asleep but before the intruder arrived, quietly extracted the items of burglarable value, a modest string of pearls, earrings, and his own gold cufflinks and stickpin, and flushed them down the toilet.

Buddy had used his time well while sitting alone and

grimacing in the office. "But," he concluded, uncomfortably eying the monkey wrench in Clarence's brown fist, "I don't want to get hit with that thing. I'll close a drawer on my hand or something."

He put the pencil again to the flattened paper bag. "Now, you got everything but the time. She generally goes to bed around eleven, give or take a quarter hour. Sometimes I go then. Sometimes I stay up a little while longer, make myself a cup of Postum or something. Tune in to *Moon River*, you know, try to relax because I don't always sleep too good. She falls right off though, soon as she hits the pillow.

"Now, tonight I'm going to bed when she does. Before I do I'll make sure that cellar door is unlocked. The door at the top of the stairs can't be locked; there ain't no key for it. I figure you show up at two sharp—you got a watch?"

Clarence shook his head in negation, then showed a questioning smile. What a moron he was. But all he had to do was follow Buddy's precise orders.

"When I'm finished you go down the street to Ziegler's and buy a dollar Ingersoll. We got to get the time straight because I'm laying there awake for one, two"—he counted on his fingers—"three hours."

Clarence shifted the Stillson to his left hand and extended the right, palm upwards.

Buddy sneered. "For Christ sake . . ." But at last he shook a dollar loose in his pants pocket and surrendered it to the Negro. Clarence took it to his jacket, from which he removed the envelope. He put the bill with the others therein and returned the envelope to the interior pocket.

"All right," Buddy said irritably. He looked at his wristwatch. "It's twenty to five already. . . . Now, you show at two A.M. The police cruiser makes their rounds at midnight and then they go back to the station and stay till morning unless called out. What I mean is, you shouldn't have no trouble being a colored person in a white neighborhood. Nobody'll see you at that hour."

Clarence's good eye seemed to revolve. Buddy went through the route and the time schedule again. Then he squeezed the paper bag into a tight ball.

"This goes down the crapper. I'll hear you tonight when you come into the hall. One more thing—you bring a flashlight."

Clarence put his hand out again. Buddy cursed, but gave him an extra fifty cents.

Buddy had got almost all the way back to the office when he remembered the only thing he had left out, and it was a wow. He returned to Clarence.

"You know where I live?" But how would he? "Well shit," Buddy said, "and you never asked. Two-two-two Sycamore. Two twenty-two Sy-ca-more, like the tree. Know how to find it?" He told him.

What he did not tell Clarence was where, when, and how he would give him the rest of the fee; nor did the ex-boxer ask for that information. From the beginning Buddy had intended to arm himself against the possibility that killing one white person would send the Negro into a sharklike frenzy for more of the same color of blood, an animal instinct that might overrule his greed for mere money.

Buddy therefore intended to keep the pistol at hand throughout the proceedings in the bedroom. It had also occurred to him that if subsequent to Naomi's death he killed Clarence, he would not only save money but also insure a perfect alibi for himself.

chapter **10**

WHEN RALPH RETURNED to the store Bigelow
denounced him for taking almost an hour to make three
deliveries and showed no sympathy when informed of the
theft of the bike.

"Should of locked it. A nigger'll take anything that's not
nailed down. They come over here from the West Side and
raid this neighborhood. Other night, one or more threw a
brick through my cellar window."

He failed to mention the money tied to it. Ralph took dull
notice of this omission, but was not nearly as interested as he
would have been were he not still under the spell of L.
Lorraine, L. Linda, L.L.L. He was weirdly thrilled that his
bike had been stolen outside her house, as if it were a sacrifice
to love.

"Whatchoo gonna do now?" asked the grocer. He held
another bag ready for delivery and poked it.

"Walk, I guess."

Bigelow enlarged his piggy eyes. "If it took you that long on a bike, the milk'll sour by time you walk."

"Then," Ralph said ebulliently, "I'll run!" Bigelow frowned at this, and Ralph added: "Tomorrow I'll borrow a bike." He felt so good he could not bear to mention the breakage. He realized this was a failure of character, but he was indulging himself in his intimate memories of Laverne: she had no need of those items, having broken off with her boy friend. Going through the possible reasons for the rupture, Ralph could only conclude that, she being perfect, the man must be a louse.

"I dunno," said Bigelow, shaking his heavy head. "I dunno if that would work out." He punched the cash register, causing the bell to sound and the NO SALE sign to appear in the window. He clattered in the change drawer and brought out a half dollar, holding it between thumb and forefinger as if he were going to put it into his eye like a monocle. "Here," he said to Ralph. "You never earned it, but if you got to save up for another bike . . ."

So he was sympathetic after all; Ralph kept changing his mind about the grocer.

"Oh, I can't take that—it was my fault." Then Ralph sensed all at once he was being fired. He politely asked Bigelow if his suspicion was correct.

The grocer rubbed his aproned belly against the counter. "That's about the size of it, kid. I got to have a boy with a bike. Even if you was fast as Jesse Owens, how would it look? Like I was a cheapskate. The A and P undercuts me on prices, and Rumbauer's, over on Maple, he's got a panel truck and delivers as far as them snobs in Wydale Hills; he charges an arm and a leg of course. Me, I'm in between. I got to work my hump off or I'll be on my uppers." His big cheeks collapsed in dramatic compassion. "Anyway, you're a little light for all the lifting I need around here."

174

It occurred to Ralph's logical mind that now no deliveries would be made for the rest of the afternoon, and he would have pointed that out to Bigelow did he not discern behind the grocer's sad-hound mien an absolute conviction that for him the matter of style superseded the claim of practicality. He was familiar with that trait of character, having identified it first in his father and then, in a juvenile cast, in Horse Hauser.

However, Ralph was not depressed by the turn of events. What a glorious day: lost my bicycle, lost my job, found my love. His memory of Laverne was an undifferentiated glow, without details and even impersonal; he could not see her face because she invested him absolutely, in a cloud of gold.

"Well," said he, "it's been a pleasure working with you." He seized Bigelow's hand and shook it.

"Same here," said the grocer, his eyebrows moving in wonderment. "Good luck to you, kid."

Ralph marched to the meat department and said goodbye to his friend Red, who couldn't shake because his hand was buried in the cavity of the fryer he was disemboweling.

"Made your million awready?" said Red when he heard the news. He peered sharply towards the front of the store and saw that Bigelow was occupied with a customer who had just entered. Red signaled with neck and shoulders for Ralph to come around behind the counter. When Ralph arrived at the butcher's block, Red said in a low voice: "He catch you with your hand in the till?"

Ralph laughed gaily, but Red for once was not joking. He pulled out a fistful of chicken entrails and dropped them onto the block. "I saw Hauser help himself a couple times. I never said nothing. This is a free country, and it's the old boy's business, not mine. But if I caught that little piss-ant stealing any of my meat, which I got to account for, I'd chop his dinkum off with a cleaver."

175

He pushed his white cap back with his left wrist. "Funny thing happened. I went down cellar first thing this morning to take a leak, and I found this brick, see, that somebody'd thrown through the window and there was money tied to it, cash, see? I never said nothing to the old boy about it, and he never mentioned it to me. Now, ain't that funny?"

"I'll be darn," said Ralph.

"I'll be goddam," said Red. "So Hauser don't show up today. I been thinking if there's a connection."

"Maybe his conscience bothered him," said Ralph.

Red suddenly threw his freckled face towards the ceiling and laughed. "Fuck 'em all but six: save them for pall-bearers." He slapped the pallid cadaver of the chicken and said: "So long, Small Change. Be good, and if you can't be good be careful."

"So long, Red."

On the walk home Ralph passed Horse's house, and as he had anyway to tell him about losing the job, he went through the side yard with its maimed wheelbarrow, busted-handled spade, and the garden hose from which the black rubber had flaked extensively from the underlying fabric: if you turned on the faucet you saw a sprinkler system of many outlets, but only dust and weeds were there to be watered.

The Hausers' back porch was screened in. Horse often slept out there in the warm season on a canvas Army cot between the washing machine and a couple dozen paint cans.

He called Horse's name four times before the owner appeared.

"Hi, Asshole," said Hauser, remaining behind the screendoor.

Three steps below, Ralph said: "You know what? Old Bigelow hired and fired me in one afternoon."

"Shit fire and save matches," said Horse. He threw the door

open and reached the bottom step before its slack spring contracted and slammed it with the report against making which he had been warned. But his old man was still at work; the truck was gone.

"Somebody hooked my bike," said Ralph.

"Well, fuck me." Behind his crude exterior, Hauser was capable of a generous sympathy. When told of the connection between the theft and the discharge, he said: "You take my bike. Show up there tomorrow and he'll hire you again, mark my words."

"But he don't want me anyhow. He was just looking for an excuse. He says I'm too light for the cellar work."

Hauser puffed out his chest and said: "It's true that takes muscle." But he gave Ralph a compassionate look and added: "But you're wiry, Sandifer, and can take care of yourself. A big hunk of flab like Bigelow ain't got no right. He can't barely climb them stairs, puffing like a switch engine." He made a fist and punched an imaginary target. "Boy, I'd like to give him one in that belly sometime, be like hitting a zeppelin though: all air behind it."

"Well, I got to go," said Ralph. "I just wanted to let you know I appreciate everything."

Hauser asked: "Hey, did Bigelow mention that brick?"

"Yeah, but not the money! Red did though."

Hauser made a face. "Red? You know how much meat that Red takes home for himself? Listen, I could tell you. Red steals that old simp blind. Course, Bigelow is the biggest crook in town."

"Who does he steal from?"

Hauser shouted: "Bigelow? The fucking public, that's who. He puts rotten apples and potatoes at the bottom of the sack. He'll sell you spoiled food that will kill you with ptomaine."

Ralph realized that Horse was merely feeding his own spite,

a favorite exercise, and even if it approximated the truth, which Ralph doubted on practical grounds, Hauser had but half a moral leg to stand on, having himself pilfered money.

"So long, Horse, and thanks again." Ralph started away but was stopped by Hauser's question.

"You reported it to the cops, I hope."

"No, but I will."

"They'll never find it. They're all nigger lovers."

Ralph turned once more, but again he was halted.

"Too bad," said Hauser, "you didn't stay on the job long enough to meet that whore!" He chortled. "You would of creamed your jeans."

Ralph had actually forgotten all about that subject. That Hauser referred to Laverne Linda Lorraine; that drunkenly they had been heading for her dear staircase on Saturday night; that his kind friend on the one hand was on the other a stinking, vile, obscene criminal whose filthy tongue should be ripped out—all this was clear.

But it could also be regarded as established truth that, except in movies and ancient narratives such as the series about Frank Merriwell, a normal modern individual did not commit violence in response to verbal attacks on a woman's honor, especially those made in innocent ignorance by an imbecile who no doubt had been home all afternoon playing with himself while perusing the little eight-page fuckbook the edges of which could be seen protruding from his back pocket as he climbed the steps.

So said the voice of reason. All the same, Ralph felt like a leper. A lesser crime against L.L.L. could be rectified: he still owed her for the breakage. His fifty-cent wages belonged to her. He fished out the half dollar and warmed it in his hand as he started back on the route to 23-B Myrtle.

But he had not quite gained the next corner when his father's Buick appeared, swerved into the gutter bordering the wrong side of the street, and came to an uneasy rest, its engine throbbing.

"Glad I caught you," said Buddy, hooking an elbow over the windowsill. "Hop in."

"I wasn't heading home yet," said Ralph.

"Ralph," Buddy said softly, "when I tell you to do something, there's always a point to it."

His plan in ruins, Ralph took refuge in a military sort of discipline. He marched around the car and got in.

"What happened," Buddy explained once the order had been obeyed, "is Leo's dear mom passed away."

"Sorry to hear that."

"The proper sentiment, son." Buddy put the car in motion and reached the right lane on a leisurely diagonal. "Now your mother and I are going to the laying-out. I think it's your place to come along."

Ralph returned to the style of his preadolescence: a writhing of features and a childish moan.

"It's not exactly fun for anybody," said Buddy. "It's an expression of respect. I believe you call Leo a friend. You owe him that much."

His father had misinterpreted his reaction. Ralph stood ready to give his due to Leo, of course. Laverne L. L. had herself stated that responsibility was paramount in her book, her eyes the color of deep water, her hand like a lily.

"Take long?" he nevertheless asked.

"As long as necessary," his father said. He frowned quickly at Ralph, then put his eyes back on the road. "You're taking short cuts again and slurring when you talk. That doesn't go over in the business world, where money might depend on you making yourself clear. Also in this instance it's pretty cynical, Ralph."

"I didn't mean it to be. I just wasn't thinking."

"I accept your apology," Buddy said, and in compensation

179

he gave an assurance: "I imagine fifteen-twenty minutes would wrap it up for you. You give your condolences to Leo, look at the cards on the flowers, and greet the other people courteously, and I'd say that was about it. You don't have to spend much time looking at the body. Everybody will understand that in a young fellow."

"Oh, that I don't mind," said Ralph, "if I don't know the person. You've got nothing then to compare. I cut Leo's grass a couple dozen times in two years, and I never once even saw his mother."

"Neither did I," said Buddy, and added piously: "But I understand she was a very fine lady." Having reached a point opposite their house, he made a nonchalant U-turn which when completed brought the vehicle in to a perfect park: a demonstration of virile skill that was not lost on Ralph. When the time came he wanted to drive well, dominating the machine but with an almost lazy sense of ease. It thrilled him to think that if Laverne drove at all, she must by definition— soft golden container of grace—do it badly, beautiful intruder on a brute mechanism.

They entered the house to find his mother sitting in the nearest chair to the door, dressed like a Mystery Woman all in black including hat-with-veil.

"See you're all set for the festivities," said Buddy, lifting one side of his mouth as if to insert a pipe or cigar. "Give me five minutes to get into a dark suit."

Ralph followed his dad down the hall, asking: "What do you think I should wear? The only dark suit I've got is for winter. I don't even have a summer coat."

Buddy turned in the doorway to the master bedroom. "Clean white shirt, Ralph. I can loan you a black tie. A clean pair of pants with a good crease. Black shoes if the pants are gray or any shade of blue; brown if the pants are brown or tan; and with a good shine in any event."

Ralph entered his own room and inspected the clothing deposited on chairs, draped on doorknobs, and hung or heaped in the closet. The only pants that agreed with his father's prescription were a pair of white ducks, in which, with black tie and white shirt, he would resemble a ballpark vendor of Eskimo Pies. He had no alternative but to remove the mothballs from the pockets of his winter suit, a dark-blue garment of weighty wool, and climb into its trousers in a temperature of some eighty degrees.

Already steaming, though the jacket yet lay on the bed, he got a white shirt from the dresser. Naked to the waist, he avoided the sight of himself in the mirror because he could not spare the time to tense his muscles, in the absence of which effort he would see more scrawniness than the wiry character kindly ascribed to his body by Hauser.

Shirt on, Ralph went into the hallway and took the four steps that brought him to the door of his parents' room. He was about to enter when he saw his father leaning in profile at the bed to insert an object under the pillow. The chenille spread was pulled back in the interests of this chore.

His father was naked. His sex organs, at which Ralph scrupulously avoided looking, were the largest he had ever seen on a man, the testicles like oranges and a banana-sized penis, sprouting from a thick black hedge. But then Ralph had no vast experience of adult male pudenda.

He withdrew instantly, silently, without detection, and made it back to his own room, where he imposed a ban on further speculations on his father's genitals and remembered his identification of the object placed under the pillow: a gun. Many householders kept one. Damn good thing to have at hand if a nigger broke in, as Hauser always said; or any kind of burglar, cheap punk, or maniac, as Ralph added. Hauser said yeah, but not to use on Peeping Toms or he'd get himself killed one of these days.

He sat upon his bed and waited while the shower roared. Before going to Bigelow's he had washed his own armpits and applied Mum. He sniffed: it was still holding. Sometime after his father had crossed the hall from the bathroom, Ralph tried again, this time with slapping shoe soles, giving plenty of warning.

When he reached the door of his parents' bedroom, his father, in shirt and trousers, was tying his tie in the mirror. When this was done Buddy took from the dressertop a golden pin and fastened it to connect the halves of his round-point collar. His shirt was made of oxford cloth, and his trousers were navy-blue, with gray chalk stripes. He was certainly more impressive when clothed; somewhere below and behind the end of his pants pleats his huge genitals were contained in the pouch of his Jockey shorts, which unlike Ralph's own had been changed.

The mirror image spoke irritably: "Do you know what you're doing?"

Ralph was scratching his crotch. He stopped abruptly once attention was called. "Sorry, I wasn't thinking."

Swinging his tie aside, Buddy slid a gold clip onto the edge of his shirt just above a button in the high middle. "One characteristic of a gentleman—the main one, in my humble opinion—is he *always* thinks." He fed the tie through the loop of the golden chain that swung from the clip. "Whereas a slob *always* has his mind in a fog."

"That knitted tie is neat," said Ralph. "Also that collar."

"Clothes make the man," said Buddy, dissatisfied with the hang of the little gold chain. He altered the position of the clip, now hidden behind the tie. He stepped to his personal chiffonier, examined his ensemble in the long mirror inside one door, then from the laden tie rack behind the other took a black tie and presented it to Ralph.

Alas, it was not of the knitted type but rather a slimy-feeling, shiny thing of silk. Ralph went to his own room to knot it. On the first few attempts the ends always came out in different lengths, and he did not want to be criticized by the well-dressed man who did everything well.

When they pulled up in front of Leo's house, Ralph assumed the idea was to pick up the car salesman and go together to the funeral home. But Buddy cut the engine and stared at Ralph in the rear-vision mirror.

"Leo's mom is laid out in the living room, Ralph, on the davenport. That might strike you as weird, but if so, don't laugh. If you feel a grin coming on and you just can't hold it, slip out to the bathroom or the porch or something."

Naomi snickered under her veil and said: "Oh, dear."

"I think that's good advice?" Buddy responded in a kind of false question.

"Very good, indeed," she hastened to say. "But it never would have occurred to me, and now I may not be able to think of anything else but *not* laughing, or else I'll laugh." She giggled again.

"I was talking to Ralph," said Buddy in a controlled way, and climbed out.

Naomi and Ralph followed him up the walk, Ralph surveying the lawn with a professional eye. Fired from Bigelow's, he would be back to grass for another month, then leaves, then snow and coal, and then another spring. Life had an inexorable quality about it, and ended with inevitable death. Sweating in the suit jacket and with this sudden tragic sense of life, he mounted the porch behind the slender black figure of his living mother, en route to view the body of Leo's dead one.

As his father opened the house door, Ralph saw the screen-door had been removed too early for the season and left leaning against the side railing of the porch. The entrance hall of this house, which he had never before penetrated, was stranger yet: utterly empty of furnishings, not even a hatrack or umbrella stand.

His father was now walking tiptoe towards a closed door. His mother had her black-gloved hand to her veil and was making faint asthmatic sounds.

Buddy opened the door and entered first. Endeavoring to suppress her giggle, Naomi stepped aside and motioned Ralph on. He stepped into a room as empty as the vestibule, with one exception: on a davenport lay a dead lady not as old as he had expected. She looked indeed like a former chorus girl.

No one else was there, including Leo. His father ignored the body to stare about in wonderment, then stepped through the archway into the dining room. He soon returned with pursed lips.

"This is fishy."

"All the while I was cutting the grass," said Ralph, "I never knew there wasn't any furniture in here."

"No wisecracks, Ralph," Buddy said, collecting himself. He nodded towards the davenport. "Just pay your respects quietly and leave." He produced his wallet. "Here. Your mother and I are going to have supper out. I know at your age it bores you stiff to sit at a table in a fancy place. Here." He gave Ralph a dollar. "Live it up in one of your teen-age dumps."

Ralph was reminded of the two dollars he had been given on Saturday night to present to Bigelow for the broken window. His father was not aware he had subsequently worked briefly for the grocer. He had of course banked the two-dollar bill before meeting Laverne Linda Lorraine. He would repay her for the breakage with the fifty-cent piece. With the dollar he would buy her the maximum assortment of Martha Washington chocolates, in a box like a jewel case of many drawers.

He went near the davenport and looked at Leo's mother. Under the paint and powder and what appeared to be a wig she was a whole lot older than she had appeared on first glance. She had a small hooked nose like the beak of a parrot, which was accentuated by a little cupid's bow of lipstick below. Hauser always said if you looked at a dead body for a while you imagined it was breathing. Ralph did not stay long enough for this effect to develop.

Buddy came out of his physical quandary—peering through windows and prowling into the dining room again—and briskly preceded Ralph into the hallway, where Naomi, veil lifted, was wiping her eyes with a hankie. She could not stop giggling.

"Buddy," she said sotto voce, "you *are* diabolical."

"I can't find Leo for the life of me," he said. "I looked all over down here. He ain't in the kitchen and I couldn't see him outside. But you know what? He took all the furniture out there. It's all over the yard."

This information quelled Naomi's laughter. She lowered her handkerchief and said: "How odd."

"Ain't it though," said Buddy. He went along the hall, opening doors. On the first try he got a closet; on the next, the basement steps. He disappeared.

"I'll look upstairs," Naomi said towards the spot from which her husband had vanished.

Ralph said, with some anxiety: "I'm supposed to leave." His mother was depositing the balled handkerchief in her black purse. "Maybe I better stay though and help find Leo."

Naomi smiled beatifically. "I'm sure there's some simple explanation for all of this." She drifted towards the staircase like a dark ghost.

Ralph doubted that there was, but selfishly did not want to be involved. He had done his duty. . . . Yet had he discharged his *responsibility*, the concept that meant so much to the sainted Laverne? There was a difference. He went back to where the kitchen should have been, found it, saw that it at least was fully furnished, did not find Leo there, and went outside.

As his father had said, the yard was full of furniture, chairs, tables, and floorlamps, all upright and, in fact, in a conscious arrangement, as one could see when his vision recovered from the initial surprise: here, a complete parlor without walls; there, near the cistern, a dining room, its round table covered with a white cloth in the center of which reposed a bowl containing two wax apples, one pear, and one eternally bright-yellow banana, and at either end a white candle in a bronze holder.

When Ralph had come close enough to count the pieces of fruit, he saw Leo sitting on the cistern cover; the man had hitherto been concealed by the high back of a dining-room chair. He wore the rumpled seersucker he was usually seen in at the lot; a black band encircled the left arm just above the elbow.

"Hi, Leo," said Ralph. "I want you to know I'm sorry."

Leo smiled in a perfectly normal way. "Ralph, you got a good head on your shoulders. What do you think I should ask for that dining-room set?"

Ralph appraised the table and chairs. "You selling this stuff?"

"You bet," said Leo, slapping himself on the thighs and rising. "They don't give funerals away free, you know."

Buddy emerged from the outside entrance to the cellar, which was the old-fashioned kind under a two-leaved horizontal hatchway.

"Could you use any of this?" Leo asked him eagerly.

Buddy pointed a finger at Leo and said sternly: "Your place is inside."

Ralph piped up: "He's selling this stuff."

Buddy raised his remaining fingers to make a flat hand. "I found that floral arrangement I sent over, down cellar."

186

"It's too big for the Frigidaire," said Leo. "That's the coolest place I could think of. Who wants to buy wilted flowers?"

"Say, Leo, did Doc Klingman drop around this afternoon?"

"No, he never—unless I was out here and didn't hear him knock." Leo's eyebrows took wing. "But, say, that's an idea. He could use some new furniture in his waiting room. And he's into me for a couple bucks for coming and signing the death certificate."

Buddy heel-and toed a complete circuit of the dining table. When finished he noticed Ralph and with one shoulder gave him the high sign to leave. Leo went to the table and re-stacked the wax fruit. Looking at Ralph again, Buddy put his index finger to his temple and traced a circle.

Leo showed Ralph a paraffin apple. "When I was three or four I bit into one of these." The very one: you could still see the tiny toothmarks.

"Say, Leo," Buddy said impatiently, "you'll have to excuse Ralph. He just came to pay his respects, but now he has to take French leave."

"Say, Ralph," said Leo, "you run into anybody who wants furniture cheap, I'd be much obliged."

"You bet, Leo." Wondering whether Leo was crazy, period, or like-a-fox, Ralph left.

Buddy said: "Look at it this way, Leo. If you don't sell everything in a hurry it's liable to rain." He refused to believe that the man was so far gone as to reject such a modest piece of practical reason.

"Nah," said Leo, squinting rhetorically at the sky. "Not a chance. Anyway, I got a couple tarps down cellar I can haul out if need be. But these things will go fast when the crowd gets here." He put back the wax apple he had bitten as a three-year-old.

Buddy said: "If you don't mind me saying so, I don't get why you want to peddle this stuff in the first place."

Leo's answer was amazingly reasonable. "The only insurance I got is on me, for *her*. Since I made the only income, I didn't have none on her. So I ain't got the money to bury her."

"For Christ's sake," said Buddy, "didn't I tell you I would help out?"

"No," said Leo, "I never borrowed a penny in my life. The old man took out a loan to buy this house and I'm still paying on it, but that ain't personal." He squinted at Buddy under his brushy brow, which in this expression was continuous, not separated above the nose. "You want to buy this furniture though, that's different."

Buddy saw the irony: Leo was blackmailing him, but unknowingly.

"How much you want?"

"Anything that's fair."

Buddy indulged himself: "What in the fucking hell can I do with two roomfuls of furniture?" But he was already separating, by touch, several bills from the roll of murder money in his pocket.

"I couldn't say," said Leo. "I'm just selling."

"Well, I'll make you a deal, Leo. I'll give you fifty bucks for the whole works. But you got to get it out of the yard right now before anybody sees it."

"Make that seventy-five," said Leo. "That table's solid oak, and that chair over there's genuine horsehide and so's the ottoman."

Buddy said: "I'll see you and raise you"—he removed his hand from his pocket and looked at what he held—"twenty-five. I'll give you a hundred, Leo, if you carry this stuff, lock, stock, and barrel, back in the house where it was."

A glowering, possibly mad expression developed on Leo's face. "I don't keep nothing that ain't mine, see?"

Buddy cried: "I got it! Stick this stuff in the basement, and tomorrow you call up the Salvation Army."

"Sure Mike," said Leo, stoically. "If that's the way you want it, Buddy."

But after a moment he went back to sit on the cistern cover, falling into a sort of coma, and Buddy had to haul the furniture to the cellar himself, wheezing and sweating. When it came to the table, he tipped it on its side and rolled it to the opening and let it fall, a leg breaking off and another splintering before it caught at an angle in the doorway below.

Damp of clothing and dirty of hands, he took upstairs the basket of flowers on which the card read: "In loving memory—Buddy and Naomi Sandifer." Buddy placed the floral arrangement in the room with the late Mrs. Kirsch. There was still no one else there. Leo had probably neglected to send the death notice to the papers. Then again, perhaps it was merely that Leo had no friends.

Buddy was wrong by one. As he left the house, Jack was ascending the stairs, wearing a properly doleful expression and carrying a bunch of weedy flowers, no doubt home-grown, wrapped in a cone of wet newspaper.

He insisted on giving Buddy a shake with an ink-imprinted, damp hand. "The wife couldn't make it," said he. "The two-year-old came down with the grippe, vomiting all over the place." Rolling his eyes, he said: "So maybe you could take a raincheck on that stopping in for coffee."

Buddy tossed his chin to the side. "Say, Jack, what would you think about coming on with me full time?"

Jack moved his Adam's apple. "Gee, Mr.—"

Buddy leaned in. "Just between you, me, and the gatepost, Leo's gone a little batty. He might have to be put away."

"Oh," said Jack, "isn't it just the shock? He's got a awfully good head on his shoulders."

"Do me a favor," Buddy said. "Don't mention to him what I just mentioned to you."

Jack quickly widened his eyes in a sissified style. He angled his head knowingly and then asked: "Is that Mrs. Sandifer I saw sitting in the car?"

"Probably," said Buddy, and went down the steps. He glanced at the Plum house. Grace never got home till well after six, given the hour's bus ride from downtown. If she was getting cock from somebody, it might run as late as ten, as it did in the old days when he fed it to her. According to her, her old man never even looked at her crossways.

He avoided looking at Naomi, sitting in the car, as he went by way of the trunk to reach the driver's side. Buddy never used the front route, around the hood, not even when the engine was at rest; he was far too paranoid. Nor did he lie on his stomach in the presence of a woman, displaying an unprotected spine. Even with Laverne this was true.

Naomi could not drive, her only male habit being one he did not practice: smoking. Though the windows were open, front and rear, on this breezeless evening the air inside the car was poison-blue. He fanned the door several times before climbing in.

Naomi's veil was lowered again, the cigarette going in and out just beneath it.

"Leo's completely cracked," Buddy said.

"He always seemed very level-headed to me," said Naomi.

"Those," said Buddy, letting out the clutch, "are the type who go to pieces first. Now, take me, I fly off the handle once in a while, I know, but it does take the pressure off."

Naomi sent some smoke towards him. "Is that true?" she asked. "How odd. I've never seen you do that."

"I guess I don't always let on," said Buddy. "I blow up in private."

Naomi murmured indistinctly behind the veil. With her it was not control but simply a character incapable of any feeling at all.

"You got supper waiting?" He knew better.

"Chipped beef won't take a minute," she said. "And I'll warm a can of limas."

"I'll tell you, Nay. We ought to get the taste of that experience out of our mouths. What say we put on the feedbag at Wong's Gardens?"

In the early years they had dined there on signal occasions like anniversaries, and the day-after-holidays, but when business had got better and Buddy acquired a concomitant taste for roadhouses with cocktail lounges, steaks smothered in mushrooms, and dance bands, Naomi in her dreary way remained enmired in an addiction to chicken chow mein. They had not therefore been to Wong's for ages. It was an appropriate locus for their last meal together.

Naomi stared at him through her veil. "Well, it *is* an extravagance. . . ."

Once again Buddy wondered, as he had for eons, whether her bland exterior, now concealed altogether, was a mask for corrosive sarcasm. And once again he decided it was not: it was humanly impossible to pose as a drone for so many years. Wong's special four-course meal, from egg-drop soup to almond cookie or pineapple slice, was priced at thirty-five cents, and Naomi never even glanced at the à la carte, resorting to which anyway you would be hard put to exceed a dollar's worth of food unless you gluttonized wildly on *both* lobster and squab. Whereas Buddy had never gone anywhere with Laverne without spending a minimum of three bucks for food alone, with more for the drinks. Laverne could run up a dollar tab at a fish-sandwich take-out place, with extra orders of french fries and cole slaw, a jar of sweet pickles, not to mention several packages of those round cheese crackers stuck together with peanut-butter putty, which she ate in the car going home. Entering a movie, she invariably stopped at the lobby machines and bought fifteen-twenty cents' worth of chocolate kisses, Milk Duds, and candy-covered licorice pellets.

"Let's go whole hog for a change," said Buddy. "We owe it to ourselves." He shook his head. "The last person I would think it of was Leo."

Naomi pushed up her veil and left it there. "I have a confession to make, Buddy." He felt a slight chill for no special reason beyond his instinctive fear of revelations, even such harmless ones as Naomi was likely to make.

"I never did go in to look at his mother," said she. "I could see no point in it if he wasn't there."

Buddy snorted in relief. "You didn't miss much."

Ralph had stopped at the drugstore and bought the box of candy, though alas the super-duper size was not in stock and the largest available was the thirty-nine-center, which however did have a red bow of satin ribbon under tight cellophane.

His route took him past Elmira's, and there, leaning against the outer wall of the high-school hangout, he saw his bicycle. Ralph was enraged at the boldness of the thief. Thrusting the candy box, in its green paper bag, as far as it would go into the cavity below his left shoulder, he prepared to enter the shop and confront the malefactor. Even in his anger he was able to reflect that finding the bike here meant no colored youth had stolen it, given the exclusion of Negroes from Elmira's; this relieved him, because he was scared of them.

Just as he reached the door however, Margie emerged.

"God," she said, "there you are! God, I've been looking everyplace for you."

"Don't bother me now," said Ralph. "For pity sake. Just get out of my way when the fur flies."

Oblivious to his purpose, she continued to block him. "I guess I was stupid. I found your bike laying on the curb over on Myrtle. When you didn't show up after a long time I figured you forgot it or some kids hooked it and left it there or something, so I took it back to Bigelow's but they said you didn't work there any more, so I took it to your house but nobody was home so I came here thinking you might—"

"Oh for Christ sake," said Ralph, "put a lid on it, will you? I might have known. You damn sap." She put a hand to her frozen face and backed up. "Why don't you let me alone? Who asked you, anyway?" He pursued her until her back met the wall. "Lucky I didn't report it to the cops, or you'd have gone to jail."

But once again he was relieved, this time of the responsibility to tangle with a boy who would have had to be tough and fearless to flaunt stolen property. The matter of his own possible cowardice in the clinch was now a dead issue. He had but a cowering, wretched girl to condemn, and could do it in perfect conscience.

Ignoble fellow that he was. "Oh, hell," said he instead, "don't act like you're being murdered. Can't you see I'm kidding?" She peeped through her hands. He made a grotesque grin and pointed to it. "See?" She sniffled. He stuck out his tongue and crossed his eyes. She giggled and wiped her nose on her wrist.

"I knew you had it all the time," said he.

"I don't think you did."

"I didn't report it, did I?"

"I don't know."

"Well, I don't intend to argue about it," Ralph said with fake huffiness. If they continued to stand there, somebody he knew would show up and think she was his girl, and his saintly decency would be rewarded with humiliation.

"Look, I got an appointment." He put the package in the basket and seized the bike.

Now that she had eluded punishment, she had no shame whatever. "I don't suppose you could give me a ride?"

"You're right. The answer is no, nix, nothing doing."

"I mean, just as far as where you turn off."

"You know something, Margie? You've got an awful lot of gall." But what could you do with somebody who regarded that as a compliment, grinning proudly?

"All right," he groaned, nodding at the crossbar. "Climb on. But watch it when we go over the creek. I might throw you in."

"Better not. I can't swim."

"Somehow I knew that," said Ralph.

"You'd just have to save me."

"Don't I know it."

"But," said she, settling her bottom on the bar and putting one damp hand over his on the rubber handle grip, "it would make you feel real big."

Burdened with this threatening knowledge of what she had on him, as well as her physical weight on the bike, and yet with a sense that he was doing the right thing in supporting them both, he shoved off. The effort reminded him immediately that he still wore the heavy suit, from which he had been distracted by his mission since leaving Leo's house.

Margie leaned forward to stare into the basket, dangerously altering the balance. He had not yet got up enough speed, and the bike veered left.

"Hey, watch it!" he said. "Don't you even know how to sit on a bike?"

"What'd you get at the drugstore?" she asked. "Wine?" She turned her head and looked over her hunched shoulder. He saw her naked blue eye between cheek and metal spectacle rim. "You're sure dressed fit to kill, too. Who's giving the party?"

"Nobody," said Ralph, sweating so copiously he could hardly see. He hoped the Mum would continue to hold under fire.

"You don't have to protect my feelings," said Margie. "Nobody ever invites me, and I've got used to it." Nevertheless she looked desolately down at the turning wheel ahead.

The self-pity made Ralph grimace at her rumpled back. "I don't go to all that many myself. They aren't much fun anyway." He was sincere in this judgment. At spin the bottle, fortune always gave him the dogs; he would for example have got Margie.

"You know when I used to run around with Imogene," said Margie, "she never even invited me to her parties."

"I wouldn't know about that," said Ralph. In pride he lapsed into Hauser tough-talk. "Her and me never have seen eye to eye. She's just a little chippie for my money."

Margie gasped at this. "Gee, I wouldn't go that far."

"Wasn't it you who told me she went off with Lester Hauser? She'll end up pregnant one of these days."

Margie's hands stiffened on the bars; she pushed herself back against his chest. "You better let me off right here."

Ralph stopped pedaling and caught the laden bike with outstretched feet. "With pleasure."

"I mean . . ." She still sat there and looked ahead.

"Listen," said Ralph in patient indignation, " 'pregnant' isn't a dirty word, and you know it."

"I can't help it."

"I can't help if you're ignorant," said Ralph. "A cow has 'teats,' and a female dog is a 'bitch.' Put that in your pipe and smoke it. For God's sake, that's the king's English, and if all the sissies and old maids who run the stupid churches around here read the goddam Bible they would find out all kinds of things, like what the word 'know' *really* means." This was one of Ralph's causes insofar as he had any. He and Hauser often discussed this matter: Horse, though fouler-mouthed, was for once less ardent.

Margie's hands went through the stringy hair to cover her ears. Ralph decided not to let her off the bike for this stupid reason, though she was making no physical move to go anyway. He started up again, and because she would otherwise have fallen, he caught her in his right arm while managing, with the fine authority of the veteran cyclist, to correct the balances with his corded left wrist. He felt a slender but smooth and vital trunk within the loose cotton dress and then, as compensating for the motion she leaned forward, his hand sliding up, a projection the size, shape, and firmness of a lemon half.

At the top of his leg, the foot of which was grinding the pedal around the sprocket, his pecker instantly went rigid. Margie on the other hand went soft in attitude though not in body: he had not dreamed she was slender-firm rather than skinny-slack. His hard-on now had swelled to touch the rounded edge of her amazingly substantial butt on every downstroke of his shoe.

She tolerated this in silence. His hand seemed glued to her breast, immune to volition. There he pedaled, along Wyman Street, flagrantly yet helplessly cupping the tit of some dippy girl, to whom furthermore he had never been attracted, sexually or otherwise, and he did not know if he was genuinely so now. In fact he doubted it, he who could get a bone-on from the motion of a streetcar in which he was passenger.

God only knows how long this would have continued had the front wheel not hit a pothole. His hand went desperately from breast to corrugated rubber grip, made it, applied corrective measures, and his balance was regained. Hers never seemed in doubt, oddly enough, though he had withdrawn her only visible support. Her narrow back was still warmly against his chest.

The physical shock broke his moral silence.

"Let me know if another hole comes up. I can't see through you, for Christ sake."

"You really ought to do something about your language, Ralph," said she. "If a person can't express themselves without being crude—"

He stopped the bike. "All right, that's *it.* . . . Go on, get off."

She complied. If he expected tears again he was disappointed. She frowned and made her mouth like a little old lady's.

Ralph said: "Let me tell you something: you're in no position to criticize." He pedaled off to see Laverne L. Lorraine.

The remarkable feature was that when he noticed his whereabouts he saw he was already only a block or two from Myrtle, with Bigelow's corner in sight. He had ridden across town in a benumbed state, his hand on Margie's little knocker. On reflection he identified something sinister in her character, which he had hitherto assessed as totally dopey. To object to a little mild cussing and then put her tit in his hand and rub her ass against his dick.

Yet it was weird and repulsive to think of such a plain girl as being horny: *she had no right.* But if this were true, was not the world completely rotten? Having abandoned her, Ralph assuaged his guilt with sentimentality: think of the poor devils born with clubfeet or as Mongolian idiots. With such melancholy deliberations he swung at high speed around the corner into Myrtle Avenue. This irked some old geezer in an ancient coupe, though he was nowhere near him. Ralph ignored the angry *oo-gah* of the old-fashioned horn.

He hopped off in front of 23. On the porch sat a tremendous fat slob in an undershirt, his belly bigger than even Bigelow's. While Ralph wheeled the bike towards the side of the house, an enormous matching woman shuffled out in carpet slippers and gave the man a glass of lemonade. They both gazed piggishly at Ralph, who favored them with the briefest of glances. He thought it amusing that a princess lived above such peasants.

But before he reached the corner the man yelled: "Hey, bud, you got a delivery for upstairs? She ain't home." The woman continued to stare expressionlessly from a face as wide as a pie. "She just went down the bus stop," the man elucidated. "Don't leave your package outside up there or some nigger might steal it. And we can't take it here. We don't want to be responsible." The woman grimaced disagreeably.

Ralph ran his bike out to the street. He assumed the bus stop would be on Jackson, the nearest arterial highway, and he was right. He was still half a block away, pumping hard, when a pair of silken limbs, topped by a golden head, between which was a fabulous figure dressed in bright green, stepped onto the bus, which subsequently roared away, leaving him in a cloud of dull blue exhaust.

He was soaked with disappointment, exertion, and his horse-blanket suit. A unique sensation was provided by a stream of sweat coursing behind his knees, now that he had stopped, with straight legs, feet planted, rump raised off a sticky seat. He fanned himself with the edges of his jacket, smelling no stench in the hot body-air that emerged, though the time for that concern had passed.

Having watched the bus dwindle to a little red dot and vanish into the converging parallels of Jackson Avenue, he remounted the bicycle. There would of course be other days, but none so right as this one could have been. His aims had been so modest: to return the money for the damage, to present the candy as a bonus, then to watch the sun rise in that glorious face.

He decided to go home, get out of the damned suit, and make himself a melted-cheese sandwich in the waffle iron. The juvenile idiocy of Elmira's would be repugnant to him at this moment.

chapter 11

LAVERNE HAD BEEN GIVEN to extremes through-
out her adult life, going helplessly where she was blown by
the gusts of chance, on the one hand; but on the other, from
time to time making irrevocable decisions. At the age of
sixteen, already full-breasted, hanging around a dance pavilion
on the shore of a man-made lake just outside her home town,
she had caught the eye of the bandleader, a thin, dapper man
with patent-leather head and hairline mustache.

When dancing Laverne would maneuver her partner into a
position below the bandstand from which she could keep a
surveillance on the leader, who most of the time kept his back
turned as his baton dominated the five musicians, but turned
occasionally to charm the customers and in one out of three
numbers himself soloed on saxophone or, more rarely, clarinet, and when he did might wink at Laverne, who was fox-
trotting with her friend Irma Grunion.

The two girls had been going to the pavilion every night,
but this being a semi-rural area, the unattached boys were

mostly hicks, with a few older tinhorn sports from town who had cars, into which if you climbed, especially the rumble seat, you had to fight for your life, which is how it seemed from the ferocity of the attacks: as if they wanted rather to kill than merely rape you. The hicks though danced at arm's length and smelled of the cloves they chewed for their breath. In the intermissions they nervously rushed away to buy pretzels and orange pop; at the end of the evening they would ride you home in the bus without a word; that is, if they had not disappeared while you were in the restroom. Many nights the girls preferred their own company.

Laverne knew herself as yet a rube, but she had a conviction that a true sophisticate neither despised nor feared women, and furthermore spoke beautifully. Therefore, when after the playing of "Goodnight, Ladies" her admirer put his little megaphone to his mouth and said: "This is Ken Canning and his Ragtime Dreamers saying a bit of a tweet-tweet, and wishing sweet dreams to you-all for always and a day," she was ready to swoon even if he had not winked for the third time that night.

"You see that?" asked Irma as they went to the Ladies' through the grove of trees, floored with tanbark and lighted with orange bulbs on strings, "Ken Canning winking at me? He was doing it all night. I never let on though. He's a real masher."

"You know that for a fact?" asked Laverne.

"By that little mustache."

"Well, I never!" Laverne said.

"I'm keeping out of his clutches," said Irma, who had never had much upstairs.

Luckily the restroom was crowded. When the first booth became available Laverne insisted Irma take it; and when the door closed on her friend she slipped out of the Ladies', circled the grove, and emerged at the rear of the bandstand,

201

from which the musicians had already departed. She groaned twice and was about to surrender to despair when a little door in the base of the stand opened and the men came out, including the one and only Ken Canning, who, the lights still burning above, saw and recognized her immediately.

He closed the door and leaned against it in his striped blazer and ice-cream pants. He put his thumb up at her and beckoned.

She had no fright or doubts. As she approached him, passing the other Ragtime Dreamers, one of them said smirkingly: "Look out. Papa spanks!" And another raked his sailor straw and cried to Ken: "Baby-rape will land you in the hoosegow."

"Kiddo," said Ken, lipping an unlighted cigarette, "you the one giving me them bedroom eyes from the floor all night, ain't you?"

Laverne simpered in silence.

"Say, listen, you ever heard the gen-you-whine words to the 'Sheik of Araby'?

> "At night when you're asleep,
> Without no pants on,
> Into your tent I'll creep,
> Without no pants on . . ."

She laughed through her nose, but not much, because he did remind her of Valentino.

Ken Canning said: "You got the time?" He held his cold cigarette elegantly between thumb and forefinger.

She realized she was on trial. "Gee, no I ain't, but I could run and ask somebody."

He leered at her and said: "You're sure a hayseed. I got a solid gold watch right here." He tapped his jacket at the point under which ran the waistband of his trousers. "You're supposed to answer, 'And I got the place,' see?"

He had lost her somewhere. She listened extra carefully to the next. "Another one is: 'You got the time?' The answer is: 'Yeah, but who'll hold the horse?' "

"Oh, yeah, I get it." She laughed again, but had the hollow sense of not doing well as she saw him nonchalantly light the cigarette with a match he ignited with his thumbnail and widen his nostrils to blow out a double stream of smoke. She closed her eyes and let it wash over her. As she opened them the lights went out on the bandstand above.

In the darkness Ken Canning said: "You like to jazz?"

"Oh gee, yeah," she said enthusiastically. She lived for dance music.

His cigarette ember flared from a hearty in-draught, briefly lighting his long upper lip and the fine line of clipped hair thereupon. He took her hand as darkness fell over him again. "Don't trip and break your leg." He opened the door to the cellar and led her down three concrete steps. "Don't fall over the trap drum."

He had long wiry fingers. Laverne was in an immaterial state. She did not believe he had taken her underground for a private recital of jazz music, but neither did she expect to find his naked male thing in her hand, as suddenly it was. She had expected he would kiss her and she would let him; then feel her and she would resist a little, but soon relent, because unlike the rumble-seat sheiks he would be deft and graceful and stylish at it.

And for whatever else happened after that, she would not be responsible. Laverne was not a carnal girl. Her sexual fantasies were cloudy, perfumed, and musically accompanied but not physically detailed. She had decided to give herself to Ken Canning, in whatever degree he wanted her.

Instead, *he* presented himself to *her*, and she knew not

what to do with him, or rather with the gristle-handle to which he was presumably attached. He had let her go altogether by now.

"Squeeze," said he. "That's my love muscle."

Suddenly his falling pants shot past her hand, the belt buckle dealing her knuckles a painful blow. She let go.

"C'mon, baby," said he, finding her fingers and putting them back on his knobbed protuberance. "Drop your bloomers."

She went up under her skirt. He moved somewhere in the dark.

"Over here," said he. She searched for him and bumped into the bass drum with a clang of the attached cymbals. He swore. She found him against the wall, at some kind of bench, on which he ordered her to sit and lift her legs. When she had carried out this command, he bent and drove his spike into her flesh. This was what Christ had suffered: the path of the pain was cruciform, going into all four limbs.

Emerging from this single thrust, Ken Canning entered her no more. Indeed, he went away altogether, and with the clink of belt buckle and rustle of fabric he could be heard to reassume his trousers: he had taken off nothing else.

Was he done with her? She decided against asking him. She felt in the place where he had been, and it was wet. What had been pain was now merely an ache. She rose and, squatting, holding her skirt away from the blood, searched the floor for the undergarment. Not finding it, she fell to her knees and explored deliberately on the cold concrete. Eventually she encountered his trousered legs.

"Hell fire," said he in irritation. "It's too late for a toot on the skin flute. Lay off!"

"I'm looking for my bloomers."

"Yeah," said Ken Canning. "It's like this, tootsie. I keep

them for a souvenir, you know? I wear 'em for pocket hand-
kerchiefs, see. You come out tomorrow night and you'll see
'em in my breast pocket. Give you a thrill, me up there onna
stage and all." He chuckled. "Fun is when some tomato is
down there dancing with her hubby, and she and I know I got
her step-ins in my pocket."

"Sure," said Laverne, getting up. "That's okey-dokey."

"You don't happen to be married, do yuh?" asked Ken
Canning in the darkness.

"I never even done it before," said Laverne.

"No lie?" said Ken. "Well, I'm a monkey's uncle. You are a
spunky one. You are O.K., kid."

All summer Ken retained a soft spot in his heart for
Laverne and every once in a while he would take her under
the bandstand and slip it to her. She was gratified to know
that she was of some use to the glamorous bandleader. On the
nights he did not use her and either took some other girl or
woman to the bandstand cellar or left with the Dreamers,
laughing and smoking, immediately after the performance,
she would go towards the bus stop but on a circuitous route
that took her through the parking lot, and now if some fellow
invited her into his automobile she usually accepted and
charged him for it: one dollar. Occasionally she was bargained
down to seventy-five or even fifty cents but not below. If
offered two bits she had a wisecrack waiting: "I ain't no
barbershop."

By Labor Day her monthly was several weeks overdue, and
Ken Canning told her that night, in the shadow of the bandstand, "Kiddo, I picked up a dose someplace. I'd figure it was
you but you was cherry when we met, so I doubt you are
spreading it around just yet. I'd like to jazz you for old times'
sake but the cannon's full of rust." He stuck out his hand and
said: "We're leaving for Chi tomorrow early, where we got a

engagement at a ritzy club in the big time, but you're a real nice kid and you gave some great laughs out here in the sticks."

They shook hands, and Laverne didn't bother with the information that it must have been he who was responsible for her being pregnant, because unless the fellows in cars had rubbers she made them finish outside in a handkerchief: theirs, if they had one. Ken went down the cellar steps for the last time, alone, and closed the door. Laverne meandered around the grove and, finding a bench, sat down upon it and wept. She would miss his stylish ways. He was a real Beau Brummell, a Gay Lothario, a Casanova, and a sheik wrapped up in one, and he was leaving to become a big muckety-muck in the Windy City.

She sat there nursing her broken heart, with a view of the deserted and darkened bandstand. At length Ken Canning came out of the cellar with a girl who in the moonlight looked like Irma Grunion, with whom her friendship had cooled after that initial slip-giving of July, but who often since, tonight included, had been her companion.

By the time Laverne reached the parking lot, the only vehicle remaining was the long touring car labeled KEN CANNING AND HIS RAGTIME DREAMERS. The drums were strapped to a luggage rack on the rear bumper, and the Dreamers sat inside. Ken, whom she was following at a distance, handed in his saxophone case, then climbed behind the wheel and drove away.

The last bus had gone too, taking Irma, if it was she. Laverne had to walk five miles home in her thin dancing pumps, and lost a heel en route. Her father, a railroad switch-man who had had to work all Labor Day, sat in the kitchen glowering over a tumbler of the hooch for which he paid the bootleggers most of his wages.

"You're up late," she said, trying in spite of everything to be nice.

"And you're a goddam little hoor," said he in his lousy brogue, the ugly, red-faced, heavy-eyebrowed, stupid Mick. Luckily her mother descended from Polish nobility, which was where Laverne got her own good looks, though her hair had begun to darken after she got her first monthlies at twelve and a half.

When she began to swell, Laverne ran away to Indianapolis and worked at a lunchroom in a bus station, not returning to the sale of herself until after her miscarriage. Throughout the subsequent decade she moved from city to city alternating between jobs concerned with food and drink on the one hand and prostitution on the other. She changed her name from Hogan to Lorraine and was often a platinum blonde. She remained in love with the idea of Ken Canning though on reflection she had identified the weakness of the man himself, which was a lack of faith in his own principles. He had every right to jazz Irma Grunion, but pretending he had the clap was a moral failure.

Every Saturday in the confessional booth, Laverne herself pretended to the priest that the worst of her sins were only "impure thoughts," but, one, she was a woman; two, she never had a moment's personal pleasure from the sexual employment of crotch, behind, mouth, or hand; and three, God saw everything you did anyway, so why go over it all again with the man on the other side of the grille, who being sexless by definition was immune to her God-given talents?

Laverne had never met a man she couldn't get up. But periodically she became bored with providing miracle cures for the impotence that remained a prevalent plague in the land, and went to serve foot-long hotdogs and fried fish, generally at roadside establishments where you got a changing clientele, and she always kept her faculties keen for the apprehension of another Ken Canning, whom she would never find in the practice of her other profession, he being a taker and not a buyer.

In the spring of '38 she became the third waitress hired by the first local example of the scheme imported from California: an asphalted area into which persons drove and parked and were served sandwiches on a tray that cunningly hooked over the window of their machine. This place was called a drive-in cafe, and what Laverne did was known as being a carhop. She wore an overseas cap in royal blue, a red monkey jacket with white piping over a high-necked white jersey blouse, a white pleated skirt to the midpoint of her thighs, and white calf-length boots of patent leather: like the getup of a drum majorette, cute but anywhere from five to ten years too young for her, as she who had no false vanity recognized. Her upper legs had got beefy while her calves had developed cords; her brassiere, with the weight it supported, left marks on her back that could still be seen on Sunday night after twenty-four hours out of harness, she no longer emerging into the world on the Lord's day, not even to go to Mass, which omission she dutifully confessed on Saturday just before reporting for work and atoned for with the prescribed number of reverent salutations to the virgin mother of Christ, with whom she secretly felt a common cause that no priest, being male, could ever understand, Laverne having taken a thousand cocks and never been touched by any, while Mary had accepted none. With such a consideration, Laverne no longer even included "impure thoughts" in her roster of peccancies.

Funny thing about a lot of fellows who came to drive-ins: they weren't anywhere near as fresh as guys in indoor places, especially those where liquor was sold. Her typical customers were high-school punks, usually a pack of them in one car; married types with wife and offspring; and middle-aged roundwaltzers. All of these were big oglers, each in their own style: the punks with jeers and guffaws and stage groans; the hubbies, on the sly; the old bastards, thin-haired and pouchy-eyed, with the insecurity of those who expected to be despised.

So when this spiffy-looking bird pulled in in the Buick on an unusually warm night in late March and swung into one of the slots she attended, Laverne at least noticed him as being different, though did not let this cut any ice as to her manner, which as always, whether serving food or taking a dick, was professionally warm and personally remote.

"Hi, how you doing?" she said automatically, lifting her order pad and taking the pencil stub from the hair just under the overseas cap.

"Real bad till now," said he, giving her a onceover that was just right; quick, appreciative, and thoroughly confident. "I was afraid I might get one of them skinny little chicks," pointing disdainfully at Millie, who was just going by with a tray of malteds, on her dreamy eighteen-year-old legs the slender thighs of which made Laverne feel like a brewery horse. "I'm gonna compliment the manager," he said, "for hiring at least one real woman." His hand was on the rim of the door; he raised his index finger. "I mean it. If he is off duty at present, I want his name and will send him my personal letter expressing same."

Laverne's face, which until now had shown the usual synthetic smile, went blank with emotion. There was nothing of Ken Canning in the substance of this speech, nor in the man's appearance, with his round, pink, boyish face and pompadour. But the uncompromising self-assurance overwhelmed her with nostalgia. He knew he was right—as did few men who consorted with her as either prostitute or waitress.

"I'd be much obliged," said he, "if you was to suggest the specialty of the house. I never been to one of these places before, and it is quite a novelty. I'm all for it, as I am in the automobile business myself, and you can look at it this way: we are scratching one another's backs, you and me." He produced a dazzling grin; he had been straightfaced until this moment. "A fascinating woman like yourself no doubt hears lots of lines, but this ain't one, I assure you." He got out an ostrich-skin wallet, with little gold corners, and took from it a piece of pasteboard. "Here's my card."

Laverne squinted and held it at an angle. The light from the globe atop the nearby standard was more than adequate, but she felt a requirement to be ceremonious. She was also getting far-sighted with age.

" 'Virgil Buddy Sandifer Quality Used Autos,' " she read aloud.

"Not the biggest in the metropolitan region," said Buddy, "but the best in the world."

"You are Virgil Buddy Sandifer?"

"One and the same," said Buddy, lowering his eyelids in mock modesty.

"Pleased to meetcha."

"Likewise," Buddy said. "Listen, I don't wanna monopolize you like they say: you got a job to do, and I admire that. You'll be giving me the bum's rush if I don't order soon. Make it a filly minion on toast; no fries or pickles or anything extra." He stopped and gave her a piercing look. "I'm gonna level with you: I ain't hungry."

"Gee," Laverne said tragically, "all we got is the plain burger or the special with chopped lettuce, onion, relish, and tomato; the fish; hotdog with chili; and the American cheese, regular or grilled."

"I'm gonna level with you," Buddy said. "I saw you from the road. I just ate a big chicken dinner. I couldn't swallow another bite." He raised his finger again, and turned on the ignition key with the other hand. This produced a certain suspense. Suddenly he jabbed his foot at the starter, and the engine came to life. He revved it. "I'll put it this way: I'm gonna pick you up when you get off. What time?"

"Eleven," said Laverne. "Make it ten past, 'cause we got to wash our hands and stuff."

"You get out of that cheerleader getup?"

"Not till I get home." She could see he was disappointed; he patronized roadhouses and cocktail lounges. "You mind stopping off?" she asked. "I ain't married or nothing. I got my own little flat. I got some real nice clothes. You wouldn't be embarrassed to be seen with me, I swear. I could go anyplace in the nice clothes I got."

Buddy raised his eyebrows as if in doubt, thrilling Laverne to her boots. He was the first man since Ken to make her feel both continuously useful and temporarily unworthy, that is, with something to aspire to: not daughter, whore, or waitress, all of them roles complete in themselves, dead ends, jobs for hire, really, in which you were paid to perform a function. She had served Ken for love alone, and he had given her nothing except the high sign with his thumb when he wanted her and a quick injection of semen.

Buddy was of the same kidney. He did not ask, demand, or order: he took. He took her home after work, took her to the couch, took off the blue underpants that went with the car-hop outfit, took out a Trojan and then his manhood, and took possession of her. Then he took his departure. He said very little during this series, and like Ken Canning he did not kiss her once.

On Wednesday, her day off, in the late afternoon Laverne put on her best dress of Kelly-green satin, platform shoes, gold pendant earrings, gold bunch-of-grapes brooch, thin gold neck chain bearing a gold cross, a string of white beads half the size of Ping-Pong balls, three rings (zircon, hammered brass, silver-

and-turquoise), and a white picture hat; and carrying a pair of white calf gloves, she appeared at the place of business called VIRGIL BUDDY SANDIFER QUALITY USED AUTOS.

A dark, hairy hook-nosed man in a rumpled brown suit came out of an aisle between the cars, raised his heavy eyebrows, and said: "Yes, ma'am, can I show you something?"

"Can I just look around?" Laverne asked in the beseeching voice she used with salesmen when she was their potential client but never when one of them was hers.

"Our pleasure," said this man, without so much as a glance at her tits or any other portion of her figure. There was not the slightest glint in his eye of guilt or even repugnance. He was either queer or neuter, in either case O.K. by Laverne, who liked fags who admitted it and even for a while in '32 lived with one, which gave them both protective coloration. As to those who had no interest in sex, as opposed to romance, she herself was one of their company.

She stared idly at the nearest machine. She didn't know beans about cars and couldn't drive one, though she had knelt, bent, or spreadeagled herself in every known make and several custom jobs including one with a dashboard of blue mirror. She hated leather seats, sticky under your bare can if beer had been spilled; also joke horns that played the first fucking four notes of "O Susanna."

The salesman went into the little concrete office, and almost immediately thereafter Buddy came out. A gust of wind threatened her picture hat, and the hand she raised to control it hid her face momentarily. With that, and the fine clothes, he showed no sign of recognition until he reached her.

"Well, say," said he, flushing with amazement and stepping back a pace and then walking around her. "Say, you look like a million dollars."

"On the hoof," said she, bending one leg and raising a heel slightly like a model.

"Hmm. You was right. You sure got swell clothes. You are dressed like Mrs. Astor's pet pony." He was impressed; he hadn't smiled once.

She said: "I figured you thought I never wore anything but the car-hop getup."

"Go on," he said, and grinned a little now. "That's bushwa, and you know it."

"Well," she said, "that's what I thought anyway."

"So you come over here to prove your point," Buddy said. "I like that. That takes class, kid, and I like it a whole lot. I like you too. I liked you the other night, but I admit I never knew you was a fashion plate."

Laverne was overjoyed. Her basic mission accomplished, she intended to go off alone to the Idle Hour, the local movie house, where a Barbara Stanwyck picture was playing. She wasn't *after* Buddy any more than she had been after Ken Canning. To a real man you just made yourself available, with the full understanding that at any given time he might well have more important claims to his attention or superior appeals to his taste. You did not lower yourself by entertaining expectations.

"Well, so long then," she said. "Maybe sometime when you haven't eaten you might show up at the drive-in and get one of my slots again, and I'll try to suggest something you would like. I asked Carl—he's the boss—about filly minion that you mentioned the other night, and he said tell everybody the fish is filly of sole though I know it ain't: it's haddock, I think. Actually, everything they serve over there is garbage, if you wanna know. If you saw the kitchen you wouldn't never eat a bite there. *I* don't, that's for sure. We get our food free, but I bring my own sandwiches from home." She stopped. "I'm running off at the mouth."

"No, you ain't," said Buddy with vehemence. "I regard nothing more important than what a man eats. I want good food. I don't care if it's fancy, you know, but it's got to be *good.*"

"You can't believe the signs they put up. You know, they all say 'Good Food.' Whereas I have seldom worked anywhere where that wasn't a damn lie, if you pardon my French." She smiled gently. "I'm like you about food."

Buddy was earnest. "Say, them sandwiches you make for yourself: what kind?"

Laverne giggled; this was getting personal. "Sometimes just cold cuts or cheese or both, but sometimes I get ambitious, you know, like ground ham and I grind cheese *into* it, and also sweet and dill pickles both and olives with pimento, and I mix the mustard in it instead of smearing it on top, and then I put that on whole wheat toast, which I think is better when cold than when hot."

During this account Buddy had by degrees lost his look of self-possession. This sophisticated individual had a true boyish quality which she had never identified in Ken Canning.

"That's the kinda stuff my old lady used to make, real original, like she would make a sandwich that sounds crazy when you hear it but by Jesus it was something to taste. You might laugh at this, but she'd fry bananas and mash 'em all up with bacon and she made her own nutbread and would make a sandwich of two slices of that, toasted, and I tell you it was something you'd lay down and lick the floor for. Though I know it sounds crazy."

"It don't to me," said Laverne, then lied: "I can make nutbread."

"I haven't tasted that in years. My old lady—I mean my mom, not the wife—died when I was a kid."

He had already, in a few brief moments, separated himself forever from Ken Canning, who had had no such vulnerability—except perhaps when lying about having the clap on that last night; if so, it was of another, a bleaker, kind.

Laverne found herself wanting desperately to feed this man. "Look," said she, "I don't want to get out of line, you probably have to eat with your missus and all, but sometime if you might want one of them sandwiches your mama used to make, I could do it. I'd need to know in the morning if it's a workday, so I could make the nutbread before I went on shift at four."

In fact she had never tried much cooking at all, let alone baking. She would buy a loaf of nutbread someplace; anybody could put bananas and bacon in a skillet.

Buddy collected himself from his reverie. "I'll take a raincheck on that." He had his authority back again. "You call in sick to the drive-in tonight. We'll go downtown to the Stardust Roof of the Maumee Hotel, or the Palm Terrace of the Chippewa. We don't wanna waste them ritzy clothes of yours."

"It's my night off, anyway," said Laverne.

"Tell you what you do," Buddy said. "Walk on down the corner, and I'll pick you up there in five minutes."

Laverne said: "I don't want to get you in trouble."

Buddy was offended. "You won't," he said curtly. He turned away, but couldn't let it go at that, and turned back. "You can't. What I say goes. I do what I want, see. It's just good taste like the fella says. That's all."

"Sure," Laverne said softly.

They ended up at the Palm Terrace of the Chippewa, at Laverne's suggestion. Already she had discovered how to influence Buddy without appearing to defy him. She pointed out that the Starlight Roof of the Maumee was neither really starlit nor a roof: it was on the second-to-top floor, and the stars were little light bulbs set in holes in the ceiling.

"You been there, huh?" This seemed to crush him.

215

She resuscitated him. "Cigarette-girl job was open last year, but I got there too late." This was true. Laverne wasn't much of a liar in important matters. What was unpleasant she rather concealed than misrepresented: for example, that she had been in rooms in both Maumee and Chippewa in the practice of her alternative profession.

She had never however been to the Palm Terrace, where the greenery was as false as the celestial display of its competitor. Buddy did not mention this though. He beamed proudly back and forth from her to the palms made of tin or papier-mâché as they entered through a kind of bower of trelliswork intertwined with celluloid bougainvillaea. Laverne had an eye for the phony even when she didn't want to.

Buddy had, already prepared, a dollar bill rolled tight as a cigarette. He took this from his side pocket and poked it at the tuxedoed headwaiter, a pockmarked Dago who stared insolently at Laverne and not at him, thinking he had her number, and but for the need not to embarrass naïve, oblivious Buddy, she might well have sent the greaseball on a flying fuck at the moon.

As it was, the cheap little prick unrolled the bill to see its denomination, and when Buddy said, with the imperiousness of which Laverne could now discern the limits, "Gimme a ringside, fella," he sneered and led them, with the place half empty, to a table just off the passage marked with arrows to the toilets.

If Buddy noticed this, he passed it off, gazing grandly around. Laverne was rapidly coming to an understanding that Buddy was nothing like Ken Canning—unless it was that she had known too little of Ken: this thought startled her. In a decade she had not had a new one pertaining to men. When the orchestra came out and began to tune up, she scanned the musicians, expecting in a mystical fashion to see Ken among them, now no longer the leader but under the domination of another's baton. But he was not there, an absence that did not please her.

The fact was that she was falling for Buddy, who once seated became strangely silent, sipping his B & L and ginger ale and playing with the green swizzle stick fashioned like a palm tree.

"A penny for them," she said, adjusting the little lamp with the orange bulb shaped like a candle flame on the tiny table-top that also held salt-'n'-peppers, sugar bowl, and ketchup bottle, the presence of which interested her as professional waitress: in a swell place every table was equipped with its own, the customers didn't have to ask.

"Oh," said Buddy, "I was just feeling blue." He brightened manfully. "How's your drink?"

She had, at his suggestion, a planter's punch. She swirled it with her own miniature palm tree. "I never saw so much fruit. They must have used a whole can."

"This is the place to go all right. I gotta hand it to you. It's got it all over the Starlight Roof, with that fake ceiling."

"Well, it was just an idea."

Buddy looked shyly at her. "You get around much?"

Laverne was touched by the question, which had no hint of possible disapproval. She had a crazy sense that she could have told him everything and he would have applauded: at this moment, at least.

"I'm not a kid any more. I don't have much time. I work six nights a week."

"Yeah," Buddy said reflectively. "A swell-looking doll like you, dressed like a cheerleader and running sandwiches to a lot of punks. It really ain't right, Laverne." He put his head down. "Listen, I wanna apologize for treating you like a chippie the other night."

Laverne's jaw fell. "My gosh," said she, "I don't know what's got into you. You behaved like a perfect gentleman."

217

Buddy frowned and shook his head. "You're nice. You're a real fine person, Laverne."

Embarrassed by his sincerity, she said: "Maybe that's because you don't know me better."

"I got instincts," said Buddy. "The way you got dressed up and came to the lot. That took a lot of gumption."

"I wanted to see you again," Laverne said tenderly. "And I wanted to look right this time."

Buddy stared wonderingly at her. "How'd you know I wouldn't just rape you again?"

"Well, my gosh." She put her hand on his wristwatch. "You are just about the funniest fella I know. Rape. Well"— she moved her fingers onto his—"I don't know where you got that idea. You didn't force me, you know."

"I didn't?"

They stared at each other through the dim orange light and then simultaneously broke into grins, Laverne's an instant earlier.

"Gee," she said, "if I thought that, you didn't look worried when I showed up on the lot."

"I was putting up a front," said Buddy. "You gotta do that in my business."

"Are you kidding? You gotta do it everywhere in life! They'll get you otherwise and put the screws to you. You can't trust most people further than you can throw them."

At last he actively accepted her fingers in his. "I like the way you handle yourself."

"Oh sure," said Laverne. "With what I got and a nickel you can get a cuppa coffee."

"Naw, I mean it. You're twenty-four carat."

They had a couple more rounds of drinks, Laverne switching from planter's punch to Buddy's B & L because all that fruit juice gave you acid, and then, deciding they weren't all that hungry, had club sandwiches, which were however enormous and garnished with bread-and-butter pickles, potato chips, a half of deviled egg, and a rosebud radish. The waiter, in his red monkey jacket and black bow tie, gave Laverne a wink at one point: colleagues could always smell you out no matter how you were dressed.

Then, coming from the toilet, after her third drink, she encountered the slimy maître-d', who went over her again with his dirty eyes, then speaking sotto voce from the corner of his mouth, said: "You wanna gimme a number? I get a lot of calls."

"Excuse me?" asked Laverne, arching one of the painted brows she had just refreshed at the dressing table in the can, presided over by a motherly old Negress, to whom she had given a dime. Knowing gratuities from the other side of the fence, she always tipped well.

"Come off your high horse, Toots," this bastard whispered. "I seen all kinds." Meanwhile he was surveying the room with his sneer.

Laverne smiled sweetly and said: "Go piss up a rope, you cheap wop."

He nodded politely. "Cocklicker."

She graciously inclined her head. "You wasn't born: your mother shit you on a rock and the sun hatched you." She returned to the table, using the most respectable walk. Nevertheless, some baldheaded fart distracted his horsefaced wife with a finger at the band, and quickly fucked Laverne with eyes swimming in booze.

"Christ, I missed you, honey," Buddy said with tremendous feeling, and now he took her hand. He hadn't leered at her tits or ass all evening. When they finally danced, she could feel his bone-on, but it nestled nicely against her belly and he didn't grind it nastily into her crotch. His face against her cheek was smooth as a baby's bottom and smelling not of crappy barber's bay rum but some classy aftershave.

"Say, what's that dandy lotion you use?" she asked once between numbers.

"You like it? It's Ed Py-naud." He sniffed at her. "What you use? Either Evening in Paris or Chanel Number Five, right?"

The contrast of Buddy's all-knowing air and her practice of knowing nothing made her heart ache. She adored this strong but helpless man, and could supply all his needs.

"You sure came close," she said. "It's Apple Blossom cologne. Anything else gives me sinus."

Then the band played "Always," and Buddy breathed the lyrics into her ear, and added the sentiments Laverne quoted to him in a somewhat altered version six months later as they lay in the bed from which he would arise and go home to his family: "I want to be with you always, baby, and have a whole lifetime."

Her immediate reaction was to nuzzle his neck. The expression of love was however soon checked by the appearance of another tuxedoed functionary, this one a gorilla with a blue jaw, who tapped Buddy's shoulder and warned him against dance-floor intimacies. Laverne knew this to be the work of the maître-d', and she would have given the bouncer at least some lip and maybe, if pressed, a platform shoe in the jewels; but nodding at the ape, Buddy obediently separated himself from her.

"That makes sense," he solemnly assured her. "This ain't no taxi-dance joint. I'm going down and get us a room."

"Why? That's awful expensive, Bud, when my place is sitting there empty."

"No," said Buddy. "I want it different this time than the other night. I want to make it up to you."

So he paid the check, which she could see was almost ten bucks, and added a tip of a dollar, and they left, her head high as they passed the maître-d's station, and went downstairs, where she stood near the newsstand while he signed in and collected a bellhop and vanished into the elevator.

Soon he was back, saying: "I signed Mr. and Mrs. Sandifer, not Smith," his face shining like a kid's. "I wanted you to know that."

Laverne would have cried did not her practical side come into play. "Buddy," she chided him, "you sure throw the money away. You should of got a single and sneaked me in."

"Laverne," said Buddy, gripping her hand, "I never will be cheap when it comes to you."

In the room he took her again and again, with only her pants off and her best green dress being crumpled and maybe stained also, and the least she could do was pretend to come even oftener than he, because if you found a good man you should make him feel able and give him a home, because you were stronger than he and could take more punishment and would last longer, whereas his assertions were short-lived and his fragility basic, not only physically but morally as well: that Buddy believed he was celebrating her by paying too much for the room was an example in point. A sense of pathos informed her love for him. She never let on that often she squeezed him as if he were the biggest dollbaby in the world, the subject of a persistent dream of her girlhood.

Buddy himself had writhed out of his own clothes by degrees until he wore only an undershirt and black-clocked tan lisle socks supported by dark-blue garters. Now he suddenly arose and climbed into his Jockey shorts, hand-ladling his damp manhood into the pouch. He had an adorable little soft potbelly and white banty legs that would break your heart.

"You going for cigarettes or something, Bud?"

"I got to get home, Laverne," he said piously, climbing into the first leg of his chalk-stripe pants and then hopping about on one foot to retain his balance.

"Huh?"

He got his other leg through and began to button his fly. "Listen, kid," he said, "I been thinking. What rent you pay for that place of yours?"

"What'd you say, Bud?"

"Rent," said he. "Listen, I'm doing all right at the lot this year, and I can swing it. I wanna pay that rent of yours, so I got some stake in your place, see. I want to make it a home for me and you so I can come there and you make meals, see, and we get a family going."

Laverne bitterly hid her eyes in both hands. "What you want with another one?"

He remained oblivious and found his shirt on the floor. She peeped and saw him at the dresser, knotting his tie.

"You mean it? You going home now, Buddy Sandifer?"

He fastened his tie pin. "I got to," he answered, still insensitive.

"Well," said she, "lotsa luck, huh? I don't wanna see you any more."

He whirled and came to the bedside. "What kinda talk is that for Jesus sake?"

"We ain't staying here all night?"

"Christ almighty, Laverne." He knelt on the bed. "How can I do that? I said I had to keep up a front, didn't I?" He leaned over and massaged her left breast, which had not been bared and in which she had no special sensation.

"Lay off," she said and rolled away.

"Be fair," Buddy beseeched. "I never said we would stay all night. I got to think of my boy." He patted her bare rump.

She rolled back and opened her eyes. "You got kids?"

"One only. He's a boy. He's a fine boy, real clean-cut. I like him. We are real pals. If it was just her, I'd stay, I swear. I despise her, but I got to think of Ralph. How'd it look to him? There ain't no lodge meeting where you'd stay out till next morning, is there? Come on, baby, try to see it my way."

Laverne asked: "How old's the boy?"

"Fourteen going on fifteen," said Buddy with a rising inflection.

She winced. "You been married since the Year One."

"Yeah." Buddy looked miserably at the pillow.

Laverne struggled up, found her step-ins where he had hurled them, and smoothed out her dress, remembering the deposit of semen at her bellybutton only when it soaked through the slip and proceeded to darken the green satin before her eyes. Sponging it with a wet towel would leave a water ring. If she couldn't brush it away when dry she would call it milk to the cleaner, who would know better.

She looked in the dresser mirror and poked her hair. Buddy rose and came behind her. He laid his head over her shoulder.

"I'm gonna work it out, kid. I ain't ever going to let you go. I'm crazy about you."

Laverne really couldn't oppose such an argument, being likewise nuts about Buddy and having anyway noplace to go except the drive-in or the streets, and next day he did begin to pay her rent and not long afterward decided she must be there whenever he needed her and not hopping sandwiches for punks, so he put her on a salary of twenty-five per, which he said he could enter in his business books as part of overhead, accounting fees or something, and considering the rent was an extra and he brought her lots of gifts besides, she was way ahead of what she would have earned at the drive-in and almost even with what she would have made hustling, given the wear and tear of clothes and shoes and kickbacks to bartenders, taxi drivers, and other free-lance pimps and bribes to cops.

And she didn't mind staying home most of the time in negligee and mules, reading *True Story* and *Modern Romances* and listening to *When a Girl Marries* and *Vic and*

Sade in the afternoon and in the evening *Lum and Abner,* who reminded her of her own hick origins.

Month after month Buddy ate her meals and took her body, then dressed and went home. She had turned out to be a good cook who from the beginning could follow any recipe and soon began to invent dishes of her own, like chopped onions in mashed Idaho potatoes, which she would then stuff back into their skins and top with Parmesan cheese and brown under the broiler. Buddy could wolf down four of these at one sitting. His little potbelly grew ever plumper, and beneath it his dick was always hard, and he took her with so much appreciation that occasionally, with an exquisitely sweet sense of his never-surfeited hunger for all that she provided, she would almost reach the threshold of a genuine climax of her own but of course always restrained herself so as not to defile the purity of her part in what they had together and so pollute their home.

Nevertheless he would always dress and go to the other one, and it couldn't be because of his wife, who he assured her mocked and reviled him incessantly. It was his son who brought him home, and therefore Laverne, who loved Buddy and was really indifferent to Naomi, with a corrosive passion hated Ralph, or rather the idea of Ralph, whom she had never seen even in a snapshot.

This little punk was the only enemy she had in the world, and sometimes when paring apples to go in her own version of chicken à la king, for which Buddy was crazy, she entertained herself with a fantasy in which she had the knife at Ralph's neck. At times the intensity of her hatred caused Laverne to collapse in tears, because for all the violence of her language to strangers who acted badly, she couldn't bear even to kill a mouse she once found in her bathtub: she filled the tub with lukewarm water, in which the tiny beast swam until the level reached the rim and he scrambled out, going down the pipe and into the floor.

And she no longer could relieve herself at the confessional, to which she no longer went, having at last become an adulteress because she did it, or let Buddy do it, for love, which constituted a sin that, being mortal, must be reported.

In the beginning Buddy talked of leaving home when the time was ripe. He gave no details, and Laverne would be the last to ask for them. But he had himself announced the general aim: he wanted to marry her. This had at first taken Laverne by surprise. She had never associated the fact of marriage with the idea of love: her old man had regularly beat up her mother, and if a client spoke of his wife it was usually to snarl or whine or, sometimes, in a self-hating way, to boast that she was too fine to go down on him, which was why he had to buy this service.

"But, Buddy," she had said at the outset, "I'll be your girl for always and cook for you and take care of you whenever you want. You got your obligations. Families make the world go round."

"But it don't make sense, Laverne," said he, pounding on the mattress, "with you here and me there and both of us dying to be together. It ain't right."

"You said that about me working in the drive-in." She smiled at him and put a loving hand on the bulge of the tum-tum she loved to fill.

"I sure did, and I got you out of there, right? Now I got to get *me* out of slavery."

Trouble was, Buddy had talked too much and too well, and soon he introduced the grand slam: he not only wanted her to be his wife, but he wanted a kid. Laverne was devastated by this information.

"I'm Catholic, Buddy," said she. "I might not work at it,

but I am. So if you talk like that, you got to be serious. If I start to bring a life in the world, I'm gonna go all the way. I ain't going to have it scraped out. I won't be a murderess."

"Baby, I'm dying of sincerity." To prove this Buddy did the unprecedented: he took her hand, which he had previously moved down from his belly, off his throbbing dong. Then he put the fingers to his lips. "I swear by God almighty." This brought tears to her eyes. She knew he was the soul of virtue, but had not been aware of this deep religious feeling at his core. "When you love somebody—" Then he broke down and they clutched each other and wept before heaven, and Laverne had a shuddering climax in the realm of pure spirit.

So this seemed to be settled, but then for more than a month Buddy never mentioned the subject, which was peculiar in that it had been his idea, and Laverne, though thinking of nothing else since, did not feel it was her place to take the initiative, being no ballbreaker. And it was Buddy, not she, who was scrupulous about contraception; he bought rubbers by the dozen and then switched to fishskins, which allowed more sensitivity but still not enough to appease his hunger for intimacy, and finally he suggested she go and get herself a diaphragm.

"I'm beginning to hate all kinds of cundrums," he said.

"Bud, I thought," Laverne said reluctantly, her eyes watering, "what I thought was we wouldn't be needing protection the rest of our life, you know."

"Let's hope not," Buddy said, looking between his legs, and then he got the point and leaned over and gently kissed her eyes and nose. "I'm trying to work it out, see, but I tell you it ain't easy. I ought to stay in this town. Maybe I could sell my business, but then even if I got a nice price I would have to pay off the bank loan and then go someplace else and get started all over, and have to borrow money again, which would be tough in a place I ain't known. Besides, you build up what they call good will when you stay in one spot for years. True, you make a few enemies with deals that go sour, but even some of them come back again in a few years. Thing is, they *know* you, which makes people feel comfortable even when they hate your guts."

One of the reasons Laverne loved Buddy was for his professional know-how. He really knew what he was doing, like Ken Canning with the sax and clarinet, and it was her assumption that most men did not, this bias based on her experience as waitress, witnessing the rotten food forked up with relish, and as prostitute dealing with clients who took off pressed pants over polished shoes to expose yellowed underwear.

"But say I get divorced," he went on, "Naomi's going to stay where she is. She'll get the house and custody of Ralph, and this is a small town: I'd be running into both of them all the time, which I wouldn't mind that much with her, but it'd be tough with the boy. He looks up to me."

"Sure," Laverne said sadly.

"See," said Buddy, "*she'd* have to divorce *me*. I ain't got no grounds against her. Christ, she's home all the time except maybe once a week she rides the bus downtown to the department stores, where she usually don't buy anything even. And she's always in a good mood, does anything I tell her to."

Laverne thought of something important: "But you said she hates your guts, Bud."

Buddy nodded vigorously. "Damn right. But it's hard to put in words, Laverne. Maybe it ain't hate. She just don't care, which is worse than hate. She don't really listen when you talk. She don't notice what matters to you. She will serve food you always despised and call it your favorite." He winced and rubbed his forehead. "I know it don't sound that bad, but all things that matter can't be explained, like why you like some smells and can't stand others and why women are scared of mice and why you get a funny chill up your back if a piece

227

of metal squeaks across concrete, see?" He peered at her with mean eyes. "One man's meat can be another man's poison like the fella says, and you can't make sense out of it. . . . She won't argue, you can't get a rise outa her. Now you and me haven't come to words, but I figure one could get under the skin of the other pretty easy if you wanted to, and I know I wouldn't wanna tangle with you, Laverne."

"Aw, Buddy," she chided him lovingly.

"No, we could, I figure, and that's the way it oughta be. But she's weird. She gives me the creeps, if you want to know. I got the definite feeling she could catch us in bed together and would apologize and leave the room."

"If that's right," said Laverne, "it's weird all right." She said that to be in sympathy with Buddy, who obviously regarded sexual infidelity as a maximum crime, straitlaced as he was. Speaking for herself, loving him madly, she might be happy to know he was getting outside nookie and thus giving her a rest. For the moment, however, she had to put up with him in bed so that he would be with her for the important things like eating her meals and judging her home-decorating ideas and talking about his business, and just *being* there, relaxing with his shoes off, naked under the bathrobe she bought him, belching after a good feed, there on her couch with the new flowered slipcover he thought was real good taste, laughing like a kid at radio comedy, Rochester giving the works to Jack Benny, Bob Hope and Professor Colonna, and the rest.

But he had a problem. "Gee, Bud, it's tough, but you'll work it out. Far be it from me to put pressure on you."

He would cheer up. "You're a sweet patootie. Hey, you know what, I'm hot for your body."

But after months of this Laverne's personality began to darken around the edges like a head of lettuce kept too long in the hydrator. Physically she was putting on weight, her

228

bazooms and behind sagging with it, and in a brassiere and girdle her flesh puffed over straps and waistband. She got no exercise, and being around the flat all day she tended to eat a lot of candy. Unless Buddy showed up for a meal she ate no real food at all, just nibbled on cheese crackers, Hostess devil's-food cupcakes, salted peanuts, and nickel blueberry pies, washing them down with Orange Crush or heavily sugared iced tea when summer came.

The top-floor flat was like a Tappan oven when the sun baked the roof all day, and she cooked within, along with the tuna-and-noodle casseroles she made for Buddy in the smaller model. She took to going about in her kimono, bare-ass underneath, which made him all the hornier on his visits and also sparkled the eyes of the little piss-willie who delivered groceries and whom she was idly amused to heat up, because already at fourteen or fifteen he was the characterless sort of jerk that some men took a couple more years to become, thinking only of dumping their loads.

Having so much time on her hands, Laverne thought about the entire male race and believed she would have had a lot more respect for them if they stayed permanently hard and did not after such a temporary friction spill and go limp.

They came and went, is what they did, all of them, and Buddy began to seem, as Ken Canning had in his time, no exception to the rule. There was one universal standard of prostitution: for the stated fee, you got the customer off, by whatever means. If he shot his wad while putting on the rubber, as some did, you had no further responsibility without further negotiation.

Laverne had wanted to be Buddy's slave and not another master like Naomi. She despised men she could dominate, but began to think there was no other kind. There might even be something radically wrong with males, with sex organs hanging out where they could be hurt accidentally. Buddy once crossed his legs while sitting on her couch and yelped in pain: his Jockey shorts had entangled his balls. Sometimes he went at it so ardently in bed that, despite the rubber, the head of his little dummy was chafed and the roll of his foreskin stayed purple for hours and if unfurled was striped in pink, orange, and ruby red, and had to be doused with Mexican Heat Powder.

Laverne began to count how long he would go without mentioning his hopeless marriage unless reminded. She always gave up before he did. The one thing in which a man had more endurance than a woman was in not defining himself. By August she had heard the same statements so often that they could have switched roles in the dialogue, with her doing his lines to a T. Her own were no longer so tolerant, so agreeable, as of yore, and what she began to resent most about him was not his doing nothing about a divorce, but rather his causing her to turn bitchy; as with Ken Canning, she despised not his lying but his assumption that she could not bear the truth.

Why were men such cowards? The only exception she knew was Jesus Christ, who never had sex and stuck by his principles and was nailed to the Cross for it. In August she began to go to Mass and take communion again for the first time in years, but it seemed the first time ever, because she had had to live a lot to taste the Flesh and Blood in the bread and wine, to accept a lot of dicks and serve a lot of hamburgers before seeing the Light in which human weakness cast no shadow.

Yet she continued, for old times' sake, in compassion and without hope, to give Buddy a chance to be more than a man. She still loved him, though gradually this love had turned from the particular, earthly sort to that with which he was regarded by his heavenly Father. By September she would not have married him had he been free, but being human she was not above the claims of spite, which alone had delayed for some days the realization of her intent to go downtown to the old red-brick convent near the railroad station and find out whether it was too late to become a novice in the Sisters of Charity.

The new delivery boy's identification of himself as Buddy's son was both a shock and a sign. It was as if God had Himself got fed up with the suspense. Laverne took a long bubble bath and then put on her best outfit: the green satin dress and the white picture hat. Going out into the yard, she saw the stout couple on the porch. They peered disapprovingly at her. They had seen Buddy come and go for half a year.

She sniffed at the piggish pair and said: "Anybody comes looking for me, tell 'em I have went downtown on the bus, willya?"

The old battleax smirked silently, but the man said: "Yes, ma'am." If he had been there alone he would have been eying her jugs in that uplift that was fastened on the last hook and yet still cut her back. But it was essential that neither those nor her behind encased in the armor of two-way stretch would wobble. She would look like a lady when she went to marry Christ.

chapter 12

ALONG WITH Buddy's saucer containing two preserved kumquats, and Naomi's pineapple slice, the moon-faced waiter brought two fortune cookies.

Taking one and turning it idly in the light of the pagoda-shaped table lamp, Naomi asked: "Did you ever know anyone who actually ate these?"

This was typical of her conversational contribution.

Buddy smiled feebly. "Ever hear the one about the guy who opened it and found a slip that said, 'Help, I'm being held prisoner in a Chinese bakery'?"

Gravely, Naomi said: "Yes, I have."

His smile strengthened with wryness. "It's a pretty old turkey, I guess. Time I was getting a new one."

"I wonder," said Naomi, "if the Chinese have their own form of wit."

"They're sure laughing over there," said Buddy, nodding at a tableful of Orientals across the room.

"There are people who will roar when somebody slips on a

banana peel." Naomi seemed to be saying this to herself while looking at the teapot.

"Don't they though." Buddy had eaten his moo goo gai pan in a state of numbness. He could not endure Naomi's presence, but neither could he depict in mind the eternal silence into which he had arranged to send her. It had been a mistake not to bring Ralph along: he would have relieved the situation by trying to use chopsticks and dropping food in his lap.

Ralph had something of the natural clown in him, which he did not get from either of them. When he was younger he stepped in dogshit a lot, and on the first day of the first grade he sat on his schoolbag, crushing the banana in the outside pocket thereof. Once when visiting some second cousin of Naomi's who owned a farm, Ralph walked through a cowpie. Another time, leaning over to see a particular goldfish, he lost his balance and stepped into the little ornamental pond made by a neighbor from a discarded bathtub.

Buddy was startled from his reverie by the brutal sound of Naomi's crushing her fortune cookie. She put the tiny slip of paper under the pagoda lamp and squinted, moving her head back to lengthen the focal range. She proceeded to search her purse.

"It seems I did not bring my reading glasses."

Buddy put out his hand.

"How kind," said Naomi, and gave him her fortune.

He put it under the lamp and read: "Confucius say, He who—" The rest was totally illegible. For an instant of terror Buddy thought his eyes, which had always been perfect, were at fault, but reason prevailed and he saw that the printing ink had run, the letters fusing into a continuous smear.

He explained and said: "Take mine."

"No thank you," said Naomi. "That's the kind of fortune I prefer." She seized the slip and dropped it in her purse. "They're usually so silly."

"They're supposed to be," said Buddy, succeeding in cracking his own cookie into two neat parts, the way he always tried, hating the mess; took the slip out; and cautiously read it first to himself. Then aloud: "See: 'He who eats soup with chopsticks never gets stains on tie.' "

Naomi began to snicker, then went into a hearty if not coarse laugh.

"Hmm," murmured Buddy. It was one of her tricks never to respond predictably to humor. He was tired of cooperating now, at the eleventh hour, and kept a straight face.

"There's a moral there, if you examine it," said she. "It's not silly at all. I withdraw my statement."

Buddy suddenly inhaled a whiff of freedom. She would be gone soon, taking with her his motive for years of diplomacy. And if he had had to boil down into one his reasons for wanting her dead, it would be: because of the way she talks.

"Why," he asked, throwing caution to the winds at last, "can't you say just: 'I take it back.' Why do you always talk in that phony way? You ain't got no more education than me, and you know it, so why can't you talk like a normal person?"

Naomi kept her aplomb though the attack was without precedent. "I apologize, Buddy. It was simply the way it came out, I assure you. It wasn't planned."

Buddy felt warm as well as damp around the collar. He put a finger there to confirm the feeling. He also felt giddy, and his feet tingled. "I think," he said recklessly, "you are making fun of me. And furthermore, you been doing it for years."

"I assure you that comes as a complete surprise," said she.

"Oh yeah?" said Buddy, snarling now. "Well, I'm onto you. You think I'm garbage."

Naomi's forehead disappeared into her hat, which she wore low anyway, old-lady style, the veil swept back over the crown.

"You figured," said Buddy, "that I was too dumb to figure that out."

She shook her head. "No, Buddy, I certainly wouldn't ever call you stupid. I don't know why you're saying this, unless you were unsettled by that morbid atmosphere at Leo's. I have often worried about all the responsibilities you have. When Leo returns to normal, and I'm sure he will, why don't you take a vacation?"

She had thrown Buddy for a loss. "What, what?" he cried.

"A weekend in Atlantic City might do you a world of good, or better yet, Tampa, Florida."

Buddy had never traveled anywhere. He cited the suggestion as another example of her incessant disparagement of him. "You know I can't swim."

Naomi smiled sanctimoniously. "You can sit on the warm sand and watch the bathing beauties."

He was genuinely shocked. "How dare you say that to me?"

Naomi's smile stayed in place while her head turned at an angle. "That's harmless enough."

"You calling me a sex fiend?" He turned to see whether the Chinese had overheard him, but they were greedily chopsticking rice into their mouths from little bowls held just under the chin.

Naomi got her cigarettes from the purse. Over the years her eyes seemed to move closer to her nose and the diameter of her nostrils had diminished. Her features were gathering together into one central vertical line. But the phenomenon was short-lived; when the cigarette was lighted they came back to normal.

Buddy was seeing things. He gulped a mouthful of cold tea from the handleless cup and got more than one bitter leaf.

He must not allow his attack to falter. "Next you'll say I been running around, is that it? You sit home there all the time, nursing a grudge. I'm onto you, though." He tapped his temple. "I'm not as dumb as you think."

Naomi was reluctant to part with the lungful of smoke she

235

had inhaled. Little wisps lurked from time to time at the corners of her mouth and finally a slow and thin blue stream emerged from her nose.

She said: "I really am convinced the situation calls for a change of scenery. Leo can manage for a week or so on his own."

Buddy could not help going on the defensive. "I'm letting Leo go, for your information. He's lost his marbles completely. He shot his parrot and he sold all his furniture. I don't even want him on the lot when I'm there, let alone behind my back. He turned out to be some kind of mama's boy." He drew back in his chair. "I got nobody to trust, let me tell you. I even caught Ralph the other night, busting some store window and making his getaway. Haha! How about that? Little smart aleck. He'll end up in reform school one of these days. That's how Baby Face Nelson started, huh?"

Naomi looked amazed, but not, as it turned out, at the information. "This exaggeration is something quite new, Buddy. And your face is flushed. Do you feel all right?"

Again she had nailed him. In fact he had a terrible heartburn. He put a hand on the resilient flesh that covered his solar plexus and gulped. The aftertaste, though he had not belched, was like the smell of smoldering celluloid. The slimy chicken fragments in the moo goo gai pan had looked weird, too white, as he chased them through the bean pods, like pieces left over from making Frankenstein.

"I'm fit as a fiddle," he however said defiantly, his eyes protruding from the effort required. He tried to relieve the pressure with a bitter joke. "But they should change the name to Ptomaine Terrace."

Rejecting as always his suggestion that she go whole hog for once, Naomi had had her usual four-course special with chop suey, into which she stirred the ball of gummy rice molded in an ice cream dipper and then had eaten it with dedication.

236

Buddy on the other hand had tried to stimulate his nonexistent appetite by resorting to the tactic, typical of his style and also notoriously effective sometimes in Chinese restaurants, of ordering a profusion of dishes: three oval platters flanked his plate. Along with the moo goo had come sweet and sour pork, and a heaped mélange of those chewy little vegetables you never saw anywhere else. The result was the reverse of what he expected: he was nauseated by the presence of so much food and merely tasted here and there. The inscrutable waiter took it all away at length, no doubt to return it to the pot.

Yet Buddy's stomach burned as if he had swallowed gluttonously. His fingers had gone cold from the terminal joints to the tips, and an excruciating cramp had manifested itself in his right thigh.

Seeing Naomi's dead-white face, framed in dead black and exuding smoke from its orifices like an inanimate incense burner, he trembled with the sudden apprehension that she had poisoned him, deftly dosed the teapot while he was looking elsewhere. One, the tea tasted excessively bitter; two, she avoided it and drank ice water; three, reaching for the tiny saucer of mustard, she had overturned his water glass, which the negligent and, now that he thought of him, treacherous-looking waiter had not refilled. Thus he had no means with which to dilute the venom.

He pried himself from the narrow booth, a constricted situation that now also seemed suspicious, and went towards the men's room, to reach which at Wong's Gardens you had to use the same corridor as the laden waiters and at one point to pass through an edge of the kitchen with its horde of sweating glossy-black heads, fanatically barking at one another in a heathen tongue and bobbing through clouds of steam.

The toilet was closet-sized. To close its door he had to elevate a buttock over the washbasin. There was just the regular sit-down can, no urinal, and Buddy leaned over it, his

hand on the wall above covering the legend saying, SOME COME
HERE TO SIT AND THINK, SOME TO SHIT AND STINK, written
purplish with an indelible pencil dipped in water. Whoever
had been there last had taken the second alternative and was
well remembered for it. Buddy had no trouble in bringing up
the small supper he had eaten.

Contrary to standard opinion, he felt no better for it. He
needed water, but not from the basin, which was glazed with
a lavender slime, suggesting that the poet and recent defe-
cator were one and the same, a degraded braggart, unless, as
was too possible, the sink had not been scoured since the
pencil point had been dampened in it weeks before.

Buddy lurched through the Asiatic hell of the kitchen,
reached the table, and seized Naomi's water glass, which had
been refilled though his own was yet empty. In his first
draught he got an ice cube, hurting his teeth with chill. He
spat it back. The water had a pronounced chemical taste, but
she would not have doped what she herself drank.

He took a grip on himself and remembered: "They get city
water here. It's full of chlorine. Fooey."

"That is why," said Naomi, "I never drink the tea, which
tastes even worse."

Buddy made himself S-shaped and reclaimed his seat.
"What a dump this has got to be, Kee-rist."

Naomi crushed out the cigarette in her unused teacup,
though a Bakelite ashtray, with slotted book of paper
matches, lay nearby. Buddy grinned in a kind of general
chagrin.

Naomi said: "I'm delighted to see you're feeling better.
That's the old happy-go-lucky Buddy I have always known."

He squinted. "By God," he said, "you never let up, do
you?" But as usual he was the prisoner of her assumptions
about him, and even shrugged happy-go-luckily and said:
"But I got to hand it to you, Nay."

"Well thank you, Buddy."

"I mean it. You can't be fazed. You live like you're all alone in the world."

"That's an interesting concept."

"No," said Buddy, "in fact it ain't. And it ain't living, either, for my money." There, it was out at last, horrifying but also relieving him strangely.

"But it's odd," said Naomi. "Because in addition to you and Ralph I have a sister, two aunts, one uncle, and a number of cousins."

"I didn't mean being alone in that way. It's your personality."

She laughed merrily. "I suppose I'm stuck with that."

"No," Buddy said again. "I am."

With a distressed look she reached across the table and scraped thin, spidery fingers across the back of Buddy's hand. "Oh, Buddy, you shouldn't ever feel that sort of burden."

"You're mocking me, you know that?" He wanted to snatch his hand away from under that claw, but lacked the will.

"I do wish you would consider taking that vacation I suggested."

Buddy said fearfully: "I don't want your pity."

Naomi brought her fingers back and put one into her cheek. "I think I have got it," she said with spirit. "Why don't you get yourself a girl?" Under the old-lady hat her face was radiant as a child's.

Buddy gripped the edge of the table with both thumbs, to keep from rising on the thrill that swooped up from the small of his back.

"Pardon me?"

"I'm no good with those old saws," said Naomi. "How does that one go, better a goat than a sheep, or whatever?" She smiled expectantly.

Astounding himself, he understood what she was saying and seized the initiative. "You make a lot of enemies in the used-car business. People will accuse you of anything if they think they got gypped. Other day, some nut even tried to murder me." That was Ballbacher. "I could of had him put away, but not me."

"Goodness, I think you probably should have."

"Not me," Buddy repeated, with even greater conviction. "I consider the source." He made a sitting swagger. "Buddy Sandifer don't run from just anybody who comes down the pike."

While Naomi looked sympathetic, Buddy said: "I guess you heard a pack of lies. But do somebody a favor, they take it as their due and never make a peep. Why, just today I gave a preacher a real good deal. But you never get thanked for that in this life." The philosophical observation gave him the tragic strength to ask: "Whajoo hear about me? Some yellow-belly sapsucker send you a poison-pen letter? Well, that won't curdle my milk. I had bum raps before. Or maybe Gladys had her yap open: a lot of filth pours outa that sewer."

Buddy deplored the loose way Naomi's sister talked in front of Ralph, saying "goddam," "crap," and "I laughed so hard my pants would never dry." She was the kind of woman he most despised: the kind who thought she was lively. She had big legs and a flat chest, piss-colored hair and dirty freckles. On her overnight visits she refused to dislocate Ralph from his room and slept on the living-room sofa. Buddy had come upon her in various stages of undress throughout the years and was about as thrilled as if he had seen Leo in BVD's.

It occurred to him, for the first time, that she may have been hot for him for eons, purposely exposing herself in slip, shimmy, bath towel, but finally gave up and was now getting the knife in out of spite.

"That's ironic," said Naomi. "Gladys is your staunch defender. More than once she has said she could not imagine you with a woman."

"That could be taken two ways," Buddy said instantly. "But wait a minute—how come she's got her nose in this at all?"

"It seems that Vern is involved with a woman on his route."

"That *mailman?*" Buddy's brother-in-law was a little twerp who wouldn't say shit if he had a mouthful. "Aw, she must be talking through her hat. Some housewife probably gave him a cuppa coffee and a fresh cruller. My mother used to do that all the time."

Naomi shook her head. "He has asked for a divorce."

"I'll be good goddam."

"His friend is a widow, and she is pregnant."

Buddy felt personally violated. "You mean it?"

"Gladys has flatly refused."

"Good!" Buddy said spitefully. "He's a skunk, and probably a fool too: the woman's playing him for a sucker."

"Well, we don't know that. She may be sincerely in love."

"Oh, sure," said Buddy, "and the moon is made of cheese. Listen, she plays around with a respectable married man, she can take the consequences. As for that Vern Bursaw, I never trusted him from the word 'go.' Civil Service bum! I got to pay his salary, you know."

"Her name," said Naomi, "is Mary Wentworth. She lives over there but drives here every day to work in the bank."

Granite-faced, Buddy said: "I sold her the car."

Naomi sniffed in wonder. "Isn't it a small world."

"Gladys never knew that, I guess." When Naomi failed to respond, Buddy suddenly reversed his previous position, with the idea that if Gladys did know that and more, and had told her sister, he would show least guilt by praising Mary in a lofty manner. "That's a different kettle of fish, then. It's still as wrong as can be, but Mary Wentworth had a lot of trouble, her husband dying so sudden. He was a friend of mine, see, and I gave her a nice deal out of sympathy. I saw her at the bank just this morning. She's a hard worker and she's got some sense in her head. Maybe I could give her a word."

Naomi however looked negative. "Oh, I don't think that's expected of you, Buddy."

"You know what, Nay: if I didn't know you better I'd say you don't seem to want to keep those folks together."

Naomi opened her purse and got out a pack of Twenty Grands. "Why should I?"

Buddy realized this was more than they had talked, at one time, in years.

"Well, knock me over with a feather."

She said mildly: "I could never understand the attraction there."

"I figure she thought he was steady. Which turned out to be a laugh."

Naomi widened her eyes. "I mean, what he saw in Gladys."

Buddy did not hear this immediately, thinking as he was, from his experience of lechery, that the first element was access, of time and then of place; Mary would be at the bank during both daily deliveries made by Vern. So they had to meet at night, Saturday afternoon, or on Sunday, none of them times when a mailman worked unless he was on special delivery. Whereas it was quite reasonable that a used-car dealer might have professional appointments at hours when customers were free of their own vocational duties. Buddy had not gone into the business for that reason, but it was true that in another calling he could not have got so much cunt with impunity—nor could he have done so if he had had another wife than Naomi.

In this light, then, she could be considered indispensable. The recognition disturbed him to the degree that he allowed her statement to travel from his neutral eardrums to his critical brain.

"What's that you say? Christ, blood is thicker than water. You ought to stick up for your own, Nay."

"Why should I?" she asked again.

After all these years he had only now discovered she had no principles. "That's basic. You just do it, for pity's sake."

"Gladys," said Naomi, making a sanctimonious mouth, "is absolutely insensitive to other people. Basically she's always remained a little girl. I grant you Vern is coarse, but that is all the more evidence that he needs a woman and not a child."

"So what's the gist of this, then?" he asked. "You want him to go off with Mary Wentworth?"

"Not at all." She still held her cigarette unlighted. "My point is simply that Gladys should not oppose him if he wants a divorce."

"That don't make sense. If he gets a divorce he'll go with Mary. Where's your logic, Nay?" Buddy didn't really give a hoot in hell what the Bursaws did, or Mary Wentworth for that matter, yet he found himself enjoying this discussion. It was a novelty for Naomi to take a stand on anything, and in all these years he had never heard her say anything meaningful about her sister. Now it appeared that she had, for her, strong feelings in this regard. Perhaps she had them in other areas as well. It was also a novelty for him to consider that other people, especially women, had ideas and inclinations that they might conceal for ages before suddenly exposing them. Leo's transformation, for example, had taken him utterly by surprise. Now it turned out that he had underestimated Vern Bursaw. Mary was no Miss Roundheels: Buddy had had virtually to rape her the first time. Unless, on the basis of her experience with *him*, she had changed. The thought gave him no satisfaction; he had no respect for naturally loose women like Grace Plum.

Naomi was pointing the Twenty Grand at him. Buddy, who often used his own finger as a kind of weapon, squirmed when under somebody else's muzzle. He hailed a passing Chinese and asked for the check. It was not his waiter, and the request was taken stolidly.

"Suppose," Naomi said, "that Gladys persists."

"O.K., I'm supposing."

"Two possibilities. One, forced to live with someone he wants to leave, he hates her for the rest of their lives. Two, perhaps this whole thing is a test." Naomi made a squinting, sinister smile. "Yes, that has occurred to me."

Buddy was at sea. To cover up, he said: "Aw . . ."

"That Vern really wants her to refuse."

"This thing is getting pretty involved," said Buddy. "You're batting your brains out over maybe nothing, Nay. The whole business might blow over." Pretending to be bored, he was actually in the grip of a peculiar dread and half rising, his thighs against the constraining table, he swiveled his head desperately, looking for the waiter.

"Buddy," said Naomi, "I have never criticized you, and I'm not doing it now. But persons with your sort of integrity are perhaps innocent when it comes to the awareness that many people are devious. They do not say what they mean, and they do not mean what they say. Often they cannot help themselves in either case. They intend no wrong. They do what they must. They may be warped."

Buddy took the cue to say eagerly: "Like Leo. I never would of—"

"Like Mary Wentworth," said Naomi. "To your mind, she's a fine woman because you knew her husband, because you sold her a car, because she's a helpless widow. But all this while she abuses you behind your back."

Buddy's back was frozen at this moment. He felt that if he

so much as altered his expression his spine would break like an attenuated icicle.

He murmured: "Is that right?"

"Therefore," said Naomi, decisively dropping her cigarette for emphasis, "Gladys would serve her own cause best by insisting on a divorce. If you see what I mean."

"I'll be damned," said Buddy with a staggering effort. "Well, I guess it's not the first time you do somebody a favor and they take it the wrong way."

"You see," said Naomi. "I predicted that would be your reaction. 'Buddy will be philosophical,' I told Gladys."

"Aw, sure . . ." He tried twisting himself gingerly on the seat, but was too brittle to go far. "The way I look at it . . ."

"Precisely. And I hasten to say that Gladys must be given a certain credit, which, childish as she is, amazed me. 'Gosh,' she said, 'I can't imagine Buddy doing anything like that. Why, he's a real Boy Scout.' "

Buddy knew for a certainty now that that bitch Gladys had been flashing her flat ass at him for years; he was happy to have denied her.

He also knew that he could not have Naomi murdered. He was too fascinated by her complex ignorance of him, in contrast to which Laverne's simple knowledge was superficial. It was Naomi alone who gave him a sense of mystery about himself.

The trouble was, he had no idea where to get hold of Clarence and call off the dog.

chapter 13

RALPH GOT an almost sexual thrill from eating certain things by himself: Leona sausage with horseradish on buttered "real" rye bread, i.e., the kind that came unsliced and unwrapped; canned chili with dry soda crackers crumbled into it; above all, melted cheese between two slices of white bread, dark-browned in the waffle iron, impressed with the griddle marks and squashed flat as a wafer, goldenly oozing.

He got the Wonder Bread from the tin box and in the Frigidaire found a package of Kraft American, of which the individual slices had fused into a solid block. He was old enough to remember back to when they had an icebox in summer, and in winter a zinc cooling-chamber that hung outside the window.

He took out a fresh quart of milk and poured off the cream into a pitcher of green glass. He then filled an opalescent tumbler to the brim and drained it into his throat continuously, breathing normally through his nose, until it was empty, feeling the solid column of milk descend through his chest. He was cooled instantly: this could not have been done with a carbonated beverage.

He placed the cheese sandwich in the waffle iron and would look at it many times before it browned and melted, his fantasies confined to the anticipation of succulence. When it was done he pried it off the grids with a fork and took a huge bite too soon and burned his mouth during the moment of indecision as to whether to spit it into his hand or drench it with milk.

After having a lone supper Ralph might well have masturbated on his bed with the door open, an unusual luxury, had not the guilty memory of his cock's hardening against Margie's butt rendered him sexless. Her failure to move away suggested that she had been benumbed with fright and/or disgust. While he was so occupied, Laverne Linda Lorraine had fled. What *she* would have thought of his despicable, obscene swelling, the advertisement of his punkhood, was too awful to imagine.

Another of Ralph's rituals when he was by himself at home was to have a smoke or a shot of booze. Though disliking both tobacco and hard whiskey, he felt an obligation to Horse Hauser to report at least a minimum of wickedness, and could never bring himself to lie. Horse's own claims were of course impossibly extravagant: half a bottle of Four Roses in three hours, two big White Owls, etc. Once he allegedly lured in Wanda Wallace, a halfwitted neighbor girl of thirteen, and showed her his dong, stemming her tears with a handful of Lorna Doones and a little ring his uncle had beaten from an Indian-head penny. Pure bullshit, though Ralph *had* subsequently seen slack-mouthed Wanda wearing a copper ring on her fat pinky.

Honoring the responsibilities of friendship, Ralph went to see whether his mother had left any whole cigarettes behind. If not, he might collect the tobacco from a number of butts and smoke it in the ten-cent Missouri Meerschaum corncob he had bought for that purpose during the summer.

The coffee- and end-tables displayed only magazines and a few books of paper matches, one hawking an art course by correspondence, showing the cartoon face of a grinning shiny-black Negro with huge white eyes and teeth, below the legend DRAW ME! Ralph headed for the catty-cornered secretary desk on the shelves of which, behind glass doors, was the permanent library of the house, a matched set of six dull-green James Oliver Curwoods once owned by his maternal grandfather, and several more recent books in paper dustwrappers, dating from the time his mother had belonged briefly to some book club, but finding it rather expensive, the charges running to as much as two dollars per volume with the charges for postage and handling, she mostly used the public library.

Ralph was fed up with reading at the moment, which he either did incessantly or not at all. Currently he was in the phase of wanting to live in reality or, failing that, in his own and not someone else's fantasy. He tried the bottom drawer of the desk, where his mother kept her supply of Twenty Grands, which she bought at a cut-rate drugstore for eighty-five cents a carton, a saving of fifteen cents per ten packs. This drawer was locked. He went to his own room and got the key to his desk, a maple piece from Sears, Roebuck that matched his bed, dresser, and night table.

Used with precision, and a tongue in the corner of the mouth, the key worked in the secretary-desk drawer, and Ralph drew it open. In the foreground were three fresh packages of cigarettes. It occurred to him that, watching her pennies as she did, his mother kept count of this supply. This consideration, along with his distaste for smoking to begin with, discouraged him from the venture.

He must find another sneaky project with which to appease Hauser. Or simply conceal from Horse that he had been alone at suppertime. He had no keen natural taste for mischief. It had always seemed idiotic to him to go about on Ticktack Night, the eve of Halloween, throwing corn kernels against people's windows and hiding their trash-can lids; then coarse and rude to appear the following night in costume and false face to collect free candy from those who had been harassed.

When he explained this to Hauser, Horse said: "Christ, Sandifer, you don't know how to have fun." Thereafter he confined his efforts to dissuading his friend, as they got older, from throwing rocks at windows and setting fire to garages, but not from giving parked cars four flat tires or strewing back steps with garbage. Horse had to be given some leeway in the venting of his strange rage against normal, decent people. Ralph saw it as his own task to keep this within the limits of sanity without showing himself up as coward, ass-kisser, pansy.

Along with the cigarettes the drawer held several of those big dull-red envelope file-folders fastened each with its own attached string. These had a deadly, legal look: no doubt they were stuffed with deeds and mortgages and tax bills signed and sealed and recorded in the county courthouse, a big solid block of dreariness, staffed by baldheaded men and dumpy women. Ralph had been there once, in the city, with his father years ago, stopping off en route to get a baseball glove at a discount from a guy who owed his dad a favor.

Ralph wondered whether prying into these documents would meet his obligation to Hauser. What people owed on their houses and how much tax they paid was confidential data. The trouble was this crap bored him so much that he could not consider its revelation a crime. However, the drawer *had* been locked, and he had opened it with an unofficial key. "I broke into the desk and went through my parents' legal records," he could say, and leave it at that. Hauser always soon interrupted anyway in his jealous urgency to go you one better: "My old man's two hundred bucks in debt to some sheeny finance company. They got him by the nuts."

If Ralph were going to say that though, he should actually do it, however quickly. He undid the string on one folder and looked within. He saw a leatherette volume inscribed in gold *My Diary*—1939 It was closed with a strap that terminated in a little brass lock.

Dropping it back inside the folder, he saw something else: a little blue bankbook. He claimed it and opened it to a page listing several deposits and interest payments, at the end of which appeared the sum of $752.87. The name at the top was Mary Joy, and the bank had a city address. He returned it to the big envelope and tied the strings.

He undid one more folder and found inside not a private diary as such but a regular book, a volume bound in purple cloth and entitled, in silver script, *My Diary, 1936, by Mary Joy*. This book he had never seen around the house. He did not as yet intrude within its covers. In the folder was also a sheaf of opened and smoothed letters, the parent envelopes secured above each by the giant-sized crisscross paperclip that held the lot.

The one on top, when the canceled envelope was bent away, was revealed to read:

DEAR MARY JOY:

Here's your copy. We trust you are well under weigh on the volume for 1937. Some early reactions from our members have come in and are altogether positive. Your feminine approach—whether or not you are actually a woman—is unique among the editions we have printed thus far. We anticipate that it will create its own demand for subsequent volumes.

Indeed, so strongly do we feel this that we are in a position to offer you a fifty-dollar bonus for the next, as an incentive that might encourage you to complete it without delay. If you could complete the current volume by the end of August, we might then go to press and have it ready for distribution to the members as the Holiday selection.

Also, another note of interest. Responding to the requests of a number of members who own personal moving-picture projectors or belong to social groups which have one in common, we are considering the making of movies, probably, at least to begin with, of the one-reel length, say fifteen minutes each of screen time. Perhaps you could think of incidents from the Diaries which might come across with special effectiveness in such a form, and prepare a scenario or two on speculation. Naturally, these should be confined to scenes involving adults. We would not have the facilities to train animals, and such episodes as the seduction of the giant colored imbecile by the eight-year-old Mary Joy, though one of the high points of the '36 Diary, would for obvious reasons not be practical. Thus far, by using only first-class mail and by proceeding with the caution of a private club whose members (including certain highly placed members of the legal profession) have a mutual interest in discretion, we have not run afoul of the law, and we wish to keep it that way.

We'll pay twenty-five dollars each for the scenarios we accept.

Yours very truly,
THE SELECTION COMMITTEE

The respective names and addresses were of more interest to Ralph than the text, which was so cryptic in essentials. How his parents got hold of a letter sent to Mary Joy, P. O. Box 121, in the city, from Continental Products, P.O. Box 537, Maspeth, L.I., New York, was intriguing in the degree to which it defied explanation.

There were two more letters in the sheaf. The bottom one said:

We like the Diary for 1936 very much, and are happy to offer you $200 for the right to print it and distribute it in a limited private edition for the members of our club. Because of its nature, this type of book cannot be registered in the orthodox manner with the Copyright Office, and our printing of it does not constitute legal publication. But if you expect to have further lucrative association with us, you will regard our right as exclusive.

May we also state that insofar as you have sent us the manuscript without solicitation on our part, that if you have another motive than you represent—that is, to be frank, extortion or blackmail, or if you are a law-enforcement officer —your procedure implicates you equally with us, if the former; and in the latter case constitutes entrapment.

The final, middle letter expressed satisfaction at Mary's acceptance and noted the enclosure of a check for two hundred dollars.

Ralph next turned to the book itself. The title page said nothing about Continental Products, but announced, below author and title, "Privately printed for the exclusive use of the members of the Eros Literary Society. Not for public sale or distribution. Of an edition of 600 copies, this is Copy No. —," no number being given.

Ralph's habit when inspecting a book was after studying the frontispiece to open to the first page of the text and read one paragraph; then turn rapidly to somewhere around the middle and scan there; and finally to swoop to the last page and read the final sentence.

The opening of Mary Joy's 1936 Diary was:

New Year's Day, 8 A.M.—Lying here upon my pink satin sheets, my black-lace nightie drawn up above the twin swellings of my creamy-white breasts, tipped with erect rubicund nipples surrounded by large roseate aureolae, I greet the fresh new year with an exploratory finger in the deepest recess of the warm, moist grotto between my heaving ivory thighs, and

think of another Jan. 1 on which, like the year, I was too a
virgin. . . . .

Ralph wrinkled his forehead: something weird here. He
was more perplexed than aroused however and therefore read
no further in this passage, but split the book at the halfway
point and read:

Again and again Wing Loo applied the vicious whip to my
apple-round, pink bottom. The massive, opium-crazed Oriental, his naked, yellow, rotund belly slimy with sweat, his eyes
narrowed to mere slits in his shaved head, was more stimulated
than dissuaded by my anguished screams. Gradually, cunningly, each blow of the steel-tipped lash fell closer to the
vulnerable cleft between my nether cheeks, until at last the
ultimate target was reached, the metal point stabbing pro-
foundly within the tender linings of my rosy labia, raking
them with fiery agony. The pain was insupportable. I swooned
. . . then returned to consciousness with the realization that
I was no longer being punished. Instead, a delicious warmth
arose from my well of womanliness and began to suffuse
throughout my limbs even unto the tips of my toenails, prick-
ling like electric current to the very ends of my long golden
tresses. . . .

This passage was sufficiently bizarre to prompt Ralph to
trace back to where it began, as an entry for July 4, 9 P.M.:

I awakened to the sound of exploding firecrackers this morning. To me this noise is inextricably intermingled with other
explosive memories of the homeland of fireworks, China,
where I spent so much of my girlhood as the only daughter
of an American missionary. . . .

Ralph wondered whether this, written so finely, could be
called a genuine dirty book. He had never seen one before.

Unlike the filthy cartoon eight-pagers, it was innocent of foul language. Perhaps that was why he was not aroused: that, along with the failure of Mary Joy thus far to get beyond stink-finger and ass-beating and get fucked—fucked by a man, that is, for now, having turned elsewhere, he saw that on September 27 she was being mounted by her pet St. Bernard.

Hauser claimed he jacked off a dog once, and also quoted a story of his brother Lester's about a petty officer who, when stationed at San Diego, went on liberty across the border in Tijuana, Mexico, where he watched a Shetland pony jazz a greaser girl in a nightclub act. Both these tales had sounded like lies to Ralph, and now, all at once, he realized that Mary Joy was lying about everything. This book was fiction; which was to say, pure crap from beginning to end about nothing that had actually happened or that really mattered.

He dropped the Diary into the folder and fastened the strings. He had no interest in the contents of the other folders, which could be imagined. What they were doing in the same drawer as his mother's cigarette supply was inexplicable. That he had never seen her write in a diary was as nothing when put alongside his conviction that she was sexless. It would also be typical of her to keep cigarettes in there for years without having the curiosity to examine the other burdens of the drawer.

She lived on a different layer of being from the rest of the race, now that he thought about it: quietly, serenely, above the battle as it were, which is why she was so suited to his father, who was always in the thick of it and seething behind his mask of apparent self-confidence. Ralph understood this consciously for the first time, although he had long instinctively felt the radiations when in his father's presence, which always made him obscurely uneasy. It occurred to him now that his father was a nervous wreck, unable to remain at rest for three consecutive minutes, unable even to speak without frantic gestures of the chin and fingers soon followed by a kind of dancing escape. His fancy clothes were also a symptom of this condition, as were his abrupt phrasings and sometimes lately even his operation of an automobile.

"Mary Joy," then, on the evidence of her texts, to characterize which there could be no other word, again, than "nervous"—being whipped by a Chinaman?—must be associated in one fashion or another with his father. That she might indeed *be* his father under a *nom de plume* was the most unlikely idea, despite the line in the letter that questioned her sex only to dismiss its importance.

He had never seen his father do anything with a pen except scrawl a hasty signature and then bite the cap, twiddle the shaft, and hurl the instrument away.

The most sensible explanation was that Mary was an actual woman, perhaps using a pen name because of the nature of her expression; though perhaps, being a mad exhibitionist, not. And in either case she was a customer of his father's or even a friend, or both, quite a good friend to put this nutty garbage into his keeping. With that thought he remembered a phrase about "extortion or blackmail," as used by the Selection Committee, and next the reference to a "law-enforcement officer."

These would certainly be real worries if you ran a dirty-book club. With the choice of blackmailer, who in the movies always lost, and FBI man, who always prevailed, one would not hesitate in the labeling of one's own dad.

That his father was indeed an undercover G-man, collecting evidence against a smut ring, would go far to explain his nervousness, as well as his frequent absences from home at mealtimes. In picture shows the Feds were depicted as cool and collected, but then neither did anyone ever seem to sustain real hurt in movie fistfights, whereas, in the real ones you occasionally saw on the street outside the Star Bar & Grill, when the rare punch connected with a face it caused damage which was still visible a week later.

Ralph and Hauser had seen a medium-sized guy named Dutch Ballbacher close the eye and break the nose of Turk Tucker, a much larger man, in that spot only last July. He might have killed him had not the cop come along and pulled him off.

"That Ballbacher is a mental case," said Horse. "He goes out of his head if somebody looks at him crosseyed. Lester went to school with him. One time he was walking across a railroad trestle when the train came along, and he had to jump down on the rocks in the gulley and he broke his skull and they put a steel plate in it. It don't pay to fuck with that monkey."

Nevertheless, a week later, Ralph zoomed around the post-office corner on his bike and ran right into Dutch Ballbacher, who had just stepped off the curb. It was like hitting a wall of masonry. With lightning reflexes, Dutch caught both bike and Ralph, who said his prayers. However, what Ballbacher said, while gently bringing his assailant into balance, was "Gee, I'm sorry, sport. You hurt?" Upon being reassured, he slapped Ralph's rump and continued across the street. Thereafter when they ran across each other, Ballbacher remembered and would say: "Hi, sport," and Ralph would answer proudly: "Hi, Dutch," impressing Hauser if he were along.

Ralph now shut the drawer and picked the lock in reverse, throwing into place the little vertical bar. In search of further evidence of his father's connection with the FBI, he went to his parents' bedroom, flipped back the chenille spread, felt beneath the pillow, and found the object he had seen his naked dad put there when they were preparing to go to the laying-out of Leo's mother.

Of course it was a pistol.

He replaced it and smoothed the bed. The only trouble

with the discoveries he had made was that they could not be revealed to Horse Hauser. The great thing though was that at long last he was fascinated by his father. Ralph had never had much interest in used cars.

At this point the telephone rang. He crossed the hall, went through the kitchen, and lifted the instrument from the little stand in the corner of the dining room.

"Hi, Ralph. It's Margie." Her voice was huskier on the wire than in the open air. "I was just calling to see if you were still mad at me."

"Mad?" In his distraction he had no clue to her concern. "No, I'm not mad."

"Well, I'm going to apologize anyway."

"For what?"

"I shouldn't have criticized you, at least not when you were doing me a favor."

"Oh, well, forget it," Ralph said generously, remembering at last. "It was an awfully hot day and I had to wear that suit."

"You sure looked real nice in it, though. . . . I took a chance on finding you home. Is that party over already?"

"There wasn't any party." He was reminded, however, of the box of candy; he might well eat it before he could get it to Laverne.

Her voice was gleeful. "Oh, really? What are you wearing now?"

He had to look down at himself. "Wash pants and a sport shirt, I guess." He really had nothing to say, so he asked: "What are you?"

This provoked a giggle. "Oh, I can't tell you."

What a bore she was. "All right," he said, "don't."

She breathed audibly for a while. Then: "I mean, because it's not much. . . . It's awful hot here and nobody else is home."

"Uh-huh."

She raised her tone in mock indignation. "Well, I'm not in the nude! I've got on, uh, you know—underwear." Her voice cracked slightly on the last word.

At hearing "nude," Ralph's pecker went instantly rigid; at "underwear," it began to throb violently. He could get an erection by looking up "vagina" in the unabridged dictionary.

Margie said in the boldest voice yet: "I guess I shocked you. But it's almost as much as you would wear at the swimming pool."

Ralph had to get back his self-esteem. "That's the point I was trying to make this afternoon about words like 'pregnant.' They just describe things that exist. Take 'underwear.' If you called it a 'bathing suit,' you could get away with it."

Margie giggled again. "I couldn't get away with this, unless I was a boy."

The blood in Ralph's member now surged so brutally that he felt as though he might be toppled from the stool. He assumed a counterfeit indignation of his own. "You mean you don't have on—" He absolutely did not have the nerve to say "brassiere" to a girl; anyway, he knew from feeling her bosom that she did not wear one when going about in the outside world.

He tried again: "You don't have an undershirt on?"

"Never in summertime."

Suddenly her brazenness annoyed him. "What about in winter?" he cried.

"Say," said she, "aren't you getting pretty fresh?"

"Well, *I'm* not sitting here naked!"

A silence ensued. His hard-on had withered.

At last she said: "I guess I got you burned up again. I'm always putting my foot in it. I don't know how to talk to boys."

She sounded so contrite that Ralph, the eternal sucker for other people's apologies, came down from his high horse.

"Look," said he, "if every time you are inclined to say something impulsive you take a deep breath first, it might come out different. Secondly, other than that, you talk just fine to boys—at least to me. *I* can't talk to a lot of girls: Imogene Clevenger for example. I guess you just have to find something in common to talk about when dealing with members of the opposite sex."

"That's the nicest thing you have ever said to me," murmured Margie.

He noticed again her tendency to make it personal when his intent was to establish general principles. "Well," he said, "it's been nice talking to you, unless you have something else to discuss."

"I never called up a boy before."

"Now that I think about it, I've never *been* called up by a girl before."

"You don't think it's too forward?"

Actually, he did think so, but she had enough troubles. "It's like anything else, as long as it doesn't become a habit."

"The first classes start tomorrow."

"Yeah," said Ralph, groaning ritualistically.

"You hate school? But you always get good grades."

"Only fair. The eighth grade was one thing; high school is another. I don't look forward to algebra. Ordinary arithmetic was always my downfall. I never did learn how to divide fractions."

"That's my best subject," said Margie, her voice taking on authority. "I'd be real glad to help you anytime. It's really a trick, you know: you just think in terms of numbers instead of in words. Know what I did this summer? I took books in algebra and plane geometry from the library, and went through them. In fact, I got all the way to trigonometry, which I think you don't get until the junior or senior year. It's easy. I could explain it if you want."

"You'll have some job," he said dolefully. He had not known of this gift of hers. In the eighth grade they had had different home rooms. He had not been aware that she possessed any virtues whatever. He admired people who could do things. Again it occurred to him that with a little grooming she could improve her appearance a lot. But now he began to believe that the result would not just get by but be positively pretty.

She might be a terrific girl when all was said and done. She already had brains and might well be on her way, with a little encouragement, to being downright beautiful. In the movies he had seen Jane Wyman among others play the mousy intellectual who was long ignored by the guy she worshiped and helped in class, and then one day he said: "Take off your glasses," and she did and proved a knockout.

"If *I* can do it, *you* certainly can," said Margie. "I'm just a girl." However, there was nothing humble in her voice.

"Say," said Ralph. "I was thinking of going down to Elmira's for a Coke."

Before he had a chance to issue an invitation, she said: "Now? Well gee, I don't know if I can make it. I'm cool and comfortable, and I wanted to start this book on trig."

To his amazement, proud fellow that he was, Ralph heard himself plead. "Tonight? Isn't it soon enough for you that school starts tomorrow? You don't want to be a greasy grind, do you?"

"You're not just feeling sorry for me?"

"Goddammit," said he, "you want to come or don't you?"

"I warned you about cursing."

She was not content just to bring him down; she had to walk all over him. Nevertheless, he groaned: "I'm sorry."

"I'll be there in about fifteen minutes." She hesitated, then added: "I really like you, Ralph."

"That's nice."

"I mean, really. . . . I care for you."

"Likewise," he blurted fearfully and slammed the receiver into its hook.

chapter 14

AFTER PAYING the check at Wong's Gardens,
Buddy had taken Naomi on a long aimless drive through the
outskirts of the suburban area, here and there reaching roads
that bordered small farms.

Now that he had abandoned his plan to murder her, he had
an appetite for reminiscence, and proceeded to feed it, recall-
ing Ralph's walking through the cowflop, his own allergic
reaction to alfalfa fields in bloom, and her cousin's wife's
homemade bread, hot from the oven and spread with fresh-
churned butter and peach preserves made from the fruit of
their own trees.

"That's the only real life, I guess," said he. "You know: no
phoniness." He was driving at 25 mph.

"Do you think so?" asked Naomi.

"*You* don't?"

She seemed startled by the question. "I have never been
able to decide what is more real than anything else."

Formerly he would have been annoyed by this statement,

finding it a subtle rejection of his point of view. Laverne would have agreed instantly, and then would have made it flatteringly personal: "Yeah, Bud, but I can't see you as a farmer, wearing overalls and a bandanna." But Naomi had actually listened to what he said, and done something with what she heard.

"Growing things," said he. "Getting up at sunrise and going to bed at dark. That seems more natural. I don't know. You get what I mean?"

"I think I do."

"Maybe after a couple more good years I'll sell the lot and buy a little farm, get away while the getting's good, before the ulcers and heart attacks."

"It's certainly worth thinking about," said Naomi.

"Free eggs and milk, anyway," Buddy said, pursuing his sentimental fantasy. "Fresh air instead of carbon monoxide. You could can fruit and make jams and jellies."

"I would be willing to learn."

Without warning he felt a strange access of affection for her. "I *know* you would, Nay." He took his hand off the steering wheel and briefly touched hers, which lay on the seat between them.

"Be good for Ralph too. Make a man out of him to be around animals." He had said that seriously, but got the inadvertent joke and chuckled. "You know what I mean. I think he might be led astray if he falls in with the wrong crowd. I don't see him developing leadership qualities living in this town. A dose of rugged individualism might do him good."

Naomi listened gravely to these ideas, and whenever he turned to her, she nodded in respect. However, it was her habit seldom to express a personal opinion unless asked, and then it might well be not at all to his intended point, as now.

"What do you think, Nay?"

263

"Ralph," said Naomi, "is a free spirit. He ranges far and wide."

Buddy frowned and increased the pressure of his foot on the gas pedal. He felt like getting home now. "I don't know," he said. "He's been getting sneaky. When I caught him breaking that window he clammed up. When I was a kid and got in trouble I talked a blue streak. I'd say anything. That's how I usually got off, even if they knew I was a bare-faced liar. At least I was *open* about it, see? Funny how most people will forgive you when they think they've got your number."

When they reached home Naomi changed into her quilted housecoat, brought forth her sewing basket, and settled down in the living room to darn a pile of Ralph's socks. However, after doing only the first pair, she squirted out the wooden egg, put it and the socks aside, and picked up a library book.

Buddy observed this with interest though ostensibly he was for once carefully reading the forward portions of the evening paper that he ordinarily rejected in favor of the used-car ads of his big downtown competitors. He discarded his own socks when they developed holes, which generally took a long time owing to his changing them daily and keeping his nails cut close. Ralph was not as diligent in pursuing either of these measures. Neither did he shower with regularity, as you could smell if you put a nose in the doorway of his room.

In an all-around mood of familial affection, Buddy dropped the paper and went to the master bedroom, where he felt beneath the pillow for his gun. He had it all worked out now about Clarence. After Naomi fell asleep he would go down to the basement and wait until the Negro arrived at the door. Trying to waylay him before he got that far would be impractical; prowling the streets by car or on foot, he might miss him if Clarence came by some furtive route, slinking through the shadows of back yards, guided by his jungle instincts. Of course Buddy had no reason to shoot him now, and no cover story for so doing, but being armed was wise in the event that Clarence took offense at losing the other half of his fee.

Thinking further along the same line, Buddy decided he was within his rights, and had the power besides, to demand that Clarence also return the advance payment.

He crossed the hall and, having opened the door on the right of the entrance to the bathroom and having thrown the light switch, illuminating the cellar floor at the bottom of the stairway, he went down the steep stairs. He was not a basement man by nature, had no workbench in the corner, no wood-turning lathe on which he made early-American reproductions from knotty pine, as did certain male neighbors; another had a ham radio and talked nightly to colleagues in Nevada and even Alaska.

At the bottom he unhooked the door to the outside. He also pulled it open, and was happy he had so done, because it resisted and squawked loudly. He left it ajar. Then he went upstairs, stripped in the bedroom and, carrying his robe over his arm, went into the bathroom and filled the tub. Ordinarily he was too nervous to bathe except by shower. The very thought of lying supine, bare rump on wet enamel, water at his nipples, caused him to quake with paranoia.

He was now however in a rare state of ease. For once he yearned to be vulnerably immersed in the engrossing element. He climbed in and slid down until his chin touched the surface of the water, his knees rising high and parting company to touch the lip of the tub on either side. At the angle, looking along the trough between the little mounds of his breasts, which had developed a plumpness in the months of Laverne's meals and were now distorted by the water, he could not see his genitals over the rise of his belly.

He was in the attitude of a woman about to be penetrated. The conceit amused him; he jazzed the water in parody. It was a ridiculous position. He had assumed it only once before,

265

then by accident, when Ballbacher knocked him to the black-top. He scrooched back, sliding his spine up the cool slope, and at last saw his floating dick, drawn back, like a boy's, inside its dunce cap of foreskin.

He decided now that Laverne would come out of her mood rather sooner than later. She was totally dependent on him, not only for bed and board, the alternative being a return to the drive-in, but also, more importantly, because of her insatiable appetite for sex. Buddy was the unique man who could feed that. Fucking was all she did, other than preparing him the occasional meal. The rest of her day was a blur of candy, movie mags, and radio serials. Unlike Naomi, she had no mind whatever.

Buddy began to develop quite a resentment against her, sitting there, and to relieve it scrubbed himself furiously with the bar of Camay gone snotty from lying in a Bakelite soap dish filled with water.

When he eventually stepped from the moist warmth of the bathroom into the cool of the hall, the time on the wrist-watch he took from the pocket of his robe was 10:20. In his congress slippers he went to the living room. Naomi was as usual reading in a cloud of smoke, but he took no offense.

"Time the boy is back, isn't it?"

She smiled vaguely. "Ralph can take care of himself."

"I don't want him flunking out."

"They don't assign homework the first night."

Again she showed she knew more than he supposed. Her apparent remoteness neither was due to, nor resulted in, ignorance. Suddenly he had the wondrous conviction that she could have listed by name every woman he had plugged in the last decade and a half, and then, without a word from him, explained away each encounter as having existed only in the malicious gossip of others.

She provided him with a secure castle from which to sally

266

forth to spear the dragons. If you owned a wife with sex on the brain, you might end up with a nympho like Grace Plum . . . or Laverne, whose rebuff of him that afternoon now seemed suspicious, given her appetites. Was she getting it from somebody else?

Buddy padded back to the bedroom and lay down in the dark. Jealousy was the emotion most alien to his temperament. What he wanted, he took. What he could not have, he did not desire. He had no sexual imagination for movie stars or princesses. With women he was not jealous, but rather jealous-making. Thus he had always regarded that feeling as, like recumbent bathing, effeminate.

He had been true to Laverne because he had nothing left for anyone else. If that wasn't love, what was? He had visited her at various hours, usually without warning. He had never seen a cigar butt or an extra glass. When the sheets showed stains, they were always those he himself had made on his last visit.

There was something wrong with Laverne if she needed more than what he gave her in abundance. Who could it be? The grocer's delivery boy? A teen-aged punk? She had after all, wearing a cheerleader's getup, worked in a drive-in that served nothing but hamburgers and hotdogs. Buddy considered it a disgusting perversity if a woman consorted with a male much younger than she. Men of course had a greater range, but Buddy himself was repelled by any suggestion of adolescence. Not till a female had put in at least two and half decades, preferably more, was her veneer of instinctive selfishness worn away; unless of course she married very young.

With Leo out of commission, and until Jack gave notice at school, if in fact he decided to come full-time on the lot, Buddy could not spare himself for a stake-out on Myrtle Avenue. He must hire a private detective to watch Laverne's staircase, especially in the hours before noon, when he himself seldom visited, and again after midnight. He realized now that these periods would not agree with the schedule of a delivery boy. If fucker there was, he was someone older, and freer—freer than Buddy, free to make free with Buddy's woman in a place for which Buddy paid the rent.

His policy being never supinely to suffer mockery, Buddy considered that he might have extra work for Clarence after all. This thought, with the memory of his bath, had the effect of a soporific, and he dozed off.

He awakened easily, with an awareness of duty and yet a peaceful sense that he could perform it well. He put on the bedside lamp and compared his watch with the clock on the dresser. By compromise it was ten to eleven. Naomi would be coming to bed soon. Therefore he got into his white pajamas with the blue stripes and piping. One of the niceties of their marriage was that, from the first, they never displayed themselves to each other in less than underwear, and for many years not even in the final layer of that, she wearing at least a slip, and he a T-shirt above his drawers.

It was an unusual intimacy for him not to tie the fringed belt of his maroon robe. He did not do so now as he entered the hall, turned towards the living room, decided to check the basement door again—he had left it barely ajar; it might yet squeak or shudder at Clarence's brute pressure—reversed himself, and opened the door giving onto the cellar stairway. He closed it behind him on the first step. Reaching the second, he felt himself detained.

An end of his loose belt was caught in the jamb. One gentle yank would not serve. He gave it another, this time applying sufficient force to free the belt but also enough to dislocate his center of balance. He fell backwards down the stairs.

Naomi was wont to work on Mary Joy's diaries in the morning after Buddy went to the lot and, during the body of

268

the year, Ralph to school. In summer, with Ralph usually around the house or yard till noon, she wrote late at night, waiting for Buddy to fall asleep, which with his clean conscience he did quickly, then rising to go to the secretary desk in the living room. Buddy drank little of any beverage; it was rare indeed for him to go to the toilet in the wee hours. He seldom stirred in bed or even breathed heavily. He was as polite when asleep as when awake.

He was indeed the perfect husband of legend. Naomi knew herself as no housewife to match. In the kitchen she could barely boil water. As laundress in earlier years she usually pressed more wrinkles into a shirt than she ironed out. Buddy calmly began to take his linen to the Chinese. Long ago he had suggested hiring a woman to clean, but Naomi dissuaded him: a pointless cost, vacuuming soothed her, polishing filled the void. In truth, if cleaning had been done at all in recent years, her sister Gladys, with the zeal of the mindless, had done it when she stayed over.

Neither was Naomi motherly by nature. In the irony of life, Gladys, who was childless, had the maternal instincts. She had cooed at Ralph as a baby, and even regarded it as a privilege to change his diapers, the more soiled the better. But then when they were girls it had been Gladys, two years older, who had wanted to mother Naomi through the onset of menstruation. Gladys was not simply immune to physical disgust; she seemed to delight in experiences which would have evoked it in others. Thus her unwitting example had suggested many scenes in the diaries of Mary Joy.

If the truth be known, Gladys was actually rather masculine in that. The Diaries were successful because men doted on what was loathsome. Buddy was the sole exception, owing no doubt to his many feminine qualities; he was gentle, generous, tolerant, and behind his mask of jolly vanity, riddled with self-doubt. His sexual drive was, mercifully, weak.

Naomi had had only one man in her life. If, when she was a girl, a tramp exposed himself, she calmly looked the other way. If, when dancing, in her high school years, a boy pressed his ridiculous bulge against her abdomen, she backed off. If a tongue was intruded into a polite goodnight kiss, she bit it; if a hand got fresh, she slapped the attendant face. Though a virgin she was well aware of vulnerability of testicles and was not hesitant to cock a knee.

Even with Buddy, to whom she had given her heart immediately because that was all he had requested in his shy courtship, she had been none too keen to share a bed. But when he appeared, that first night of the honeymoon they took at home in the little flat, because he had just been hired by the local Essex agency, after he had pulled the Murphy bed from the wall and gone discreetly into the kitchen while she used the bathroom and pulled on the same flannel night-gown she had worn for some years as a maiden (it was January and the coal-oil heater exuded more stink than warmth), after she had climbed in and covered up with the gray U.S. Army surplus blankets, Buddy came out, attired—well, she could not resist him in brown derby, a huge red bow tie with white polka dots, a suit of long underwear, and rubber knee boots. He carried a ukulele, which he strummed to no tune, and was singing, abominably, "The Yanks are coming . . ."

Naomi's was not a sheltered imagination: it was afforded great range by the restrictions of her life, which were happily self-imposed. She had always been notorious for her modest wardrobe and her disinterest in cosmetics. The mirror-sight of herself wearing jewelry caused her to smirk. What moved her was written language. Among the furniture of her memory were the names "Chesebrough," the company that made Vaseline, and "Burroughs Wellcome," who produced Empirin Compound. She read every label, whether that cemented to the Castoria bottle or that, forbidding its removal under pain of law, which dangled from anything stuffed with Kapok.

If while walking on the pavement she stepped first in chewing gum and then on a detached page of a magazine, she peeled off the latter and read it while awaiting the bus. One such fragment comprised pp. 29–30 of a publication entitled, according to the running head on one side, *Hotdog*. Much of page 29 was occupied by the photograph of a young woman with tremendous bare breasts. On page 30 was a column of jokes, concluding with a special notice, in a printed box, to the effect that the editors of *Hotdog*, in charity to victims of the Depression, would be happy to give a free goose to any girl who called in at their offices.

The column was flanked on either side by a number of advertisements: the "draw-me" darky of the correspondence art school, the taxidermy institute's stuffed-squirrel-holding-ashtray, the novelty company's exhortation to "fool friends and policemen" by purchasing a device with which to throw your voice inside locked trunks and closets, and an offer of ten of the "kind of books men like" for one dollar, postage paid by the seller, Continental Products.

Naomi had been a wife for almost a decade and a half, and a mother for almost as long, and yet had no sense of the kind of book men liked. In Buddy's grasp she had never seen any volume but the telephone directory. Her father had been a plumber and though deft with his hands when they manipulated a wrench, with a pen he was at a loss, hardly able to scratch his signature, and when holding a newspaper he was generally asleep behind it.

Her own addiction to the printed word had been acquired on the model of her mother, who went regularly to the public library and also belonged to a little group of like-minded women who would get together over coffee and cake once a month and discuss the poems of Ella Wheeler Wilcox ("Laugh and the world laughs with you") and Felicia D. Hemans, authoress of "The Boy Stood on the Burning Deck."

In school Naomi's peculiar strength was in English. Her composition on *Black Beauty* was read aloud by the teacher; she could recite from memory twice as much of *Evangeline* as was required; and at quite an early age she began to read adult books such as the novels of Gene Stratton Porter.

Many diaristic episodes were suggested by memories of the favorite books of her childhood, *Rebecca of Sunnybrook Farm* and *Girl of the Limberlost* (relations with animals), and, in honor of the taste of her young-womanhood, the romances of Maysie Grieg and Ruby M. Ayres (gentlemen suitors with whips and manacles). Perversions and corruptions, that is, of what Naomi found good and true. Because, except for Buddy, that was what men liked—the realization of which confirmed what she had believed her life long, but with the difference that she had never before seen the utility in it.

And had not yet with the arrival of the first plain-wrapped parcel from Continental Products, addressed to "Mr. N. Sandifer," which when opened yielded ten "books" that were really little pamphlets filled with the kind of jokes printed in *Hotdog*, most of them mildly scatological, concerning flatulent fat ladies or the preacher's wife seen dusting her aspidistra in the window of the manse.

But included in the packet was an announcement of yet another series for those readers who craved "spicier" fare, and the quoted price implied as much: a dollar each, two-fifty for any three. Never profligate with the household money Buddy gave her, Naomi was wont to accumulate quite a little fund by the end of each month, enough usually so that she could refuse one week's allowance in four, and with pride accept Buddy's affectionate reproof. As to her personal consumption, two housedresses, bought on sale, lasted her a year, and

Twenty Grands, at ten cents a pack, were inferior to fifteen-cent Lucky Strikes only on the gauge of snobbery.

However, a motive that she neither questioned nor explored caused her to invest still another precious dollar in Continental's latest offer. This arrived as a thirty-two-page booklet entitled *Clothed in Innocence*, with no explanation as to why it had replaced her choice, *What the Butler Saw through the Keyhole.*

The slender paperbound volume proved to be a singular work concerned primarily with the wardrobes of its characters and only as an afterthought with anatomy.

When I arrived at Wyndham Manor to take my new employment as upstairs maid, I was directed by the housekeeper, clad in severe black bombazine, to the servants' quarters and instructed to exchange my serge traveling-costume for the clothing laid out in readiness on the counterpane of my garret bed. To my astonishment, this raiment consisted not of the customary uniform of those in service, but rather of a short, many-pleated skirt of the design of that worn by a ballet-girl, but made of mauve silk; an extremely abbreviated jacket, hardly long enough to extend over my adolescent bosoms, and constructed of an utterly transparent white lawn; flesh-coloured stockings of the finest weave and an elaborate ribboned harness which, studying carefully, I understood at last to be a suspender-belt. Finally, a pair of maroon-coloured high boots of supple Russian leather, with lacings of lemon-yellow ribbon. No intimate garments having been provided, I retained my own, side-closing knickers and an underwaist, both of simple but clean cotton cambric. When I was fully attired, I had only just turned to inspect my ensemble in the full-length pier-glass, an unusual piece of furniture to be found in a servant's mean room, when the door was flung violently back on its hinges, and a tall, imperious, hawk-nosed gentleman strode in, wearing a burgundy-hued velveteen jacket embroidered with black clocks. . . ."

After announcing himself as her master, the hawk-nosed gent demanded the removal of her wretched underwear before his eyes and the resumption of the transparent jacket, directed her to replace the boots according to a complex scheme, strolled around her, lifting the ballet skirt here and there with the tip of his gold-headed walking stick to pluck at the "suspenders," which from their location seemed to be garters, discoursed on fabrics, buttons, buckles, and the like, and only several pages farther on drew from his pocket a tin of shoe wax, fell to his knees, and polished her boots to a mirror gloss.

Then, his fingers stained with red wax, he removed from his fawn trowsers his massive virility and with a few quick strokes of his lace-cuffed wrist brought it to a rigid stand and then to a spasmodic disgorgement of its copious, creamy secretions. Soon my Russian-leather toes were inundated in his rich spendings.

Subsequent chapters struck the same note with various other members of the manorial household, both family and servants, and the narrative culminated in an orgy of costume in which the classes, and sexes as well, were extravagantly confused, cook wearing the master's shooting suit, groom donning the nanny's uniform, and the mistress dressed as a male Highlander, her kilt cut away in front to display her natural sporran, a rare display of genitals in this company.

"By Lady Penelope Clavering" appeared on the title page. Whether or not this was a pen name, Naomi did not question that the style and the theme treated were those natural to a woman: the gracious language, with its limpid rhythms, the displacement of focus from vile anatomy, willy-nilly common to all, to its coverings, which could be regulated by taste, reflected much the same sensibility and cultivation as that of her favorite respectable authoresses.

Was it sacrilegious to suppose that were Mary Elizabeth Braddon to try her hand, in mischievous caprice, at erotica, the product might resemble *Clothed in Innocence?*

Naomi had written nothing but letters since her last high school book report, on *The Four Million*, by O. Henry. At the Christmas prior to her discovery of the fragment of *Hotdog* three months later, Gladys had given her a blank diary, the first she had ever owned, though when they were girls Gladys had kept one for a while and in it recorded crushes, invariably unrequited, on successive boys. To hear such passages read aloud was unbearable.

At the time she found the ad placed by Continental Products, Naomi had yet to inscribe a word in the blank journal. It would have been nonsensical to enter the events of her typical day, which though never boring her while in progress would, abstracted and falsified in language, look otherwise to the reader, who in utter philosophical absurdity, must by definition be only the writer thereof, namely herself—else it were no diary. Naomi always had a firm command of identity. "Nay knows her own mind" had long been heard throughout the family.

In possession of *Clothed in Innocence*, however, she was caused to believe, as she had never been by the work of Ruby M. Ayres, *et al.*, with its realistic delineation of romantic love, that when it came to lust, a totally fictitious subject, she herself could do as well as Lady Penelope Clavering, what was required being merely the unleashing of fancy. The result brought a dollar for each thirty-two pages. Naomi had married Buddy the day after graduating from high school. She had saved but never earned. All her life such money as she received had been given her by men, merely, as it were, for existing as daughter and wife.

It amused her to think of serving as noncorporeal prostitute to anonymous and undifferentiated hordes of men; to be paid and not to be touched; to infect them like a succubus. In this spirit she began the fluent account of Mary Joy's assault on the virilities of half the world. For it was indeed Mary who, beginning at age eight with the seduction of the huge Negro, set her partners in motion, including even those, like the whip-wielding Chinaman, to whom she might for her own ends temporarily relinquish physical command but over whom at all times she retained moral authority.

The composition went as fast as Naomi could move her fountain pen, requiring little deliberation and no pretext; her imagination proved to be a miraculous pitcher always brimful of slime. Having backtracked to January 1, she came forward to March 15 in a week's writing, alternating between reminiscences of earlier times and current adventures.

At the accumulation of seventy-four pages she halted and wrote a letter to Continental Products, giving as return address the postal box she took downtown.

DEAR SIRS:

I am a woman of 30. During the past 22 years I have had every type of sexual experience, and I am still going strong today. Recently I decided to set down, in diary form, an account of my activities, both present and, through flash-backs, past, including much childhood material. I enclose for your consideration copies of ten pages of the diary in reference.

Should you be interested in publishing the entire work in book form, please let me know. In any case, it is not necessary to return the manuscript, the original of which is an actual diary, in my possession and maintained daily.

Sincerely yours,
MARY JOY

Naomi had not intended to inscribe another word in the private volume until Continental responded, but to her amazement she found that the day on which she did not write was emotionally barren and physically attended by headaches, indigestion, and muscular cramps, from none of which she had ever suffered before and from all of which she got relief almost as soon as she lifted her pen. Therefore she proceeded with Mary, and by the time the answer came, three weeks later, her heroine had sailed around the calendar on an ocean of semen and was currently in port for Christmas, having a go at her long-lost father, who was dressed as Santa Claus.

The letter to Continental Products was answered on the stationery of the Eros Literary Society.

DEAR MISS JOY:

The specimen pages of your Diary have been read with great interest by each of the several members of the Committee, and without exception have met with approval. We would definitely like to reserve a look at the finished work when it becomes available. We're afraid we can offer no financial encouragement at this point, but we await the completed Diary with some eagerness. If it realizes the promise of these ten pages, we may be in a position to make you a generous offer for the rights to its publication.

A word of explanation: the Eros Society is a subsidiary of Continental Products, specializing in the private printing and distribution of high-quality works of erotica. Our subscribers pay an annual membership fee that entitles them to receive one selection each quarter of the year. These are luxury volumes, handsomely bound, often gilt-edged and with marbled end pages, and sometimes profusely illustrated by leading artists.

It might be of great use to you to become yourself a subscriber. An awareness of what your predecessors have accomplished in this field could not but be encouraging; many of them bear the celebrated names of World Literature. Our selection for this past Winter was THE WHIPPINGHAM PAPERS, by the great poet Algernon Charles Swinburne. For Spring we have chosen UNDER THE HILL, or *Venus and Tannhäuser*, by the renowned artist-poet Aubrey Beardsley.

As a (prospective) author you would qualify for a discounted subscription, at a reduction of fifty dollars from the standard fee. On receipt of your certified check for $100 —made out to Continental Products, *not* the Society— we will enroll you and send you by return mail the Beardsley volume.

Meanwhile, our best wishes,

THE SELECTION COMMITTEE

Naomi passed up this offer, but in three days she finished her record of 1936 and sent it off to Maspeth, L.I.

The letter of acceptance was pleasing, the check less so: $200 against an anticipated thousand or more, considering the fee paid by the Eros subscribers. But she was new at the profession and not an old hand like Swinburne and Beardsley; and it was also the first payment she had ever earned for anything.

And the suggestion that she try her hand at motion-picture scenarios appealed. During the summer and fall, then, she applied herself to characters and plots for movies to run the specified quarter of an hour each. These efforts were not successful. Her specialty, the outlandish conjunction of a young girl with a partner dissimilar by reason of age, race, species, etc., had been disqualified by the letter from the Society, and Naomi's vision turned fallow when asked to envision the kind of encounter that could be depicted by living actors, who would be constrained by common sense from whipping themselves raw and could not by nature display the colossal organs essential to her type of storytelling, with its reliance on the preposterous.

In desperation she arranged a situation or two in which a man in his years of maximum vigor met, stripped, and topped a girl in the full flush of sexual maturity, but the results were

278

excruciatingly banal, no matter the positions represented, the orifices employed, which after all were finite in number. A certain quality was absent, and was not to be provided by filling the imaginary room with more fanciful personages of the same breed; an orgy of these automata was even more tedious than the grapplings of the lone pair. Naomi was at a loss when not allowed to be fantastic.

Eventually she admitted as much to the Selection Committee, who in fact agreed, confessing they had had the same complaint from their other living authors and had given up the project.

Next she made several attempts to write fiction in another form than the diaristic, taking as model the English-lady's novels of which she had long experience as reader—even copying out certain sections verbatim, to which she then supplied erotic content. But lust and romance were as oil and water. She learned formally what she had always known by instinct: that because sexual congress was ludicrous in life, its depiction must necessarily follow suit, nay, go it more than one better if interest were to be provoked from the reader, who having come into the world with genitals was himself a born clown. Pornography was a form of farce, inspiring neither terror nor joy, representing neither aspiration nor achievement, proceeding towards no goal.

Time being Mary Joy's sole structure, then, the chronicle was the only format that would serve. The seasons as they came, the passing holidays, the very modes of time, even as simple morning, afternoon, and night, were inspiring. Mary Joy lived in a world that seethed with possibilities.

Recently, having grown bored with exotic male characters, gadgets, and animals, Naomi had for the first time given Mary an episode with another woman, a robust Swedish masseuse named Helga. This had proved so satisfying that she was eager to compose a sequel. Having gone to the bedroom for a handkerchief and found Buddy sound asleep, she believed she might chance a session with the current diary at an earlier hour than usual, though of course he might wake up and Ralph was due to return.

But it had occurred to her long since that neither of the men in the household posed a threat to her privacy. Since the onset of his adolescence, Ralph had never looked at her. If she were replaced with a window dummy he might not know the difference by Thanksgiving, and not then if someone else served him the plateful that matched his tastes (all white, lots of gravy because it's dry). As to Buddy, he was attentive to anything but, being a talker, the written word. To him the secretary desk was as sacrosanct as a ladies' room; he had never approached it in all their years together. The bookshelves could have held the grosser, cheaper wares of Continental Products: he would not have seen a title. Coming upon her as she wrote in a diary, he would retire as discreetly as if he had accidentally entered a bathroom already occupied.

Naomi worked clandestinely for the sake of the secret itself, not from fear of discovery. She had always been an intensely private person, often when they were girls concealing from Gladys, driving her sister mad, knowledge of, say, where she had disappeared to on Saturday morning (the public library) or Sunday afternoon (the attic, where she read the library books she had hidden). Naomi despised the aboveboard, the revealed, the known, and with the character of Mary Joy, who had no secrets, whose essence was accessible to all, she was complete.

Thus she was happily writing away—Helga's great bulk, muscular but not obese, was laboring over the recumbent body, trim, lithe, but not skinny, of Mary—when in the rear of the house Buddy fell down the basement stairs.

He missed the first three treads, but struck the fourth with his shoulders and the edge of the fifth with his head, snapped on the whip of his neck, which broke, so that he would probably have been a goner even if he had not continued to descend rapidly to the concrete floor, meeting it finally with the sound, which he did not hear, that a sugar melon might have made if dropped from the same height.

A certain excitement of creation had caused Naomi to gulp more cigarette smoke than could be managed by her windpipe. She coughed elaborately, clearing her irritated throat, obscuring with these noises the sound of Buddy's fall. Therefore he died in secret, apprising nobody.

chapter 15

CLARENCE THOUGHT the least he could do was say goodbye to the widow who lived down the hall and sometimes fed him. However, on reflection he decided it was more than he could accomplish. Given the aroma in the hallway, it seemed likely she was cooking supper. He had swallowed nothing since the dry baloney sandwich he had as usual taken along for lunch. Leo would on request bring him back coffee and pie from the Greek's, in which he was himself unwelcome, but Leo had not appeared at the lot that day.

Once Clarence hit the road he would be able to get no hot food until he reached another town with a colored district, and so far as he knew it was solid farmland for a good many miles west. But one thing leading inevitably to another—if she fed him she would, and with justice, expect compensation—he would end up with a full belly and empty balls, in which condition he would no doubt fall asleep and not get started to California until the next morning. By that time the man for whom he worked would be looking for him with a gun.

So he picked up the shopping bag into which he had packed all his possessions except the Sunday suit, which he wore, and sneaked past the widow's door and down the stairs. He walked the two miles back to the lot, found the '38 Packard where he had left it after buffing its body to a splendid sheen, unlocked it with the keys from his vest pocket, and slid onto the leather under the steering wheel.

He rolled gravely through the local streets. Buddy had never permitted him to drive a car farther than from the gravel service area into the garage; the machines were brought around from the front lot by the white men. He had no bill of sale, no registration, and no driver's license. He had however screwed on a set of plates he had taken from Buddy's personal car that afternoon, replacing them with dealer's tags on the Sandifer Buick.

For his own credentials he took from the shopping bag a much more useful passport than any made of paper for the alien country through which he would drive for many days: a chauffeur's black cap, which he had bought with the money Buddy had given him for the pocket watch and flashlight he would not need. There was a clock on the dashboard, for that matter. There was also a radio. He had no idea of how long it would take to reach California, but if he was still on the road next Sunday morning he intended to listen to a religious broadcast.

Laverne knocked for a long time at the door of the convent before noticing the pale rectangle on the brick wall alongside, indicating that a sign had been removed. The place was obviously deserted. She had to walk four blocks, leaving the area of warehouses, lofts, and small wholesalers, to locate a drugstore with a telephone. The directory was missing from the little shelf outside the booth. Also, she did not have a nickel with which to call Information. Neither could she find in her purse a piece of money smaller than a two-dollar bill, gambler's bad luck. Being a proud, independent sort, she was averse to asking that a note of this denomination be changed without a purchase.

She went to the marble counter and ordered a hot-fudge sundae from the soda jerk, a pimpled teen-aged kid in a white overseas cap, who was closing the containers in the ice-cream wells.

Like Buddy's son, he blushed when he had to talk to her.

"Sorry, ma'am, the machine that heats the fudge is on the blink."

Suddenly she knew it was one of those days when she would be frustrated in every fucking thing she tried.

She shook her head in the picture hat. "I guess you better tell me what you got. If I wanna banana split you'll be outa bananas, right?"

He shrugged and looked miserable, throwing one shoulder at the wall clock and his chin towards the prescription department, where some old baldy in a gray jacket was locking drawers and cabinets with an officious clatter.

"It's closing time, and he likes to be on the dot. Maybe a cherry Coke or something to go?"

Laverne climbed wryly off the stool. "Naw, I never drink on the street. I don't want to get run in."

"I'm real sorry." He looked it.

Laverne gave him a glorious smile. "Gee, kid, it ain't the end of the world. Buck up."

"You're a good sport, ma'am." He was scarlet from forehead to neck.

Twisting from the waist to emphasize her breasts, she wondered how much longer she could produce that effect on males.

On a whim she mounted the iron footrest of the stool, leaned over the counter, and beckoned to him as if to share a secret. When his wondering face came close enough, she gave him a great big red-hot smooch on the mouth, jumped nimbly down, and left, hips rolling, before you could say Jack Robinson.

Ralph waited forever at Elmira's, but Margie didn't show. Imogene Clevenger did though, alone, looking the worse for wear. He had never before noticed that she was somewhat out of proportion from the waist down: her legs seemed shorter than they should have been, given the length of her trunk, and her ankles were rather sturdy. His preference was for the suggestion of vulnerability given by fine bones.

She wore a rumpled skirt and a blouse in which you could see the impression of the big safety pin that secured her slip strap above the right bosom.

Pausing opposite his booth, she smiled in a weird, crinkled way and said: "Hi, Ralph."

This was unprecedented, and if it had happened a few days earlier Ralph would have been overwhelmed. Now he was rather suspicious. He gave a distant nod.

"Mind if I sit down?" she asked, and then as if in afterthought put a wearily coquettish hand on her hip and simpered.

"Waiting for somebody," Ralph said, frowning.

"Not Horace Hauser, I hope." She was so dispirited she had to put a hand on the booth top to support herself. "They just picked up his big brother."

Her face, which Ralph had previously believed unbearably delicate, now looked beefy. It was also wearing an expression he would have called peevish had her mouth not begun to quiver.

"What for?"

She breathed heavily, her lumpy, ill-defined breasts rising and falling like something in a laundry bag. "For deserting from the Navy."

"Izzat right?" said Ralph. "How about that?"

She started to slide into the facing seat, slowly, seeking his permission with watery eyes.

"You got to go when my friend comes," said Ralph.

"Sure thing, Ralph. I don't want to intrude."

He thought it might be a good thing to have Margie see him sitting with Imogene when she came in, Margie having been a bit arrogant on the phone to somebody who still had not altogether moved from the position in which *he* was doing *her* the favor. You had to keep one-up on women. He would also enjoy throwing Imogene out when the time came.

Imogene put her cheeks in her hands, elbows on the table, and said tragically: "We were engaged."

"Hmm."

Defensively she said: "I couldn't wear a ring because I'm underage and my parents would kill me, but we were, all right." She wiped her eyes with her short, rather stumpy fingers, the nails flecked with fragments of red polish. "But now I guess they'll shoot him."

"Naw," jeered Ralph. "That's only in wartime. He'll just be sent up for a long stretch."

She dropped her hands and stared. "How long?"

"Oh . . ." He looked at the ceiling fan, its big blades lazily circulating. "Twenty-thirty years, anyway." He chuckled. "In the good old days, you know, Captain Bligh and all that, he would have got a hundred lashes and then made to walk the plank or been keelhauled. You know what that was—"

But she did not listen to this historical lore. She murmured, "Oh, God," and buried her face in her hands.,

"Well, easy come, easy go," said the sadistic Ralph.

286

Her grieving countenance emerged. "You swear?" she asked.

Ralph's compassion was at last mildly stirred, and he changed his tune. "I don't really know about court-martials in peacetime. Maybe he'll cop a plea or something and get off light. It's probably serious but not hopeless, Imogene. You really stuck on that guy?"

She screwed her face up horribly. "I hate him!" She leaned across the table and took his wrist. "You swear you won't divulge this to a soul, Ralph Sandifer?" Without waiting for an answer, she then said at a low but intense pitch: "He got me in trouble."

Ralph leaned back, his head against the wall of the booth. He decided it was not decent to gloat publicly on the confirmation of his prediction.

Imogene was still attached to his wrist. "He turned out to be a real rotten egg," she said.

"So what are you going to do now?"

She lowered her dirty-yellow head almost to the tabletop; he saw the brown roots of her hair. "Kill myself, I guess."

Ralph pulled his wrist free. He patted her on the scalp, which felt like a bale of hay. "Cut the noise," he said sharply. "Don't be a dope. You got to get yourself taken care of."

She came up for air. "How? I don't know anything about stuff like that. I never knew anything about the whole business. I just let Lester do what he wanted to. He said he'd beat me up if I didn't." She was too desperate to cry. Ralph was grateful for that.

"Well," said he, "if you want, I'll look into the matter for you, Imogene. There's this colored fellow who works for my dad. He used to be a boxing champ. I bet he'd know where you could go and get fixed up. He's been around, see. I'll ask him for you, not mentioning any names of course. Probably someplace over there where they'd do that for you and nobody'd be the wiser." He pointed his index finger at her in the well-known gesture of his father.

As he talked on, her tense face relaxed, and when he finished it was almost worshipful. She took his hand again, this time with her fingers into the palm. For a moment he thought she might tickle him there, in the legendary fuck-me signal that Horse was always claiming to get from girls.

"That would be sure swell of you, Ralphie." She turned her head and peeped at him sidewise. "I always have liked you, but never had the nerve to let on, because I thought you'd think it was fresh. I would of asked you to my parties if I thought you would of come, but I didn't dare. Some people think you're stuck up, but I always said no, he's too sophisticated for the hicks around here, and—"

Seeing Elmira heading their way to take an order, he cut this off. "I'll get back to you soon on this matter, Imogene. Now, if you don't mind, my friend is supposed to show up."

She grimaced in disdain. "Horace isn't going to show his face tonight, I can guarantee that." Then her lips protruded as if to whistle, but instead she said softly: "You wanna walk over in the park? I'm real grateful for all you're doing."

Ralph got up briskly. She was no longer precisely to his taste, but having been warmed up by the call from bare-breasted Margie, and then left here to cool for an hour, he was not immune to this offer. He had read, in some sex manual Hauser had borrowed secretly from his old man, that women could do it for months after they became pregnant. Also, Imogene had revealed herself as a complete whore to begin with, and he now had total control over her. She was no longer a beauty, but neither was she a dog by any means.

Elmira was not offended that they were leaving without having spent a cent. She merely asked: "Hey, Ralph, didya ask your dad about that car?"

288

Ralph had forgotten the request, but he said: "Sure did, Elmira, and he'll see what he can do."

Imogene took his hand and held it as they walked to the door. He did not look to see what impression this made on the kids in the booths along the route. It might not be good by tomorrow, when everybody would know about Lester; it might not be good right now. But if you had nothing better to do than worry about popular approval, you were a horse's ass.

However, as he stepped onto the sidewalk, two things happened. The first, to his pride, was a sudden decision that he could not follow Lester Hauser: he might get syphilis. The second was that he saw Margie, leaning forlornly against the outside wall.

He extricated himself from Imogene. "Listen," he said, "you go on home and get your rest. You got to take it easy in your condition. I'll see that person tomorrow and let you know what he says."

He abandoned her with that, and went to Margie, who for all her attitude of distress, was all dolled up in a type of Sunday frilly dress, robin's-egg blue in the light coming from Elmira's, and with high heels and silk stockings. And wearing some kind of uplift brassiere, stuffed with Kleenex or socks, because her knockers looked bigger than Imogene's. In fact, had she not been in a hangdog attitude he might not have recognized her quickly.

Now he was fearful she would think the worst when seeing him with Imogene, but she gave no indication of so doing, her eyes fixed on the pavement. Glancing over his shoulder, he saw Imogene had crossed the street and was proceeding, with a voluptuous stride, into the darkened park.

He took the initiative. "So there you are! God, I was waiting inside for an hour."

She did not raise her head. Another woman in trouble. "Come on," he said. "What's eating you now? How'd I know you would stand out here?"

Without warning she threw her arms around him and put her head against his chest. "Something awful happened on the way over here. I just can't get it out of my mind."

Ralph thought: If she was raped, I know where my father keeps his pistol. But then she did not look disheveled. In fact her hair was clean, brushed, and shining. She was also wearing lipstick that had not been smeared until she pressed her face against his sports shirt, leaving, when he pulled away slightly, a big red blotch.

He noticed another novelty, and wondered that it had taken him so long: she was not wearing her glasses. But there was not that much difference: she had not suddenly become Jane Wyman.

He asked: "Where's your specs? Don't you need them any more?" Which in fact was what he always wondered about the Jane Wyman character; gorgeous, true, but blind.

"I took them off!" she wailed. "I don't want to see any more awful things."

He took her hand and began to walk.

At the corner she had recovered sufficiently to say: "Aren't you going to ask?"

"I'm asking."

She shuddered dramatically and said: "I can't tell. It's too horrible."

"Then don't."

She stopped and said indignantly: "You men are all alike. If it was a woman, you'd sing another tune."

"Margie, I honestly don't know what you're talking about." Those big tits he saw under the streetlamp couldn't be her own.

"That terrible man you were with the other day, coming

out of the Greek's. I mean, he was there and so was I, but he left first and you were talking to him when I came out. Remember?"

"Oh, yeah, Leo. He's not terrible. He's a nice guy. Works for my father. His mother just died. Funny you should mention him. I was just over there. He had her laid out on a sofa. That was weird, I grant you, but you can't shoot him for that."

"You don't know the half of it," said Margie, who furthermore seemed to be wearing some orangey pancake make-up like an older woman; it darkened her complexion but did hide the discolorations left by acne. "I was on my way here, peacefully walking along the street, passing some old house down on Hickory, when I suddenly heard a kind of hissing, you know, 'Pssst! . . . Pssst!' It was getting dark but the streetlights hadn't come on yet, and there was some rustling noise in a bush. So I stopped and looked, and then this man, this awful man, all of a sudden steps out from behind a bush and says, 'Hi, girlie,' And it was that Leo."

"Yeah," said Ralph, "he's been acting peculiarly all day. He's really upset by the death of his mother—which I guess is reasonable."

"He was stark naked," said Margie.

"Wow," said Ralph. "I didn't suspect he was that far gone."

"He was all covered with hair, like an animal."

"Did he do anything else?"

"No, he ran back in the house when I screamed."

Ralph shook his head. "Poor devil. He showed me a wax apple he bit when he was a baby."

Margie reared back, hands on hips. "*Poor Leo!* He's a criminal!"

"Well, I wouldn't say that," said Ralph. "He is under pressure."

"Ralph Sandifer! Are you going to tell me you don't intend to do anything?"

"What could I do?"

"Ask him for an apology."

Ralph's voice rose to a higher pitch than hers: "An apology?"

"Well, am I or am I not your girl?"

Ralph took the crook of her elbow and started to walk her again. "Let me explain something, Margie. That wasn't personal, see. Leo's gone off his rocker."

"If I was a man I'd give him a good horsewhipping."

"That wouldn't do any good. He's not responsible for his actions, you see. He's more to be pitied than censored, like the fella says."

"That's an easy out. Neither is an ax-murderer."

He sensed it would be useless to continue the argument. He might even sour her against himself if he did. Therefore he said, after a pause: "I guess you're right at that. Tell you what I'll do: I'll get hold of him tomorrow and by God, unless he apologizes, I'll beat him within an inch of his life."

Margie pulled him against her. She was amazingly strong for such a small girl. "Don't do anything foolish, Ralph. He may be dangerous."

Ralph could handle women, yet they often bewildered him. The next thing that Margie did was to lead him across the street into the park. Under a tree that kept dropping seeds that had a funny, not unpleasant stink, he kissed her with closed lips. She forced her tongue into his mouth and pressed her hard belly against his erection. He went into the bodice of her dress and with some difficulty among all the straps there, though with no resistance from her, he found that her breasts were indeed padded with what felt like toilet paper. He could toy there at will, but when, ablaze, he reached down and started up under her skirt, she pulled away and slapped at his face.

"If you want that, try Imogene Clevenger!"

Ralph kissed her again. "Maybe I'm in love with you."

"Then try to act like it," said she, pulling her clothes in order.

"I apologize."

"Accepted," said she. "It might interest you to know I've been crazy about you since the seventh grade. But I have my self-respect."

"And you've certainly got a right to it," said Ralph. "Come on, I'll walk you home."

The journey proved longer than anticipated, Margie turning out to be a monologist on inconsequential subjects—spats with her mother about the possible indecency of flaming lipsticks and nail polishes; thefts by her brother, twelve going on thirteen, from her supposedly secret cache of Mars bars; the ten-o'clock curfew imposed by her father and piously defended by her as "strict but fair"—family stories of the type in which Ralph himself never dealt and which he found tedious to hear unless told by Horse Hauser, whose examples were disgraceful, violent, hilarious. It seemed better taste to an outsider if a family was mocked by one of its members than if represented humorlessly.

When they finally reached her neighborhood, well beyond Bigelow's store in a westerly direction though not apparently bordering Darktown—he was somewhat disoriented by night and by her presence—Margie announced she was just about home, stepped behind a curbside tree, and beckoned to Ralph to join her.

Nodding at the nearest bungalow, he asked: "That your house?"

"Up the street." She gestured vaguely.

No doubt her folks, who emerged as puritanical in her long-winded account, were not supposed to know she was out with a boy without permission. But Ralph believed parents were quite right to take precautions against the Lester Hausers of the world. At the proper time he must go to Mr. Heppelmeier, Margie's father, shake hands, and introduce himself. He must get a haircut and shine his shoes, so that his clean-cut, hard-working character would be evident.

"Well," said Margie, leaning against the tree, hands behind her. She wore a thin, superior smile in the light from the streetlamp just across from them. "In the morning I am always grouchy, so if we see each other before class tomorrow, be prepared. But I'll be in my usual good mood by noon, so I can meet you in the cafeteria. Go there as soon as you can after the bell and get a table for us before they're gone. I might be a little late, because I generally have some things to discuss with the teacher. If so, just wait—no, if they've got cheese fondue and carrot-'n'-raisin salad, get a tray for me. And milk, and layer cake. Not pie. Don't get pigs in a blanket though. Stew is O.K., or chicken à la king—"

Ralph said quietly: "I go home at noon. I live only three blocks from school."

"Well, I don't," said Margie. "I live way over here. It's too far to go home, and I don't like to eat by myself. It's not fair."

He threw up his hands. "What can I do about it? I can't afford to pay for lunch every day."

"I didn't mean for you to buy mine!" she cried. However, he suspected her excessive indignation was due precisely to the fading of that hope. "Besides, you've got all those jobs of yours. What do you do with your money?"

"I don't make that much," said Ralph. "And what I make, I don't mind telling you I salt away."

Margie quizzically closed her lips in the center, but opened them slightly on either side to show the tips of her canines. It was a sort of trick expression, which Ralph would have been hard put to characterize, except that it made her look about forty.

"What do you salt it away *for*? Maybe you're just stingy."

She hit the target. He knew himself for a miser. Looking at the sum in his savings book, with the flanking interest payments in red—money born magically, not by work but from the copulation of one dollar with the next in the dark vaults of the bank—he enjoyed a swelling erection of soul. But he would have assumed that as his girl she could admire and not condemn that passion.

"Oh yeah?" said he. "Maybe I'm saving up for a ticket to New York. I'm not staying in this tank town forever."

That threw a scare into her. She brought her hands across her stomach and said feebly: "You're only fifteen."

"I didn't say it would be tomorrow. It's just something I'm keeping in mind."

"You're sure ambitious, Ralph. . . . I'm sorry I said you were stingy. I guess one day you'll just think I'm some hick. You'll drive through here in a limousine and won't even recognize me." She looked as if she might cry; though, true, without her glasses she tended to look that way anyhow. He much preferred her when she was being vulnerable and not critical or demanding. However, he had begun to suspect that her quick changes of style were not altogether involuntary, that she would take as much as she could get after trying for all. He must stay on guard at all times. She was indeed a worthy opponent. Her yielding was valuable in that it represented a resistance momentarily overcome but not destroyed: it would be back to keep him keen.

Therefore he did not give her elaborate reassurances now. He did not say that his fortune consisted of $19.77 and that he would need at least a hundred before moving East. He said merely: "There'll be a lot of water under the dam before that happens."

He placed his hands not on her shoulders but on the rough, cold bark of the tree just above them, leaned forward at the waist, and kissed her partially opened mouth with his own closed lips. Result: no bone-on.

She tried to pull him closer but failed. She sensibly accepted the situation, as he had known she would.

"I might walk you home after school tomorrow," he said in compensation.

"Ralph," said she, dropping her arms from his neck, "there's something I have to tell you." Her back still against the tree, she moved around to the shadowed side of the trunk. He too, feeling stranded, got out of the light. "My brother comes home the same way. So what that means is if he sees us he will find out who you are, and tell."

"So?"

"So, my father doesn't like your father."

"For heaven's sakes, why not?" asked Ralph, who had never heard his own father speak ill of anyone.

"Don't ask me," said Margie. "He just hates his guts. He'd never buy a used car from him, that I know."

"What's your father do?"

"He's a bookkeeper at Universal Playing Card."

"Uh-huh."

"Look, Ralph, that shouldn't make any difference with us. Did you ever see *Romeo and Juliet*, with Norma Shearer?"

He shook his head. "Leslie Howard was in that, wasn't he? I like Englishmen like Errol Flynn and even Ronald Colman in an action part, but Leslie Howard's sort of a sissy."

"Their parents had a feud, so they had to meet on the sly," said Margie. "I saw that when I was about twelve. My mother took me. She likes love stories, the sadder the better. I didn't understand it all, but it was sad. We both cried."

"Maybe we'll have to read it in English," said Ralph. "I'm not looking forward to it, I'll say that. I don't go much for poetry. I prefer modern writings: adventure, stuff like that. Also history, about real people and events."

He wanted to get off the subject of their fathers, but Margie wouldn't let it go: "So we've got to watch our P's and Q's." He detected a certain excitement in her voice. "If my father knows about you, he'll slay me. So if you call me at home and I'm not there or if I'm taking a bath, just say 'Ralph.' If they ask 'Ralph who,' make up another last name, and I'll know it's you and call back soon as I can."

Ralph was himself appalled at the thought of such a sneaky association. Besides, if their fathers were on the outs, it might be because his had caught hers in some criminal enterprise: for example, fiddling with the books he kept for the playing-card company.

"Better forget about the telephone altogether," he advised her. "*Your* name might be mud at my house too." Having recaptured the initiative, he decided to escape before her next offensive. "See you in school."

Margie refused to say goodbye, holding him there with her silence. Maybe she wanted to be kissed again, but he was determined not to be aroused.

"Well, I guess I'll say so long," said he, resting one gym shoe on its snub toe and lifting a hand into the light outside the shadow. "I better get on my way."

"I think it's because my father thinks your father was fooling around with my mother," said Margie at last.

Ralph brought his hand into the darkness and replaced his foot flat upon the earth.

"I heard them fighting once," Margie said. "My folks, I mean. It was really awful."

Ralph was on the sidewalk now and moving in the direction of home.

Behind him she cried: "There might be some mistake!" Then, as he put more distance between them: "I'm crazy about you, Ralph!"

But after that, he having broken into a run, she would have had to shout to reach him, and it was a quiet neighborhood and she a discreet daughter. He heard no more. He wondered whether her mother's first two names were Mary Joy.

chapter 16

LAVERNE TOOK HER OLD STOOL at the short end of the bar, against the wall and near the door, and when Vinnie waddled up unwittingly, she said: "I never let a day go by. I stop all Italians."

His eyes disappeared and his peg teeth went on display. "I din't reckonize yuh! Holy hell. Laverne!" He put a set of hairy knuckles across the bar. "Kid, you look like a million onna hoof."

"See you still walk like you got a load in your pants," Laverne said, affectionately fondling his warm fat paw.

He winked, looked around stealthily—a lone morose man sat at the other end of the long side of the bar, and a quiet couple occupied the rearmost booth—took back his hand and grasped his crotch. "It's the load I carry here," said he. "I got enough for three men." He was already tentatively wheezing, but reserving the big belly laugh for her comeback.

"Yeah? Well, your old lady tole me you was two hundred and fifty pounds of dynamite with a two-inch fuse." His shoulders began to heave. "She says it looks like the neck of a balloon."

He gave a great roar, at the sound of which the solitary drinker looked sourly towards them and the couple, sitting on the same side of the booth, stared in brief alarm.

Vinnie said, eyes full of water: "What I can't figure is where she's getting it. Bread in the oven again."

"How many's that make now?"

"Shit sake, *seven*," said Vinnie in proud exasperation, hooking a thumb on one pocket of his black satin bar vest.

"Boy, it *is* a long time since I seen you," said Laverne. "You had only five then. The ice man's been mighty busy." She made a sober face and began to count her fingers. "Dom, Connie, Treese, John, and Marie."

"What a memory you got, Laverne," Vinnie said, shaking his blue jowls. "I couldn't name-um no faster. So last spring, Rocco."

"I gather you never heard of the Rhythm, Vinnie." The man at the end of the bar drained his glass, then just sat there staring bleakly into it.

"Rosie's got the book, with the archbishop's imprimer in it and all, but we never been able to figure it out. I ain't got no head for numbers unless it's dollars and cents."

"Yeah," said Laverne, "you got enough money you don't need to count anything else."

"I always say I'm working on my own ball team, you count the girls."

"You gotta keep your eye on Catholic girls though," said Laverne. "Get-um married quick or in the convent." She was sorry she said that. Vinnie wasn't terribly amused and neither was she. "Hey"—she leaned over—"Hot Dan the Mustard Man down there could use a refill. Get out and earn a dollar. You go broke talking to old Laverne."

Vinnie's wide body moved down the slot. He resembled

Two-Ton Tony Galento. She hadn't seen him since Joe Louis slaughtered Tony, so when he came back she would crack him up by saying: "I see the jigs got you back for Ethiopia." Being in Vinnie's affectionate presence brought out her sense of humor, which had gone unused for too long.

He poured a fresh one for the guy and then came back with a bottle of Four Roses in one hand and a Seven-Up in the other.

"He's buying," said Vinnie.

Laverne made a moue. "He ain't hardly looked at me." She had to get fortified by the time she started to work, so she threw down the first jigger in one swallow, had a sip of Seven-Up, the bubbles stinging her nose, and then took the refilled shot glass in two gulps.

"That one's on me," Vinnie said.

"Now I'll pay for one," Laverne said, and he poured a third. She lifted the little vessel between thumb and middle finger, crooking the index to salute Cock Robin down there, but still he wasn't looking.

"So where you been all my life?" asked Vinnie. "I ain't seen you since Hector was a pup."

"I been hauling it elsewhere." All of a sudden Laverne felt like crying on his shoulder, but she restrained herself. "Hey, you heard this one? I know a girl who can speak English and French at the same time?" She leaned back until her throat was vertical and dumped the booze down it.

Vinnie's face was swarthily concerned. He pushed the Seven-Up glass towards her. "Take a little chaser, willya?"

"I don't want to get drunk." This was true: diluted whiskey went more quickly to the brain; she wanted to keep it warm in the belly. She took a five-spot from her purse and leaned forward. "You hang on ta that," she said to Vinnie. "You buy a rattle for little Rocky from his Aunt Laverne."

"Awww . . ." Vinnie was touched.

"C'mon," Laverne said, forcing the bill into his big mitt. "One of these days the world'll be all wops, and I wanna keep on their good side." She got up and went around the corner of the bar and along to where Herman Hotdog was chewing his cud and climbed on the next stool beyond him, where she could watch the door for the bulls or better prospects.

He was long and skinny and dark. It was the curve of his nose where it met his lips that gave him the sour feature. He wore a pale-gray fedora like Dick Tracy.

"Much obliged for the free juice," said Laverne to his inscrutable profile.

"My pleasure," he said, lifting his glass and drinking from it, slitting his eyes towards the blue mirror behind the bar.

"Please to meet you," said she. "I'm June. Who are you?"

His hat slowly turned. He had the palest eyes in a murky, lined face. He seemed about forty. He looked like the kind of bird who would show his cock to a Campfire Girl in the park. Laverne could handle him.

"Doc Savage," he said.

"I seen your name on a book."

"You bet. The one and only." He produced a crumpled bill from his pocket and carefully smoothed it on the polished wood, thumbs traveling away from each other. "I'm gonna get on my horse. The silence here is deafening."

"Maybe you just got coffee nerves," said Laverne.

"I'm going down the morgue for a few haha's," said he. He wore a gray suit and a gray tie, and his sideburns matched his gray hat.

"I been called funny as a crutch," said Laverne. She slid her hand along the bar and asked levelly: "Did you want a giggle?"

"I dunno," said Doc Savage. "Depends on what you got,

sister. But"—he looked critically at her hand—"don't touch me unless you love me."

Vinnie was futzing around at the other end of the bar, watering his stock or something, and Laverne's back was to the couple in the booth. She lowered her hand and finger-walked up the inside of his left thigh until she touched the lump.

He said immediately: "O.K.," and rose. She tucked her purse under her arm and followed, ignoring and ignored by Vinnie.

Doc's car was parked nearby. It was an old heap, an Auburn or something, so old she worried he might be a piker, so after he got in the driver's side, leaving her to wrench at the corroded handle of the passenger's door, she thought she'd better get the price settled pronto.

The upholstery felt ripped as she slid her ass on it. She asked: "Five O.K.?"

He started up the engine, which sounded like a wash machine, then stared at her angrily.

She wrinkled her nose. "We better get this straight," she said. "I ain't a pickup. I'm a prostitute."

He snorted. "Congratulations." And eased away from the curb, drove four blocks, and glided to a stop just beyond the twin green lights that flanked the doorway of a police station. He let the engine idle and showed her his badge.

"Oh no." She grasped her picture hat in two hands.

"You must be a tenderfoot," he said. "You sure don't know the ropes. You feel me in a intimate place, you quote your price before I say nothing, and then you name your profession. It's like you was reading from the rules of evidence."

She made a crazy grin. "I swear I was kidding! I thought you was a fruit. Can't you take a joke?" She put her face into her hands. "Would you believe, this is my first time?" She came up. "That's why I never knew the procedure, see? Think I would of done that if I was a real hustler? Like you said."

"Maybe not if you was sober, huh?"

"That's it!" cried Laverne. "My old man busted his hand at the plant today and he ain't covered by Accident—"

"Pigshit," said the detective, yawning cavernously and then for good measure sounding a shattering raspberry from which she felt the spray. "I got you cold, Sister Sue. So don't tell me about your kid with infantile paralysis."

"Yeah," Laverne agreed dolefully. "Today has been some cocksucker."

"Show me one that ain't, kiddo, and you win the gold toilet seat."

Believing that she detected a note of bitter compassion for all of God's creatures, she said: "I don't suppose you'd want to talk a little business?"

"Talk."

She took the change purse from her bag and, holding it to the nearest lighted dial, withdrew and counted its contents. "Seven dollars and thirty-nine cents. That's the works." With her free hand she overturned the little purse and shook it.

He put the car in gear, drove around the corner, entered an alley, and parked halfway along it. He turned off headlights and engine, but left the dashboard aglow. He hooked a finger into his side pocket and pulled it open. She dumped the money in.

"Looky," he said, holding his badge to the light. She leaned forward and read JUNIOR G-MAN.

He caught her claw in mid-air and fished out his wallet with his left hand, flipping it open to show the real badge.

"I took that phony one off a punk tonight who was shaking down bartenders." He dropped her wrist and put both badges away. "In case you think I'm nothing but a cunt cop."

"Hey," said she. "Can I have a nickel back for carfare? I ain't got no way to get home."

"Sure thing," he said, leaning against the seat back and probing for his fly-zipper with an insolent finger. "Soon's you play a little tune on my meat whistle. Don't bite, and maybe I'll slip you a dime."

"Lemme," said Laverne. He wore BVD's under the gray serge, and she unfastened the appropriate button, gathered his squirmy balls in her hand, and squeezed as if she were cracking one walnut against another.

He let out a rush of air and slammed his head on the steering wheel. She jumped out of the auto and ran up the alley in the impossible direction for his pursuit, the passage being one car wide. Reaching the street, she shrewdly walked in the direction of the police station. She might even have had the guts to go in, report a robbery, and borrow a nickel from the desk sergeant, but in the next block she saw a taxi stand with an attendant Yellow Cab. The driver was happy to get a fare out to the Valley, seventy-five cents on the zone chart.

She told him, "Cheap at half the price," took off her big hat, and scrooched down on the seat till they had cleared the downtown. When they reached her house, a half hour later, she told the cabbie she had to go in and get the money, and he didn't even give her a funny look. Going on the offensive had changed her luck.

"You just take your time, ma'am," said he.

Sitting on the bottom step of her stairway in the dark was Buddy's boy, chin on hand like The Thinker. They were both startled. He recovered before she did, sprang up, and began to jabber about owing her money.

She caught her breath and said: "Gimme a dollar then." He dug one from his pocket, and she took it out to the taxi.

"Keep it." She walked away from the profuse thanks and returned to Ralph. Only he was gone now. She wondered whether he was a mental case. She found him more or less hiding behind the steps.

"C'mon," she said. "I give you your dollar back."

"I don't want to intrude."

"I'd sure tellya if you was," said Laverne. She climbed up and opened the screen, unlocked the door, and, reaching in, chose the wrong switch of the pair and put on the outside light. They blinked at each other in the gnat-filled glare.

He took the pressure of the screendoor off her hip. She extinguished the outdoor globe and got the inside sconces lighted.

"C'mon," she had to tell him, "you're letting the bugs in."

She went to the bathroom and got from the top of the medicine chest the Kotex box in which, behind the pads, she banked. She had thirty dollars there, give or take, between her and the poorhouse. She couldn't hustle downtown any more after tonight, and she was now much too heavy of upper leg for the car-hop outfit: with six months of the kind of food you eat when home all the time and no exercise, her thighs were like the pair of toy zeppelins, when the flat folds were inflated, that she had once bought for Vinnie's boys. Her keester felt like a loaded garbage can. Her girdle was killing her. And so were her shoes.

Crossing the hall to her bedroom, she called: "Get yourself a Coke in the icebox." Teeth clenched, she peeled off the elastic tube, forgetting to free the garter clips, so the stockings came down as well. For a moment there was a big mess of alien material around her ankles. She sat down on the chintz-covered chair and, feeling her breasts, still brassiered and thus firm, press against the liberated swell of her belly, she pulled the whole works, shoes and all, off her feet and threw it at the stuffed elephant on the bed. Her skirt was at her waist, and she still wore the picture hat. Buddy had always liked to see her snatch when she was otherwise fully dressed. She could whistle for the kid to come and pop his eyes, probably his cork too. But she was incapable of vindictiveness, being devoid of envy.

She skimmed the hat at the closet door and got into her mules. But without high heels and stockings the dress looked sluttish, and without the girdle her stomach bulged even when she was standing, so she removed everything, her tits falling to the red corrugations left by the waistband of the girdle. She quickly wrapped herself in the pink satin negligee.

When she went to the living room he was still standing in the middle of the carpet. "I just got comfortable," she said. "Here's your buck."

He backed away. "I owed *you*."

She threw the bill onto the coffee table. "Suit yourself. I'm sick of that subject." His paralysis annoyed her because she too suddenly felt ill at ease in her own front room. She glared at him. "Why'd you really come here, kid?"

"I was in the neighborhood, and I remembered what I owed you, and—sorry, you're sick of that, though."

"Aw," said Laverne, artificially taking the strain off herself by dropping her shoulders, "I was just ribbing you. You're sure serious for a boy your age. You ever have any fun? You got yourself a girl?"

He grimaced. "I had one. For about an hour. But it wasn't much fun. It was more like work."

"Ha!" Laverne said, twisting away and addressing the radio set, "then don't tell me about it. I don't wanna hear no sad stories tonight." She brought her trunk back, hands on hips. "I had a real ornry day. I'm just lucky a bird didn't do his dirt on my hat. You know the kind of day I mean?"

"Yeah," he said eagerly. "I've had them like that."

"Is that right? Well, you're starting out young. Now how

about that Coke? And sit down, huh. You give me the willies standing there. It's like you was making a delivery or something. You're company now."

He looked around bewilderedly and chose the hassock. She shrugged and went to the kitchen. Along with the Coke she took, after a few jabs with a table knife to chop it free, the ice-cube tray from the Frigidaire and loosened its contents under running water. Buddy had also promised to bring her one of those trays with rubber compartments; she had intended not to think of him. She filled a soup bowl with potato chips and took it and the glass out to Ralph. With dainty fingers he accepted one chip.

"You're a cheap date," said Laverne. "Listen, I'll put it here, and you help yourself." She meant the coffee table, on the other side of the room. There was no nearer surface but the rug, and she had a traditionalist's aversion to seeing on the floor the vessels of eating and drinking.

Ralph had sprung to his feet when she entered. He now bent forward slightly from the waist and asked: "Aren't you joining me?"

"Why? You coming apart?" When he laughed out loud, he lost all dignity. His tongue showed, and his ears fanned out. She decided now that she preferred him when he was a bit formal.

"I kid a lot," she said, "but I don't mean it. You got real nice manners. I appreciate that in a fellow." She lowered herself to the couch. A kneecap poked out of the wrapper, but she soon concealed it.

"My father is always after me about that," said Ralph, sinking to the hassock with a wary eye on the level of his glass. "He harps all the time on that subject."

Laverne said quickly: "Know who's a perfect gentleman in the movies? Warren William."

Ralph nodded. "I guess that is a specialty of the English. Leslie Howard, for example."

"Well, I always thought he was sort of a pans—" Laverne caught herself; hell, he was a better model for a boy than Wallace Beery, scratching and blowing his nose in his hat. "Actually, I ain't—haven't been to the movies in ages. Been too busy. Who are your favorite girl stars, though, while we're on this?"

"Merle Oberon and Olivia DeHavilland," he said as if in response to the pushing of a button.

"Is that right?" Laverne said doubtfully. "I really like Bett Davis."

"She's certainly a good actress," Ralph said pompously. "She plays a lot of difficult parts."

"You don't really go for her, you mean."

"No, I wouldn't say that. I wouldn't say that at all."

"You prefer the ones who are always real ladies."

"Well," said Ralph, "maybe they're not as good actresses."

"Be hard," said Laverne, "to find yourself a girl like that around this burg." She put back the foot she had eased from her slipper: the big toenail showed cracked paint, and the whole hoof was red and puffy from its hours of confinement in a shoe one size too small. Her feet were anyway not her long suit. She also regretted having climbed into the satin wrapper, which hadn't been cleaned since the Year One.

"Oh, I don't know," Ralph murmured, hiding his face with his glass.

Laverne said: "You can't go around all dolled up all the time if you got to earn a living. I'm on my feet the livelong day." She primly brought her mules together.

"What happens to be your profession?" He lowered the Coke without having drunk much; he was still ruminating on the little crescent of potato chip he had nicely severed and holding the remainder in space.

"Hostess in a tea room. But I'm on vacation at this time. I might not go back to work. I might get married."

Now he took a long drink, swallowing several times with the glass still at his mouth.

"Then again, I might not. I can't make up my mind. This person is nuts about me, and he's quite a catch, I have to admit that—handsome, well-to-do, the whole kit and caboodle." She gracefully smoothed the satin over a thigh, but feeling the sponginess beneath, took her hand away and let it droop across a back-rest cushion. She had put on new polish before going out, and her fingers were still an attractive feature, long and slender and not discolored from smoking. She looked from this hand to him intermittently. "I just don't like the idea of giving up my independence."

He wiped his lips on his wrist. "You said— I don't know if you recall, but I believe this afternoon you said you weren't going to see that gentleman again."

She rounded her mouth and put an index finger into the little roll of flesh under her chin. "Oh, *that* gentleman. Yes, that's right." She smiled. "I guess I play the field." She frowned earnestly. "You got to, if you're popular."

He rose, marched across the carpet, and put the empty glass on the coffee table. "Thank you for the refreshments."

She had not been prepared for this. No little punk, no son of Buddy's, would walk out on her unless she dismissed him. "You get spanked if you stay out after eight?"

He was obviously hurt, but reacted in a manly fashion. "I don't want to take up your time."

She threw herself up from the couch and, changing gears, said huffily: "Far be it from me to waste your evening for you, sir. Kindly call again when you can spare a minute."

He assumed the burden. He made a face and flapped both hands at the level of his waist. "I guess I put my foot in it somehow. I'm sorry. I can stay if you want."

He looked so young and vulnerable that Laverne was instantly ashamed of herself. She had gone too far to call it kidding again.

"My fault," she said. "I had a real bad day. I oughtn't to take it out on you. What I oughta do is to get me a drink."

She came back with a glassful of ice and the entire fifth, three-quarters full, of B & L. Ralph had taken a seat on the couch.

"You could use another Coke." She returned to the kitchen and got it. Entering the living room, she saw him desperately screwing the cap of the whiskey bottle in a clockwise direction. His glass was clean as a whistle: not even any dregs of Coke or nuggets of melted ice.

She seized and smelled it. "Oh, no, kid. You don't do that in my house!"

His face was warped in a combination of guilt and defiance. "I drink all the time."

"Well, then you do it someplace else." She put the glass down and sat alongside him. "No, you don't do it at all, see. It ain't right." He turned his head away. "Look at me." She grasped his chin and brought his face around. She rubbed her hand all over his cheeks. "You ain't even started to shave, for God's sake. Why you want to ruin your stomach, huh?" She was smiling in fond remonstrance when he put his lips on hers. She could taste the whiskey.

It surprised her that she was not surprised. She pushed him slightly away after a moment and said, in the same tone as before: "You don't even know how to do *that*." She put his head in her neck.

"Why you in such a hurry to get old, huh?" He was almost as big as a man but her fingers felt the skinny nape and the funny thin ears of a child. "Let me tell you, when you get there you'll find nobody's to home."

She felt a strange tickle on her nose, brought her hand

there to rout the fly, and discovered it was a tear: her own. What a stupid thing. She never cried except when mad. She had not realized she felt so sorry for him. With his sensitive temperament, he would think he had offended her again somehow. To distract him she opened the bosom of the wrapper and lifted a breast to his mouth.

In shifting weight, his knee was gone, not only from her thigh but from the couch as well, taking with it the rest of his body. He had slipped to the floor; she heard the thump as if a long time later. It did not seem funny to her, though he grinned immediately. He knelt there, and she missed him awfully.

His mouth was blotched in red. She had been wrong: he wasn't grinning, he was making the kind of face that comes from swallowing with a strep throat. In another situation he would have looked completely ridiculous. He was also glistening with sweat.

She put her hand on his hot, wet cheek. He seized it and pressed its palm to his stained mouth. "What are you trying to prove, sweetheart?" she asked.

"Sweetheart," said Ralph, going all over her fingers with his nose. "You called me sweetheart."

"Like the song," said she. "It's just something you say."

"No." He grasped her hand and said firmly: "No, you meant it."

She threw his hand away. "Goddammit, don't tell me what I mean. I can take care of myself. If I couldn't, who would? *You?*"

He thought about that and seemed to grow disheartened.

With the noblest motives she exploited the advantage, indignantly covering her breast. "You can't be nice to some people. They'll walk all over you."

"You kissed me back."

"I was just being polite, for God's sake."

312

With youthful vigor and grace he came up from the floor, using no hands and applying no discernible effort. It was like a flower shooting up before your eyes. As it turned out, he wasn't discouraged at all. "You don't have to do a thing," said he, gleaming. "I won't try to kiss you any more. I won't hang around if you don't want me to. You don't ever have to even see me again. But what *I* think is my own business." He was walking backward. "And I don't care what you say: you kissed me back." He had almost reached the screendoor. He shouted: "I'll love you all my life."

Her responsibility was unbearable. If he backed out the door he might keep going across the landing and through the rail, breaking his skinny, goofy, sweet neck. What a sap he was.

She raised her arms before he got away. "How about just for tonight?"

Now of course he looked scared, lifting a gym shoe as if he would run off for the opposite reason. So she had to go and get him and lead him back, and he wanted to stop off at the sofa, but she said no, that wasn't the place, and she had his shame to contend with in the bedroom and he surely would still have taken French leave had she not quickly got the crucial clothes off him first, and he wouldn't go far in a sweaty T-shirt and the wool athletic socks that stank sweetly of his gym shoes, and she couldn't help kissing his darling wiggling smelly feet.

Forever his little root just hung there, or lay there, or dangled there, or just was squeezed between the softness of her belly and the flatness of his, and she wouldn't do anything whorish to it, else this right thing would turn sordid, and he would be distracted from her to what she did, and having finally found an idealist she would not throw him away. So what they did was just hold each other and breathe together as if their lives depended on it.

313

At some point she fell asleep, a state of which she was aware only retroactively, being brought awake by a body-sense of deprivation. He had separated himself from her and rolled to face away. She raised her head to peep over his slender shoulder, looking down that hairless plateau of chest and belly. His manhood was enlarged now, quite stiff and domineering, with him asleep. But before she was able to fall back and contemplate the loveliness of this in pure mind, she saw his hand sneak out from beneath his hip, and enclosing the base of the projection, begin to—

"No, sweetheart," she said, turning him to her, he pretending to be asleep with squeezed eyes. "That will give you pimples."

He kept his lids lowered. "I'm sorry. I just couldn't help it."

He was in her now, and she moved her hand out and around his narrow hip and into the small of his taut, boyish back.

"Neither can I," she said. "I want you to remember that when you are grown up and I am dead."

But when their eyes flared in unison, she forgot, for the first time ever, her habitual self-pity.

Ralph did not come back to real life until, rounding the town-hall corner on wingèd feet, five minutes from home, his eye was distracted from the celestial semen of the Milky Way by the clock on the fire-department annex. The time was 1:25.

As had always been his wont, he had told the truth when apprehended after breaking Bigelow's window: and been taken for a liar. Manliness was sometimes mere folly. He must be shrewder now and do something like steal in through the outside basement door, go boldly upstairs, and if his father was staked out in the living room, profess to have gone down cellar in early evening to find a certain old issue of *Open Road for Boys* and to have fallen asleep over it, concealed behind the high stacks of discarded papers awaiting the junkman; to have awakened only now, disoriented and dismayed.

If all was quiet, the same narrative would serve in the morning. The essential thing was to deliver it with an air of confidence, so that though his father would hardly accept the details he might well, if Ralph knew the man, himself so suave in manner, bold in deed, at least respect the authority with which it was told.